John Eadie

Life of John Kitto

John Eadie

Life of John Kitto

ISBN/EAN: 9783337333140

Printed in Europe, USA, Canada, Australia, Japan

Cover: Foto ©Raphael Reischuk / pixelio.de

More available books at **www.hansebooks.com**

LIFE

OF

JOHN KITTO, D.D., F.S.A.

BY

JOHN EADIE, D.D., LL.D.

I argue not
Against Heaven's hand or will, nor bate a jot
Of heart or hope, but still bear up and steer
Right onward '   MILTON

EIGHTH THOUSAND,

EDINBURGH: WILLIAM OLIPHANT AND CO.
LONDON: HAMILTON, ADAMS, AND CO.
———
MDCCCLXI.

'Perhaps no one ever was in my circumstances, or being so, ever retained or gathered spirit to surmount his difficulties. I think more and more, that a statement of those difficulties, as I could make that statement, would be felt to be a thing of no common interest.'—KITTO.

MURRAY AND GIBB, PRINTERS, EDINBURGH.

PREFACE.

How a brave spirit may not only conquer obstacles, but
climb by means of them to unrivalled eminence and usefulness; how a mysterious providence originated a hard and
healthful discipline, and by it, wrought out its own benignant purposes; how deafness, privations, and disappointments could not 'choke the life from out' a tender and
manly heart; how the love of literature fed itself amidst
rags and wretchedness, and ultimately realised its boldest
dreams; and what perseverance, armed with courage and
leaning on faith, can achieve,—may be learned from the
following biography.

Dr KITTO always purposed to write out his own life, and
unfold its great lessons. When he first resided at Islington,
the plan was so far matured, that he proposed, in a letter
to Mr HARVEY, October 17, 1826, to divide the sketch into
three parts—1. From Birth to the Workhouse; 2. From
the Workhouse to Exeter; 3. From Exeter to leaving
England. A month afterwards, he wrote to the same

friend—' Perhaps there is sufficient of interest, I had almost said romance, in my past life, to render the narrative of it attractive to the many; and it will be my business to employ that attraction as I best can, for the glory of my Master's name, and the real welfare of my readers.' This design was never executed, and though, in subsequent years, it was allowed to fall into abeyance, yet it was never abandoned, and towards the close of his life, it was revived in its original ardour.   In a letter to the Rev. Mr LAMPEN, dated Woking, November 5, 1845, he says, in reference to the experiment of writing some personal notices in his little autobiographical work, ' The Lost Senses,' ' it has sufficed to throw me back very strongly upon my previous impressions, that a biography, such as I should wish mine to be, is a work which cannot now be efficiently executed, or rather advantageously published, but should be reserved for a later period of life, when more of the tasks of that life have been accomplished, and more of its labour done.' Lastly, in his correspondence with his Edinburgh publisher, September 21, 1851, he repeats the avowal in these decided terms : ' the reception of " The Lost Senses," and the desire for further information which it has awakened, have confirmed me in a purpose I previously entertained, of hereafter preparing or leaving materials for a full account of my early experience, my travels and sojournings, and my literary labours since my return.   I have reason to hope there is yet much for me to do, which may render this

memorial of an eventful and laborious life, no unbecoming
intrusion on the public notice.' What Dr KITTO was pre--
vented, alas! by an early death, from doing, we have endeavoured in these pages, to do for him; though, certainly,
we could not hope to invest the work with those charms
and attractions which he, in his own style and way, would,
as author and subject, have thrown around it. Still, Dr
KITTO told his story so often and to so many persons, and
so voluminous are the papers and correspondence which he
has left behind him, that from its free use of this wealth of
material, the following volume may be regarded as virtually
an autobiography, with some comments interspersed for the
sake of connection and illustration.

We come into no invidious comparison with Mr RYLAND's
full and excellent Memoirs, the form and object of our
labours being so different in their nature and design. Mr
RYLAND's selections and unpublished transcriptions from
Dr KITTO's Letters and Journals, have saved us much
trouble and time, and we accord him our hearty thanks.
It will be seen, however, that we have not only made an
independent use of such papers as our predecessor has employed, but have added, from other sources, numerous new
incidents, extracts, and illustrations of character. The
whole of Dr KITTO's manuscripts were confided to us by
his family, at whose request and that of the publishers of
the previous Memoirs, this work was undertaken. We
were also kindly favoured with the use of numerous parcels

of letters, which have been preserved by the various friends to whom they had been originally addressed. Our object has been, to tell the story, develop the moral, and recount and estimate the labours of Dr Kitto's life, within a brief compass; and if we have not wholly failed, the book will be found to be one, not only of interest in the strange vicissitudes which it pictures, but one also of profit in the impressive teachings with which it is so signally fraught.

13, Lansdowne Crescent, Glasgow,
May 22, 1857.

CONTENTS.

CHAPTER VIII.
RETURN FROM THE EAST.

CHAPTER IX.
LONDON—FIRST LITERARY ENGAGEMENTS—MARRIAGE —PICTORIAL BIBLE.

CHAPTER X.
BIBLICAL AND LITERARY LABOURS—SOCIAL AND DOMESTIC HABITS.

CHAPTER XI.

DAILY BIBLE ILLUSTRATIONS—LAST DAYS—DEATH.

CHAPTER XII.

GENERAL REVIEW OF CHARACTER AND CAREER.

ILLUSTRATIONS.

LIFE

OF

JOHN KITTO, D.D.

CHAPTER I.

BIRTH AND BOYHOOD.

JOHN KITTO, the eldest son of John Kitto and Elizabeth Picken, was born at Plymouth on the 4th of December 1804. So small and sickly was the infant, that but a few hours of life were expected for it. Though nursed with uncommon tenderness and assiduity, it was long before the child was able to walk. This original feebleness was never surmounted. His stature was considerably below the average height, and his limbs were defective in vigour ; while a headache, recurring at longer or shorter intervals, accompanied him from his cradle to his grave. As this constitutional frailty unfitted him, to a large extent, for the society of other boys, and debarred him from their sports, it must have prevented, or at least greatly retarded, a healthful physical development. Bodily exercise was his grand necessity all his days, but he never relished it, and, indeed, never took it, till he had partially paid the penalty of neglect. Distaste for it may have originated in his incapacity to run and riot with his childish comrades ; but it clung to him, and grew upon him as he advanced in years—nay,

led him, when charged by his physician to walk so many
miles a day, and when his life depended on punctual compliance, to seek, by various shifts and pleasantries, to lessen
the amount of his pedestrian regimen.

If a boy that has not sufficient strength and hardihood
to keep pace with his fellows in their boisterous pastimes, should be often seen with his book behind a hedge,
or on a sunny slope, or found quietly seated in his own
corner of the domestic hearth, it would naturally be concluded that he had been well educated; that since he reads
so much, volumes are freely at his disposal; that he meets
with parental encouragement; that no misery preys upon
his heart; and that there is no undue demand for labour
upon his youthful sinews. But Kitto's condition was
exactly the reverse. He was not sent to school till he was
eight years of age; the majority of his books were begged
or borrowed, by continuous and untiring effort; his home
was a scer of misery and degradation; and, by the time
he was twelve years old, the dwarfed skeleton was yoked
to the heavy drudgery of a mason's labourer.

It is scarcely possible to estimate the amount of evil
influences that were thrown around Kitto from his childhood. His parents, both in humble life, had married young
—the bridegroom, a mason by trade, and doing business
on his own account, being in his twentieth year, and the
bride in her eighteenth. But alas! the gay ' morning,
with gold the hills adorning,' was speedily overcast, and
there closed in a dark and stormy afternoon. The young
husband and father soon fell into intemperance, and his
heart and home became a wreck. Character was not only
lost, but the love of a good reputation died away within
him. He was, as his son has said, of ' the class of men
whom prosperity ruins;' and from being a master, he
sank into a servant. The curse of poverty fell upon his

family, for what he earned he consumed upon his lusts. Swiftly pursuing his reckless and downward career, he found himself more than once in 'durance vile,' and at length, and at a later period, a more serious misdemeanour threatened such consequences, that his poor boy writes, in the bitterness of his soul—'What will they now say of Kitto, the felon's son?'[1] To snatch the delicate child out of this wretchedness, he was transferred, in his fourth year, to his grandmother's poor garret. She, 'dear old woman,' nursed him with more than a mother's tenderness, and her he regarded with inexpressible affection. She, too, had been blighted by intemperance. Her second husband, John Picken, though usually reckoned a sober man, had gone from Plymouth to Bigbury, a distance of thirteen miles, and spent the evening to a late hour with friends in the alehouse; so that, as he was riding home somewhat intoxicated, his horse trotted into a pond, and its rider falling from its back, was drowned in his helplessness. Kitto's mother was born a month after the melancholy event. 'Alas!' says her son, on a comparison of his grand-mother's and mother's fate—'My mother has the sad pre-eminence in misery.' For the shadow which had fallen upon her birth gathered over her wedded life in more terrible gloom. Intemperance had made her a posthumous child, and now it made her an unhappy wife, and a broken-

It may be added, that Kitto's uncle, who had got a superior education, fell a victim to intemperance, as well as his father. The uncle had some local fame as an engineer, having 'constructed the Upper Road across the Laira marshes from Plymouth towards Exeter, and embanked a great portion of this road from the tide.'—*Lost Senses,* p. 7. Both brothers had come from their native parish of Gwennap, in Cornwall, to Plymouth, attracted by the high rate of wages. Mrs Picken, with her two daughters, Mary and Elizabeth, lived in the same street with them, and the result was, that the two Kittos courted and married the two sisters about the same period. Kitto, in his Workhouse Journal, fills some pages with the sad story of his uncle, who was at length so reduced that he wrought on the Hoe as a pauper, and he concludes by saying, 'Drunkenness is the bane of our family, and the name of Kitto is synonymous with drunkard.'

hearted mother. Menial offices of the lowest form, she was at length glad to do, working, as she once tells her boy, 'from five in the morning to ten in the evening,' that she might have something to put into the mouth of her babes.

From his fourth to his eighth year, though Kitto enjoyed a partial asylum with his grandmother, who 'pinched herself to support' him, yet he got no schooling. True, he enjoyed another kind of education, perhaps as essential to his welfare. He strolled through the fields and lanes with his venerated relative, and gathered the flowers and plucked the fruits, which grew around him in wild luxuriance, his grandmother deftly using her staff to hook down the clusters of nuts and berries which were beyond his reach. At other times they turned their course to the sea-beach, and both were nerved by the breezes, which carried the surf to the feet of the aged pilgrim and her tiny charge. As they returned from these frequent and happy excursions, she usually supplied him liberally 'with ginger-bread, plums, apples, or sugar-stick,' her indifference to the sweetness of the last article often filling his young imagination with great amazement.[1]

At the age of eight Kitto was sent to school, and he remained, for various periods, and at various places of tuition, during the next three years. The congenital malady of headache was perpetually attacking him, and destroying the punctuality of his attendance. But there was another reason for his irregularity. His grandmother was too poor to pay the requisite fees, and his father either would not, or could not, spare a few pence for the purpose; so that when the fees could be saved from the ale-cup, the boy attended school, and when not, he stayed at

[1] The record of his abode with his grandmother is given at full length in a letter by Kitto, dated Bagdad, June 25, 1832—an interesting piece of autobiography, from which our knowledge of this portion of his life is derived, so that the source of the subsequent quotations needs not be again referred to.

home.[1] Perhaps this circumstance may account for the changes made in the schools he was sent to; for he was 'placed, for short and interrupted periods, at the schools of Messrs Winston, Stephens, Treeby, and Goss.'[2] Probably, at first, he lost as much in these forced recesses as he had gained in the previous weeks of attendance. Still there must have been great carelessness on the part of his parents, 'for they might have availed themselves of the opportunities which the many charity schools of the town afforded, for the instruction of poor boys in elementary knowledge.'[3] But such neglect was inevitable—the father still drank, and the mother was obliged to go out and char. Kitto did not gain a great deal by this desultory schooling; his early attainments not extending further 'than reading, writing, and the imperfect use of figures.' The first specimens of writing which we have, about four years after this date, are legible, but by no means very elegant; and as the occasional blunders in spelling and syntax in the same papers indicate, his English acquired at school was not to be measured by a very high standard. His 'granny' once boasted that he was the best scholar in Plymouth; but he blushed at the unmerited honour, and rejected it, adding, however, as her apology, 'she did it ignorantly, but affectionately.'

But his real, as distinct from his formal, education began under his grandmother's roof. The little fellow, seated quietly at her knee, was, for his amusement and occupation, taught by her to sew; and such was his assiduity, that he exulted in having done the greater portion of a 'gay patchwork' for her bed, besides having finished 'quilts and kettle-holders enough for two generations.' His fingers might, indeed, soon fall out of practice with needle and

---

[1] Letter addressed to Sir Walter Scott, found among his papers.
[2] Preface to his first publication.   [3] Ibid.

B

scissors, but he was unconsciously training to that retired
and patient industry which characterized his subsequent
life of seclusion and silence. Then, too, from his grandmother's lips, he came first to know the current lore of
ghosts, hobgoblins, fairies, and witches; and a lively shoemaker, named Roberts, who dwelt in the same tenement,
added his contribution of nursery literature, and repeated,
with awl and cord in hand, the tales of Bluebeard and
Cinderella, Jack the Giant-killer, and Beauty and the
Beast. 'Assuredly,' says Kitto, in 1832, 'never have I
since felt so much respect and admiration of any man's
talents and extent of information as those of poor Roberts.'
The young listener was charmed. By and by, he found
out that such wondrous stories were not mere traditions,
to be heard only from the lips of his grandmother and the
cordwainer, but that they might be actually seen in print,
in Mrs Barnicle's shop-window, ay, and be had for a copper
trifle. 'This information,' he says, 'first inclined me to
reading.' He was at once induced to buy them, as often
as he could afford the small expense. The passion grew
upon him, and every spare penny went for the purpose. He
willingly denied himself the dainties which his doting
grandam would have provided for him—no confections so
witching as a picture-book, and no fruit so sweet as a
nursery-rhyme. His desire of reading was indicated by
his growing love of quietness, and by his decreasing relish
for amusements out of doors, while it was nursed by the
zealous watchings of his relative, who, when he was permitted to go out for a brief period to play, soon interrupted
him by her loud call from the garret window, of 'Johnny,
Johnny!'—a sound, he pathetically adds, more than twenty
years afterwards, 'which, notwithstanding my deafness,
rings in my ears at this moment.' It was surely a kind
Providence which was so disciplining him, that the work

of his subsequent life did not necessitate a sudden and
violent change of habit. He was thus, at a very early
period, thrown much upon himself and upon books for his
amusement, a proof, as he was wont to argue, that his love
of literature was certainly not created, though it was ripened
and confirmed, by his subsequent deafness. The books in
his grandmother's possession were speedily explored—'a
Family Bible, with plenty of engravings; a Prayer-book;
Bunyan's Pilgrim; and Gulliver's Travels.' 'The two
last I soon devoured,' says he, 'and so much did I admire
them, that, to increase their attractions, I decorated all
the engravings with the indigo my grandmother used in
washing, using a feather for a brush. Some one at last
gave me a fourpenny box of colours, and between that and
my books, I was so much interested at home, that I retained
little inclination for play ; and when my grandmother observed this, she did all in her power to encourage those
studious habits, by borrowing for me books of her neighbours.' All the books in the street passed speedily through
his hands. Prior to his twelfth year, he had got into a
new world, and he was at first bewildered by its variety.
Nothing would satisfy him but book upon book. The
voracious student was not at all backward in maintaining
a supply by pen or tongue. His first efforts at composition were written to the kind and obliging mistress of a
neighbouring charity school, and were either requests for
the loan of a volume, or apologies for putting the lender
to so much trouble. 'Many of the old neighbours,' he says,
' will remember what a plague I was to them in this respect.'
In fact, if he heard of a book being within reach, he pestered
everybody about him till he got it. What he calls his 'first
literary effort,' was at this time also achieved by him, and he
has thought it of such importance, as to place it on record
himself. Nay, when looked at in the light of his subsequent

career, it might be regarded as a propitious omen. The following is his amusing account of the transaction:—

'My cousin came one day with a penny in his hand, declaring his intention to buy a book with it. I was just then sadly in want of a penny to make up fourpence, with which to purchase the history of King Peppin (not Pepin), so I inquired whether he bought a book for the pictures or the story? "The story, to be sure." I then said, that in that case, I would, for his penny, write him both a larger and a better story than he could get in print for the same sum, and that he might be still further a gainer, I would paint him a picture at the beginning, and he knew there were no painted pictures in penny books. He expressed the satisfaction he should feel in my doing so, and sat down quietly on the stool to note my operations. When I had done, I certainly thought my cousin's penny pretty well earned; and as, at reading the paper and viewing the picture, he was of the same opinion, no one else had any right to complain of the bargain. I believe this was the first penny I ever earned. I happened to recollect this circumstance when last at Plymouth, and felt a wish to peruse this paper, if still in existence; but my poor cousin, though he remembered the circumstance, had quite forgotten both the paper and its contents, unless that it was "something about what was done in England at the time when wild men lived in it"—even this was further than my own recollection extended.'

As the boy occasionally sauntered through the streets, and had so much time on his hand, he read all the play-bills posted on the walls; and though he had never read or seen a play, he resolved to get up one—the 'price of admission being, ladies eight pins, gentlemen ten.' Dresses were prepared, such as ribbons and sashes, caps and feathers, and the play was acted; the value of the pins collected amounting to three halfpence. The drama was a tragedy, so sweeping in its mimic massacre, that only one little actress remained alive at the end; and the audience, consisting of fifteen boys and girls, were perfectly satisfied with the performance. The whole affair was sufficiently childish, though Kitto was disposed to make his share— the play-bill and the plot—a proof of his literary progress.

It is plain, from these statements, that Kitto's early love of reading was no whim, or mere childish curiosity, but that there was a craving for information awakened within him. He rose gradually, even in his boyhood, to a more select and useful class of books. The cousin referred to, and for whom the booklet was extemporized, was as fond of books as Kitto, and could far more easily procure them; but his love of reading soon passed away from him, and in his manhood he scarce turned the leaf of anything, 'save a jest-book or a song.' With him, literary relish was only a variety of juvenile caprice, and the ball and the book might, at any moment, change places in his fancy; whereas in Kitto's case, the thirst for knowledge had really been excited, and, no matter how often baffled, it was never to be repressed. He enjoyed, at the same time, some religious education, and could answer a few questions from the Church Catechism. He also attended church so often, as to have caught the manner of Dr Hawker the vicar, and be able to imitate it, to his grandmother's vexation, when he read the Bible to her. Yet no serious impression seems to have been made upon him : 'After,' says he, 'I had studied the engravings, and read so much of the text as seemed to explain these, I felt then no disposition to study the Bible further.' There was much in it to interest him, had he chosen to read it—many scenes and stories that might have fascinated him both in the Old and New Testament ; but the time had not yet come when he was

to find it a refuge to the weary, and a balm to the smitten
in heart, and when its illustration was to form the daily
business of his life.

But the sky was gradually lowering around him. His
grandmother ceased, in 1814, to have any separate means
of support, while age and disease were leaving their traces
upon her. Reduced to poverty and attacked by paralysis,
she was forced to go to live with her youngest daughter.
Under his father's roof again, Kitto soon felt the sadden-
ing change. The boy must do something for his maintenance, and, in the spring of the year 1815, he was sent
as a species of apprentice to a barber's shop. 'Old Wigmore,' as his facetious underling records, 'had practised on
board a ship-of-war, and related adventures which rivalled
Baron Munchausen;' had a face so 'sour,' that it sickened
one to look at it, and 'which was beside all over red by
drinking spirituous liquors.'[1] While in Wigmore's service,
he learned only so much of his art, as to be able to shave.
For want of better occupation, he seems to have practised
so frequently upon himself, as, by the age of sixteen, to have
induced a growth of no ordinary thickness on his upper
lip, while, by the repeated application of the scissors to his
eye-brows, they acquired also a similar premature 'bushi-
ness.' But, from this occupation, he was summarily dismissed. His master's stock-in-trade, or at least his best
razors, were put under Kitto's charge, and taken home by
him every night. One morning, as he came up to the
shop, with the precious implements of his calling under his
arm, a woman in front of the unopened place of business,
professed to be anxiously waiting for Wigmore, and that
no time might be lost, she induced Kitto to leave his parcel
with her, and run and call his master. As might have
been anticipated, she was off before Kitto returned, and the

---

[1] Workhouse Journal.

surly old fellow discharged the little craftsman on suspicion
of his being an accomplice of the thief. Kitto keenly felt the
imputation, for his mere simplicity was branded as knavery.
And thus ended his first and curious engagement.

What, then, was the boy to do, but occasionally put on
a smock-frock, and go out and assist his father? He
did so, both in town and country—the grieved witness and
reporter of his parent's profligacy. When left at leisure
at any time, he usually took to wandering in the fields, and
among the rocks. He felt himself growing out of harmony
with his home and the world around him. As his mind
opened, he became more and more conscious of his unhappy lot. He confesses that he first 'knew what happiness was, by his own exclusion from it.' He pined for
solitude with book in hand—

> 'Away, away, from men and towns,
> To the wild woods and the downs;
> To the silent wilderness,
> Where the soul need not repress
> Its moaning, lest it should not find
> An echo in another's mind.'

In fact, morbid imaginations began at this time to gather
upon him. Having picked up a dog's head, which had
been long bleached on the sands, he at once determined to
make it a sort of symbolical memento, and having given it
a more ghastly appearance, by .reddening its jaws, and
replenishing its eyeholes and mouth with artificial orbs
and tongue, he hung up the grotesque teraphim at the foot
of his bed. He had long sought in vain for a human skull,
that he might place it in the same position. The abode
of his father was old and tall, and John's dormitory, in
the very apex of it, was of small dimensions, seven feet
by four. It was ventilated by an aperture that admitted
the wind, and could not exclude the rain, and was furnished

with a rickety table, framed originally to stand on three feet, but now sustaining itself with difficulty on two. This dark oak table was an old heirloom, and highly prized even in its decrepitude. The bed was in keeping with the table, and was by turns a seat and a couch, according as the strange inmate of the den wished to work or sleep. A chest was there, too, having its appropriate uses, with a box of smaller dimensions, holding pebbles and shells, and the other contents of his museum, and which was fastened with a string, passing through a huge and rusty padlock— 'a satire on security.' The walls were spattered with such prints as he could afford to buy, and such drawings as he was able to execute. Here was his library of a dozen volumes, having among them a Bible 'imprinted by Barker in the days of Queen Elizabeth,' and here he continued, so far as his intermittent toil allowed, his habits of miscellaneous reading. His spirit was gladdened, amidst all his oppressions and wrongs, by such literary vigils. He made indexes to his books, and even then he delighted to hang over the lines of Young and Spenser. We can easily imagine the sorrow of his grandmother, at the changed condition and shrouded prospects of her favourite. Perhaps she regarded his position in life as fixed, and suspected that, if his strength at all permitted, he would naturally follow his father's occupation. Who, at that moment, could have gainsaid such a prediction? But Providence interposed, and suddenly changed the entire current of events.

On the 13th of February 1817, the elder Kitto was engaged in repairing the roof of a house in Batter Street, Plymouth. His slim and ragged son was, about half-past four in the afternoon, engaged in carrying up a load of slates, and, when in the act of stepping from the top of the ladder to the roof, he lost his footing and fell, a distance of thirty-five feet, into the court beneath. There he lay insensible, bleeding profusely at mouth and nose. On being lifted, about five minutes after, consciousness returned for an instant, and he could not divine why he came there, or why so many people were staring at him. For more than a week, he continued in prostrate insensibility; for four months, he was obliged to keep his bed, and he did not entirely recover his strength, till other four months had also elapsed. But the accident had deprived him wholly of the faculty of hearing. What injury was done to the organ was never ascertained, and no possible form of treatment could remove it. He was subjected to every variety of surgical torment and experiment, but all in vain. The action of the auditory nerve was completely paralysed, perhaps, as has been surmised, from the entire internal apparatus being gorged with blood. The sense was not simply dulled, it was extinguished. He became deaf, not comparatively, as if he could hear only a little, and that even with extreme pain and difficulty, but absolutely, for he could not hear at all. The base of the skull had also sustained some fracture beyond the reach of detection or reparation—a sad supplement to his constitutional headache.

In after years, Kitto often reflected upon the accident, and he virtually assigns no less than three causes for it. His first account of it in his Workhouse Journal (1820), enters into no such details, and the probability is, that the reasons ultimately urged, had really little to do with the matter, but are rather the suggestions of an inquisitive and introspective mind, which tried to connect the fall with some previous mental associations, through which he might have been thrown off his guard. The phenomenon has happened too often to be one of mystery. Any one may stumble, after he has often mounted a ladder, under a heavy burden—much more a feeble boy like John Kitto

who never enjoyed great power of limb or firmness of step.
It does not need any analysis of his previous thoughts
to açcount for his mistake. He had climbed repeatedly
with a portion of mortar and slates during the day ; and
familiarity with the pathway may have induced a momentary carelessness. Or the frequent ascent may have so
wearied his sinews, that when he had reached the summit of the ladder, and a different muscular action was
required, he had not the complete control of them. Or
his knee-joints, stiffened with the short and hard jerk of
so many steps up and down, repeated for so many hours,
may not have stretched so far as he imagined, when he
attempted to throw his foot on the eaves. In one account, he refers to the anticipation of a wonderful book,
which had been promised him by the town-crier for that
evening ; and in another, to the prospect of a smock-
frock, on which his grandmother had been a long time
working, and which he greatly needed, for he was in
tatters, ' out at elbows, out at shoulders, out at breast, out
all over ;' and, lastly, he seems to impute the accident to
the *post mortem* examination of a young sailor's body, going
on in one of the rooms of the house on which his father
was employed, the effect of which he had happened
to notice, as he was ascending the ladder, in the form of
bloody water spouting from the gutter. Were the last the
true version, there would have been a physical source of
unsteadiness—vertigo or momentary faintness, which, however, he does not affirm, but speaks simply of a ' shock ;'
whereas the two former reasons adduced by him, could
only have produced absence of mind. Besides, the third
hypothesis would supersede the other suspected causes,
which are purely mental, and which, moreover, had been
just as powerful during the whole day, as at the fatal moment. All the three could not well co-exist, and the cir-

cumstance of a *post mortem* dissection could hardly affect so deeply the nerves of one who had long tried, in various ways, to get the skull of a human skeleton, for the guardian symbol of his couch.

On being carried home, the stunned youth lay in a trance of nearly a fortnight. At length he wakened up 'as from a night's sleep,' and perceived that it was two hours later than his usual time of rising, but he could not even move in bed. Many an hour he spent in 'trying to piece together his broken recollections,' so as to comprehend his position. How he learned that he had become deaf, is thus particularly related by himself. There was profound silence in the room in which the pathetic scene took place, and alas! that silence reigned around him ever afterwards.

'I was very slow in learning that my hearing was entirely gone. The unusual stillness of all things was grateful to me in my utter exhaustion; and if, in this half-awakened state, a thought of the matter entered my mind, I ascribed it to the unusual care and success of my friends in preserving silence around me. I saw them talking, indeed, to one another, and thought that, out of regard to my feeble condition, they spoke in whispers, because I heard them not. The truth was revealed to me in consequence of my solicitude about the book which had so much interested me on the day of my fall. It had, it seems, been reclaimed by the good old man, who had lent it to me, and who doubtless concluded that I should have no more need of books in this life. He was wrong, for there has been nothing in this life which I have needed more. I asked for this book with much earnestness, and was answered by signs, which I could not comprehend. "Why do you not speak?" I cried; "Pray, let me have the book." This seemed to create some confusion; and at length some one, more clever than the rest, hit upon the happy expedient of writing upon a slate, that the book had been reclaimed by the owner and that I could not, in my weak state, be allowed to read. 'But,' I said in great astonishment, "Why do you write to me? why not speak? Speak! speak!" Those who stood around the bed exchanged significant looks of concern, and the writer soon displayed upon his slate the awful words—"You are deaf."[1]

A more complete case of isolation can hardly be imagined. Had it not been for the boy's previous acquaintance with books, into what misery would he not have fallen? How many, with such an infirmity, without education, and in his rank of life, taunted as useless, and tormented as semi-maniacs, would have sunk into objects of pity or contempt, would have fallen into the dregs of society, and disappeared in a nameless tomb—in the pauper's or stranger's corner of the graveyard! Had there not been a powerful principle within him, nursed and sustained by his eagerness for reading, he might, as has been the case with not a few in his social position and with his defect, have become sullen and discontented, out of harmony with himself, and in antagonism with all around him—first a burden and then a pest. His own idea was, that 'such trials and deprivations have been generally found to paralyse exertion, and reduce the mind to idiocy, inducing a mere oblivion of thought and feeling.'

What circumstances, then, could be so discouraging as those of Kitto—a poor deaf boy, with none to care for him, none to guide him, or stimulate him to healthful mental exercise? Such an inmate of such a home—how helpless and how hopeless! He was able to do little for himself before, and he could certainly do less now. The father might gain a penny from his son's toils once, but now he left him wholly to his own vagaries. His grandmother's

---

[1] 'Lost Senses—Deafness.' By John Kitto, D.D., pp. 11, 12.

resources were exhausted too, and not a farthing to buy a
book came into his possession. He resorted, therefore, to
what he has graphically called, a 'Poor Student's Ways
and Means.' He went down to Sutton Pool,[1] where the
'fishing trawlers' and small coasters discharged their
cargoes, and, wading among its black and fetid ooze and
mire at low water, he groped, along with other boys, for
pieces of rope, iron, and other nautical fragments. Some
of his comrades could gather as much in a day, as amounted,
when sold, to threepence ; but Kitto was never very nimble
in his movements, and his weekly profits only swelled up
once to fourpence. But he happened, on one occasion, to
tread on a broken bottle, and such a wound put an immediate end to this form of industry. Then he turned to his
box of paints, and bethought him of artistic employment,
wondering, all the while, at the vulgarity of his previous
occupation. Having laid out his capital sum of twopence
on paper, he set about a series of paintings—human heads,
houses, flowers, birds, and trees. Grotesque they were,
according to his own account—'faces all profiles, and all
looking the same way ;' birds sufficiently weighty to 'bow
to the dust' the branches on which they were awkwardly
perched ; and flowers, 'generally in pots,' with a 'centre
in all cases yellow, and with any number of petals.' But
in describing this handicraft, he subjoins, with a simple
honesty, 'Thus far I can *now* smile, but no further. I
cannot smile when I recollect the intense excitement with
which I applied myself to my new labours, and the glorious
vision of coppers and reputation which attended my progress. How knew I but, in process of time, my pictures
might be pasted on the walls or over the mantel-pieces of
most of the rooms in the lane where I lived ! This was

The details are given by Kitto in two papers in the fourth volume of the Penny
Magazine, pp. 218 and 227.

the extent of my ambition ; for I do aver that I did never,
even in thought, aspire to the dignity of being framed.
The boyish ambition that might thus be acquired among
my compeers, was, however, a perfectly secondary object ;
that which I wanted was money.' But his pictures were
painted for sale, and not for criticism ; and being arranged
in all their glory in his mother's window, he sat down
behind it, and anxiously awaited customers. Few were
attracted, for few passed the court, and fewer came in to
buy. Yet, the average weekly income of the artist, from
this source, was about twopence-halfpenny. Then he resolved to have a 'standing' in Plymouth Fair, and wrought
hard to provide his stall with an adequate supply of goods.
The character of his wares attracted many spectators, and
it was probably for his comfort, that he could not hear
their remarks. Their staring curiosity annoyed him, but
he gained a larger sum of money by this public sale, than
he had ever before possessed. Certain labels in the windows of the lanes and outskirts of the town, had long been
an eyesore to him. The spelling and writing were equally
wretched—' Logins for singel men,' ' Rooms to leet en-
quair withing.' He prepared neat and accurate substitutes,
and took many a long and weary journey to dispose of his
productions. Occasionally he succeeded, but as often he
failed from bashfulness. The boy's infirmity sometimes
secured him sympathy, and sometimes led to a testy
rebuff; and his inability to talk about his articles made
his customers, in one place, kind and generous, and in
another, brief and surly in their dealings with him.

The money gained from employment so precarious, was
spent on books. Attachment to study might well have
been chilled in a stripling who seemed to himself the most
forlorn and helpless of human beings. Yet he read and
pondered, frequented Mrs Bulley's circulating library, and

contrived to plod his way through numerous volumes—
many, indeed, of an inferior class, but others of a higher
stamp and excellence. Still he loved to stroll into the
country, or recline among the shelving crags with the surge
beating at his feet, and to create for himself, through his
reading and reverie, a temporary Elysium. There was a
stillness around him, unbroken even by his own footfall.
Wearied out after a day's solitary wandering, heart-sick at
the misery and privation of his home, with bitter memories
of the past, and dreary anticipations of the future, his
only refuge was with his books, and in his little attic, where
many a tedious hour was beguiled, and where the growing
consciousness of intellectual strength could not but frequently cheer and sustain him. He used, at this time, and
after being sent to the Workhouse, to go to Devonport,
once almost every fortnight, to visit a bookstall in the
market. He feasted among the volumes, and the keeper
not only did not disturb him, but gave him books at the
cheapest rate, in exchange for the few pence he had scraped
together.[1] This man he reckoned a prince in generosity,
and a perfect contrast to a 'sour old woman,' and a 'surly
little man,' by whom two other stalls were kept, and who
did not relish the sight of so 'shabby a fellow' handling
their literary wares. And he naively adds, 'I had another
more logical mode of reasoning on the matter, which
settled it in my mind beyond any·possibility of dispute,
that my friend of Devonport market, and others of his
kind in general, were, and must be, the happiest men in
the world. If, I used to say, they sell the books, they
are happy in the money they get; but if they do not sell
them, they are happy in the books they retain.'[2] This

[1] Old Aubrey, the antiquary, says of Hobbes, 'He took great delight to go to the
bookbinders' and stationers' shops, and lye gaping on mapps.'
[2] Letter to George Harvey, Esq., January 19, 1827.

period has been described by Kitto himself in the following
eloquent terms :—

'For many years I had no views towards literature
beyond the instruction and solace of my own mind ; and
under these views, and in the absence of other mental
stimulants, the pursuit of it eventually became a passion,
which devoured all others. I take no merit for the industry and application with which I pursued this object,
nor for the ingenious contrivances by which I sought to
shorten the hours of needful rest, that I might have the
more time for making myself acquainted with the minds
of other men. The reward was great and immediate ; and
I was only preferring the gratification which seemed to
me the highest. Nevertheless, now that I am, in fact,
another being, having but slight connection, excepting in
so far as "the child is father to the man," with my former
self ; now that much has become a business which was
then simply a joy ; and now that I am gotten old in experiences, if not in years, it does somewhat move me to
look back upon that poor and deaf boy, in his utter loneliness, devoting himself to objects in which none around
him could sympathize, and to pursuits which none could
even understand. The eagerness with which he sought
books, and the devoted attention with which he read them,
was simply an unaccountable fancy in their view ; and the
hours which he strove to gain for writing that which was
destined for no other eyes than his own, was no more than
an innocent folly, good for keeping him quiet and out of
harm's way, but of no possible use on earth. This want of
the encouragement which sympathy and appreciation give,
and which cultivated friends are so anxious to bestow on
the studious application of their young people, I now count
among the sorest trials of that day ; and it serves me now
as a measure for the intensity of my devotement to such

objects, that I felt so much encouragement within, as not to need or care much for the sympathies and encouragements which are, in ordinary circumstances, held of so much importance. I undervalue them not; on the contrary, an undefinable craving was often felt for sympathy and appreciation in pursuits so dear to me; but to want this was one of the disqualifications of my condition, quite as much so as my deafness itself; and in the same degree in which I submitted to my deafness as a dispensation of Providence towards me, did I submit to this as its necessary consequence. It was, however, one of the peculiarities of my condition, that I was then, as I ever have been, too much shut up. With the same dispositions and habits, without being deaf, it would have been easy to have found companions who would have understood me, and sympathized with my love for books and study, my progress in which might also have been much advanced by such intercommunication. As it was, the shyness and reserve which the deaf usually exhibit, gave increased effect to the physical disqualification; and precluded me from seeking, and kept me from incidentally finding, beyond the narrow sphere in which I moved, the sympathies which were not found in it. As time passed, my mind became filled with ideas and sentiments, and with various knowledges of things new and old, all of which were as the things of another world to those among whom my lot was cast. The conviction of this completed my isolation; and eventually all my human interests were concentrated in these points, to get books, and, as they were mostly borrowed, to preserve the most valuable points in their contents, either by extracts, or by a distinct intention to impress them on the memory. When I went forth, I counted the hours till I might return to the only pursuits in which I could take interest; and when free to return,

how swiftly I fled to immure myself in that little sanctuary, which I had been permitted to appropriate, in one
of those rare nooks only afforded by such old Elizabethan
houses, as that in which my relatives then abode.'[1]

This condition, so well depicted, did not last long. It
was a cold gleam of sunshine in the last hour of a wintry
day. Nor was it wholly beneficial to Kitto. He was becoming too much the lord of himself, for he seems to have
been gratified in all his caprices that did not involve pecuniary outlay. The sympathy so naturally felt for him by
his relations, inclined them to fondle and humour him.
Nay, the child author and artist, was in danger of being
admired as a prodigy. But a severe and curative probation was before him. About the end of the year 1818,
his grandmother was obliged to leave Plymouth, in order
to reside at Brixton. The darling grandchild could not
accompany her, and he was left alone with his parents, and
entirely dependent on them. Ah! then did he suffer. His
father was unreformed : vice had turned his heart into a
stone, and he was insensible alike to his own disgrace, the
degradation of his wife, and the cries of his young ones for
bread. It was certainly no merit of his that his famishing
children preserved their honesty, and did not stray into
those courses toward which temptation is ever pointing so
many in quest of food and raiment. For months was the
boy a pitiable spectacle—pinched with hunger, shivering in
rags, and crawling about with exposed and bleeding feet.
A picture of more abject wretchedness could not be found,
than this deaf and puny starveling. Every prospect was
closed upon him, and to screen him from 'cold, and hunger,
and nakedness,' he was, on the 15th of November 1819,
admitted into the Plymouth Workhouse.[2] The sorrow

---

[1] 'Lost Senses—Deafness,' pp. 76 78.
[2] This workhouse, originally founded in 1630, was called the 'Hospital of the

and want of his home had been long notorious; the neighbourhood was scandalized at his daily and hopeless privations; charity was roused at length to interfere without
regard to his wishes and feelings; and, therefore, as the
last and unwelcome resource, he was seized and sent to the
common receptacle of aged and juvenile pauperism and
wretchedness.

Poor's Portion.' A new one has now been erected in a different part of the town.
The old building stills stands, however, in its comparative desolation, as when we
saw it in the beginning of last year. It had been tenanted a short time before by
about fifty Emancipadoes from Cuba—negroes who had purchased their freedom,
and who were on their way to Lagos and Abeokuta. Our friend Dr Tregelles and
his lady, with others, were very attentive to them. Services in Spanish were held
with them every Lord's Day, as well as many meetings during the week. The old
workhouse seemed alive again with its sable inmates, and the Christian efforts did
not appear to be without fruit.

CHAPTER II.

Some stratagem was necessary to secure the lad's entrance into the workhouse, for he was wild and shy; and when he learned that he was in virtual captivity, his sorrow was without bounds. But the wayward and defiant pauper submitted, in course of time, to the salutary curb; and he was in need of it, for he had long moved simply as it pleased him, and acted under no law but that of his own moods, which brooked neither challenge nor control. Not only were the order and discipline of the workhouse of essential service to him, but his fellowship with the other boys was also of immense advantage. It revealed to him various aspects of human nature, and tended to soften such misanthropic asperities as solitude is apt to produce. It gave employment also to his pen, and his facility of composition eventually drew attention to him. He had been going down the valley of humiliation, and the workhouse was the lowest step but one in the descent. For there was still another, and a deeper one; but it was the last, and the next step beyond it commenced the up-hill journey. Kitto's desultory life, prior to his entry into the workhouse, would never have brought him into observation; but now his power was more concentrated, and he gradually came into closer contact with the benevolent Governor and the Board of Guardians. If he felt acuter misery, he had also acquired a keener power of telling it; and such a power in such a narrator, could not but excite surprise. If he had to make complaints, his fearless utterance usually secured redress; and if he was obliged to enter into self-vindication, the cleverness of his advocacy was at least as conspicuous as the rectitude of his conduct.

Mr Roberts, who was governor of the workhouse at the time of his admission, treated him kindly, and permitted him some indulgences, even so far as sleeping at home; and Mr Burnard, his successor, was Kitto's kind friend and sympathizing correspondent through his whole eventful career. The youth was set to learn the making of list-shoes, under Mr Anderson, the beadle, and he grew, in no long time, to be a proficient in the business. Probably his friends were happy that now he might be able at least to maintain himself, and that there was something between him and abject penury. Within a year of his entering the workhouse, he began to keep a journal, and this curious and extraordinary document[1] is the best record of this portion of his life and progress. For this purpose, therefore, we shall freely employ it.

It might perhaps be supposed that a lad, brought up as John Kitto had been, in comparative pauperism, should be a stranger to delicacy of feeling. It might be imagined that the hardship of his condition could not but blunt any mental refinement, and that therefore now, within the walls of a workhouse, he had more than ordinary reason for contentment among boys of his own years and class. What is thus surmised might be true of many, perhaps of the majority, in Kitto's circumstances; but it was certainly not true of him. He was painfully conscious of his degra-

---

[1] Kitto mentions, in a letter to Mr Burnard, from Bagdad, that he had found some of his early papers, which had escaped the flames to which, some time previously, he had committed his early MSS. The papers thus accidentally preserved, seem to have been the Workhouse Journal.

dation. In spite of all he suffered, he never sank into callousness. What he might have been ever stood out to him in sad contrast to what he was, and his present condition was out of all harmony with his ideal prospects. He felt, and he keenly felt, so that in his Journal, when he becomes sentimental or sketchy at any time, or describes what enjoyments he coveted, or what anticipations feasted him, he suddenly and testily checks himself, and cries, ' But what has a workhouse boy to do with feelings?' or, ' The word pauper sticks in my throat.'

The interesting quarto is styled, ' Journal and Memorandum, from August 12, 1820, by John Kitto, jun.' The motto on the title-page, might have been ascribed to undue self-appreciation, had it not been vindicated by his subsequent career—

> ' Full many a gem of purest ray serene,
>   The dark unfathomed caves of ocean bear,
> Full many a flower is born to blush unseen,
>   And waste its sweetness on the desert air.'

The volume is, ' with reverence, inscribed to the memory of Cecilia Picken, my Grandmother, and the dearest friend I ever had,' etc. It was an odd thing for a pauper boy to think of such a project as keeping a diary. It shows, at least, that his mind was stirring, and that he was resolved to exercise himself in observation and in composition. When was a journal compiled in such circumstances— amidst such physical and social disadvantages—by a deaf boy in a poorhouse, of whom no higher estimate was formed, than that he might be a passable shoemaker, and for whom no loftier wish was entertained than that he might be able to maintain himself by his craft, and without being an expense to the community ! Compassion was felt for him, but no hopes were cherished about him. Men blamed the father and pitied the child, and then thought no more of him, but as the victim of complicated and re-peated misfortunes.

As to his motive in writing it, he says, that as he had no time to finish his drawings, and they did not sell when finished, and as he could not command a sufficient quantity of books, so he thought that writing was a good substitute, both for painting and reading. He adds, too, that he adopted the plan of a journal as a useful thing—as something to instruct others years hence (if he should be spared), in the misfortunes and sorrows of his early years, while he admits that there may be a little bit of human vanity in the resolution. But the Journal has realized its purpose. What, in fact, would the record of his early life be without it?

The following is his description of himself—racy and rather picturesque, though several features of the external portraiture were subsequently modified or toned down by the higher physical culture which he afterwards enjoyed:—

' Yesterday I completed my sixteenth year of age, and I shall take this opportunity of describing, to the best of my ability, my person, in which description I will be no egotist. I am four feet eight inches high; and, to begin with my head, my hair is stiff and coarse, of a dark brown colour, almost black; my head is very large, and, I believe, has a tolerable good lining of brain within. My eyes are brown and large, and are the least exceptionable part of my person; my forehead is high, my eyebrows bushy; my nose is large, mouth very big, teeth well enough, skin of my face coarse; my limbs are not ill-shaped; my legs are *well*-shaped, except at their ends they have rather too long a foot; when clean, my hands are very good; my upper lip is *graced*, or rather disgraced (as in these degenerate days the premature down of manhood is reckoned a dis-

grace !—how unlike the grave and wise Chinese, who envy
us fortunate English nothing but our beards) with a beard.'

There was indeed something peculiar in his appearance :—

'*March* 30.—I observe that my decorated lip exposes
me to observation, and that when I walk along the streets,
all men, women, and children, do me the honour to stare
me in the face. I got leave to come out this afternoon,
and shaved myself with my father's razor.' In a fragmentary autobiography, dated June 26, 1823, he writes,—'My
manners are awkward and clownish. I am short in stature,
stoop much in walking, and walk as though I feared I
should fall at every step, with my hands almost always,
when I walk, in my pockets.'

'*October* 7.—When I go any where, I am almost afraid
to meet any of my own sex; there is, it seems, something
about me that exposes me to observation, and makes me
stared at; and I find, by experience, that the best way to
come off well, is not to avert the face, but to look uncon-
cerned, stare at them in return, and assume an impudent
look. What a world is this, in which modest bashfulness
is contemned, and impudence caressed !'

His deafness, 'laboured asthmatic breathing,' and apparent powerlessness, often made him the butt of the other
boys in the hospital, and he was obliged to make sudden
and smart reprisals.

'*October* 12.—When afterward, in the evening, Torr was
making faces at me again in the court-yard, I could bear
it no longer, but gave him such a blow as made him fall
down. You cannot imagine, Madam,[1] how this seeming
trifle provoked me.

'*October* 22.—I to-day experienced the truth of the maxim,
that *meanness* is a medal, the reverse of which is *insolence.*

---

[1] The diary often addresses some ideal personage.

When I was waiting under the porch till Mr Burnard should pass by, to ask leave to come out, one of the blue-coat boys, named Peters, kept making faces at me. At first I treated his foolery with the contempt it deserved, by taking no notice of it. But at last he provoked me so far, by attempting to pull my nose, that (though no boxer, and not over courageous) I gave him a blow on the forehead, with such good will, as made him reel to the opposite wall, and brought the water into his eyes. When I had done so, I fully expected a return of the favour, but he, so far from resenting it, desisted from his foolery, and soon sneaked off.

'*March* 21.—At eight o'clock, as we were going to prayers, Rowe gave me an unprovoked blow on the back, and ran away. I pursued him, and hemmed him into a corner, when, finding he could not escape, he placed himself in a pugilistic attitude; but a few blows made him stoop to defend his ears, and at the same time to pick up a bone and a large cinder to throw at me. While I was disarming him of those missile weapons, I was attacked in the rear by ten or twelve boys, who delight in mischief. Having disarmed Rowe, I turned against my new opponents, and, discharging a bone at one, and a cinder at another, and some blows among the rest, put them all to flight.'

Sometimes, when bad boys were flogged, Kitto was selected to hold their legs, probably because, from his inability to hear their cries, he was under no temptation to slacken his grasp. The next extract is a reflection, in his own style, upon his early disaster.

'*October* 9.—I found, on coming to my senses, that I had just been bled, and that by my fall I had lost my hearing, and from that time to this there has

"Not to me returned
The sound of voice responsive, no feast divine

Of reason, nor the 'flow of soul,' nor sports
Of wit fantastic : from the cheerful speech
Of men cut off, and intercourse of thought
And wisdom."[1]

'I did not entirely recover my strength till eight months after, four of which I kept my bed from weakness, during which time I had leeches applied to my temples and under my ears, also an issue on my neck, besides taking plenty of nauseous physic—all to no purpose as to my deafness, for I do not expect to hear any more. Ever since, after dark or sunset, and in a great measure in the day, I have always had an irregular uneven pace and a labouring gait, and after dark I stagger like a drunken man. Thus, you see, no sooner had youthful fancy begun to sport in the fairy fields of hope, than all my hopes anticipated, and present pleasures and happiness, were, by this one stroke, destroyed. O! ye millions, who enjoy the blessing of which I am deprived, how little do ye know how to appreciate its enjoyment! Man is of such a fickle nature, that he ever slights the pleasures he has, to sigh for those he has not. However, I will attempt to give you an idea of my deprivation. Fair lady, how should you like to forego the incense of flattery (so gratifying to female vanity) offered you by the admiring throng? I believe, my Lord, you would regret being deprived of the fulsome adulation offered you daily by abject (pardon me, my Lord) sycophants. Sir, who are you? What are those who extol you to the skies? You are a wonder, I must own—a rich poet. Yet, remember, it is not to your poetical or personal merit they pay homage, but to your wealth you owe it; nor forget that such men as those who flatter you, could suffer, unmoved, an Otway, a Chatterton, and many others, to die " unpitied "—I had almost added, " unknown "—the for-

[1] Imitated from Milton, by Miss Palmer.

mer of want, and the latter of ——— ; but let me not withdraw the veil benevolence has thrown over his memory.
Should you, Sir, like to be deprived of this degrading
flattery ? Ye men of genius, and of wit ! Ye patriots and
statesmen ! Ye men of worth and wisdom ! Ye chaste
maids and engaging matrons ! And ye men of social minds !
Should you like to be

> " From the cheerful speech
> Of men cut off, and intercourse of thought
> And wisdom?"

If not, guess my situation, now I am grown somewhat
misanthropic, with no consolation but my books and my
granny.'

He had passed through the fire, and the smell of singe-
ing was upon him. But he never sank into

> ' A grief without a pang, void, dark, and drear,
> A stifled, drowsy, unimpassioned grief,
> Which finds no natural outlet, no relief
> In word, or sigh, or tear.'

Strange it is to find the editor of the Pictorial Bible
thus recording of himself :—

' I was to-day most wrongfully accused of cutting off the
tip of a cat's tail. They did not know me who thought
me capable of such an act of wanton cruelty.

' *June* 2.—I am making my own shoes.

' *June* 9.—I have finished my shoes—they are tolerably
strong and neat.

' *August* 14.—I was set to close bits of leather.

' *August* 15.—Said bits of leather that I had closed, were
approved of, and I was sent to close a pair of women's
shoes, which were also approved of.

' *August* 16.—I was most unaccountably taken from what
I had just begun to learn, to go to my old work (making
of list shoes), in which I am perfect as it is possible to be.

S—— who, without being acquainted with the structure of a list shoe, dictates to us who are, without any authority but that of being a man (a very little one too), and bids us, under pain of the stirrup, make a pair of shoes per diem, which is particularly hard on me, who, besides doing my own work, am obliged to teach the rest.

'*November* 14.—I forgot to mention that, on Monday, I had been a year in the workhouse, during which time I have made seventy-eight pairs of list shoes, besides mending many others, and have received, as a premium, one penny per week.

'*November* 20.—Set to tapping leather shoes to-day.'

In striking contrast with these revelations about list and leather, tapping and closing, waxing and sewing, occurs the following entry, which proves that the mind of the pauper shoemaker was not only busy, but stretching far above and beyond the walls of the workhouse :—

'I burnt a tale of which I had written several sheets (quarto), which I called "The Probationary Trial," but which did not, so far as I wrote, please me.'

The discipline of the workhouse was occasionally administered in profusion, and on a somewhat miscellaneous principle.   He records that, on one occasion, having finished his shoes, and when he was waiting for the soles of others to be cut out, he began to '*write a copy*' for Kelly, and had only written one letter, when the beadle came in, and 'gravely gave us a stirruping all round '—idleness being the alleged ground of the castigation.

Among the most interesting entries in the Journal, are those relating to his grandmother, who had nursed and watched him with more than maternal fondness and self-denial, and whom he regarded with more than filial affection.   On the first page occurs the following entry, which we copy as it stands :—

' 1819.—Granny has been absent in Dock this 2 days. Tho' but for so short a period I severely feel her absence. If I feel it so acutely now, how shall I bear the final seperation when she shall be gone to that "undiscovered country from whose bourn no traveller returns?" She cannot be expected to live many years longer, for now she is more than 70 years of age. O, Almighty Power, spare yet a few years my granny—the protector of my infancy, and the . . . I cannot express my gratitude. It is useless to attempt it.'

His interviews with this relative are the epochs of his life. He carefully notes her gifts to him, is rejoiced when she is pleased, and sadly dismayed when he hears of her being in a ' fine taking' about any domestic occurrence. After numerous incidental allusions, he writes :—

' *April* 16.—Granny is worse again. She seems almost unconscious of everything ; yet she knows me, for she held out her hand to me when I was going.

' *April* 17.—She does not know me !—she is speechless. Aunt tells me that the surgeon has given her over—that— she is dying.

' *April* 18.—She is dead.'

This was the sensitive and affectionate boy's first great sorrow.

' *April* 20, *Good Friday.*—Being now a little recovered from the first shock, I have, after several attempts, summoned courage to detail particulars. On Wednesday evening, when I came out [from the workhouse], I trod softly up stairs lest I should disturb her repose. Useless precaution ! Aunt met me at the head of the stairs, in tears. I entered ;—a white sheet over the bed met my view. She was dead ! Think you I wept ? I did not weep ! Tears are for lesser sorrows ; my sensations were too powerful for tears to relieve me. The sluices of my eyes were dried !

My brain was on fire! Yet I did not weep. Call me not a monster because I did not weep. I have not wept these four years: but I remember I *have*, when a boy, wept for childish sorrows. Then why do I not weep for this great affliction? Is not this a contradiction? Am I hard of heart? God forbid that tears should be the test, for I felt —I felt insupportable agony.

' Even to an indifferent person the sight of a dead person awakens melancholy reflections; but when that person is connected by the nearest ties—oh, then—when I saw the corpse—when I saw that those eyes which had often watched my slumbers, and cast on me looks of affection and love, were closed in sleep eternal!—those lips which often had prest mine, which often had opened to soothe me, tell me tales, and form my infant mind, are pale and motionless for ever!—when I saw that those hands which had led, caressed, and fed me, were for ever stiff and motionless—when I saw all this, and felt that it was for *ever*, guess my feelings, for I cannot describe them. Born to be the sport of fortune, to find sorrow where I hoped for bliss, and to be a mark for the giddy and the gay to shoot at—what I felt at the deprivation of my almost only friend, the reader can better conceive than I can describe. Yet that moment will ever be present to my recollection to the latest period of my existence. Gone for ever! that is the word of agonizing poignancy. Yet not for ever—a few short years at most, and I *may* hope to meet her again—there is my consolation. Joyful meeting! yet a little while to bear this

> " Fond restless dream which idiots hug,
> Nay, wise men flatter with the name of *Life*,"

and we may meet again. Already I anticipate the moment when, putting off this frail garb of mortality, and putting on the robe of immortality, of celestial brightness and

splendour, in the presence of our God we may meet again;
—meet again, never to part;—never again to be subject
to the frail laws of mortality—to be above the reach of
sorrow, temptation, or sickness—to know nought but happiness—celestial happiness and heaven! Accursed be the
atheist who seeks to deprive man of his noblest privilege—
of his hopes of immortality—of a motive to do good, and
degrade him to a level with the beast which browses on the
grass of the fields. What were man without this hope?
I knelt and prayed for her departed spirit to *Him* in whose
hands are life and death, and that He would endue us
with resignation to His decrees, for we know that *He* had
a right to the life which *He* gave.[1] Her countenance is not
in the least distorted, but calm and placid, like one asleep.'

'*April* 23, *Easter Monday.*—The day before yesterday
being the day prior to my grandmother's funeral, and not
being certain that I should be able to come out early
enough to be present, as it would take place at nine
o'clock, I determined to take what might eventually be a
last view of the revered remains. I raised the cloth—it
was dusk—the features were so composed that I was for
a few moments deceived, and thought it *sleep.* I pressed
my lips to her forehead; it was cold as monumental mar-
ble!—cold for ever! A thousand recollections rushed
upon me, of her tenderness and affectionate kindness to
me. She, who was now inanimate before me, was, a short
time since, full of life and motion; on me her eye then
beamed with tenderness, and affection dwelt in each look.
When I was sick, she had watched my feverish pillow,
and was my nurse; when I was a babe, she had fondled,
caressed, and cherished me; in short, she had been more

---

[1] This language is only, in Kitto's case, the vehement expression of attachment
and sorrow. It meant little more than an earnest hope that his grandmother had
gone to heavenly glory.

than a mother to me. And this friend, this mother, I never was to behold again. A thousand bitterly pleasing instances of her kindness to me occurred to my recollection, and I found a kind of melancholy pleasure in recalling them to remembrance. I gazed on each well-known feature. I kissed her clay-cold cheek and pallid lips. I remembered how often my childish whims had vexed her. I remembered how I had sometimes disobeyed her earnest and just commands. I mentally ejaculated,

> " O that she would but come again !
> I think I'd vex her so no more."

Fruitless wish ! Will the grim tyrant death give up his prey ? Will the emancipated soul return to its dreary prison ? Ought I to wish it ? " No !" said reason ; " No !" said religion : such a convincing " No !" they uttered, that I blushed for the wish. Shall I, a frail mortal, wish that undone which my *Maker* has done, and by implication censure His decrees ? If (as we may hope) she be happy, will she not grieve to see us repining at her bliss ? I will try to be resigned. I thought of all this ; but yet I did not weep ; for 'twas not a *tear*—my eyes water sometimes ; I did not weep ; it certainly was not a tear that fell from my eyes as I leant over the open coffin, but it was probably caused by my looking stedfastly at one object. I continued bending over the coffin till darkness hid the features entirely from my sight, and then tore myself away.'

Who would surmise that these paragraphs, so fluent and correct, so vivid and tender, were written within the walls of a workhouse, by a deaf and disabled stripling, almost uneducated, wholly unpractised in composition, and seated, in pauper livery, on a tripod from morning till night, working at a list shoe on his lap ?

'*April* 24.—About a quarter past eight on Easter Sunday, my father went to Mr Barnard, and got leave for me to come out. Crape was put round my hat. . . How unable are the trappings of woe to express the sorrow doubly felt within! I looked once more and for the last time on the corpse, once more and for the last time pressed her cold lips, and then she was shut from my view for ever! I felt a something at my heart that moment, which baffles description. I felt as though I could have freely given my life to prolong hers a few years. What! had I viewed for the last time her who was my only benefactor, parent, and friend, and was I never to see her more? "No!" whispered doubt; "Yes!" said faith; and she was right. . . At the appointed time we walked in "sad array" behind the coffin—first, Uncle John and Aunt Mary. . . There were about forty persons present : the service was read by Dr Hawker's curate; the coffin was deposited in the grave and covered with earth. . . The moment in which the coffin which contains the remains of a beloved relative, is hid from our sight, is, perhaps, a moment of greater agony than at their demise, for *then* we have still the melancholy consolation of contemplating the features of the beloved object; but when that sad and gloomy comfort is taken from us, the feelings of our loss occur with accumulated force; we consider what, a short time since, the contents of the coffin *were*, and what, in a short time, they *will be ;* we consider that, in our turn, we shall be conveyed to a similar, if not to the same place, and in our turn be wept over with transient tears, and soon be forgotten. I thought the man almost guilty of sacrilege, and could have beaten him, who threw the earth so unconcernedly on her remains. "Why does he not weep?" I internally asked. "Why does not every human being join with me in lamenting her loss?"'

D

But I shall not attempt to describe my feelings; they were such, that the moment when I stood on the brink of the grave, eagerly looking on the coffin till the earth concealed it, I shall never forget till the hand that writes this shall be as hers, and the heart that inspires it shall cease to beat. When we came home I felt a kind of faintness coming over me, and if Aunt Mary had not timely rubbed my temples with cold water, I should have fainted. Grandmother is buried on the left hand side of the aisle, opposite the steeple, near the church door (Charles' Church), beneath the headstone erected to the memory of her grandchildren.'

Still Kitto could freely criticise the perfunctory manner in which he thought the funeral service had been gone through. But the next entry reveals the lacerated state of his heart, and opens up a glimpse of his unhappy home.

'*April* 27.—In consequence of the loss of this revered relative, I already begin to feel a vacuum in my heart, which it is impossible to describe. Who shall supply her place? Nature points to my mother. . . While she (grandmother) lived, I had no cause to regret the want of kindness in any other person. But now, alas! she is gone, and I feel myself an isolated being, unloving and unloved; for whom this world, young as I am, has few charms. . .

' When I return from the restraint of the workhouse, the rooms look desolate, for she is not there. She who greeted me with looks and smiles of affection is not there ! She who prepared my tea, and rejoiced if she had some little delicacy to offer me, is not there ! She who chode me if I left her even a short time, is not there ! In short, she who loved me, is not there ! Who shall supply her place? My mother, or my aunt? My mother! it must be so, it shall be so. To do her justice, she has been very kind to me since the sad event, and so has aunt. Yes, mother has been very kind. She knows, amongst other things, that my grandmother's death would deprive me of the means of getting almost the only thing I value—*books:* therefore, with great kindness and consideration, my father wrote, by her direction I suppose, "I will give you the money to get the books." "Indeed," I said, "but do you know how much it will come to?" "No." "Why, you know," I said, "I have got a penny per week at the work-house, and I change my books (two vols. small, or one large vol.) three times a week, and pay a penny each time; that penny will pay but for one of those changes." Father wrote, "You shall never want twopence the week." Was not this kind? very kind, I think. I shall have no occasion to put their kindness in this last instance to the test as yet; but will this kindness last? Will they not, when they think the edge of my grief is blunted, relapse into their former indifference? I expressed this doubt to my mother. She assured me of her continued kindness, and that she would see this last act of it duly performed. I would have said, but did not—O, my mother! representative of the dear friend I have lost, would that I were certain that this kindness would continue; would that I were certain that your present kindness would never cease, and that while I am in need of your aid, you will continue to accord it to me; and then, when manhood shall have nerved my arm, and age have enfeebled *yours*, and you will need the aid of your children, how happy shall I be, and how shall I exult to be able to step forward and say, "My father, and my mother! while I was yet a boy and needed your help, you granted it me; then, O my parents, how I longed for opportunity to show my gratitude! The time is come, and now you need it; as you once offered me your aid, so now I offer you mine, henceforth let all mine be yours." . . I think I could love my mother almost as well as I did love

my grandmother.' And in his mother's old and infirm
days he did verify his wish.

· ' *June* 10.—I have been to aunt's ; was received kindly;
before I came away uncle wrote, " You must come out
here as often as you can, for it was the dying request of
your grandmother that *we* should be kind to *you*." And
did she think of *me!* to the last anxious for me—interested
even in death for my welfare! and making friends for me !
My only friend! my revered benefactor! my dearest grandmother! in death didst thou think of *me !* Oh that I had
been present! Yet, no, I could not have borne it. Father!
receive her soul into Thy mercy, and guide my steps in the
intricate paths of human life, beset as it is with thorns and
briars, with temptations and sorrows : and if it be Thy
pleasure that I should drink the cup of human misery and
affliction to the very dregs—even then, Lord, in the midst
of all, grant me strength that I may not swerve from Thy
will, nor murmur at Thy decrees; for well I know that
whatsoever Thou doest is just and right, and that, though
Thy commandments teach me to resist the dominion of my
senses, they, in the end, lead to the eternal mansions of the
blessed. I humbly pray Thee, my God, that there I may
at last arrive, through Jesus Christ, and there meet her who
has gone before me.'

He had sad doubts that the affection now shown by some
of his nearest relatives would soon cool, and he felt that then
he should be desolate indeed. Thus he sobs—' Why do I
feel? why dare I think? Am I not a workhouse boy?
My father, if you could but imagine what, through your
means, I suffer, you would—Begone pen, or I shall go mad.'

Whatever appealed to Kitto's eye gratified him ; and
among his ocular amusements, the ' shows ' at Plymouth
fair occupied a prominent place. A fair was great or small,
in his boyish estimation, in proportion to the number and

splendour of such exhibitions. What he saw he describes
in his journal with picturesque minuteness : the transpa-
rencies and pictures; an 'ill-looking pock-marked dwarf,'
or a giantess so plump and fleshy as to 'make the mouth
of an anatomist water.' The various devices and blazon-
ries, stars and fireworks, first on the conclusion of Queen
Caroline's trial, and then at the King's coronation, were a
special treat to him. But his deafness occasionally filled
his soul with sad regrets. The constables had on one occasion collected into the workhouse all the unfortunate
women of the town. Kitto gazed on the scene with melancholy, and moralized upon the lost creatures 'covered with
shame, abandoned by friends, shunned by acquaintances,
and thrown on the wide world—insulted with reproach,
denied the privilege of penitence, cut off from hope, im-
pelled by indigence, and maddened by despair.' After service, 'one of the best gentlemen in Plymouth addressed
them, so that many of them wept, as well as five-sixths of
all the people in the room. Even I,' he adds, 'had almost
wept from sympathy.' In recording this, there came upon
him at once the overpowering sense of his own desolation.
And he writes, October 15, in touching moans :—' Yet I
alone was insensible to the inspiration that flowed from his
lips. To all, insensible ! Devotion ! oratory ! music ! and
eloquence ! To all of ye alike insensible !'

In a similar cheerless spirit he soliloquizes :—

'. . . I should be inconsolable under my great misfortune, were it not for the conviction, that it is for wise
purposes the Almighty Power has thought proper to chastise me with the rod of affliction. And dare I, a worm,
the creature of His will, to repine at His behests? Besides,
He has declared, " Those whom I love I rebuke and
chasten." But whither do I wander? Dare I to think
that an accident was His infliction? Dare I to hope that

the Omniscient will deign, when I pray, to attend to my supplications? I dare not—'twere presumption—'twere almost impiety—to think *He* would incline His ear to such a one as *me*—*me*, of all my species created the inferior—*me*, whom each eye views with contempt—who am mocked, buffeted, and despised. And why am I thus treated with contumely? Because I am—unfortunate! And does misfortune render me inferior in Thy eyes, O my God? No, for Thou hast said, Thou art no respecter of persons. Thou hearest alike the king on his throne, and the beggar on his dunghill. Though man treats me with contumely, Thou wilt not be less merciful. Pardon my doubt, which had dared to prescribe limits to Thy mercy, and endue me with resignation to kiss the salutary rod with which Thou (I dare almost say it) chastisest me. . . I fear I am deplorably ignorant in religious matters.'

The language employed in the preceding and succeeding paragraphs is scarcely that of a quiet resignation, but rather of a stubborn acquiescence. The youth who had suffered such degradation from a father's intemperance as now to be a pensioner on a public charity, and who had, by a mysterious Providence, been suddenly bereft of a precious faculty, succumbed, indeed, to his lot, but at first with seeming reluctance, and with a strange curiosity to ' cast the measure of uncertain evils.'

' 1821, *January* 1.—Welcome 1821! Though thy greeting is but rough (uncommonly cold), boding a year of as great events as thy predecessor, I pray God that, as I am conscious I have but ill performed my duty as an accountable being the preceding year, and that my lot in life is but low, He will deign to look on the most humble of His creatures, and blot out of the book of His remembrance the sins I have committed heretofore; to endue me with fortitude to bear with resignation whatsoever misfortunes may yet assail me, and to enable me to resist temptation, the allurements of vice, and even my own thoughts when they lead to ill; and to enable me, if it be His pleasure, to drink the cup of misfortune to the very dregs, without repining; and, finally, through all my life to make me bear in mind that this life is but a probationary trial, to fit us for a greater and a better state hereafter.'

Kitto's powers of composition were in the meanwhile improving, and he criticises public characters in a free and independent style. The first sentence of the following description is felicitous. It was inserted in his diary on learning the Queen's acquittal. Many glowing sentences were written at the period: the eloquent declamation and satire of Brougham and Denman thrilled the nation; but the hearty and stirring tribute of the obscure workhouse cobbler has never been printed before.

'*November* 14.—Bells ringing, flags flying, and almost every person rejoicing, on the occasion of innocence and the Queen being triumphant; for the bill of pains and penalties was withdrawn on Saturday, November 10th, by the Earl of Liverpool, from the House of Peers. The day on which the Queen was victorious over slander and revenge will ever claim a distinguished place in the annals of this country—a day on which slander, perjury, and guilt were vanquished by innocence and truth. This trial has been such a one continued scene of iniquity as has not been equalled since the time of the Tudors (except in the instance of Charles I. and Louis XVI.) Last week has shown these are not such days as those unenlightened days in which the tyrannic Henry swayed despotically the symbol of mercy—those days when Britons could tamely see an innocent Queen (Anne Boleyn) led to the scaffold on a pretended charge of adultery. No! Such days are over; and now the generous character of Britain will not suffer

an unprotected female to be persecuted with impunity.
Not unprotected neither! She cannot be called unprotected who has the hearts of two-thirds of all Britain
warmed with enthusiasm in her cause; and experience
has shown that their hearts are no despicable protection.
The conclusion of this iniquitous transaction has over-
whelmed the enemies of the Queen with shame and confusion.   Greater part of Britain will be illuminated in the
course of the week—Plymouth on Wednesday.

'16th.—Plymouth was illuminated last night.'

The next excerpt, in a different strain, is a meditation
on the death of Napoleon.   It betokens the interest taken
in public matters by the young recluse, who never 'saw a
newspaper to read till he was nearly twenty years of age.'

'July 6.—Learned that Napoleon Buonaparte died on
the 6th of May, of a cancer in his stomach.   He was ill
forty days.   I doubt not but that the public journals,
newspapers, etc., have detailed all the particulars of his
exit from the theatre of the world, in which he has shone
as a meteor—a meteor of destructive influence; and I shall
only give a few observations on his character, according
to my idea of it.[1]   That he had talents, no man who has
attentively considered his conduct and character can doubt;
but such talents!   He was an innate tyrant—he introduced
himself to notice by his eminence in adulation and cruelty.
That he was a cruel man, his conduct has always shown.
Witness the dreadful Bridge of Lodi, the massacre of Jaffa,
and the poisoning his own sick soldiers.   He was more
than suspected as the murderer of the Duke d'Enghien.
I consider him as a man who, from the earliest period of
public life, was resolved to let no considerations of honour,
religion, humanity, or any other consideration, to interfere

[1] The page is adorned with a portrait of Napoleon, done in glaring colours, and
looking rather fierce, and is said by Kitto to be copied from a plate in Barre's
Rise, Progress, etc., of Buonaparte's Empire.

with his advancement. Nor did they interfere. He certainly had not always thoughts of obtaining the sovereign power; but his ambition for sovereignty arose from circumstances, step by step. After the abolition of royalty and nobility, and the declaration of equality, he was resolved to admit of no superior. That he was ungrateful, may be seen by his treatment of his former patron. One or two centuries hence, and even now—if we knew not its reality—it would be considered as an improbable fiction, belonging to the ages of romance, that a man of obscure origin should thus become the ruler of nearly all Europe—thus realize the visions of Don Quixote, and reward his Sanchos with kingdoms at his pleasure—thus spread desolation, fire, and sword, where nought but peace was known before;[1] that a man—a simple man—an unsupported man should thus make princes crouch at his footstool, and should have his will obeyed as a law. How many thousands of widows and orphans has he not made? A lesser villain would have been hanged for the thousandth part of his crimes; yet he has his admirers. Notwithstanding what has been said by many to the contrary, I allow him the meed of personal courage, and that he was grateful when he could gain nothing by being the contrary. He was an hypocrite and an infidel; for he has different times been of almost all religions, Mohammedan included. He was generous by starts—condescending when Emperor—irritable, hasty, insolent, and choleric. It will not be considered as the less extraordinary part of his story, that, in the end, he was unfortunate — obliged to abdicate his throne, and was twice banished; but, above all, that this man—this Napoleon Buonaparte—died in his bed of a cancer, while the great and the good Henry died by the hand of an assassin, and the meek Louis died on a scaffold !!

[1] Switzerland.

On the whole, it may be said of Buonaparte, that he was a glorious villain !!'[1] And yet, amidst all the youth's dejection, there were forereachings of spirit, anxious anticipations, the picturings of possible propitious circumstances. His highest ambition at this time was to have a stationer's shop and a circulating library, with twelve or fourteen shillings a week. His anxious question was, ' When I am out, how shall I earn a livelihood ?' Shoemaking could yield but a slender remuneration ; and as he had been taught to make coarse shoes alone, he could only expect small wages. Yet he thought that he might travel, and that some kind gentleman might take him, even though it were in the humble capacity of a servant, ' to tread classic Italy, fantastic Gaul, proud Spain, and phlegmatic Batavia'—nay, 'to visit Asia, and the ground consecrated by the steps of the Saviour.' This odd anticipation of Asiatic travel was wondrously realized, for a 'kind gentleman' did afterwards take him to the banks of the Tigris.

The long and heavy affliction of Kitto had brought him under religious impressions. He had felt the Divine chastening, and stooped to it. It was a necessity to which he was obliged to yield, and, as he could not better himself, he bowed, though he sometimes fretted.

' O nature,' he exclaims, ' why didst thou create me with such feelings as these,' which spring from ' superiority

[1] It would seem that Kitto had been reading a well-known passage in Milton, one of his favourite poets :—

'Might only shall be admired,
And valour and heroic virtue called;
To overcome in battle, and subdue
Nations, and bring home spoils with infinite
Manslaughter, shall be held the highest pitch
Of human glory, and for glory done
Of triumph, to be styled great conquerors,
Patrons of mankind, gods, and sons of gods.
Destroyers rightlier called, and plagues of men.'

of genius ?' 'Why didst thou give such a mind to one
in my condition ? Why, O Heaven, didst thou enclose
my proud soul within so rough a casket ? Yet pardon my
murmurs. Kind Heaven ! endue me with resignation to
Thy will.'

But a quieter emotion gradually acquired the ascend-
ency within him, and he strove to feel that it was the
hand of God his Father which had placed him beyond
the reach of sound or echo. His knowledge of the Bible
began to produce its quickening results, and spirit was
infused into the forms of religion. He wished earnestly
to be confirmed, and made the necessary application. He
was found to be deficient, when first examined, in some
portion of the Catechism ; but he adds, ' I learnt the Catechism perfect,' and he was then approved by Mr Lampen,
the officiating minister of St Andrews. Yet at the first
occasion on which he attended, he was not confirmed ; the
bishop, and 'the man with the gold lace cloak,' with the
crowds about him, divided his attention, while his want of
hearing prevented him from understanding and following
the order of the ceremonial.

Mr Nugent, teacher of one of the schools in the hospital,
began at this time to pay special attention to him, wrote
out some theological questions for him to answer, and
promised to be his friend. Mr Burnard's interest was also
increased by reading certain papers of Kitto's, suggesting
a plan of judicature among the boys. He proposed to
the thoughtful projector, a short time afterwards, to write
lectures to be read to them, ' respecting their duty in the
house, and their future conduct.' This proposal agreeably surprised Kitto, and he could not contain himself:
' You can scarcely imagine, my friend, how this letter
delighted me, and set me a walking up and down the
court with uncommon quickness, eagerly talking to myself.

Take a bit of my soliloquy : " What ! I, John Kitto, to write lectures to be read to the boys ! Mr Burnard seems to think me competent to it too !" rubbing my hands with great glee.' The youth was filled with gratitude to both these gentlemen, formally adding Mr Nugent to the list of his benefactors, and saying, in the fulness of his heart, of Mr Burnard, ' I wish, I wish his life was in danger, and I could risk my own to save him. That won't do either— too much danger for him.' This feature of Kitto's character grew with his growth, and in his last work he lays down the true doctrine : 'He who most clearly sees God as the source of his blessings, is the man who will be most grateful to the agents through whom these blessings come to him.'[1] Kitto, on one occasion, hints that he did not like to see Mr Burnard whipping the boys, for it was so unlike his generous nature.

The boys used to teaze Kitto a good deal, when the eye of their superiors was withdrawn, till his patience was at length exhausted, and he made a formal complaint to Mr Burnard. The 'frisky letter,' as one of the accused styled it, was at once acknowledged, and his tormentors were severely cautioned as to their misconduct, and prohibited from indulging any longer in such wanton cruelty and sport.

He was becoming, as we have said, more and more anxious about his religious duties. He speaks, under date of October 12, of its being one of the inconveniences of the workhouse, that he was not able to kneel when prayers were publicly read, but resolves to begin on that day to pray ' with himself' in the morning, 'inclining one knee against a chest' which was under the window.

Kitto's dealings with his father are much to his credit. We give two extracts, the first a specimen of humour, and the second of integrity :—

[1] Daily Bible Illustrations, vol. I., p. 393.

'*February* 17, 1821.—The week before last, father wrote on the table with chalk, " You never gave me anything to drink yet." I went, gravely, and emptied out a cup of water, and gave it to him, and said, " There—drink." He blushed deep at this pun, and said no more about it.'

'*October* 7. — Father wrote a paper as follows, and wanted me to give it to Mr Burnard :—" Sir, I should be much obliged to you if you will be so good as to give a ticket for a shirt, as I am out of work.—Ju. Kitto." "Father, thou sayest the thing that is not—you are not out of work." "You must give this paper to Mr Burnard." " Are you out of work, father ?" " No." " Then, do you think that I will deceive my benefactor, and permit you to say, through me, that you are? I will not give it to him." So I said, and so I did. . . . I am inclined to think that I was right. My duty to my parents shall never interfere with that to God.'

Though Kitto felt the restraint of the workhouse, he had become reconciled to it. He was at times, indeed, anxious to quit it, and at other times willing to remain when liberty was offered him. His father on one occasion held out some hopes to him, and, though he refused at first to leave, yet he soon altered his mind, and became very desirous to get out. But his father had changed his purpose, if ever he had seriously entertained it, and the lad was sorely disappointed. The father put forward a variety of objections, but the excited son rebutted them all in succession. 'Liberty,' he cries, ' was my idol—liberty, not idleness. If it were not for the bounty of the kind Mr Burnard, the workhouse would be insupportable. Methinks when I am out of the house, I breathe almost another air. . . . Like the wolf in the fable, I would rather starve at liberty than grow fat under restraint.' Believing that his father was only 'seeking causes' against his getting out, he waxes warm, and tells him, 'There is no fear of my starving in the midst of plenty—I know how to prevent hunger. The Hottentots subsist a long time on nothing but a little gum ; they also, when hungry, tie a tight ligature round them. Cannot I do so too ? Or, if you can get no pay, take me out without, and then I will sell my books and pawn my neckerchiefs, by which I shall be able to raise about twelve shillings, and with that I will make the tour of England. The hedges furnish blackberries, nuts, sloes, etc., and the fields turnips—a hay rick or barn will be an excellent bed. I will take pen, ink, and paper with me, and note down my observations as I go—a kind of sentimental tour, not so much a description of places as of men and manners, adventures, and feelings. Finally, me and father said much more.' The debate was resumed a couple of months afterwards, and Kitto still thought himself ill-used, his father having raised 'false hopes' within him. He admits, that, in displaying such pertinacity, he was in the wrong ; 'for, upon the whole,' he writes, 'I am not dissatisfied with my present condition.' But he drew up what he calls 'articles of capitulation,' and presented them to his parents, insisting that his father, when he agreed to any of them, should write 'granted' opposite to it, while his mother was to make a cross to signify her assent. The principal heads were—that he should be taken out on the 1st of April 1822, or sooner if he was maltreated ; that his boxes and papers were not to be rummaged at home ; that he was not to be interrupted in his studies ; and that, if he died, his body was not to be taken from the workhouse to the grave, but first carried home, and thence conveyed to the place of interment, 'in New Churchyard, beside granny.' The last of the stipulations reveals his suspicions, for it is, 'that you be kind to me.' To all these articles the parents agreed. The curious document thus solemnly concludes : — 'We, the undersigned, do hereby promise to abide by what we have in the above promised to perform, and if we in the least tittle infringe it, we do consent that John Kitto, junior, shall do as he has said; as witness our hands this sixth day of August, in the year of our Lord one thousand eight hundred and twenty-one. On the part of John Kitto, junior, John Kitto, Jun.

On the part of J. and E. Kitto, seniors.

Jn. Kitto.

+ Elizabeth Kitto, her mark.'

He adds, however, that by this formal arrangement he 'gained nothing more than before.' But he was soon released in a manner, and with a result, that he little anticipated.

It was quite common with the guardians of the poorhouse to apprentice the boys under their care to tradesmen in the town. They were anxious, as Mr Burnard expresses it, that Kitto should 'learn a trade, so that he might be able to support himself without parish relief.'[1] This was a kind and considerate motive on their part. It was, in fact, the only design which they could legitimately entertain. That the lad should not be a burden to society or to them, that he should be able to maintain himself by honest handicraft, that at least he should not return to them and be a pensioner on their bounty—was the loftiest purpose they could form for him. Therefore Anderson, the beadle, taught him shoemaking, and he made great progress. To perfect him in his trade, he was then indentured, on the 8th November 1821, to one John Bowden, who had selected him for his proficiency, and in spite of his infirmity. He was to remain under this engagement till he was twenty-one years of age, and he was now about

---

[1] Letter to Mrs Kitto, written after Dr Kitto's death.

seventeen. The guardians probably congratulated themselves that they had done their duty to their ward, John
Kitto, and that they had fitted him to be a useful member
of society. They had got him capricious and wayward,
and now they turned him out a quiet and thoughtful youth,
who had shown some mental power, was inordinately fond
of reading, and had subjected himself to an excellent moral
discipline. Probably they lamented, at the same time, that
his deafness would exclude all rational hopes of elevation
and progress.

By this time, as we have seen, Kitto had subdued his
spirit to the routine and degradation of a poorhouse life.
He was even comparatively contented among his pursuits
and associates. And yet, though he had found such an appreciation of his talents as might have ministered to his
youthful vanity, and not a few indulgences were given him,
still he seems sometimes to have regarded the hospital as a
species of Bastile, and he rejoiced in the idea of quitting it.
He was periodically anxious to be gone; grumbled that
his father had not kept his word and taken him out; nay,
he threatened again and again to run away, though he
usually laughed to himself at such a clumsy mode of exit
and escape. The first offer to remove did not tempt him,
for it presented, in fact, few inducements; so that he hesi-
tated, but afterwards consented. And then the idea of
finally quitting such a domicile filled his spirit with exultation, and, with a flourish of his pen—not elegant, indeed,
but expressive—he writes :—

EPOCHA.

'I am no longer a workhouse boy—I am an apprentice.'
He felt that he had risen a step in society, that he had
ceased to wear the badge of serfdom, and that he was once
more master of himself, save in so far as he was bound by

the terms of his indenture. What we have said is quite consistent with his indifference when the proposal was originally made. He said ' No' to Bowden's first invitation ; but some of the boys, 'aside,' held out the inducement ' of food, clothes, money, and freedom ;' 'I pleaded deafness.' ' I do not care,' he replied to repeated questions, ' I would as soon stay as go.' Some time was spent in negotiations, and at last his coy reluctance was overcome. He never was easily induced to change his habits, and this inflexibility of nature did, for the moment, almost conquer his oft-expressed desire to get out of confinement. His own exclamation, however, leaves no doubt of his rapture—' I am no longer a workhouse boy !' The going home at night, the possession of his evenings for himself, the power of reading in his own garret without molestation, the dropping of the poorhouse uniform, food in plenty, and good clothes—these formed an irresistible temptation. ' Therefore, on Friday 2,' he records, ' I gave a paper to Mr Burnard expressing that desire, and ·soliciting his aid to my being apprenticed.'

The only objection to Kitto's leaving the workhouse was made by Anderson, and that was because the hospital could not afford to dispense with his services, since he was the only boy perfect in the making of list shoes. Nay, Anderson afterwards wished to get him back for the same reason, but Bowden was too shrewd and selfish to part with him.

Kitto had, during his residence, become attached to many things about the workhouse ; and, in the prospect of quitting it, he relates—' So I went and took a farewell look of the bed on which I used to sleep, the tripod on which I had sat so many hours, and the prayer-room. I shook hands, in idea, with the pump, the conduit at which I washed, the tree against which I leaned, nay, the very stones on which I walked. . . I then took a final leave of the

E

hospital, and we went to Mr Bowden's house again, when I was aproned and seated, and set to rip off the old tap of a boot.'

But the hopes of the buoyant apprentice were soon and terribly blasted. His next year's journal opens in a tone of hopeless anguish. He had been delivered into the hand of a brutal tyrant—one who hoped that the infirmity of his apprentice would disable him from making any complaint, and prevent him from obtaining any redress. Bowden's previous apprentice had also been deaf, and we cannot suppose that his treatment differed from that suffered by his successor. But the poor creature had not a tongue to tell, nor a pen to reveal his woes. Bowden, on looking round the busy inmates of the hospital, selected John Kitto, not simply because he discerned him to be the best workman in it, but because he imagined that his deafness, like that of his predecessor, might enable his master to work him beyond right, and punish him without limit, and yet run no risk of being himself detected and exposed. A speechless apprentice he had found to be a helpless victim, who could neither murmur under exhaustion, nor appeal against stripes. The six months of his apprenticeship with Bowden formed the most miserable period of Kitto's existence. He groans mournfully indeed :—

'*January* 19.—O misery, art thou to be my only portion! Father of mercy, forgive me if I wish I had never been born. O that I were dead, if death were an annihilation of being ; but as it is not, teach me to endure life ; enjoy it I never can. In short, mine is a severe master, rather cruel.' The retrospect of two months is sad as he gives it. Bowden threw a shoe at his head, because he had made a wry stitch, struck him again and again— now a blow on the ear, and now a slap on the face. He wept at this unkind usage. 'I did all in my power to suppress my inclination to weep, till I was almost suffocated: tears of bitter anguish and futile indignation fell upon my work and blinded my eyes. I sobbed convulsively. I was half mad with myself for suffering him to see how much I was affected. Fool that I was! O that I were again in the workhouse!

'*December* 12.—My head ached, and yet they kept me to work till six o'clock, when they let me come away. I could eat nothing.

'*January* 14.—He threw the pipe in my face, which I had accidentally broken; it hit me on the temple, and narrowly missed my eye.

'*January* 16.—I held the thread too short; instead of telling me to hold it longer, he struck me on the hand with the hammer (the iron part). Mother can bear witness that it is much swelled; not to mention many more indignities I have received—many, many more; again, this morning, I have wept. What's the matter with my eyes!

'I here leave off this Journal till some other change, or extraordinary misfortune takes place!'

Such is the melancholy end of the Workhouse Journal.

He did not know what awful thing was to happen him, for he had been tossed about like a ball, and he could not predict where next he should either alight or rebound. He could not bear up. He had already suffered much. He had felt in former days the pang of hunger and the cold of nakedness. But now he was oppressed, overwrought, and maltreated,—for sixteen and often eighteen hours of the twenty-four, did his master force him to drudge, and all the while strike and buffet him without mercy. Workhouse boys have few to look after them, and fewer still to interfere for them. And why should Kitto be any exception? The slavery could not be endured. He had been

all the while devoting his spare hours to mental labour—
and even this luxury was at length denied him. To keep
himself awake for study, he had to torture himself by several
cunning appliances. He was willing to have wrought
twelve hours, so to have some time for reading, thankful
to snatch a brief period for sleep. But to toil from six
in the morning to ten at night left him so exhausted, that
only by a painful effort could a little space be given to
reading and thought. This tyranny preyed upon his
mind, such castigations galled him, the long hours of
labour, and the short intervals left for study, oppressed
and fretted him. His nervous system was shattered,
trains of morbid reasoning usurped supremacy over him,
conscience was perverted by sophistical ingenuities, and
his spirit, weary and worn out, looked to suicide as its
last and justifiable refuge. The crisis came; but, as in
the case of Cowper, a watchful Providence interposed,
and Kitto lived. In the volume of essays which he
published on leaving the workhouse, there are two papers
on suicide. In the first, the sin is set in its true light;
in the second, it is described more leniently, and much in
the way in which, in the period of his misery and gloom,
he had gradually brought himself to contemplate it. In
illustration of his remarks, he gives, under the assumed
name of William Wanley, a portion of his own biography,
detailing his dark sensations, how he formed the purpose
of self-destruction, justified it, and resolved to carry it out.
But the attempt failed. The valuable life which was
about to fall a sacrifice to wretchedness and despair, was
preserved for higher ends, and did work them out, till
God's time came for its final release.

The Life and History of Wanley were his own, and he
formally identifies them. He tells Mr Woollcombe, some
years afterwards (December 1825), that 'his mind was

darker and more wretched than anything he had ever
read of'—that 'the letter of Wanley was no posterior fab-
rication, no picture of imagined anguish, but emanated
from a warm and loving heart, every vein and fibre of
which seemed lacerated with misery too highly for the
highest powers of language to express.' In sending the
Essay and Letter of Wanley to Mr Woollcombe, prior to
their being printed, he wrote this admission:—

'*January* 8, 1824.—You will experience no difficulty
in discovering the identity of Wanley. Though he is
happier, very much happier, now than at any period during the last half of his life, all his endeavours cannot prevent the occurrence of that melancholy which predominated
once so absolutely over him.   .   .   The event which I
have narrated is one which he now contemplates with
grief, and on which he looks back with the greatest repentance.' In a brief sketch of his early life, written just
before he left the workhouse, he confesses more explicitly—
' The life of misery I led reduced me to such a state of
despair, that I twice attempted my liberation from his
[Bowden's] tyranny by a means that I now shudder to
think of.'

The complaints of Bowden's apprentice against his
master became at length the subject of judicial investiga-
tion. The trial was adjourned in the first instance, and
one of those times of 'despair,' to which Kitto refers in
the previous sentence, happened in this interval of suspense, when, misunderstanding the forms of procedure, he
believed that he had been formally condemned to be
sent back to undergo, without hope or respite, Bowden's
cruel and lawless oppression. But at length he obtained
redress. The instrument of his slavery, ' with its formidable appendage of seals and signatures,' was cancelled, after
his case had been fully heard before the magistrates, with

whose sanction he had been originally indentured.   In his
appeal to them Kitto acquitted himself to admiration.   He
wrote so fluently and so correctly as to astonish the bench.
His pen delivered him from bondage, and gave him the
consciousness of possessing an undeveloped power.   He
became aware that he could not only think but express
his thoughts—that he could not only feel, but give fitting
language to his emotions.   The gentlemen, who tried the
case, wondered, questioned, sympathized, applauded, and
set him at liberty, but did not trouble themselves much
more about him.   They must have thought him a bold
and bright little fellow, who was armed with a rare power
of self-defence, and would not be easily put down; but,
while they delivered him from the tyrant, they took no
steps to improve his condition.   They had only a very
partial acquaintance with him, and probably judged that
the workhouse was his happiest asylum.

Thus Kitto returned to the hospital, and was set down
again to his former occupation to be perfected in it—still
for the avowed purpose of enabling him to earn an honest
livelihood.   He received many minor privileges, for which
he was thankful.   Bright visions of the future began, however, to cheer him.   He thought himself destined to something.   What might he not do?   Might he not write or
compose a work?   Be it in poetry or in prose, might it
not immortalize his name?   What should hinder the
achievement?   Might not every obstacle be surmounted,
and John Kitto become an author known to fame?
Thanks to Bowden's outrage.   It stung him into life.
He began to criticise some things he had written, and
pronounce them trash,—the first sign of growing taste and
judgment.   He had proposed a higher standard for himself,
and now laboured to come up to it.   His reading had enabled him to judge of style, and had supplied him with

many illustrations. His awakened power longed for exertion, but he knew not as yet where to find the proper field for it.

The experiences of this period are thus delineated by him :—' I had learned that knowledge is power; and not only was it power, but safety. As nearly as the matter can now be traced, the progress of my ideas appears to have been this—Firstly, that I was not altogether so helpless as I had seemed; secondly, that, notwithstanding my afflicted state, I might realize much comfort in the condition of life in which I had been placed; thirdly, that I might even raise myself out of that condition into one of less privation; fourthly, that it was not impossible for me to place my own among honourable names, by proving that no privation formed an insuperable bar to useful labour and self-advancement. . . . To do what no one under the same combination of afflictive circumstances ever did, soon then ceased to be the limit of my ambition.'[1]

But he must, in the meantime, learn his craft, to please Mr Burnard and commend himself to the guardians. He and they, however, were fast diverging in purpose. They thought of him as a shoemaker; he pictured himself as an author. They saw him on ' the tripod;' he beheld himself at a desk. They strove to give him the ability of making a shoe; he dreamed of the power of producing a book. But immediate duty must be attended to, and Kitto passed more months in the workhouse. Again and again did he enjoy his solitary walks—a favourite scene of recreation being the Hoe, a magnificent parade, with the sea and breakwater before it, the ships and docks on one side of it, and, to the right, the classic groves and shady retreats of Mount-Edgecumbe.

The style of his correspondence at this epoch indicates

[1] Lost Senses—Deafness, pp. 82, 83.

higher moral health, and a more refined taste. The cloud was passing away, and his mind was possessing itself 'in patience.' His fevered brow was cooler, and the dew had fallen on his parched heart. He knew not what was before him, but he was becoming equal to anything that might occur. Though he was conscious of talent, there was no inflation of pride, for he was resolved to refuse no offer that might promise to be of advantage. He knew that only step by step could he reach the summit; nor did he seem to be devoured by eagerness for elevation. Probably, however, he was disappointed that nothing further was done for him. But he had awakened interest on his behalf—such interest as sufficed, when a project was started for his benefit, to crown it with success. His case was matter of wide notoriety; yet no one stepped forward to lend a helping hand to the deaf and lonely aspirant.

But Mr Harvey came at length to the rescue. This famed mathematician and man of science had observed Kitto's demeanour in a bookseller's shop, and anxiously inquired about him. Learning his history and circumstances, his benevolent heart knew no rest till he had interested others on Kitto's behalf, and induced them to contribute something, either money or stationery, to the studious youth's assistance. Mr Nettleton also, of the 'Plymouth Weekly Journal,' inserted some of his compositions in that paper. So that Kitto became known, was more and more asked after, and a deeper anxiety being excited, a few friends issued a joint circular on his behalf, the language of which shows the favourable impression which his character and talents had created. The following is the circular referred to :—

' The attention of the public has lately been drawn, by some Essays published in the Plymouth Weekly Journal, to the very extraordinary talents of JOHN KITTO, who is now a pauper in the Plymouth workhouse. He is about eighteen years of age, and has been nearly four years in the workhouse, to which he was reduced by the inability of his parents to maintain him, after his having lost his hearing by a fall from a house in Batter Street, where he was employed as an attendant on the masons. This loss of hearing has been accompanied with other bodily infirmities; but he has been thus so entirely thrown on the resources of his mind, that he has cultivated his intellectual faculties with singular success, and gives promise of making very considerable attainments. An inquiry into his conduct and general character has proved most satisfactory to the undersigned, who are thus led to believe that he must greatly interest those who feel for the difficulties under which virtue and talents labour when they have to struggle with poverty and misfortune. He has of late been employed as a shoemaker in the workhouse, and in that capacity he has given proofs of great skill and industry; but it seems desirable that he should be placed in a situation more consistent with his feelings and abilities, and to which his deafness might not render him incompetent. It has been suggested that, as a temporary measure, application should be made to the Committee of the Plymouth Public Library, to employ him as a Sub-Librarian; and that a sum might be raised, by small subscriptions, to enable him to obtain board and lodging in some decent family, until something permanently advantageous should be suggested. In the meantime, although he could not be in the receipt of a salary, he would have opportunities of improving himself, and would be enabled to direct the powers of his mind to those pursuits in which he is so well qualified to excel, and in which, perhaps, the world may find his usefulness, and he himself a merciful and

abundant compensation for all his deprivations. Great reliance may be placed on his industrious habits, and it is
confidently believed that small contributions from several
individuals would enable him to get over the chief impedi-
ments to success in a way for which he seems so peculiarly
well qualified.   The undersigned, who have carefully examined into his character and acquirements, are anxious
to give the strongest testimony in his behalf; and will
receive, with great pleasure, any contributions, pledging
themselves to use the utmost discretion in their power in
the application of any money that may be thus intrusted
to their management.   JOHN HAWKER, HENRY WOOLL-
COMBE,[1] WILLIAM EASTLAKE, THOMAS STEWART, JOHN
TINGCOMBE, GEORGE HARVEY, ROBERT LAMPEN.—*Plymouth, 26th June* 1823.'

This modest narrative and appeal were successful, and
the governor and guardians of the workhouse subscribed
five pounds to the fund.   On the 17th of July, the following entry is found in the workhouse Minutes :—' John
Kitto discharged, 1823, July 17.   Taken out under the
patronage of the literati of the town.'   Kitto was then
boarded with Mr Burnard, and had his time at his own disposal, with the privilege of using the public library.   A
great point was thus gained for him.   He was released
from manual labour, and had all his hours for reading and
mental improvement.   He must have been aware that efforts
were making for him; and this knowledge, acting on a sanguine temperament, seems to have originated and moulded
the following dream, as he calls it, and which, though probably a waking reverie, is very remarkable as a true pre-

---

[1] Mr Woollcombe, whose early and continued attentions to Kitto were as stimulating as they were kind, was the founder of the Plymouth Institution, a promoter
of literature and the arts, and connected with all the philanthropic movements and
societies of the neighbourhood. He was a highly respectable solicitor, and an alder-
man of the borough, in which he had great and merited influence.

sentiment—a correct delineation of his subsequent career. It is dated three days prior to his discharge, and occurs in a letter to Mr Tracy :—

'Methought (this is the established language of dreamers I believe) I was exactly in the same situation in which I really was before I slept, and indulging the same reflections, when there suddenly appeared before me a being of more than mortal beauty. He was taller than the sons of men, and his eye beamed with celestial fire; a robe of azure hue, and far richer than the finest silk, enfolded his form, a starry zone of glittering gems encircled his waist, and in his hand he bore a rod of silver.

'He touched me with his rod, and gently bending over me, he said, "Child of mortality, I am the Angel Zared, and am sent to teach thee wisdom. Every man on his outset in life proposes to himself something as the end and reward of his labours, his wishes, and his hopes; some are ambitious of honour, some of glory, and some of riches. Of what art thou ambitious, and what are the highest objects of thy earthly hopes?"

'I was astonished at the visit and the words of the angel, and replied not to his demand.

'"Thou canst not readily find, O child of the earth, words to express the scenes which thy fancy has drawn. It matters not; I know thy wishes, and will give thee possession of the state that is the highest of which thou art ambitious."

'He touched me with his rod, and my form expanded into manhood; again he touched and then left me. On looking around me, I found myself seated in a room, two of the walls of which were entirely concealed by books, of which I felt myself conscious of being the owner. On the table lay letters addressed to me from distant parts of the Island, from the Continent, and from the New World:

and conspicuously on the chimney-piece were placed
several volumes, of which I was conscious that I was the
author, and was also sensible that the house wherein I was,
was mine, and all that was in it. I went forth into the
street. Ridicule no longer pointed her finger at me;
many whom I met appeared to know and esteem me, and
I felt conscious that I possessed many sincere and disinterested friends. I met a blind fiddler, and placing my
hand instinctively in my pocket, I found that it lacked not
money. I returned, and exclaimed, as I took Cæsar's
Commentaries, in their original language, from the shelf,
"Now at last I am happy!" but before I had concluded
the word, the Angel Zared again appeared before me, and
touching me with his silver rod, restored me to the state
in which he found me.

' I felt a momentary sensation of disappointment and regret at the transition, till the angel spoke to me, and said,—

' " Listen to my words, O child of mortality, while I
withdraw, as far as I am permitted, the veil of thy future
destiny. Thou hast been afflicted with misfortune, and
taught in the school of adversity. Think not that HE
who made thee and me also, regards with displeasure
those whom He purifies by sorrows, or that those are His
peculiar favourites who are permitted by Him to enjoy
the good things of this world. Whenever thou findest
thyself inclined to murmur at the dispensations of Providence, recollect that others, greater, better, and wiser
than thou art, have suffered also,—have suffered more
than thou hast, or ever wilt suffer.

' " The time approaches when thou shalt attract the
notice of thy superiors, who shall place within thy reach
the means of acquiring that knowledge for which thou
thirstest. They will transplant thee into a soil fit for thee,
and if thou attendest well to the cultivation of thy intel-

lectual and moral faculties, thou mayest perhaps become a permanent occupant of a station like that which I have permitted thee to enjoy for a moment. I say, *perhaps*, for only HE knows, in whose breast is hid the fate of worlds, whether thou art to live beyond the day on which I visit thee; but of this I am permitted to assure thee, that the period of thy sojourn on earth will not be, at the furthest, very many years.

' " Be not, O son of earth, dejected, if thou again meetest with disappointments and misfortunes; neither suffer prosperity too highly to elate thee; and in every situation, and in every moment of thy life, remember that thou art mortal, and that there is a God and a hereafter. So live, that thou mayest not fear death, at whatever moment he may approach thee; and if thus thou livest, thou wilt have lived indeed ——." Zared perhaps would have spoken longer, but a book falling from the shelf upon my head, I awoke, and, as honest John Bunyan says, behold it was a dream !'

One might say to such a wondrous dreamer—

> ' Thy life lies spread before thee as a sheet
> Of music, written by some gifted hand,
> Unsounded yet : to longing, listening hearts,
> Translate its small mysterious silent notes
> Into full thrilling chords of life and power.'

He was now afraid of being overrated, and to show that he was not unduly lifted up by his good fortune, we may quote what he says to Mr Harvey :—

June 15, 1823.—' I sometimes doubt the efficacy of any trifling abilities I possess to retain that patronage with which you honour me. I have not mentioned my unattractive person or clownish manners as likely to operate in the least with a gentleman of your good sense to my disfavour.' Or again, he writes to the same correspondent, Sept.

30, of the same year, 'I apprehend that you are not
disappointed on discovering that I am not one of those
meteors which sometimes emerge from darkness, and illu-
mine the hemisphere of science with their blaze. On two
subjects I am not indifferent. I wish to be known in the
world. I wish to get myself a name, and to be esteemed
by the wise, the learned, and the good. But even this
wish is inferior to that which I have to extend my knowledge, and to compensate, by literary acquirements, for the
deprivation under which I labour.' On June 23, he
chides Mr Burnard, for having altered his style of address
to the pauper boy who had risen in rank :—' Will you
permit me to find fault with the address, " Mr John Kitto ?"
—how cold and formal ! From any other person I might
not object to it, but from *you*, my earliest and best friend,
it must not be. Call me, I entreat you again, plain John
Kitto, or, if possible, by some more affectionate appellation.'
His hopes were not yet very high, and this is his humble
solace—' I am perfect in my trade ; and should circumstances send me back to the workhouse, I hope in Mr
Burnard for all his former kindness and attention.'

Kitto's mind was at this time specially sensitive, and
somewhat irritable. There was the prospect of relief, but
it might not be realized ; the blessing of elevation was close
upon his grasp, but yet not within it. A few of his Essays
had appeared in the papers, and some people suspected that
he had been assisted in their composition. On this point
he was exceedingly tender, as the following letter to Mr
Burnard indicates :—

'*July 22.—Public Library.*

' Sir,—I am not happy : I am very uneasy—more than
uneasy, or I should not now write to you. Pardon me,
sir, if I write incoherently, for I address you under the
impulse of feelings that have recently been wounded to the

quick. Those gentlemen were in the right who foretold that I should meet with disappointments. I went down stairs to read last evening, when it grew dark. I had not been there long before a gentleman came in, who, after having read a few minutes, asked me whether I could hear loud sounds? My answer to this, and other interrogations much more disagreeable, were perused with so evident an intention of finding fault, that it mortified me in the extreme. The pencil was slowly traced beneath the lines; each word was weighed in the scale of grammatical nicety, and one was found to be improper. I observed, in answer to one of his questions, that I had not, till within these few days, begun to study grammar, and that I did not think it fair that I should be judged by rules with which I was un-acquainted. He replied, "You are in the right, I believe; but how came you to write so correctly in the Essays in the newspaper? Did any one correct them for you?" I leave you to judge, sir, whether this was a proper question for a gentleman, and a stranger, to make. I replied in the negative, adding, that "I repeatedly transcribed them, improving and correcting them each time, till I thought them sufficiently accurate. In the two first Essays, how-ever, the editor corrected some errors in punctuation, and he prefixed the quotation from Anon. to my Essay on Home; but, in the Essay on Contemplation, he, at my desire, made no correction or alteration whatever, further than adding three lines from Shakspere to it as a motto." Yet I believe that Essay is the best. Do you not think so too, sir? . . . It was very evident, by his triumphant exhibition of a grammatical error and other circumstances, that he was, beforehand, determined to find fault, and that he departed with a very contemptuous opinion of me and my abilities. Whatever was his intention, it is certain that he has made me very uneasy, and greatly discouraged

me; for, undoubtedly, "the scoff of pride" is not celebrated for its powers of stimulation.'

At this juncture, and while his plans of life were still
uncertain, a proposal was made to publish a volume of his
Essays.   But he scrupled at the censorship of his friends,
and wished the papers to be left wholly to his own taste
and selection.   He had no objection that Mr Lampen
should read and revise them, provided that he himself
might finally bestow upon them 'additional corrections and
improvements.'   But before the volume was published
another change had taken place in his social position, and
he had mounted another step upwards.

His time, meanwhile, being fully his own, was principally
spent in the Public Library, and he was not less miserly in
the distribution of it than formerly.   He devised various
means of economising it, such as forming a diagram of
method, marked with different colours; lamented that of
late he had been in bed full seven hours, while six were
quite sufficient; resolved against heavy dinners; would
like a little ale, but would prefer a small quantity of wine
to his frugal and solitary meal, and so hoped to be able to
read or write, with little interruption, from nine in the
morning till five in the afternoon.   Conscientiously did he
occupy his leisure.   While he was free to choose any line
of study, he decidedly preferred literature to science.
Opening his mind to Mr Harvey (June 1st), he declares of
Natural Philosophy, 'I have no desire to make any particular branch of it my study.   As I have but few hours in
the day at my own disposal, and when I attain to manhood
am likely to have still fewer, it would be absurd in me to
hope to succeed (even if I had the inclination) in such
branches of philosophical and scientific research, as geome-
try, chemistry, electricity, and others equally abstruse,
which are calculated only for men of great talents, and those

who have been blessed with a liberal education.' 'Mine,' he explains to Mr Woollcombe (Sept. 25), 'is a mind not adapted to scientific pursuits. *Man*, I have repeatedly said, and that which relates directly to him, shall be the chief subjects of my research. Let chemists analyse the elements in their alembics, but let me analyse the passions, the powers, and the pursuits of man in the alembic of the mind.' Accordingly he gave himself to reading chiefly in metaphysics. 'The novels, the poems, and the periodicals slept quietly on the shelves.' History, also, occupied a portion of his time, and he retained through life his liking for it. But the metaphysical theories with which he came in contact, ultimately perplexed him, and he abandoned the pursuit. Yet, before he laid it aside, he had gathered from it 'some useful knowledge, acquired some useful habits, and drawn some useful conclusions.' His mind liked to store itself with information, rather than penetrate into profound questions, or range among subtile hypotheses. His intellectual nature was not fitted to deal with such subjects, and his metaphysical studies were pursued, not for the love of mental science, but for the sake of general knowledge. Instinctively he valued the palpable more than the abstruse, and immediate utility outweighed, in his estimate, every form of speculation. He was, indeed, in danger of being injured by the desultory nature of his exercises, for when any mental pursuit ceased to delight him, he was at once inclined to abandon it. He did not relish mathematics, for 'he pursued the steps to the demonstration without pleasure or curiosity.' He resolved to go through Euclid, but was easily seduced from the task; and at length confessed, that whenever he ventured over the Asses' Bridge, he usually 'fell into the water.'

But he thought of 'beginning Latin,' and of 'possessing the Greek language also.' Though he had been, and was

F

still, so voracious a reader, he knew that the mere perusal of books was not to be identified with intellectual improvement.   He puts the case strongly :—'Were it possible for one man to read all the books which have been printed, from Caxton to Bensley, that man might still be a blockhead.   For reading the thoughts of other men will not in itself enable us to think justly ourselves, any more than the wearing of a Chancellor's wig would endue us with the legal knowledge of a Lord High Chancellor.'[1]

He had not been long boarded with Mr Burnard, when his constitutional monitor spoke to him, as it afterwards did, periodically, till his death.   In a letter to Mr Harvey, August 13, he laments :—

'Since Tuesday night I have experienced more illness than within an equal space of time since my fall.   Sickness is well calculated to produce wise reflections and conclusions in the mind.   In the fervour of my hopes, and in the anticipation of future attainments and subsequent usefulness, I had almost forgotten that it was in the power of death to prevent their fulfilment.

'You may, perhaps, sir, also say, that my trifling illness does not justify an anticipation of early dissolution. On such a subject no one can speak with certainty ; yet I may be permitted to say, that I believe my demise will be at no distant period ; and, indeed, I think that, at no other time, it could be more eligible than now.   Were my decease to take place at present, sympathy might shed a tear over my grave, and I might be lamented by the benevolent, the pious, and the learned, as one who, had he lived, might have been a useful member of society.   In after life I may be exposed to criminal temptations, which I may not have power to resist.   I may form ties which it would be agony to tear asunder ; and I may have miseries to endure of which I have now no conception, all of which my demise *now* would prevent. I imagine you pause here, and take up your pen to ask me, " Are you then tired of life, and do you wish for death?" Oh no, sir, I wish to know, and to communicate my knowledge. I would live, could I command it, till time shall have covered my head with hoary honours. I would live till I had learned how to die with a well-grounded hope of future bliss. The reasons above alluded to are by no means such as to make death desirable. It would be absurd to wish for death in order to avert evils, the occurrence of which is no more than probable. However, the frequent thoughts of death will certainly render his approach less terrible when he ultimately arrives.

' Considered abstractedly from the probability of my early dissolution, I think my future prospects very invigorating indeed. Henceforth I shall not look too anxiously on the future, but rely on that Great Being who has been so merciful to me, and hope that He will enable me to be happy in any condition which I may be called to occupy.'[1]

With all his high prospects, a feeling of gloom occasionally stole over him—the shadow of his earlier sensations. To such despondency he makes frequent allusion. He was tormented by fears, and he wisely advised himself to take long walks, and unbend his mind, by partaking of any harmless amusements.[2] But, with all his dark tendencies, his gratitude was great. When he looked on what he had been, felt what he had become, and hoped what he might yet be, his spirit was filled with thankfulness ; and he describes his emotions, in a letter, published in his earliest volume :—

TO MR WILDE.

Plymouth Public Library, Oct.·16, 1823.

' DEAR SIR,—With much pleasure I avail myself of the

[1] Essays, p. 30.   [2] Essays, p. 48.

first opportunity of returning my grateful acknowledgments for the attention you have shown to my accommodation and comfort in the library; and, at the same time, of
saying something about myself. When I recollect (and
can I ever forget?) how miserable I once was; how I was
exposed to ignominy, to insult, neglect, and oppression,
my joy is great to have escaped such evils, and my heart
expands with gratitude towards those disinterested individuals who have rescued me from them.

'In the most enthusiastic of my reveries, I never imagined
that I should ever be as I now am, or that I should attract that attention which has been, and is directed towards
me. I wrote; I endeavoured to acquire knowledge, because my deafness had divested me of all relish for common
amusements, because I could find no other enjoyment or
occupation equally interesting, and because the employment of my few leisure hours and moments gave me the
satisfactory consciousness of spending my time well, without having the most distant idea that this occupation of my
leisure would lead to the beneficial results to which it has led.

' An unprepossessing exterior, and deportment somewhat
singular, made me to be persecuted and despised by my
equals and superiors in age, who knew me no further than
as they saw me, or thought me a being not far removed
from idiocy. Misery, sir, had rather quickened than
blunted the native sensibilities of my heart; and great as
my sufferings were, I probably felt them more acutely than
many others would have done in the same circumstances.

' Amidst all these troubles, however, my thirst for knowledge was not destroyed. My closet was my only refuge,
and a book, when I could procure it, my only consoler;
for there were none to enter into my feelings or sympathize
with me, and by deafness I was cut off from social intercourse with every human being.

'Thus unhappy as I was, if you can form an idea of my situation, you can also conceive the satisfaction which I felt when I suddenly became an object of attention and commiseration to those who have assisted to rescue me from the state in which they found me, and placed me in that which I now occupy. I, the lowly being who, a few days before, was unnoticed and unknown, now became an object of curiosity and wonder to persons who would never have become acquainted with my existence, or have heard my name mentioned, if some trifling circumstances, which I should denominate *accidents* if I had not been accustomed to trace the finger of an overruling Providence in many of those events which the irreligious, the ignorant, and the careless, call by the name of *chances*, had not introduced me to the notice of those who have made me known to others.

'It must be evident, however, that this is not my final destination; and I feel no other anxiety or uneasiness than as it respects futurity. The vast ocean of human life lies before me, and my only wish is that my little bark may in future escape those dangers by which it was once assailed, and that it may proceed in peace and comfort, undisturbed by the blasts of adversity, till it ultimately rest in the quiet haven of the grave.'

One can scarce wonder at the following wish, expressed by such a child of misfortune and poverty, who had never handled a piece of money of any value. It occurs in a Journal that dates from February 19, 1824, to April 3 :—

'I have some time been desirous of consulting my kind and zealous friend, Colonel Hawker, on the propriety of my desiring to have at Whitsuntide and Christmas, or any other two periods of the year, a sovereign, but I have been loath to mention it to him, for he has lately, and indeed always, been so attentive to my wishes, that I am unwilling again to make so great a claim on his consideration. I do not think that Mr Woollcombe or Mr Lampen would make much if any objection to it; but, perhaps, Mr Hawker might, and I am not willing to make a proposal which there is any probability of his rejecting, for if he disapproves of it, I shall not mention it to any other person. I should not be so reluctant, if it were not for the great increase which has been kindly and spontaneously made to my weekly stipend. Well, and what do you want with twenty shillings twice a year? Why, as to that, it is partly a wish of having what I never had before, for I *never* touched a note in my life, nor a piece of gold coin, but once, which was ten years ago, when I was permitted to hold a seven-shilling-piece in my hand for a few seconds. I wish also to have a small sum always at hand, to answer any particular want which may occur. I should also, with part of it, purchase some old books, and thus gradually increase my little store. With half of it, ten shillings, I have no doubt of being able to purchase, at my old acquaintances, ten or twelve volumes of books. I could also supply myself with some minor articles of clothing out of it, and thus prevent the necessity of too frequent applications to Mr Hawker and the other gentlemen on that account.'

Amidst all this anxiety for himself, his wants, and prospects, it is pleasant to find Kitto ' looking on the things of others.' His favourite subjects of composition had been, and still were, childhood and affliction.[1] He wrote of the former with a kind of melancholy pleasure, and of the latter in a tone of earnest commiseration. His life had been a companionship with grief, and such an experience taught him to enter readily into the trials of ' brethren in tribu-

[1] A series of brief essays on ' Childhood ' were addressed by him to Mr Woollcombe, and many of his earlier compositions take the form of letters or addresses to the afflicted.

lation.' Sickness had often visited him, and death had once 'come nigh unto him;' nay, had laid in the tomb his aged and beloved grandparent. He had often craved for sympathy toward himself, and therefore he was forward to express his condolence with those who sorrowed, and mingle his tears with those who wept. He records in his Journal the death of Mr Burnard's son, and adds, under a twinge of despondency, 'I consider his fate as enviable; and nothing but the consciousness that it is my duty to support the life which my Creator gave, prevents me from being absolutely weary of my existence, and anxious to quit it.' But he who had called himself 'John, the Comfortless,' essayed to comfort the bereaved mother :—

April 29, 1824.

' DEAR MADAM,—That at the present moment I write to you with reluctance on the subject you suggested, I must candidly acknowledge. At an earlier period it would have been more proper than now, and I should at such a period have written, had I not been deterred by the reasons I mentioned to you. The natural effect of time is to soften that grief which every afflictive occurrence inspires ; I should therefore have deemed it a duty to avoid the mention of any circumstances likely to revive that intensity of sorrow which time must necessarily in some measure have ameliorated, had you not expressed a willingness to receive any communication on the subject I might make. That your son should be lamented by you, is natural—perfectly natural. Robert was a son of whom any parent might be proud ; and had he lived, and enjoyed health, there could be no doubt of his proving a blessing to all connected with him, and an honour to human nature, if, as nobody denies, human nature can be adorned by piety, talent, and virtue. These are just causes for the sorrow you felt and continue to experience ; but I cannot persuade myself that any

causes can justify unjust repinings, overstrained lamenta-
tions, and rebellious murmurings at the dispensations of
that Almighty Providence which never acts but for the
good of its creatures. Let it not be imagined that I suppose you feel in this manner. Far from it! you feel only a
just and natural grief. But if I indeed thought so, I would
say so. Recollect the state in which he spent the last year
of his life, and say whether you should have preferred to
have had him live for years in this state of mental and
bodily anguish? for, doubtless, independent of his personal
sufferings, he endured much in being cut off from nearly
all the gratifications and enjoyments which render life desirable. Do you believe him happy? Undoubtedly. Well
then, is it kind to repine at his happiness? Supposing, and
there is no absurdity in the supposition, that his immortal
part be conscious of your actions, can it be thought that
his felicity receives any increase from seeing the relatives
whom he loved, lament as those who have no hope, and
murmur at the dispensations of that Gracious Being who
has mercifully seen fit thus early to reward his virtues, by
taking him from a state of anguish to one of unutterable
felicity? Far from it; on the contrary, I conceive this
consciousness, if it be indeed possessed by disembodied
spirits, to be the only alloy of which their present happiness is capable; and, therefore, if it were possible that any
being should have rejoiced in the death of your son, that
being would be in reality less his enemy than you who
thus bewail his loss. Loss! Who has lost? What is
lost? Has *he* lost anything? Yes, he lost mortality, he
has lost pain, he has lost all the miseries of human life,—
these are his losses; but he has in compensation for these
losses, gained,—but his gains I will not attempt to enumerate, for only a disembodied spirit can describe those pleasures, which only a disembodied spirit can enjoy. And

you, have you lost anything? No, nothing has been *lost*, your son has gone a journey, and you know that he is happy, eminently happy, in the country which he inhabits. You know also that a great many years cannot elapse before you will be sent for to the same happy regions, where you will dwell *for ever* with him, without fear of further separation. But supposing for a moment that *you* had *lost* anything by the demise of your son, you are certain that *he* has gained; and could you in that case be so selfish as to repine at your own individual loss, when the same cause has rendered your child so supremely happy? If you could, it would not be acting the part of a mother and friend. Such, my dear madam, are some of the reflections which I would have suggested to your consideration, if I had supposed that in your instance they had been requisite. As my own sentiments respecting death are pretty well known, I shall not now intrude on you any longer than to assure you that I am, yours most respectfully,

'John Kitto.'

'To Mrs Burnard.'

Kitto's continued and prayerful study of the Bible, with the assistance of the best Commentaries which he could procure, was greatly blessed, for there seems to have been all this while the steady growth of religious principle within him.

'*April* 2.—I am in a state which I cannot exactly describe. I become every day more sensible of my own neglect of the duties due to the Almighty, and of my offences against His commandments. I have not that due sense of His mercy, His love, and His benevolence, which I ought to have. I do not form a proper estimate of the vanity of human life, and the contemptible nature of human pursuits, compared with those of a spiritual order. I have not that

overwhelming sense of my own religious and moral crimi-
nality which I ought to possess, nor have I that effectual
and lively faith in Jesus Christ without which everything
else is of no value. It is true that I believe Jesus Christ
to be the Son of God, that He existed with·the Father
from all eternity, and that it is only through His atoning
blood that we can hope for mercy and forgiveness; I believe all this, but this *theoretical* faith I feel to be utterly
insufficient, unattended by practical results, and these practical results I do not experience. There is an internal
monitor within me, independent of the written words of inspiration, which makes me fully assured that of myself I
can do nothing—that my own efforts are contemptible—
and that through a Mediator, and a Mediator only, I can
hope for salvation. That Mediator is Jesus Christ; through
Him I may obtain mercy and pardon, and His righteous
blood can wash away my sins. But I do not feel myself
sufficiently grateful to Him, having sufficient faith in Him,
sufficiently desirous of living only for Him and to Him, or
feel Him absolutely necessary to me. Should I not pray
for all this? I have—I have—but I cannot pray as I
ought to pray. I cannot draw nigh to God in spirit and
in truth. I do not approach Him with a humble and contrite spirit, and with that awful veneration which I ought
to experience. The busy thoughts of the world and literary subjects intrude, and call off my attention from the
solemn occupation in which I am engaged, and thus I
rise from my knees more guilty than when I began to
kneel. O my God! Enable me distinctly to discern the
path in which I should walk, and give me strength to
pursue it.'

He reveals also to Mr Burnard, April 9, the nature of
the emotions which gave birth to such sentiments. 'My
uneasiness is not the cause, but the effect of the humiliating

sense under which I labour, of my own moral and religious imperfections.' 'It originates in a lately awakened sense of my unworthiness. I am afraid that mine is a cold theoretic belief, rather than an effectual and saving faith.'

This anxiety of soul quickened him, taught him from experience the value of prayer as a means of relief, and led him to read the Scriptures with still greater relish and constancy. The idea of becoming a missionary struck a chord in his bosom. When he heard the question thrown out, 'Might not Kitto become a useful missionary, if he studied with effect the only book of sound principles and perfect science ever written?' he caught at the suggestion, and nobly expressed himself on the character and aims of the missionary enterprise, in a letter to Mr Flindell on the subject.[1] Nay more, he was on fire at the thought of becoming a minister. In his Diary, March 31, we note this meditation—

' *Apropos* of Kirke White—I learn that his deafness was one of the reasons which induced him to relinquish the study of the law for the clerical profession. Till I had learnt this, I had understood that a defect of hearing was an insurmountable bar to entering into Holy Orders. Were it possible, O my God! that I could become a minister of Thy Word; that I could be permitted to point out to erring sinners the paths of peace and salvation, what more could I desire of Thee? If an ardent zeal for the salvation of souls, if an unshaken belief in the faith promulgated by Jesus Christ and His apostles, if a fervent attachment to the Scriptures, and if a deep sense of the *natural* depravity of human nature, are qualifications for the ministry, then I am so qualified. How truly happy should I be in some retired and obscure curacy, where I should have no other business but the delightful one of instructing others in their

[1] Essays and Letters, p. 49.

duty to God and their fellow-men, and in which I should
have sufficient leisure to read, to study, and to write!'

Gate of the Hospital of the Poor's Portion

CHAPTER III.

WHILE his mind was in this propitious state, Kitto was introduced to Mr Groves, a dentist, residing at Exeter. Mr Harvey had hinted at a University education for him, and believed that he had sufficient interest to obtain a fellowship. But Kitto's other friends would not entertain such a proposal. He was, therefore, left free to form an engagement with Mr Groves, who had heard something of his history, and had judged favourably of him, from having seen one of his letters to Mr Flindell, editor of the *Western Luminary*. Mr Groves offered to instruct Kitto in his profession, to board him, and give him for his services, £15 the first, and £20 the second year, with prospect of higher remuneration. Kitto accepted the offer, and this engagement was the turning point in his career. It deepened and sealed his piety, and ultimately led him to the East, in preparation for the great work of his life. He had already written a paper on the Antinomianism of Dr Hawker, which shows some familiarity with Scripture, though not a very distinct conception of some portions and aspects of the scheme of grace. But the example of Mr Groves quite electrified him, and every fibre of his heart vibrated under the living impression. A vital and decided change passed over him,—the result of long preparation and prayer.

His mind had been always susceptible of religious impression, but it had not yet quickened into life. The blade had shot up, but there now began to appear the 'full corn in the ear.' He had put on record, before he left the hospital, a specimen of his prayers, in a style of no ordinary magnificence—a specimen which becomes a moral and intellectual wonder, when we consider the upbringing and the circumstances of him who wrote it—a boy, rendered totally deaf by an accident, suffered to grow up uneducated, made a pauper by his father's vices, and now learning an humble trade in a workhouse :—

' MORNING PRAYER.

'King of the Universe! I, an atom of that universe, dare humbly pray Thee to incline Thy ear, while at Thy footstool I confess that I am a wretched sinner; that I have broken Thy laws, and Thy commandments I have trodden under my feet; that I have slighted Thee, my Maker; that I have not done my duty to Thee, my neighbour, or myself; that I have deserved nothing at Thy hands but Thy displeasure. I have wasted the precious moments which Thou gavest me to improve. I have murmured at Thy decrees, because Thou, in Thy mercy, wast pleased to afflict me, and because Thou gavest me to drink of the cup of affliction. I have not loved Thee as Thou oughtest to be loved. I have suffered impure desires and evil passions to influence my actions. In short, O Lord, I am a miserable self-convicted sinner. I have deserved Thy wrath and fearful indignation; and I do not remember one good action that ever I did, which makes me know that Thou alone canst save me. Therefore, Almighty God, overburdened as I am with sin, I dare humbly sue Thee to pardon my sins; remember not against

me my iniquities, but blot them from the book of Thy
remembrance, and erase them from the tablets of Thy
memory. Hear me, O God, when I cry to Thee for that
mercy I do not deserve. Give me, most merciful Father,
the gifts of Thy grace. Give me repentance, for, without
Thy aid, I cannot repent of my sins nor abide by my
purpose of leading a new life; without Thy aid I cannot
know myself. Give me, Eternal King, faith, that no
doubts may obtrude themselves, that I may believe in
Jesus Christ, and keep Thy law. Do Thou also grant
unto me, O Lord, content, that I may be satisfied with
whatever situation in life it be Thy pleasure to assign me,
and that I may be convinced that whatsoever Thou doest
is for my benefit; and that I may thank Thee even for the
rod with which Thou dost chastise me.

'I most humbly entreat Thee, Omniscient God, to grant
me strength to resist the allurements of sin, Satan, my
own flesh, and mine own thoughts, that I may not give
way to temptation, but resist it. Take from my breast,
O Lord, this heart—harder than adamant, black with
impurity, and stubborn—and, O Lord, substitute in its
place a heart purified in the blood of Jesus.

'Inspire Thou those under whom I am placed with
kindness unto me, and give me, O Lord, power to please
them. Shed over me Thy grace, and reveal Thyself unto
me, through Jesus Christ, in whom alone we can know
Thee, and that I may become a new being, casting off all
evil habits and unholy feelings, and conduct myself as be-
seemeth a being whom Thou hast redeemed. Guide Thou
my steps in the way which, though to mortal eye it is
rough and unpleasant to the sense, leads to everlasting
life. And do Thou, Almighty Power, give me strength to
avoid the road which appears to abound with unalloyed
pleasure, but which leads to eternal death.

'If it be Thy pleasure to give me hereafter affluence, grant that I may not abuse Thy bounty; if poverty, grant that I may not murmur;—but I pray Thee, O Lord, grant me not riches nor poverty—yet not my will, but Thine always be done, for Thou knowest what is for my benefit better than myself.

'Bless, O God, my benefactors, relatives, and friends. Teach me how to pray unto Thee, in spirit and in truth.

'Grant me, O Lord, I humbly entreat Thee, grace that I may so conduct myself here on earth, that when it is Thy pleasure to take me hence, I may die with the conviction that my sins are pardoned, and that at the last I may be able to exclaim, "O death! where is thy sting? O grave! where is thy victory?"

'Lord! be merciful to me, a sinner, and grant that I may be one of that happy number to whom it shall be said, "Well done, good and faithful servant, enter thou into the joy of thy Lord." I ask from Thee not, O Lord, worldly blessings. I ask of Thee neither fame, nor riches, nor honours, but, Lord, I ask of Thee a pure and contrite spirit. I ask of Thee patience, to bear with resignation whatsoever afflictions Thou art pleased to send me.

'I thank Thee, O Father, for the manifold favours I have received from Thee. I thank Thee for life, health, friends, connections. I thank Thee that Thou hast forbore hitherto to punish me as my sins have deserved. I thank Thee for all the good I have enjoyed, or may enjoy hereafter; particularly for the protection Thou hast afforded me heretofore, especially in the past night; and I humbly pray Thee to continue my Protector through the coming day, and grant that at the end thereof, I may look back on a well-spent day. These, and all other favours, which are for my good, I pray Thee grant in the name of Thy beloved Son, Jesus Christ, Who loved our souls so well, that He took upon Himself our sinful nature, bled for our sins, bore Thy anger in our stead, and suffered death for our iniquities, and Who taught us, in the perfect form of words, to say, "Our Father Which art in heaven," etc.

'The above is not all that I pray for, only a brief view of the principal heads. What say you to it, dear Harry? Not worthy the Being to whom it is addressed?'

But in Exeter a great spiritual advance had been made, experience had ripened, and he discloses himself to Mr Burnard, June 1824 :—

. . . 'When I look back, I am surprised at the very great change which has taken place in my views since I came hither—a change which I had never anticipated—a change which clearly convicts me, in many former instances of my life, of folly and impropriety—and a change which, ' I hope, will ultimately, under Divine teaching, make me wise unto salvation, and enable me to become a Christian, and an useful member of society. To what is this change to be imputed? Perhaps to a more exclusive contemplation of Divine things, to a more attentive study of the Word of Life, to abstraction from many temporal things which at Plymouth too deeply interested me and engrossed my thoughts, to my intercourse with Mr Groves; but chiefly, I conclude, to the grace of God, who has at length permitted that "day-spring from on high" to arise, for the *appearance of which I have long prayed,* and which, when fully risen, will enable me to behold the beauty of holiness in all its glory and perfection, and by the strengthening influence of the Holy Spirit, to pursue that light which will then be revealed more completely than at present.'

Again, writing to the same correspondent, in September, he reverently marks his first sacramental enjoyment :—

'Since I wrote last, I have for the first time partaken of

G

the Communion, and the day in which I did so was one of the most pleasant in my life—most particularly was it distinguished by that absorbing and sublime devotional feeling which it is my most earnest desire may ultimately become the continual feeling of my daily life, repelling worldly affections and earthly wishes, and making me perpetually act and think from the simple motive of love to our Divine Master.

. . . . 'You must be sensible, from the tone of my letters to yourself and those which you may have seen of mine to other persons—that the John Kitto you will see, is rather a different person from the John Kitto you have seen; and I am sure you will rejoice with me when you understand that this is not a mere alteration of the external manners or appearance, but an alteration most deeply felt in the heart, and entering into every feeling, every passion of the mind, insomuch that I should now be disgusted with much in which I once delighted, and many things are now most pleasant and delightful, which once were indifferent to me.'

Kitto got on well with Groves, as his Diary shows :—

'*May* 19.—Troubles of Latin.—Surely this inaptitude must lower me in Mr Groves' estimation.

'*May* 22.—Mr G. desired to know if I was happy in my situation with him. I replied "that it was beyond my anticipations, and equalled my wishes." It would be ungrateful were I to express myself dissatisfied with his disinterested and zealous endeavours to promote my happiness and comfort. He added, "That it would be a subject of great regret, if any consideration should induce me to wish to leave the bosom of a family, to every member of which I was an object of interest and attachment." '

During his residence at Exeter, Kitto corresponded regularly with his Plymouth friends, upon a variety of themes, and treats, for example, in a series of letters, the topic of capital punishments. Subjects seem to have been proposed to him from time to time; and his style, through exercise, acquired considerable freedom and energy. He was in the habit of distributing tracts in Exeter, and he was often pained by the scenes of profligacy which he witnessed— such as 'fellows emerging from a beer-house, and fighting in the street.' 'My dear sir, my heart is quite sick when I contemplate such scenes of brutal violence. Reflecting on this state of things, it is the duty of every one whom the Holy Ghost has enlightened, whatever his rank or degree may be, to devote himself exclusively to the service of his Master, and to aid His great cause to the utmost stretch of his power. . . . Now, my dear sir, of what I have said I would make personal application, and addressing the Master, say, Behold me, then, my Father! I offer myself, and all that Thou hast made me, to Thee. Send me where Thou wilt, do with me what Thou wilt, and require my services as Thou mayest, I thank Thee that Thou hast made me willing to obey Thy summons; and, Eternal God, so prosper me, as by Thy grace I seek, above all things, Thy glory and Thy honour.'[1]

The portion of his Diary which describes his sojourn at Exeter, concludes with the following prayer :—'Almighty and ever-living God, who madest all things, and lovest all that Thou hast made, deign to incline Thine ear to the prayer of a sinner, who thus humbly, at Thy footstool, entreats of Thee, not this world's goods, or its pleasures, or its honours, but that portion of Thy grace, that infusion of Thy Spirit which maketh wise unto salvation. Grant me these, Righteous Father, and nothing more do I entreat of Thee, for in these all lesser blessings are included. If it be Thy good pleasure that I should drink to the dregs that bitter cup of adversity, of which I have already drunk so largely, proportion my strength to the trials which Thou givest me to undergo ; make me submit, in humble acquiescence, to Thy chastening rod, and make me, in circumstances of apparent sorrow, to exclaim, " Father, if it be Thy pleasure, take this cup from me ; nevertheless, not my will, but Thine be done."   But if, on the other hand, Thou bestowest upon me those things which men so highly seek and desire, O grant that they may have no injurious effect ; that they may not draw my heart from its hold on Thee, and that I may feel myself nothing more than the steward of Thy bounties, and the deputed dispenser to the poor, the unhappy, and the destitute, of a portion of those blessings which Thou mayest give to myself, or rather which Thou hast deigned to give me in trust.   If what I have asked be for my good, grant it, O Father, for the sake of Jesus Christ.—Amen.'

That Kitto had surrendered the ' fortress of his silence,' prior to the time he left Plymouth, is evident from some statements in what he calls his ' Private Diary.'   Who his ' little flame ' was, we know not, except by name.   He was always fond of female society—he loved sisterhood. An impression had been made upon him, which cost him no little pain, when with ' many terrible conflicts ' he sacrificed it on what he believed to be the shrine of duty, and in obedience to the warnings of Mr Groves.

' April 24.—Visited H. this evening ; communicated as much as I thought necessary of my Exonian destination. She did not seem much more pleased with it than with the more superb University plan, an insight into which I gave her.   Well, whatever happens, God preserve her, and make her happy, and while she is so, I can never myself be completely miserable.'

We have given the previous extract, simply to show

that, while so many painful circumstances had conspired to make Kitto solitary and dull, and force him into a lonely and self-devouring asceticism, he had neither sunk into moroseness, nor avenged himself by a scornful misanthropy. He could not exclaim, 'man delights not me, nor woman neither,' for, to his benefactors of the one sex he was sincerely grateful, as his letters testify, and there was one in the other sex who had power to attach him, and charm him out of his solitude, and of whom he says, after the correspondence had been broken off,—' she clings to my heart with a force almost irresistible.' He had pleaded, and that powerfully, for this attachment, against the remonstrances of Mr Burnard. This susceptibility of a first love shows that his heart had not been utterly wrecked by his bitter experiences. He had been saved from himself even when a hard and dry incrustation seemed sometimes to be gathering about him. 'Nay,' he says in his volume of Essays, published soon after (p. 85), 'marriage is in general the principal component part of a happy home.' In an Essay on Beauty (p. 102), he declares, ' I am an enthusiastic admirer of personal beauty. Expression is to beauty what the soul is to the body. I now repeat, I am an enthusiastic admirer of female loveliness. . . . Mental charms in a woman will give pleasure and excite admiration, when the attractions of beauty and youth exist no longer.' . .

About this time, in the beginning or spring of 1825, the volume of Kitto's Letters and Essays just referred to, was published.[1] Neither title-page nor preface has any date. The duodecimo, of 210 pages, was patronised by above 400 subscribers. It is premised that the volume does not ' consist of papers composed expressly for publication.

---

[1] Essays and Letters by John Kitto, with a Short Memoir of the Author. Plymouth.

They are selections from letters which he wrote in the
workhouse, and essays with which he exercised his fond ·
ness for literary occupations, and they were chosen from
the mass of his writings, rather to give an impression of
the character of his mind and talent, than as conveying
any particularly striking or original views of the subjects
of which it treats. . . The volume is now offered to
the public in the hope that it may justify the attention
that has been paid to the merits of this deserving young
man, and that it may be the means of affording him encouragement in the pursuit of that line of conduct by
which he now gratifies his friends.'

It may be well to pause for a moment over Kitto's
earliest production, as the index and fruit of his mental
progress ; and as many of its sections are autobiographical,
we may find confirmation of the statements we have
already made, and learn how, in the dawn of his release,
he regarded his previous hardships, what trains of reflection they suggested, what circles of emotions they produced, what lessons he extracted from them, and what
share they had in directing and moulding his subsequent
career.

And first, there was realized, to some extent, another
and early dream of Kitto, which he has given in his Workhouse Journal, with considerable picturesqueness and
power. He represents himself as being in a book-shop,
'and well-dressed'—a sly hit at the poor-house uniform.
He is surveying on the counter his own journal in a published form, when a family enter the shop—a sage father,
' a flauntily-dressed elderly lady, with their son and
daughter, both dressed as a dandy and dandyzette.' The
young coxcomb laughed outright as he took up the volume.
' When asked what excited him, he read the title-page of
my unfortunate book—" Journal and Memoranda of a Man

with Four Senses, by John Kitto, Shoemaker, Pauper,"
etc. " Was there ever such a thing heard," continued he,
" as for a pauper! a shoemaker! to write anything proper
for the perusal of a man of sense!" adjusting the ribband
of his quizzing-glass, with the air of a person well satisfied with his own sense. " No, certainly," said his mother,
" and I would wager a guinea that it may be classed
among the Methodistical jargon which the authors are
pleased to call Journals, and of which so much has been
obtruded on the public." " I, too, would wager a guinea,"
said the young lady, "that in this bantling of *wax* there
are no tender embarrassments—no ghosts—no tears of
sensibility—nor any duels—for nothing but the most gross
vulgarity can be expected from this son of the awl."—
" Yes, indeed! was ever such extravagance heard of, as
for a shoemaker, an occupation found only among the very
dregs of the vulgar, to pretend to write a book? I should
not now wonder, 'pon my honour, if the barber should
favour us with a treatise on beards—the sign-dauber with
a history of painting—or even the catgut-scraper with a
history of music," concluded the young gentleman, with
a loud and long "He! he! he!" at his own wit; "for,"
added he, "they may as readily do it as a pauper write a
Journal." The grave looking old gentleman, who had
attentively listened to all that had been said, advanced
towards the rest and said, " Ladies and young man, I
must dissent from what all of you have said " (an angry
and satirical " indeed!" proceeded from all three at the
same time)—The old gentleman, not noticing this interruption, proceeded—" Particularly with regard to what
has been said about the incapability of mechanics. For,
from my own experience, I can assure you that I have
met with genius, probity, and honour, in many instances,
among what you are pleased to call the dregs of the peo-

ple. I have always looked upon an honest mechanic, though even a shoemaker, as a much more useful member of society than he who, blessed with affluence, holds time a burden—who lives merely to circulate that which would make hundreds happy, and who spends every hour, every day, in what is falsely called pleasure, and who lives for not one of the ends of his creation; who, so far from improving that *time* which every hour shortens, thinks himself happy when he has hit on an idea to kill that time of which he is not certain of a moment's continuance. But the best way to convince you of your error is to give you examples of genius amongst the lower classes. I will mention but a few names of the many that occur; as, for instance, R. Bloomfield, Burns, Chatterton, G. Morland, Savage, Lloyd, Otway, and Shakspere. I scarce need have told any but you that most of these were poets—very celebrated poets, and more particularly that Bloomfield was a shoemaker—the fourth was one of our best English painters—and yet none of these were bred in affluence, nor were their talents cultivated by education. But with regard to the book, the merits of which you have decided without opening its pages, I have read it, and though written by a pauper, it does not sink *much* below mediocrity—the misfortune of the author renders it in some measure interesting; the language is simple, the orthography not very incorrect; it has some humour; learning cannot be expected; yet the author is not ignorant, and he seems an honest youth, with sentiments much above his condition. Upon the whole, it is better than could be expected from one of his years and situation; and if it does no good, it will have the negative merit of doing no harm, and it shall be placed in my library." '

He who could so express himself was on the high way to write a book, and leave behind him the ' flannel jacket

and leathern apron'—the badge of poverty and St Crispin,
and must soon cease to be 'shoemaker and pauper.'

The volume bears witness to his multifarious· reading.
One wonders how he had found time to run through so
many books, and read them so carefully as to be able
to make such frequent and pertinent allusions to them.
The amount of his reading would not have dishonoured a
university student; nay, few of them lay in such a stock
of general information. In metaphysics, intelligent and
distinctive reference is made to Malebranche and Hume,
Reid and Stewart, Berkeley and Des Cartes, Locke and
Stillingfleet. Lord Bacon and Madame de Stael are fami-
liarly quoted. In an essay on Sublimity, where he refers
to the fine arts, he contrasts the Tuscan and Doric orders
of architecture with the Gothic, especially as seen in West-
minster Abbey, and in the ruins of Tintern and Glaston-
bury; tells what the pencil of Salvator Rosa achieved,
and what Gainsborough could effect; assigns their respective positions to Titian and Raphael; then passes on
to sculpture, criticising the Apollo Belvidere, the group of
the Laocoon, and the Choragic monument of Lysicrates.
His papers, entitled 'Rabnah and Abdallah,' are rather
happy imitations of the once famous Jewish apologues of
Hawksworth and Johnson, and many of the 'desultory
reflections,' which conclude the volume, are terse, pointed,
and memorable. Kitto denies imitation in style, but
many of his first compositions controvert the statement.
He fell unconsciously into such imitations. What he
had been reading deeply interested him, and left its impress on his next composition, while inability to hear his
own sentences prevented him from detecting the similarity.
Does not the following sentence sound like a piece of a
Saturday Spectator?—

'When we consider the numberless claims that the

Deity has to our gratitude, our adoration, and our love—
what a great Friend, a merciful Father, and a bounteous
Benefactor He has been to us, and that on Him depends
everything we value and desire—the coldness with which
we sometimes perform our religious duties appears to me
truly strange and unaccountable.'

Would not the following pass for a portion of the
Rambler?—

'It were well, perhaps, if the wealthy and the prosperous could have a periodical fit of misfortune, which, independent of its other uses, would give them an opportunity
of discovering who were their real and who their pretended
friends.'

There occurs also in the Workhouse Journal a pretty
good imitation of Sterne, in an account of a real occurrence. Kitto describes a poor fellow who, from a double
amputation, shuffled along on his knees, but did not beg.
A marine, passing him, poured the whole contents of his
pocket into the maimed man's hand, went away, and wiped
his eyes, as if he thought a tear disgraceful. 'Thou wast
wrong, generous soldier! That tear, that action did thee
more honour in my eyes than if thou hadst slain with thine
own hand thousands of thy fellow-men, and wert therefore
called a hero! Thou, noble veteran! wast more charitable
and more praiseworthy than a rich man if he had given fifty
pounds. Thou gavest thy little all. In the perils of war,
and temptations of peace, God be with thee, generous
marine!' Kitto was fond of Shakspere, and specially
fond of Spenser; and his proneness to form allegories, and
shape his fancies into dreams, arose probably from this last
predilection.

His deafness laid him under the necessity of writing.
The thoughts of his heart struggled for utterance; and
what could not be spoken, must at least be written. Had

he been able to converse freely, his feelings would have sooner expended themselves, and when afterwards committed to writing, would have lost somewhat of that intensity which characterised them. But his emotion, unwasted by oral expression, appears on paper with undiluted strength. Even his ordinary thoughts, pent up within him, and turned over again and again, and examined on all sides, in prolonged and undisturbed reflection, assumed a mature fulness and symmetry when his pen gave a deliberate and final utterance to them. This record of his inner history is striking and characteristic :—'I never was a *lad!* From the time of my fall, deprived of many external sources of occupation, I have been accustomed to *think*, to find sources of occupation within myself; to think deeply; think as I read, as I worked, or as I walked. Even in my sleep I dreamt ; the addresses, letters, sermons, puns, bon-mots, and tales, I have composed in idea, would, if committed to paper, fill a folio. While other lads were employed with trifles, I thought as a man, felt as a man, and acted as a man.' Yet the appetite for human intercourse led him again and again to write as if addressing another party in an ideal dialogue ; and the same yearning for social speech prompted him to write formal letters to himself, specimens of which are inserted in this published collection. The solitary boy created an imaginary companionship. Some of his letters and papers, illustrative of previous parts of his life, have been spoken of already, such as his letter to Mr Flindell on the moral dignity of a missionary, and his essay on suicide. There is, in fine, an excellent paper in the volume, suggested by a passage in Bishop Hall's ' Balm of Gilead,' which unfolds much of his inner thoughts. In harmony with what the good bishop has said, he delivers his own experience :—

'Next in pre-eminence in the list of misfortunes, after

blindness, comes deafness. To me the whole world is dumb, since I am deaf to it. No more the music of the human voice shall charm. All around, below, and above me, is solitary silence—ever-during silence—stillness unbroken. Words of advice, of comfort, of instruction or reproof, to me convey no knowledge, nor make me wiser, better, or more happy. For me the feathered warblers tune their little throats in vain! To me the violin or the harp gives no music; the deep-toned bell and the pealing organ, no sound. Behold the people crowd to the house of God, to hear the preacher display the riches of redeeming love; but if I go I hear not his words, which to me alone are profitless; I hear not his voice, which only to me is mute. I am now a mere cipher among men—of no value, importance, or estimation. My door is shut, and ever barred against the entrance of knowledge; and in no capacity can I hope to be a useful member of the community. Liable to continual mistakes and mortification—cut off from social communication — incapable of receiving pleasure from many of the impulses of sympathy, and of enjoying congenial intercourse—a being completely solitary and desolate, life would be robbed of all its sweets did there not exist some

"Motives for consolation."

Some of these consolations are mentioned by the pious prelate:—"Had it pleased God to 'shut up both senses from thy birth, thy estate had been utterly disconsolate; neither had there been any access for comfort to thy soul: and if He had done so to thee in thy riper age, there had been no way for thee but to live on thy former store: but now that He hath vouchsafed to leave the one passage open, it behoves thee to supply the one by the other, and to let in those helps by the window which are denied entrance by the door." ' Kitto then proceeds with his comment :—'An anonymous author tells us that "The way to be happy, is to look down on those who suffer, and not up to those who shine in the world." This I hold to be an excellent maxim, and, to be consistent with it, though I cannot look much lower than myself, instead of lamenting the loss of my hearing, I will rejoice that I am not blind. I thank Thee, O my Father! that Thou didst rather.close the doors than the windows of knowledge and delight; and that, having barred the doors, Thou didst not also darken the windows. If I were both blind and deaf, in what a wretched situation should I be! If both the windows and doors were shut, whereat could knowledge enter? It has been my earnest endeavour, since my fall, to "supply the one sense by the other," and to give entrance at the window to as much information as I could possibly obtain. If I could not read, how deplorable would be my condition; and I earnestly entreat all who may chance to read this, of whatever condition, sex, or degree, that they will not be backward in lending me *books;* for if they attentively reflect on my situation, they will perceive that no other sources of information, knowledge, or instruction, and, I might add, of amusement, are left open to me than those which books afford. Without books, I should quickly become an ignorant and senseless being, unloving and unloved, if I am not so already. I apprehend that I have sometimes offended my acquaintance, by the importunity with which I have solicited the loan of books. But if I had a house full of books myself, and knew any person to whom they would be so necessary as to me, and who would make so good a use of them as I do, I would not stay to be entreated, nor scruple to lend any, or all of them, in succession, to such a person. What earthly pleasure can equal that of reading a good book? O dearest tomes! Princely and august folio! Sublime quarto!

Elegant octavo! Charming duodecimo! Most ardently
do I admire your beauties. To obtain ye, and to call ye
mine, I would work day and night; and to possess ye, I
would forbid myself all sensual joys. . . . The Almighty
afflicts but to bless. Notwithstanding that His judgments
often seem harsh and severe to those who are afflicted,
they are in reality just and merciful. It is mercy in Him
when He sends us one evil to preserve us from some greater
and more serious ill. How do I know but that God permitted my deafness, as an instrument through which I
might be saved from some far worse evil, which He fore-
knew would have happened to me if I had continued possessed of my hearing. But be that as it may, while I
regret the loss of a valuable sense, can I ever forget to
thank Thee, O my Father! that, when I fell, I did not
lose my reason or life instead of my hearing? Never!'[1]

Such, then, was Kitto in his twentieth year—an unfortunate and feeble stripling, who had sunk into poverty
and wretchedness, nay, had fallen so low as to dwell in
a workhouse to acquire a trade, and thus become, as the
guardians thought, provided for. Now, through his talents
and character, he has emerged into a position of respectability, has turned his busy reading to good account, is
the author of a handsome volume, patronised by many of
the clergy, and by peers and peeresses of the realm, and
is talked about as a kind of prodigy. The Hospital of
the Poor's Portion is proud of him, and he is in the way
of higher preferment, though as yet his friends discern not
his ultimate career, nor does he himself foresee the rugged
and devious path by which he must reach the great labour
of his life. Yet he hints to Mr Burnard that he is in
high hopes of prospective authorship. 'If my days be
lengthened, nothing is more likely than that I shall publish

---

[1] This Essay is dated Plymouth Workhouse Feb. 16, 1823.

again ; but never will I publish, unless it be something far
more worthy of attention than this ; but I question whether
my next publication, however superior to this it may be,
will be equally well supported.' Right, and yet' wrong.
His next publication was both vastly superior and far
better supported. But he did not as yet even dream of
it, for it was the Pictorial Bible with which his name has
become identified, nor was he then trained and equipped
for such an undertaking.

A fortunate change speedily took place in Kitto's condition. Mr Groves had been for some time contemplating
the work of a missionary for himself, and had kept terms
at Trinity College, Dublin, to prepare for episcopal ordination. As, therefore, his residence in Exeter could not be
of long continuance, he was anxious to secure some settled
mode of subsistence for his assistant. Several plans were
proposed, to enable him, if he should abide by his vocation
as a dentist, to practise either in Plymouth or the metropolis. But a wise Providence had otherwise determined.
Mr Groves had learned that the presses at several stations
of the Church Missionary Society were in need of hearty
workmen, and, knowing the devotedness of Kitto's spirit,
and his vast admiration of evangelical labour, he proposed
that he should take part as a printer in the great missionary enterprise. Kitto caught at the proposal, and thus
addressed Mr Woollcombe :—

Exeter, June 1825.

'Sir,—To you and my other friends I feel it necessary
to write, before the recurrence of the periods respectively
assigned, in order to communicate a circumstance, for
which you are more prepared than any of the other gentlemen to whom I am about to write. From something
which passed when I had the honour of waiting on you
whilst I was at Plymouth, in November last, you are, I

presume, sir, sufficiently aware of the high interest which
I felt in relation to the general subject of missions. And,
indeed, from a letter written before I had the least idea of
coming' hither, it will probably have appeared that my
mind was early impressed with a sense of the great privileges and importance of the missionary character. Will
not these circumstances, sir, have operated on your mind
as preparatives for the intelligence, that I hope myself to
be permitted to occupy the high station of a labourer in
the vast field of missionary exertion? That is the intelligence I write to communicate. And, requesting to be
allowed to suppose, for a moment, the existence of a common feeling in relation to *one great object* between us, I may
be allowed to anticipate your sympathy in the gratification
which I derive from having enlisted under the banners of
The Church Missionary Society. Attached as I am to the
soft domestic charities of life, and open as my prospects of
being permitted to enjoy them were, it cannot be necessary
that I should inform you, sir, that nothing but a deep sense
of the duty which I owed to Him who has been so very
good and merciful to me, and an ardent desire to contribute the humble offering of my individual exertions to
the great, the noble cause, of assisting to dispel that darkness which is so deeply to be deplored, could have induced
the offer of my services to that Institution. At a time
like this, which may not improperly be considered a *crisis*
in every point of view in which it can be contemplated, I
think it very essential that every Christian should assist the
mighty energies now in active operation, by the practice
of that absolute and exclusive self-devotion to the service
of the Almighty, the principles of which the Scriptures so
strongly inculcate and enforce. Hence I rejoice in an
occasion of practically demonstrating the *reality* of that
willingness, which I have not been backward in professing,

to appropriate myself, and every talent which God has committed to my trust, to the cause of Him from whom all things are derived, and whose right they therefore are. To do this is my honour, the highest honour I can attain—my privilege, my duty ; and to it every rational consideration suggested to my mind—every *proper* feeling of my heart—irresistibly impels me, in spite of a certain degree of reluctance which I have naturally experienced at the idea of entering on a career of high moral responsibility and active exertion.   Instead of these general statements and reflections, it will, perhaps, sir, be more necessary that I should enumerate the leading features of the circumstances under which I live.   It having been discovered that the Church Missionary Society was in want of printers in various of its stations, the idea occurred to Mr Groves that I might be very useful in such a capacity, and that I seemed peculiarly adapted for such a situation.   When I had properly considered the suggestion, I eagerly entered into the idea it contained.   Being satisfied, then, that this must be a most *useful* sphere of action, it of course became my duty to labour in it.   Mr G. therefore wrote to Mr Bickersteth, the secretary, offering my services to the Society.   No answer was immediately received, but Mr Groves received an intimation from a third person, which induced him to go to London.   He was there enabled to put the affair in a more desirable chain of operation than it had previously been ; but the question was reserved for the decision of the Committee, which was held the week before last.   On Friday evening information was received that the Committee did not consider my deafness as any material impediment to my usefulness as a printer at one of the Society's stations.   They wish me, therefore, to come to London, where I am to be instructed in the business by Mr Watts, their printer.   Printers are much needed.

in Calcutta, Malta, and several other places ; and if I go
out under the Society, my employment will be to superintend the operations of the natives in the printing esta-
blishments.   I know nothing, sir, in which I could be more
useful than this ; and to be useful is the only object, if I
had any preference at all, for which I should wish to live.
Even in a temporal point of view, if my mind had even
adverted to such a consideration, this would be no unde-
sirable provision, as the Society takes care of its labourers
in cases of inability arising from sickness, age, or any other
cause equally unavoidable with these.   Certainly I do not,
sir, expect that, either in London, or on any of the Con-
tinents, I shall not have many trials and difficulties to support ; but I hope and believe that He who has hitherto
been with me will give strength and patience sufficient for
me in *all* the varied circumstances of action and of being
to which He may see fit to call me.—I remain, Sir, your
greatly obliged and obedient servant,

                                             ' J. Kitto.'

Kitto was accepted by the Board in London, Mr Groves
making a liberal offer of fifty pounds a year, for two years,
towards the defraying of his expenses.   In July 1825 he
took up his residence at the Missionary College in Islington,
and was assigned to the care of Mr Watts to learn printing.   What trades he had passed through already—barber, shoemaker, dentist, and now a printer !   The last,
however, was viewed by him in a spiritual aspect.   He
was qualifying, as he imagined, for the purpose of circulating the Bible and religious books.   The work was, therefore, to his liking.   He had thought of various projects
before he left Mr Burnard's, and suggested to Mr Harvey[1]
' that active measures should be taken to procure me some

                 [1] Library, September 30, 1823.

situation, before the money be exhausted, which you have with so much trouble collected.' . . . 'Food and clothing are my only objects.' He had at that time a strong desire to be attached to some gentleman's country residence, as he was willing to work for his maintenance in any humble capacity, provided all his time was not occupied, but some of it left for his own literary pursuits. He had a strong aversion to either editorial or subordinate connection with a newspaper, but would not have demurred to being 'connected with Mr Drew and the Imperial Magazine.' Other schemes were afterwards started in his fertile ingenuity, but none of them were adopted. Such a place as that which he had so recently held under Mr Groves had never once been thought of, and his position in Islington as a printer, in connection with the Church Missionary Society, was as remote from his usual anticipations. The calculations of his own prudence had all been defeated, and he could not but feel that, as a ward of Providence, his steps had been under the leading of a kind and invisible Hand. The unschooled cobbler of the Plymouth Workhouse was now an honoured inmate of Islington College.

CHAPTER IV.

KITTO was highly gratified with the attention shown him by all the persons connected with the Institution at Islington, and he speaks very decidedly of the piety and zeal of the eighteen students resident in the house. He tells his friends in Plymouth of a great meeting, Lord Gambier in the chair, when fifteen missionaries received parting addresses. It was 'the most grand and impressive occurrence' he had ever beheld, and, he adds, 'a finer delivery than that of some of those speeches I never *witnessed.*' In Mr Watts' printing-office he learned first to set Greek types, and he enjoyed much 'delightful contemplation while working at his Greek cases.' Then he tried Persic on Henry Martyn's translation of the New Testament. This manual labour was fatiguing, but still he gave himself to reading. He enjoyed what he called 'pocket-reading'— that is, taking one of his volumes and reading it as he walked to and from the place of business, and at every spare moment he could snatch during the day. The reader will remember how the boy, either in rags or in the dress of the workhouse, prowled about the bookstalls in Plymouth and Devonport, and pored over their miscellaneous and tattered contents. Now, when he had come to London, this passion met with an ampler gratification. He revelled in the luxury, and philosophised upon its superior delights.

The paradox which he maintains is evidently a relic of his early vagrant life. He rejoiced in his perambulations, and seemed to prefer such half-hours of literary license to undisturbed and sedentary study. 'Bookstalls,' he writes, in high glee, to Mr Harvey,[1] 'are very numerous in and about the town; bookstalls, the least of which will not admit any comparison with any provincial bookstall I have ever seen; and if I had formerly lived here, I might have had many hours of comfortable reading every day, merely by going from one bookstall to another, and spending half an hour or so at each; and by the time I might have visited the last in my circuit, I should have been long enough absent from that with which I had begun, to venture thither again, and so on, circuit after circuit. Now, if this state of things be compared with what I have already mentioned to have been the case in Devon, the advantages of a residence in London, to a person of literary habits, is sufficiently obvious in the instance I have selected. Few, on this plan, would be able to boast a larger library than myself. The advantages of such a library are obvious also. *First*, No money is paid for the privilege. *Secondly*, The usual effects of sedentary occupation are prevented, as the student is obliged to stand while reading, and to walk both before and after. *Thirdly*, The opportunity of studying human character is one of peculiar importance; for the character of the book-man or book-woman, when they form the accompaniment of the stall, which happily is not always the case in London, is a subject of such essential importance to ourselves, that we study them with an anxiety the most intense, and penetration can never be more strongly excited by circumstances than in such an instance. And, *Fourthly*, there are peculiar benefits attending this mode of reading. When

[1] Islington, January 19, 1827.

we have books in abundance of our own, or have them in
any way at our own disposal, we are apt to neglect them,
knowing we can read them at any time we please; and
when we do read them, we are apt to do it cursorily,
knowing that we can turn to them again whenever we
wish to do so. But at the bookstall we read for our lives.
We know that no time is to be wasted. We know that it
is not likely we shall ever see the book again. Stolen
reading, too, is sweetest; and, upon the whole, there is
probably nothing we ever read which is so impressed on
the memory, and so treasured up in the mind, as that
which is read at the bookstall. This is easily accounted
for. We know that the only future benefit we can derive
from the volume, is that which the memory may afford;
and hence the effort of the mind is strong to retain that
which it has taken in. The person likely to avail himself
of such a system, has also so little else to read, that the
little he does thus read is the more easily retained. *The
best readers are not those who read most.* I read a great deal
in the Plymouth library, but I remember less of that than
of what I had previously read at my friend's bookstall,
and in the windows of booksellers' shops. A person who
has many books of his own, or who can get books to read
without difficulty, will never understand the advantages of
bookstalls as I have related them, because he will want
that intense and powerful stimulus which the bookless
student possesses.'

In the meantime, his eye had not been idle, nor was his
heart seared. The pain he had suffered in relinquishing his
early attachment did not prevent him from forming another.
His heart yearned for affection. He was continually striv-
ing, as he tells us, 'to win the affection of children, and
was often disappointed in their caprices and fickleness.'
Three months after coming to Islington, he had seen a

lady at church, who invited him to the joint use of her hymn-book, and he had been pleased by her appearance.[1] He could tell nothing about her. Neither her name nor residence was known to him : nor does he seem to have made any anxious inquiry about them. But one of his periodical illnesses overtook him. He had been leeched on the temples, and during his convalescence he went out and walked one afternoon in Barnsbury Park. As he was returning to the college, he happened to enter a shop and engage in conversation with the lady who kept it, and who was a 'respectable and serious-looking woman.' The talk was about Sunday Schools, and 'she supported her part of the discourse on a slate.' She invited her customer into the parlour, which was 'hung round with prints of eminent ministers, framed and glazed.' She showed him the prize-books which her children, six in all, had got at a neighbouring Sabbath seminary, and he naturally wished to see the family. The reply was, that they were all at school but one, and when that one obeyed the maternal summons to appear, Kitto was agreeably surprised to recognise in her the object of his previous admiration. She did not, however, recollect him. A courtship naturally began, and proceeded, on successive visits, to his great satisfaction. A matrimonial union was ultimately agreed on. Mr Groves did not now attempt to reason down his passion, but approved of the project, and Mr Bickersteth, the secretary, gave also his formal consent. He lost no time in informing Mr Burnard of his choice, for 'he who has rejoiced in my joy, and sympathized in my distress, will assuredly rejoice with me in this ; and great will be my pleasure, my dear sir, in introducing to you no common character— a Christian wife, a Christian daughter, a Christian woman.'

---

[1] The incidents are given by himself, somewhat minutely, in a paper entitled, 'A Memorial of Two Years and a Half of the Life of J. K.'

Marriage was no new idea to him. Even when he was
the immediate protegè of charitable friends in Plymouth,
and before any door was opened to him, he avows, if
he should get a curacy—'Then I shall marry, and shall
enjoy domestic comfort and my favourite pursuits at the
same time.'

Kitto's spirit glowed into poetry when it felt the 'new
sense,' or laboured under the 'madness' which he ascribes
to his love, and he sent the following meditation to Mr
Burnard. The prelude is—'My dear Sir;—Though you
know that John Kitto is no poet, still I hope that, at a
leisure minute, this may give you pleasure :—

A REVERIE ON MARRIAGE.

COMPOSED WHILE SITTING TO A PORTRAIT-PAINTER.

Full many a man has sunk to rest
With social kind affections blest—
A heart to cherish and enjoy
The tender, soft connubial tie.

And yet these men have seldom known
The social happiness *of home;*
But, served by menial hands and rude,
Have mourned in cheerless solitude.

Say, such be I, then. Shall I sigh,
And sunken and dejected die,
Because to human joy unknown,
Gently to soothe me there is none?

None to sympathize in glee,
And, when I weep, to weep with me;
None to ease life's weary load,
And walk with me the narrow road;

None near me in the trying hour,
Soft balm into my wounds to pour;
None in pain to hold my head;
None to mourn me when I'm dead.

    .   .   .   .   .

His hand shall soothe me when in pain ;
That hand can make me whole again.
In death my God will still be nigh ;
Yes ; He'll be with me when I die.

Domestic sweets—the social band—
Are doubtless present ; but the hand,
Which them and other blessings lends,
Can give a bliss that never ends.

Why, then, should I complain and moan,
As one quite cheerless and alone ?
When, having God, in Him I've all
We justly happiness can call.

Human delights, I ask them not ;
Be Thou the guardian of my lot ;
And give a heart to count but loss
All, all things for the Christian Cross.

Give, Lord, a heart of warm desire,
Touch it with coals of living fire,
And kindle there a radiant flame
To burn for ever to Thy name.

And Thou, O Man of Galilee,
Who bled and agonized for me,
Through the strength that's only Thine,
Be victory and triumph mine.'
' *December* 30, 1825.'

The lines that succeed were addressed to the object of his
devoted attachment. It is now the betrayal of no secret,
that if Hannah were substituted for Mary, the poem would
stand as originally composed. Kitto himself published it
in the ' Lost Senses,' with the fictitious name :—

' In silence I have walked full long
    Adown life's narrow, thorny vale,
Deaf to the melody of song,
And all music to me mute,
    From the organ's rolling peal
    To the gay burst or mournful wail
Of harp, and psaltery, and lute.

Heaven's dread answer I have heard
  In thunder to old ocean's roar,
As while the elements conferred,
  Their voices shook the rock-bound shore :—
I've listened to the murmuring streams,
Which lulled my spirit into dreams,
Bright hopes, and fair imaginings ;
But false as all that fancy flings
Upon a page, where pain and strife
Make up the history of life :
And so, beneath o'ershadowing trees,
I've heard leaves rustle in the breeze,
Which brought me the melodious tale
Of the all vocal nightingale,
Or else the cushat's coo of pride,
O'er his own new-mated bride.
Yes : I have heard thee—Nature, thee—
  In all thy thousand voices speak,
Which *now* are silent all to me.
  Ah, when shall this long silence break,
And all thy tides of gladness roll
In their full torrent on my soul ?

But as the snows which long have lain
  On the cold tops of Lebanon,
  Melt in the glances of the sun,
And, with wild rush, into the plain
Haste down, with blessings in their train :
So, Mary, gilded by thine eye,
  Griefs melt away, and fall in streams
  Of hope into the land of dreams,
And life's inanities pass by
Unheeded, without tear or sigh.

True, that the human voice divine
Falls not on this cold sense of mine ;
And that brisk commercing of thought
Which brings home rich returns, all fraught
With ripe ideas—points of view
Varied, and beautiful, and new,
Is lost, is dead, in this lone state,
Where feelings sicken, thoughts stagnate,

And good and evil knowledge grows
Unguided and unpruned, and throws
Too often a dull sickening shade,
Like that by trees of Java made,
O'er hopes and o'er desires which might
Have lived in glory and delight,
Blessed and blessing others, till
The gaspings of this life were still.

But, Mary, when I look on thee,
   All things beside neglected lie :
There is deep eloquence to me
   In the bright sparkle of thine eye.
How sweetly can their beaming roll
Volumes of meaning to my soul,
How long—how vainly all—might words
Express what one quick glance affords.
So spirits talk, perhaps, when they
Their feelings and their thoughts convey,
Till heart to heart, and soul to soul,
Is in one moment opened all.

Mary, one sparkle of thine eye
   I'd not exchange for all the gems
    That shine in kingly diadems,
Or spices of rich Araby.
My heart would count th' refined gold,
Which Eastern kings have left untold,
But as a beggar's price, to buy
One sparkle of my Mary's eye.'

What Kitto had already avowed, was still true of him—
'I cannot accuse myself of having wasted or misemployed
a moment of my time since I left the workhouse.' All his
hours were carefully spent. The frugal youth usually had
for his dinner, on the days he did not fast, a roll and a
sausage, which he bought at a shop in the vicinity of
Temple Bar. From a brief journal, in which he wrote
occasionally during his residence at Islington, we learn
some other particulars of interest.

'*April* 4, 1826.—At the outset I had best make such an arrangement of my time, and form such resolutions, as I have, for a considerable time, had in contemplation, and I pray God that if it be for His glory, I may be enabled to adhere to this arrangement and keep these resolutions. I am sure that it is more than I should be able to do in any strength of my own.

' WORK.

' 1. When business is regular, I purpose to leave Islington for town before breakfast, and leave the office directly after tea.

' 2. Stay at home every alternate Wednesday, and the forenoon of the other Wednesday—when not practicable, the earliest opportunity occurring subsequently.

' HOME.

' 3. When at home from any cause, to spend the morning in writing till dinner. After dinner call on Miss A.,[1] and spend the evening as occasion may require—reading if possible.'

He then specifies the days of the week, with their peculiar duties. Thus, as a sample :—

' *Wednesday.*—I have for some time observed this as a day of abstinence and humiliation. But finding that it is very injurious to my head to go without breakfast, I hardly think myself justified in abstaining from it. I shall therefore take breakfast, and content myself with the omission of dinner and tea.' It may be added, that Friday was observed, like Wednesday, as a fast-day.

' HOURS OF REST.

' My hours of rest have been very irregular since I left Mr Groves. Sometimes I have gone to bed early—some-

---

[1] The visits to Miss A. are set down as very frequent, almost daily, occurrences.

times late, but generally very late, so late that I have not thought it worth while to put off my clothes, but have lain down in them, and on an average I have seldom risen earlier than six. I propose, therefore, to go to bed from eleven to half-past, and to endeavour to get into the habit of rising at five. Thus I allow one-fourth of my time, six hours, for sleep, rather more than I can afford.

'SCRIPTURES.

' My method has been to divide my Bible into four parts —from Genesis to Job, from Psalms to Malachi, from Matthew to Acts, from Romans to Revelation; and it has been my general rule to read in two of these parts, one of the Old and one of the New Testament, daily, in alternation, so that if I read in the historical part of the New Testament on one day, I read on the same day in the didactic and prophetic part of the Old; and if I read on another day in the epistolary part of the New Testament, I the same day read in the historical part of the Old. I have found this method more useful and pleasant than any other, and therefore I shall continue to pursue it.

' I appropriate the first half-hour after rising to my Bible, that is, till half-past five, when I am dressed by five, and another half hour in the evening is to be employed in the same way. . . The Bible will be read of course at other times, particularly on Sundays.

'DEVOTIONS.

' The half-hour succeeding those appropriated to the Scriptures, I propose to apply to the purpose of prayer, prefaced generally by the reading of a few hymns; and I have thought it would be very desirable to apportion the different objects which intercessory prayer should embrace on the different days of the week—a plan which I consider as presenting many advantages and great facilities for the due discharge of this important duty.   I adopt, therefore, the following arrangement :—

SUNDAY.	*Morning.*—For clergymen, and ministers, and their congregations — a , blessing on the preached Gospel.
„	*One o'clock.*—At this time, on the two first, or when there are five in the month, the three first Sundays in the month, my dear H—— and myself will be engaged in simultaneous prayer for each other.
„	*Evening.*—Church of England, and the Christian Churches in general—a catholic spirit among the different denominations.
MONDAY.	*Morning.*—England and its authorities.
„	*Evening.*—The States called Christian.
TUESDAY.	*Morning.*—Religious Societies.
„	*Evening.*—Children—Sunday Schools.
WEDNESDAY.	*Morning.*—Parents and Relatives.
„	*Evening.*—Friends and Enemies.
THURSDAY.	*Morning.*—Jews.
„	*Evening.*—Turks, Infidels, and Heretics.
FRIDAY.	*Morning.*—Missionary Societies and Missions.
„	*Evening.*—Simultaneous Prayer.
SATURDAY.	*Morning.*—Missionaries and Students.
„	*Evening.*—Outpouring of the Holy Spirit on ALL flesh.'

A few disclosures from his Diary at this period, will throw light on several interesting points of his experience and character :—

'10.—On the sixth I was so very ill when I came home, that I was obliged to lie down immediately, and the next morning continued so unwell, that Mr Yates thought it necessary to send for the medical gentleman who attends the house.   He directed that twelve or fourteen ounces of blood should be taken from the back of my neck, by cupping, and furnished me with some medicines.   I have not been to town since, but I think I feel better to-day than I have done since Thursday. I have often, during this time, experienced excruciating pains in the head and breast. But I do not repine. I have no cause to do so. I feel and am persuaded that it is sent me for good and not evil, and most truly can I, from experience, say that those periods of indisposition to which I am subjected, have been, and are, visits of mercy, seasons of refreshing to me, from the presence of the Lord. The retirement of a sick cham-ber, too, is pleasant to me, if only from the contrast with the bustling nature of general engagements. Here I can commune with my own heart—here I can read, and write, and pray, and, when pained and weary, can lie down in my bed unmolested, and unseen by any but by Him whose presence I seem almost sensibly to enjoy. Oh may these seasons be more and more sanctified to me! May my Master, my crucified Master, appear thus to me more and more the fairest among ten thousand, and altogether lovely! May I more and more enter into the *chambers of imagery* in my own mind, and be more and more strengthened by the Holy Spirit, in tearing down and demolishing every idol, whatsoever it be, which has there exalted itself against the knowledge and the love of God my Saviour.

'12.—I am better to-day than I have been since taken ill; and, if I do not go to town this week, hope I shall not be detained longer. I have experienced much kind atten-tion from Miss Hart. She has done everything to meet my wishes and render me comfortable, and the very ser-vants, too, have laid me under much obligation, by their uniform manifestations of every little kindness that they may have had it in their power to exhibit. That it is the same with many of my dear fellow-servants, it is super-fluous to say. All are very very kind to me: thus, for in-stance:—Brown has come to my room every evening, to dress my neck while it needed dressing, and my dear

Marsh has called up frequently to see me. When I came,
I anticipated that I should be quite among strangers, and
was prepared to find it so. But my kind and gracious
Master has ordered things otherwise for me than I had
expected. I feel that I am among brethren and friends,
and that there are several within these walls who feel a
most affectionate regard for me. What cause, then, have
not I for thankfulness and gratitude to Him who thus far
has made crooked places straight, and rough places plain
before me? Oh that this cold heart were more alive and
open to all those thankful emotions and impressions which
such a continued course of mercy and loving-kindness from
my heavenly Father should communicate!

' 15.—Hoping my health would allow me to return to
the discharge of my regular duties on Monday, I determined to terminate my keeping at home by a long walk
and tract distribution. After breakfast, therefore, I stored
my pockets with about eighty tracts, an equal number of
handbills, and some fifteen little handbooks. This, with
my Testament, pocket-book, and the last number of the
"Register," completely filled my pockets. I walked out
about four miles from Islington, and returned by another
road. I distributed tracts chiefly in returning, as my walk
out was in a very retired direction—a road in which I had
never been before. I have seldom had a more pleasing
excursion than this. The weather was beautiful, and my
mind had attained to that exquisite tone of feeling and of
thought, of which it is indeed susceptible, but which it
is so unfrequently permitted to enjoy. Under a different
modification of feeling, I might possibly have contemplated
all the objects I beheld, without experiencing that interest
they have now communicated; or without deriving any
improvement from them. But before I went, my heart
was prepared to respond to the language of the Psalmist,

and to say, "Thou, even Thou, art Lord alone. Thou hast made heaven, the Heaven of heavens, with all their host, and all things that are therein; and Thou preservest them all, and the host of heaven worshippeth Thee. O Lord, how manifold are Thy works! in wisdom Thou hast made them all! The earth is full of Thy riches." And hence I was interested—hence I was instructed and improved. My walk out, as I have said, was retired. It was one also in which I had never before walked. It lay sometimes on the bank of the canal, sometimes beneath the shade of trees, sometimes through fields and pleasant lanes, and at others, over steep hills, from which I had extended and beautiful views before me, and could distinctly discern objects which lay at a very great distance from me. My Testament was a most valuable companion to me, and did not leave my hand till I turned my face towards Islington again, and began to distribute tracts in good earnest. While I soared with the eagle-minded John, or rather with the Divine Master whose words he records, the various objects spread around me, and the blue skies above my head, seemed softly to speak to me a sweeter and more exalted language than that which the natural man can hear. The spirit seemed to enjoy a freedom it never had before—to breathe an air it never before imbibed—and, for a short and fleeting moment, to experience the foretaste of another world's enjoyments, in holding communion with beings of a higher world; yea, with Him who, of all beings and all worlds, is the Cause and the Creator! I think that God, the Holy Ghost, has been graciously pleased more to enlighten my understanding in reference to many things in His sacred Word, which had not appeared to me before, than in any equal period of time within my recollection. Oh! it is most pleasant to feel and know that the self-same hand which wrote the beautiful and

I

splendid volume of nature, wrote also the far more precious
book of Revelation for us; that the High and Holy One,
who called into being and arranged—

> "The pomp of groves, and garniture of fields,
> And all the dread magnificence of heaven,"

is not an abstract quality—an awful, unknown something,
—but the very same Friend, Guide, and Father, who in
mercy and in love has revealed Himself in Christ Jesus,
—the very same whose loving-kindness and whose truth
has followed us through all the devious and intricate paths
of our pilgrimage, and has brought us hitherto, and who
Himself has promised that He will be with us still—that
He will never leave us nor forsake us, but bear and carry
us even to the end. I am fully aware that a man, not
duly impressed with a sense of the amazing value of the
Christian verity, may yet be capable of contemplating the
sublimities and beauties of nature, with exalted emotions
of wonder and delight. But he cannot have the interest
and kind of property in them which a Christian has—he
cannot recognise in them the hand of his best and dearest
Friend—he cannot, oh, he cannot experience that undefined
and inexpressible emotion with which the Christian philo-
sopher can look below, around, above him, and, laying his
hand upon his breast, can say, " My Father made them
all." I had a very pleasing success in the distribution of
my tracts—and I pray my dear Master to let His blessing rest on the seed which I have thus been enabled to
sow by the way-side. I am looked up to as an authority
on tract matters here.'

It happened that there was not in the printing-office a
sufficiency of Persic types, and Kitto, unwisely using his
own discretion, sometimes stayed at home all day, and occasionally left the office before the appointed hour. These
absences began to be marked, and to form the subject of

suspicious comment.   Kitto hastened to explain, but his explanation was not reckoned wholly satisfactory.   He vindicates himself to Mr Watts thus :—

'Sir,—I am sorry to be obliged again to intrude on you, but I feel it necessary to mention distinctly that, although I recollect to have said *once* that I did not think *setting up pie* was a useful employment of my time, or much calculated to promote my knowledge of the business, yet, I added, what your informant has seen proper to omit, " That if I could obtain nothing better I should·do that of course."   I *never* did object to anything else, nor to this more than once.   On this subject, however, I hope I shall be pardoned for saying that I think now as I did then. . . .   As you are pleased to refer to your apprentices, I would just remark that it seems to me, that as I have so much to acquire in a period so much more limited than theirs, the same system of instruction cannot well apply to both. . . .

'In reference to the irregular attendance you mention, I must be contented with what I said yesterday, that it arose from insufficient employment.   I have generally gone to the office every day, even when I expected to find no work.   I have waited there, a longer or shorter period, frequently the best part of the day, and if I could get nothing to do, have returned home.   I wish to state distinctly *now*, since I have been misunderstood before, that regular attendance may be expected from me when I have regular work.'

But the truth is, that Kitto and the Committee did not understand one another.   He was never fond of control, and could scarce endure it in Exeter, where he laments, ' I am less a free agent than formerly.'   He wished very much to be master of his time, conscious that he ever made a due and diligent improvement of it.   The Committee thought that he was neglecting the main point for which they had engaged him, and that he was slighting the business for which they had hired him.   The terms of agreement must have been somewhat loosely made, and Kitto's deafness prevented him from entering into any minute inquiries or stipulations ; for, certainly, had he known that he was ex- pected to give up his entire time to mechanical labour, foregoing his precious and coveted hours of reading, he would rather have remained at Exeter, and cut the ' tusks of certain foreign animals' into the semblance of human teeth.   His belief was, that he was bound to learn to print, but bound, in a higher sense, to prepare for writing some- thing that might be printed.   He aspired to be at least a translator.   Authorship for men's spiritual good was his aim ; and every other vocation was, in his opinion, to occupy a subordinate place.   The Committee, on the other hand, not knowing what was in him, and not, perhaps, fully acquainted with his habits and his ambition, resolved that he should simply be a printer, and that the setting of types should be the one present employment, and the ulti- mate business of his life, at least in connection with their Society.   On being challenged, he made an honest confes- sion, telling how he thought and felt, praying not to be judged harshly, narrating his early experiences and hard- ships, and how the love of books grew so strongly upon him.

' I should have been, perhaps, much gratified if my im- mediate duty to the Society could have been more identi- fied with those habits and pursuits, or rather, that they be brought to bear more immediately upon that duty than it appears they can, in the line of employment now chalked out for me.   As it is, however, I am very desirous of being informed whether it be indeed, as seems to be intimated, required of me that I should relinquish these pursuits *altogether.* If it be, I am sorry to say, that I cannot think myself called upon or justified in making any promise to that effect. As the Society could devise no line of service for me which would harmonise more fully with the peculiar bent and tone of my mind, is it therefore necessary that this should be wholly merged in the other? I do myself think not. I cannot believe, although I have tried to believe it, although I have earnestly prayed that the Lord's thoughts for me, and my own thoughts for myself, might coincide, and although I know that a gift to the service of the Lord's house, would not be estimated according to its intrinsic value, but according to the spirit in which it might be offered, yet I cannot believe that it is designed by Him, whose dispensations towards me have been so strongly marked, that the maximum of my service should depend upon that degree of manual exertion which another—a mere printer—might perform much better and more efficiently than myself.'[1]

He was then distinctly told what was expected from him, and that he could not be sent abroad 'till his altered conduct should show his cordial compliance with such regulations.' This resolution unduly pressed the matter to a crisis; no sympathy was shown him; there was no appreciation of his peculiarities; nothing would be accepted but formal and unreserved submission. Aye or no—select the alternative at once, and abide by it. Kitto was irritated, and resigned his situation.

His friends were exceedingly angry at him, and some of his Plymouth patrons were prepared to cast him off. He was inundated with counsels, and cut to the quick by harsher words and rebukes. But he met with special sympathy from the students, whom he delighted to greet as

[1] Letter to the Rev. J. N. Pearson, President of the Missionary College,—December 1826,

'brethren and friends.' On the second anniversary of the
Institution, he had delivered an address to them, and they
had tendered him their hearty thanks by a unanimous and
unprecedented vote. Now he sold his books to them, and
wrote them a farewell address, which winds up as follows:—

'I am permitted to remain a short time at the Institution, till I have arranged matters for my departure to the
place whither He, who has led others through the wilderness before, may lead me. I leave you, and I do most
truly lament that I leave you in a manner so very different
from any that I had foreseen or anticipated. Brethren,
suffer me to hope that I shall be followed by your prayers.
Permit me to believe that you will not consider the bond
to be quite broken which bound me up together with you.
Forbid it not, that I still look upon myself as a fellow-
labourer with you ; indeed, that I still shall hold the sickle
of the reaper, to gather in the harvest of God, although I
no longer have a reaper's name.'

At this period, when so much was at stake, and he must
find some employment for himself to live by, he applied to
the London Missionary Society ; but his deafness was held
to be a barrier to his usefulness as a foreign evangelist.

That Kitto was conscious of no such breach of contract
as was laid to his charge, may be learned from some incidental expressions in his letters. He had written to Mr
Woollcombe in June—'I scarcely recollect the time when
I have read so little as I do now, certainly never since I
left the workhouse.'

But he soon regretted the hasty step he had taken, and
to Mr Burnard he poured out his spirit :—

'I have essayed my own will and my own way, and I
have found that will and that way to be bitter. I have
therefore endeavoured to return to His way and His will
for me. I have thrown myself upon Him again. I have

said to Him, " Thou seest I fall except Thou help me. I cannot walk by myself. I will no longer try to do so. Lead me and guide me." I am satisfied that I sinned in relinquishing my connection with the Church Missionary Society. I did not, however, sin with my eyes open. It was the sin of blindness. I do not wish to extenuate. Most of my friends have been offended, chiefly because I gave up a good temporal provision. But that was not my sin, nor was it the real ground on which others should have been angry with me. It was the proud heart, the lofty mind. My offence had been chiefly spiritual, intellectual ; chiefly against God, at least more against Him than against man.'

In the journal to which we have referred, he also put down these words of mingled bitterness and hope :—

' *February* 29, 1827.—What am I now? What have I been doing? I awake as from a dream. In what difficulties am I not involved? Friends dropping away from me on every side, and stripped thus by degrees of human consolation, comfort, hope. Hope, yet I have hope—hope not fallacious and delusive, because it is built on the Rock Christ. How desolate now do all things earthly seem to me! I look around; all things seem dark, and black, and gloomy — and what were I, could I look nowhere but around me! I look to Thee, O my God! I wait for Thee more than they that wait for the morning. Arise, arise, O light! and shine upon me, and enlighten the darkness of my way. I have dealt very treacherously against Thee from my youth up. Yet Thou wert long-suffering, and barest with me, and lo! Thou hast brought me hitherto, and now wilt Thou leave me—now? Thou wilt not. Thou hast promised that Thou wilt not, O my God! Look down upon me in pity, and let not the enemy triumph over me! Whom have I but Thee—to whom can I look but Thee. O, then, teach me to look to Thee indeed, to lean upon Thee indeed, to the end of my journey. I go forth, O my Lord, into the wilderness of this world, and know not whither I go. Thou art my hope. Go with me —lead me—guide me. Direct my steps and my wanderings by Thy providence. Watch over me for good; and when I have finished my appointed course, receive me to Thy bosom to live, and there be cherished for ever. Do not leave me; I throw myself upon Thee for guidance and protection; and when I am far away from those charities and ties with which men do surround themselves—when I have no home to shelter me, no pillow on which to lay my head, be Thou my Shelter, my Refuge; and when my wanderings are finished, do Thou plant me where I may grow, and live, and die to Thy glory,—where I may be fruitful as the vine, verdant as the fir, strong as the cedar.'

Kitto, four years afterwards, added a note to this extract:—

'*March* 21, 1831.—When I wrote the above, I recollect it was my intention to set out on foot and travel in England, till I should find some way or other of subsistence. How little experience, how little knowledge of the world I had then! I was as a child in every respect. Most likely it would have ended in my being sent to the House of Correction as a vagrant. . . That prayer is better than I thought would be in my heart at *that* time. The Lord's dealings with me have been wonderful from a child.' It is probable that the example of Goldsmith suggested this desire to wander through the country—a desire which had already been keenly expressed by him when he was in the workhouse.

Mr Groves, the Rev. Mr Hatchard of Plymouth, and other friends, interfered for him, and the Society restored him to his place. But he gave a rash pledge, to abandon literary pursuits—a pledge which, unless his intellectual nature had been changed, he could not redeem. He praises Mr Hatchard highly, and Mr Groves very highly, for the pains they had taken to secure his reinstalment. He contrasts Mr Groves with others of his friends, whose coldness had keenly wounded him. ' He did not say, like others, "Lie in the bed of your own making;" but, though himself the most aggrieved, has come forth repeatedly to my help.'

It was deemed advisable that Kitto should be sent forthwith to a foreign station, and Malta was selected as his field of labour. When he was in suspense as to the decision of the Committee, we find him urging not only his own anxiety, but also that of another, as a reason why he should like to have speedy intelligence. He says to Mr Groves, ' for *her* account, it is therefore my hope to find that the matter is to be decided, or will be soon.' It was resolved, however, that he should go to Malta alone, but that the bans should be proclaimed prior to his departure. This preliminary step was taken, and Kitto expected to be followed in a few months by his betrothed.

It may be added, in conclusion, that, during his residence at Islington, and when he was worried so much about his own affairs, which at one time looked dismal, he busied himself in various efforts to find a comfortable situation for a young man, who had recently married Betsy, his eldest and favourite sister. This brother-in-law had come to London in quest of employment, but failed to find it. Kitto notes some of the counsels and comforts which he set before him at one of their interviews, and concludes :—

' I spoke of the nature of trials and adversities, the blessed purposes they were calculated to answer ; on trust in God, and casting all our care upon Him, knowing that He careth for us; on seeking first the kingdom of God and His righteousness, and having all other things necessary to us. I adverted to my own case. I had once nothing.

The bread I ate, the water I drank, was bitter; and that bitter bread and water was procured with trouble and difficulty. I had not sought then the kingdom of God and His righteousness; but since I have been enabled to do so—since I have sought, in the first place, objects of pre-eminent and absorbing importance — the living water which cometh down from Heaven, the bread which perisheth, and the raiment which waxeth old, have been added to me, and I have lacked nothing. I recommended the seeking of this above all things, and could assure him that if he did so, He who arrays the lilies of the field, and feeds the fowls of the air when they cry, would not fail to take care of him, to feed and clothe him and his also. I went on, at considerable length, in the same strain. I was heard with attention, but not, I fear, with interest. Indeed, I have seen so little out of myself of the Holy Spirit's operations in softening the hardness of the human heart, and I contemplate that heart as so deplorable, and everything but hopelessly bad, and disinclined to the things of God, that I labour under very great discouragement in speaking and acting, and exert myself, in either way, less from the hope of being instrumental in bringing a blessing to those whom I address, than from the conviction that it is my duty to declare the truth of God on such occasions, and speak and act for Him.'

Kitto left England on the 20th June 1827, rejoicing in the work that lay before him, and hoping that the bride he had left behind would soon come out to Malta and be his wife—the ornament and joy of his home. The Wilberforce (Captain Deuck) was detained for some time at Torbay by contrary winds, and Kitto had the satisfaction of feeling that the last land he set his foot on was that of his native county of Devon.

CHAPTER V.

MALTA.

KITTO's mind had, for some time, been steadily under the power of a motive to which it was originally a comparative stranger. The desire of usefulness had supplanted or outgrown the mere love of fame. He craved to be known, in the first instance, and 'get himself a name;' but now his soul was bent on imparting benefit to his fellow-creatures. In a letter to Mr Pearson of the Missionary College, he confesses, '*Fame* was the idol I was taught to bow down to and worship. I hope that in reference to myself it is on the throne no longer, and that I have no other wish on this point than that my light may so shine before men that they may glorify my Father who is in heaven.' Let us listen for a moment to his deeper self-analysis, made at a period of subsequent and leisurely meditation :—

' It has often occurred to me that the stimulant which the desire of fame offers is specially adapted to one's youth, in which it is indeed most entirely in operation, and that it has been providentially given to that period of life to supply the absence of the more sedate stimulants which advancing life introduces. Rightly understood, it is then an incentive to good and a curb to evil, which, in the spring-time, are so much needed, for he who, in his sanguine youth, hopes that the world will hereafter take

notice of his course, will not be unsolicitous to keep his
garments clean.

'The desire to be honourably known among men—the
craving for approbation—the wish to do something which
might preserve one's memory from the oblivion of the
grave—and the reluctance to hurry on through this short
life and disappear along with the infinite multitudes who

> "Grow up and perish as the summer fly,
> Herds without name—no more remembered :—"

these things savour, seemingly, of that "love of fame" of
which so much has been said or sung. I cannot say that
this, as a motive to exertion and to perseverance in the
course which I had taken, did not find a way to my mind.

'I have confessed that self-advancement eventually became one of the objects which I contemplated as the possible result of my exertions. Very few of my readers will
complain of this ; but considering the generally sacred
character of my pursuits, which, I will venture to say,
have been, however tremblingly, directed not less to the
glory of God than to the use of man, some will be disposed to ask, whether self-advancement is a legitimate
object of exertion ; and whether it was not rather my duty
to have been content in the station to which it had pleased
God to call me. Now, by "self-advancement," I mean
melioration of the evils of my condition ; and no one can
object to that without affirming that it was my duty to
lie still, to be content and happy, under the unmitigated
calamities of the condition to which I had been reduced.
I believe that *this* was not required of me. I am persuaded
that the state of life to which the Almighty calls every
man is that for which he is fitted, and to which he may be
able to rise by the just and honourable use of any and
every talent which has been confided to him. In *that*
station let him be content, and not waste his heart in aim-

ing at things beyond his reach. I have read the Bible ill,
if this be not its meaning. Saint Paul enjoins the Christian slaves to be content in their stations; and yet he tells
them, that "if they be made free, *to use it rather.*" Was
ever any slave in so hard a bondage, bondage so hopeless
as that into which deafness brought me? and if I might
by exertions not degrading but elevating be free, should I
not "use it rather?" Let the answer be found in the contrast between the uselessness of my first condition, and the
usefulness of that to which I have now attained.'[1]

It was with the view of taking an active and honourable part in what he reckoned the highest function of redeemed humanity, that Kitto left Islington. He felt that
he was going out to Malta to labour in Christ's cause, for
the Master had said to him, 'Son, go work to-day in My
vineyard,' and he gladly, and to the best of his ability,
obeyed the charge.

The institution at Malta had for its object to supply tracts
to the Church missionaries, in Greek, Arabic, Maltese, and
Italian. It had three presses, and employed six individuals. Mr Jowett and Mr Schlienz were the principal
labourers, accomplished, scholarly, and devoted. Of Mr
Jowett Kitto says, 'He is second to none; or if second to
any, only to Mr Groves; and Mr Schlienz works, in another
way, far harder than we printers do, for he preaches, and
that frequently, twice on Sunday.' Though there was not
a bookseller's shop in the island, the Romish clergy were
their principal opponents, and the circulation of tracts
was forbidden by sacerdotal authority. But the works of
the missionary press at Malta were largely circulated in
other countries. Kitto rejoiced that, in sailing to join such
an institution, he was assuming, though in an humble form,
the coveted character and position of an evangelist.

[1] Lost Senses—Deafness, pp. 84 87.

But his sojourn in Malta was, in Scottish religious phrase, a ' crook in his lot.' The voyage to the Mediterranean was, however, of lasting service to him. His deafness had been accompanied by a growing reluctance to speak, and indisposition to use his vocal organs had almost produced inability.

' When I first went to the Mediterranean, the companions of my outward voyage were Dr Korck, a German physician, who had lately taken orders in the Anglican Church, and Mr Jadownicky, a converted Polish Jew, lately arrived from America, where he had been completing his Christian education. These well-informed and kind-hearted men, being always with me, soon perceived how the matter really stood; and, after much reasoning with me on the matter, they entered into a conspiracy, in which the captain of the ship joined, not to understand a word I said, otherwise than orally, throughout the voyage. In this they persevered to a marvel; and as I had much to ask, since I had not before been at sea, I made very great progress with my tongue during the six weeks' voyage, and, by the time we reached our destination, had almost overcome the habit of clutching a pen or pencil, to answer every question that was asked me. From this time I usually expressed myself orally to those whom I knew, in the ordinary intercourse of life; but when my communication required many words, it was usually conveyed in writing. This also I at length dropped, and strangers only were addressed in writing. Finally, I ventured to accost even strangers with the tongue; and it was only when not understood that I resorted to the pen. At first, strangers could rarely understand me without much difficulty; but, under the improvement which practice gave, my voice was so much bettered, that the instances in which it was not readily understood, gradually diminished; and, at the pre-

sent day, I rarely find even a foreigner to whom my language is not clear.'[1]

The gain to Kitto from this voyage, therefore, was
immense ; and he felt under no little obligation to his kind
and earnest friends, who broke his pernicious habit, and
won him back to the use of speech. The voyage was
pleasant to him, for he was a stranger to sea-sickness.
He felt, indeed, what sometimes terrifies or distresses a
landsman, the instability of cabin furniture and dinner
equipage from the blowing of smart breezes; and while
he had made up his mind to such annoyances, and could
smile at them, yet he liked an occasional calm, and rejoiced
over ' the capture of two fine turtles.' His letters to his
friends, Woollcombe, Harvey, Lampen, and Burnard, contain such details as, in his opinion, would be most relished
respectively by each of his correspondents.

He states generally, that his mind was no stranger to
those emotions which men so often feel on leaving their
native shores—that a ' feeling of desolateness' had occasionally come over him, but that he felt each evening
' Whose presence was with him,' and he hoped that such
feelings ' threw him more upon God.'

His first sensations, off the coast of Portugal, are detailed to Mr Woollcombe, July 10 :—

'I fetched my bolster from the cabin, and arranged a
bed for myself on the tafferel, by laying Mr Jadownicky's
thick cloak along, to lie upon, and then wrapping myself
in my own cloak and fur cap, to defend me from the dew.
I remember walking about the deck, or sometimes leaning
on the gangway, till between twelve and one o'clock, when,
feeling sleepy, I retired to my new bed, and lay there, so
that I could look the moon in the face till I fell asleep.
An accident awoke me about a quarter past two, and then I

[1] Lost Senses—Deafness, pp. 20, 21.

got up and walked about for nearly an hour, went to bed
again, and slept till a few minutes before sunrise, which of
course is considerably later here than in England. The
sun rose with great splendour from behind the Lusitanian
Mountains, but I have seen far more gorgeous risings of
the sun than this, from the Hoe, at Plymouth, and from
the Catdown. Both the risings and settings of the sun do
not seem such slow and majestic affairs as in England ;
and, indeed, I understand that the farther we advance to
the south, the shorter is the morning and evening twilight,
and the less time the sun takes in rising and setting. I
have just inquired at the captain, and find that, as I suspected, the mountains adjoining the Rock of Lisbon are
those of Cintra, of which Lord Byron speaks, in the four-
teenth stanza of the first Canto of Childe Harold :—

> " Cintra's mountains greet them on their way."

And, indeed, it was to us, as to him, a pleasant greeting,
after having been, for so many days, out of sight of anything like land.'

The good ship Wilberforce, with a ' gilt effigy' of the
senator at her prow, entered at length the straits of
Gibraltar ; and as Kitto looked alternately on the African
and European land, so close on each other, many trains
of meditation passed through his mind. He reached Malta
in safety on the 30th of July, entering the harbour of La
Valetta in the evening, and disembarking next morning.
The accommodation provided for him was not of the best
description, for he slept several weeks on the floor, and
some time elapsed ere he enjoyed the luxury of a chair and
a table. At length he got two rooms, a study and within
it a bedroom—' the highest in a high house'—but abounding in windows, which commanded a fine marine prospect.
He had also a bookcase, with a good collection on its
shelves. But who will wonder at his confession, that of

an impatient bridegroom—'My heart was in England, and my mind continually travelled thither?' He set to work with ardour, and especially occupied himself with Asiatic types; nay, he spontaneously entered, at the same time, upon Arabic studies. The literary departments were filled by the clerical missionaries, and the translators were natives of the countries into whose languages they were rendering Christian books and tracts. From half-past seven till half-past four was he occupied every day in the printing office. He liked his work; and he rejoiced in its prospective results. He declares, in his letters, how happy he was that his connection with the Society had been renewed.

'It is easy,' he says to Mr Burnard, November 13, 'to *talk* about missionary service when we are at home, or even when we are preparing at home for personal service in the cause, and yet understand very little of what it really is. In this, as in other things, an ounce of experimental knowledge is worth a pound of speculation or conjecture. . . . Believe me, it is not my wish to magnify any sacrifice I may have been enabled to make; far from it. I only mention this that I might say how "the consolations of Christ" do abound in these situations, notwithstanding the difficulties and sacrifices with which they must be obtained. In my own case, I feel that my most ordinary employments, even my daily occupations, are, with the blessing of God's Spirit, calculated to be the means of great usefulness to the Christian cause. This is what few, but those in our situation, can say of their most *ordinary* duties.'

Kitto saw the carnival, with all its puerile follies, which he alleges were on the decline—not more than a fourth part of the people wearing masks, and the maskers being prohibited from tossing sugar balls at the unmasked, or in any way molesting them. 'Sweetmeats, generally small comfits, were thrown about in great abundance, chiefly by

English and Russian officers, who had small bags full, which
they frequently replenished at the stalls. These were generally thrown into the coaches, in the faces of the ladies,
who commonly returned the compliment with zeal, and often
were the first to give it.'

The Committee in London, by one of their minutes, dated
March 20th, 1827, on readmitting Kitto to their employment, and sending him to Malta, gave a conditional sanction to his marriage, ' on the understanding, that, at a
future period, should he conduct himself to Mr Jowett's
satisfaction, H. A., to whom he is under matrimonial
engagements, may join him at that place, with a view to
their marriage.' But the lady of his heart, whom Kitto
had left behind him in England, proved faithless to her
engagement.   He was disposed to blame the Committee at
home for being careless about forwarding his correspondence. ' I have now,' he says, ' been absent from England
for something more than eight months, and have not, in
all that time, had one letter from Miss A. ; and therefore
I feel assured that several successive letters have been left
with the Society, on the understanding that they would be
sent out.   If the separation, for a short time, between us,
to which I was unwillingly induced to assent, was at all
necessary, this surely is not also necessary.   This surely
might have been spared.' He did not know what to think
about her whom he calls his ' ladye faire'—' she whom
I had trusted before all earthly beings—she who was
dearer to me than all other things my heart ever knew or
cherished.'

His suspicions, at the end of these eight weary months,
were at last confirmed, by the intelligence that she had
deserted him, and had been married to another person.
His hopes were in a moment dashed to the ground, and
his heart was oppressed with sad and bitter thoughts.   He

had loved intensely, and was in daily expectation of being married. He was ever picturing the comforts of home, when she should fill it and grace it; but, alas! she had plighted her troth to another. On receiving the tidings, he went at once into his room, shut the door upon him, and did not leave it for more than two days, not even for his meals. During that dark period no one saw him. The servant became alarmed, and told Mr Jowett. Knocking was vain; but a ladder was got, that the servant might, by means of it, see in above the door, and ascertain whether Kitto were dead. On his friends looking into the chamber, he was discovered sitting on his desolate and solitary hearth, with his head bent on his knee. The intelligence grieved him beyond any former affliction which he had been called upon to suffer. 'My spirit is bowed down indeed.' 'I am alone,' he says to one correspondent, 'but what else I am I cannot tell.' 'I often found myself,' he says to another friend, 'engaged in the repetition of two lines, which I must have picked up somewhere at a former period—

"No more, no more, oh never more on me
The freshness of the heart shall fall like dew."

'. . . I know I can never again confide as I have confided. . . . I have read over what I have written. It is not all good. There is an unhealthy spirit in it. True, my own spirit is diseased, for it has been deeply wounded, and the wound is not yet healed. May Almighty God give me the spirit of health and strength—give me a sound mind—bind up again that which is broken—heal that which is wounded. He can, I doubt not; that He will, I am willing to hope and believe. In outward nature He revives again in the spring that which the winter seems to wither away. Does God take care for plants, for trees,

for flowers, and shall He not take care for me? Shall not
I revive again also? I will hope that I may, and, believe
me, I do endeavour to cast myself and all my cares and
troubles upon Him in whom I have never vainly trusted,
by whom my confidence and trust have never been be-
trayed. I trust He will make good to me all these evils;
and that they may be made instrumental in drawing me
still nearer to our crucified Lord, who can give me *here*
comfort, strength, things in my spirit, far better than all I
can now lose, than all that can be taken away from me;
and who can give me hereafter " quiet and enduring
chambers" in His Father's house, where none of the things
that now trouble and distract me, can vex me further.'

To his mother he thus unbosoms himself :—

March 7, 1828.

' MY DEAR MOTHER,—I write this letter to you in very
great sorrow of heart. I received news yesterday from
the Society, which has given me a blow that it will be
very long before I shall recover. It was this—that H——
A—— is married to some person in England! Oh, my
mother, you cannot imagine what this has made me suffer!
I had expected that she would soon come to me, and hoped
that we should be very comfortable and happy together in
this place—when all my hopes and happiness in this life
were at once destroyed by this intelligence. I hardly
know how to believe it. But it was the Secretaries of the
Society themselves who wrote to tell it to Mr Jowett, and
they would not have written it had they not been quite
certain about it. They wrote very kindly, and assured
me of their sympathy and prayers, and my friends here
have also been very considerate and kind on this occasion
to me. But the kindness of man can do little for such a
wound as this. I am very unwell, my dear mother, and
my spirit is quite broken up. It is a very severe trial to

me, and I should quite sink under it, if the Lord were not graciously with me, to support and strengthen me, under the heavy burden I have to bear. I hope it will be sanctified to me, as my other trials have been. I wish you were with me now, that I might talk with you; for I am desolate indeed, and my cup of sorrow is very full. The Lord is with me, however, and puts a little peace into my heart, else I could not live. Indeed, I do not care to live at all. I have had nothing to make me love life. My life has been quite full of disappointment and sorrow, and I shall be very, very glad, when my labours are ended, and I am permitted to go to my home in heaven—to that quiet rest from all these troubles, which the Lord has prepared there for His people.'

His mother replied in a letter which has the genuine maternal stamp upon it. Indignation at the lady's conduct, and sympathy with her son, struggle alike for utterance. She tells him that God, for some wise purpose, had not designed her for him, and, descending from this altitude, she affectionately advises him to walk a good deal, take plenty of exercise, and converse pleasantly and often with his associates.

In a letter to the lady's cousin, he sends the following message :—

Malta, March 7, 1828.

'. . . Tell her that I have no wish to reproach her. God can bear me witness, that I have desired her happiness above all things; and although she has wounded me so deeply, and made me desolate indeed, I shall rejoice if she prove to be happy in her new situation. But I doubt whether she will. They who can sport so with the happiness of others, are seldom happy themselves. They may seem to be so for a season, but, in the end, they are not. Their happiness passes away like a dream. Believe me,

it is my prayer that hers may be lasting.   But mine would
not in her situation.   I do not think I could rest quietly
upon my pillow if I had served her, or any other person,
as she has served me.   To murder the peace of another is
the worst of all murders; and she has murdered mine.   I
think, however, that I can forgive her, and I pray God to
forgive her also.'

We do not know all the reasons which induced the lady
to withdraw her pledge to Kitto.   We find in his Islington
Journal, in an incidental record of his most secret thoughts,
the following complaint :—

'Went to Hannah before coming to the Institution.   I do
not really know what to think about her.   That she loves
me I have very great reason to believe ; yet, on this supposition, and knowing that she is *not* naturally volatile, I
have felt much at a loss to account for a degree of inatten-
tion to me when at her house, which has very frequently
distressed my feelings much, very much indeed.   The most
trivial and unimportant circumstance has the power of
diverting her attention from me, even though I should be
speaking of something which may seem to me peculiarly
interesting ; and I have seen her chatting and laughing,
for a long time occasionally, without seeming to be in the
least conscious that such a being as John Kitto was present.   I am very foolish to mind such things, yet I cannot
help minding them—lovers are very foolish beings.   . . .
That she is faultless, I am not obliged, by the most ardent
affection, to believe.   . . .   If she do not experience
that warmth for me which I do for her, that surely cannot
be imputed to her as a *fault*—it is my *misfortune.*'

We should be inclined to lay no great stress on this
lover's lamentation, for Kitto was very sensitive in society ;
and, from his deafness and isolation, was apt to think himself slighted.   He never ascribes to her any alteration of

affection, but says, some years afterwards, that her conduct 'admitted of much extenuation, owing to the awkward predicament in which the Society had placed them both.' We have learned, on good authority, that Kitto's letters from Malta were studiously kept back from the lady ; that she was taught to believe that he had forgotten her ; that it was under the pressure of maternal authority that the match was broken off; and that the instability of his connection with the Society was a topic principally insisted on.   What Kitto calls the ' deep repentance' of the lady's death-bed, was the result of her coming too late to a knowledge of these painful circumstances.

The result was, that a severe illness overtook him.   His heart had been crushed, and his health now failed.   In fact, he was fast sinking into that morbid state which had oppressed his early years.   He felt as if he had been cut off from the world, and as if some curse had fallen upon him.   He had suffered much already for sins not his own —had been the inmate of a workhouse, had lost one of his senses, had been twice misjudged, as he thought, by his Committee—and ' all these things were against him.'   Was he never to enjoy the sunshine ?   Was a sudden eclipse for ever cruelly to interpose?   Providence had been mysterious in its actings towards him, and was man, in addition, continually to thwart him ?   His spirit sank under such reflections, and sickness preyed upon him.   ' I became dangerously ill,' he tells Mr Frere, ' and we all thought that my cares and my afflictions, my miscalculations and my errors, would now at last be terminated.   It pleased God, nevertheless, that I should be again restored.'[1]   Such was his lassitude, even when recovering, that he had no heart for his duties ; nay, his physical strength was not equal to the task.   A peculiar weakness of his ankles, which he had felt

[1] Letter to the Right Hon. J. H. Frere. Malta, Dec. 4. 1828.

ever since his fall, and more than once described and lamented, disabled him from standing at a case ten hours a-day. He began to perceive that he was not giving satisfaction to his superiors. He had rashly bound himself to relinquish literary pursuits. But his own explanation seems to have been—that literary pursuits and literary relaxation were different things—that he might safely indulge the latter without devoting himself, heart and soul, to the former. Though, therefore, he spent his hours of leisure in reading and meditation, he did not think that he had broken his pledge. The Committee, however, judged that the way in which he passed his evenings, did not leave him sufficient time for exercise and sleep; and that, in consequence, he must come to his employment under them, with a jaded mind and an exhausted frame. Mr Jowett, when about to leave Malta for England, had told him so; and Mr Bickersteth, the Secretary, sent him a lecture on the 'Sacrifice of self-will and self-gratification.' The Committee gave it as their opinion that his 'habits of mind were likely to disqualify him for that steady and persevering discharge of his duties, which they considered as indispensably requisite.' 'It is clear,' writes the unflinching Secretary, 'that the Society cannot continue in its service those who will not devote themselves to their engagements.' Kitto had been under espionage in Malta, for his previous breach with the Society had been only partially healed. He was, in fact, on trial, though he was not aware of it, and, perhaps, no one put him on his guard. He accordingly thought himself unjustly used, and affirmed that he had kept his pledge,—that his general hour of retiring to rest was eleven o'clock, and that if he remained out of bed longer at any time, it was because painful feelings would have scared sleep away, had he lain down to woo it. He adds with some degree both of tartness and truth—'If I

had employed an equal portion of my evenings, lolling on
the sofa and smoking my pipe, it seems all would have been
well—no blame would have been imputed to me.' It was
allowed, that when in the office, he was faithful to his work
as a compositor, but it was surmised that his studies out
of it must unfit him, to some extent, for its manual labours.
The Committee and he were both in error. He had made
too large a promise, and they were too exacting and dic-
tatorial as to his performance of it. An expression of
sympathy would have done more to accomplish their end,
than the stern declaration of authority. He might have
been led to more exercise and earlier hours, but he could
not be forced to them. Kindness might have moved him,
but rigour only confirmed him. He was not to be con-
cussed into what he deemed a species of helotry. The
Committee were resolved to keep him to his place, for he
had already offended, and a second misdemeanour could
not be tolerated. They would not put up with insubordination on the part of such a servant, and the unconscious
Kitto was, therefore, warned, rebuked, and virtually dismissed. We cannot blame the Society so deeply as some
have done, though, certainly, according to their own premises, if they acted toward the misguided lad in equity,
they showed him but small lenience. If he was 'out of
the way,' they exhibited but slender 'compassion' for the
invalid at once fevered in body and bruised in heart.

Kitto's residence of eighteen months in Malta was nearly
lost time to him, and it was the most miserable portion of
his maturer life. He had been disappointed where he had
'garnered up his heart.' He had tried to please his em-
ployers, and had failed. His views in life were darkened.
He had hoped to rise to a position of honour on the missionary staff, but he had been sharply severed from it.
And what, then, should he do? What would his former

patrons say of him now? Would they not disown him, and reckon their confidence in him misplaced? In what 'line of things' could he promise himself success? No wonder his spirit preyed upon itself, for even Mr Groves did not, in this instance, justify him. In this forlorn and unhappy condition, and with the horizon lowering all around him, Kitto embarked for England, on the 12th of January 1829,[1] in the Maria, Captain Tregarthen. The ship was first detained for a while in port, and was also long on her voyage. When she was off the Lizard, Kitto composed a letter for Mr Harvey, which might be sent to Plymouth in some fishing-boat. His object was to assure his Plymouth friends of his safety. He was the only cabin passenger, and the voyage had improved his health. He is thankful that his detention in Malta enabled him to get a resolution of the Society, in which they promise to 'make it their business to assist me in the best way of doing well for myself. . . . God make me very thankful and grateful to Himself first.' On the voyage out, Kitto had been in raptures as he gazed upon the mountains of Granada, and he thought that the eyes of another coming after him would admire them too. But, on his return, the magnificent scenery made no impression on him, for 'his heart was too hard and cold to care two pins for all the snowy mountains in the universe.'

Before Kitto set sail, he had proposed to Mr Frere to write at length a history of the island.[2] Concerning another literary composition, relating to missions and Scripture, we find among his papers the following prayer :—

[1] In the Missionary Register for January 1829, it is simply stated, that 'Mr Kitto's health has suffered much; and on this, and on some other accounts, he is about to retire from the Society's service.' In the printed Report for 1828-29, it is mentioned, quite as vaguely, that 'Mr Kitto, on account of his want of health, and other circumstances, has relinquished his connection with the Society.'

[2] Letter to Mr Frere, just before leaving Malta, in which he signifies his wish to lay his case before the king—his early misfortunes and his literary desires.

'ON COMMENCING MY BOOK.

'Almighty God! without Whom nothing is good, nothing
is holy, without Whom all my best designs are vain, I pray
Thee bless this undertaking to Thine own glory and the
blessing of many.   To me, also, may it be sanctified.
Grant that I be not led astray by the poor lust of literary
honour and distinction.   Fill my heart with Thyself, and
out of the fulness of my heart may I be enabled to speak
to others in the book which now, with this promise, and
by Thy grace, I purpose to write and to send forth into
the world.'

In the prospect of leaving Malta, he composed a farewell in verse.   Though not certainly of a high order, it
was written with some care; and it is rather quaintly
topographical and minutely antiquarian in its allusions.
Place after place is saluted, and its ancient history glanced
at.   Copious notes in prose illustrate the poem and conclude the paper.   It opens thus :—

> 'Dear isle, farewell!   I had not though
> To find so soon my bark afloat—
> So soon to have again to spell
> That short but painful word, farewell!
> Less had I thought, with much regret,
> To speak that word to thee.   .   .
> Farewell, then, Malta; yet, once more,
> Why linger my feet on thy shore?
> To thee, a few months since, I came
> With heart in love, and hopes in flame,
> Trusting to find in thee a rest,
> In others blessing being blest.
>
>   .   .   .   .   .   .
>
> But now I leave thee.   Soon England
> I tread upon thy smoother strand;
> Yet, sooth to say, I little care;
> For what have I to bless me there?

The hopes, which once around me flourished,
Have faded all away and perished. . .
So, then, can I be anxious whether
I dwell in this clime or another?
No; regions all alike we call
When misery we find in all.
England to greet I shall not grieve,
Nor Malta do I gladly leave.'

On his arrival in London, Kitto met with Mr Groves,
who was about to embark on his mission to the East. His
faith had not been shaken in his former apprentice, and he
proposed that the cast-off printer should accompany him.
Before coming to a decision, the forlorn adventurer went
down to Plymouth, and there he resolved not to go out
with his benefactor. He said 'No' most firmly to the
very proposal which moulded his subsequent life, and raised
him to his ultimate position of usefulness and honour. But
a mysterious Providence brought him suddenly to another
decision, and he then hastened to be gone. Meanwhile
his sojourn in Plymouth was far from being comfortable.
Many who had helped him in former days, refused further
assistance, and taunted him with his repeated breaches
with the Missionary Committee, as a proof that he was
proud and intractable. Conscious of his integrity, and
disdaining to volunteer such a minute and lengthened explanation as might be construed into an apology, or interpreted as a confession, he seems sometimes to have
wrapped himself in dignified reserve, and thus offended
another class of his friends. The case did appear suspicious; and many seem to have thought that their high
opinion of his talents had been unwarranted, as being the
dictate of sympathy rather than of judgment, that they
had erred also in their estimate of his character, that his
promotion had turned his head, and that a self-willed
obstinacy, or a hasty temper, was evidently the fatal bar

to his advancement. Now that he was again flung upon them, they resolved that he should be left to his unaided resources; for if he were determined to throw away such auspicious opportunities as he had already enjoyed, they concluded that their money, influence, and advice, would be grievously misspent.

Kitto, in a letter to Mr Harvey, as far back as 1823, mentions an unknown gentleman who had made him a present of 'Butler's Analogy,' and warned him that, when he ceased to be a novelty, then would come the great test of his abilities. Kitto mused, and acquiesced so far— 'When novelty has ceased, and curiosity has evaporated, and after I have had my hopes raised by the transient attention shown me, I shall be neglected, laid upon the shelf, and forgotten.' Was he now doomed to realize his own prophecy? In his moments of melancholy, he looked upon himself as one 'marked out for pain, trouble, and bitterness, to whom expectation is delusive, and all hope vain.' He seemed, in short, to embody the poet's description :—

> 'I am all alone, and the visions that play
> Round life's young days have passed away,
> And the songs are hushed that gladness sings,
> And the hopes that I cherished have made them wings,
> And the light of my heart is dimmed and gone,
> And I sit in sorrow, and all alone.'

He was galled excessively by this procedure on the part of so many of his friends; and the following paragraph is, perhaps, the only instance in his whole correspondence of something like a querulous and ungrateful spirit. It was in the worst of testy moods that he wrote it, and the fact of his being so misjudged and frowned upon is his apology. It occurs in a letter to Mr Lampen :—

Plymouth, April 6, 1829.

'. . . . I lament to have perceived that those gentlemen

of Plymouth, to whom I most naturally look at this juncture, are less willing than I had hoped and expected, to afford
me the advantage of their powerful influence, in obtaining
for myself a future provision.   I certainly did not expect
much assistance of any sort; but whilst my expectations
were not of a pecuniary nature, I thought there might be
a readiness to exert so cheap a thing as *influence* on my
behalf.   It appears that I have been mistaken in this, as
in many other things.   I regret to have seen, that the
friends to whom I am so much indebted for the kind inten-
tions on which they have at former periods acted towards
me, seem now to be apprehensive lest I should again become burdensome to them.   *They* know best whether I have
been so or not.   If I have, I am sorry for it; but it will
be borne in mind, that so far as I may have been so, it was
not I who threw this burden on them, but *they* who voluntarily, unsought of by me, and with kindness which can
never be forgotten, took it on themselves.   They did so,
perhaps mistakenly, perhaps on hasty impressions.   I do
not know.   It is not for me to judge.   But I had been
happier, perhaps, if they had not done so; and now I cannot again be happy, as I have been, or as I might have
been.'

He still wished to justify the measure of kindness which
he had received, and which he frankly acknowledges in the
previous sentences; and as the Society had not only given
him a quarter's salary, but voted him £30 to enable him to
find some remunerative situation, he resolved to set up a
stationer's shop or circulating library, at Moricetown, in
the vicinity of Plymouth.   ' The gentlemen of Plymouth,'
he says somewhat caustically, ' have studiously proved to
me that I am fit for nothing—for no regular employment,
for none of the common businesses of life ; and, indeed, I
do not myself know what regular employment there is, to

ENGAGEMENT WITH MR SYNGE.

say nothing of my deafness, the duties of which the present state of my health would allow me to fulfil. What, then, remains for me but *this?*'

But his funds were soon exhausted. 'He drank to the dregs again the cup of misfortune and poverty.' He became anew what he once called himself, *J. Lackpenny*, and was obliged to pawn his watch and other articles, as he confesses in a brief note to Mr Harvey, where he states a plan of redeeming them—that plan being to proceed to London, and draw the thirty pounds which the Society had kindly set apart for him. The bookselling project, about whose expenditure and income he made many grand calculations, and all upon the side of profit, came to nothing, or rather was superseded by a note from the indefatigable Mr Groves, in which he offered him a situation in Teignmouth. John Synge, Esq., of Glanmor Castle, County Wicklow, who had been residing for some time with his family in Teignmouth, was busy in printing, at his own private press, ' some little works in Hebrew and Greek,' and wished to engage a practical assistant. Mr Groves, knowing the rock on which Kitto had split, wisely advised him that Mr Synge's object was ' *simply printing*,' italicizing the words, and asked his determination. Kitto, warned by many, and by Mr Groves himself, that his mercantile enterprise would be a failure, at once agreed to the offer, and pledged himself to enter into Mr Synge's employment on the 1st June.

Man proposes but God disposes. In the month of May Kitto went up to London, to make preparatory arrangements ; chiefly to see Mr Groves, and take a long farewell of his kind and considerate guardian, who was on the eve of departure for Persia. But while he was in London on this errand, the lady who had disappointed him and married another, died, and died, as he affirms, 'under mysterious circumstances, which seemed in a striking manner to counect her demise with her conduct towards me and my return to England.' What he had learned of her bitter remorse in her last illness, induced him to go and look on her corpse; and the spectacle excited such a terrible train of thought in his mind, that when Mr Groves asked him a second time to accompany him to the East, he returned an immediate and affirmative reply. 'Will you come:' said Groves, 'Yes,' said Kitto—question and answer alike remarkable for conciseness and practical aim. Anything to afford relief to his spirit, Kitto would have grasped at. He longed vehemently to be away

'From the wreck of hopes so scattered,
                    Tempest shattered.
Floating waste and desolate.'

In a letter to Mr Harvey from Bagdad, Sept. 25, 1831, he explains this period,—'I returned from Malta with a desire not to leave England again. But I left Plymouth in great bitterness of feeling, which, combined with some heart-rending scenes of death and sorrow I had to pass through at Islington, rendered odious to me the only two places in England in which I had any interest.' In the short space of three days Kitto prepared himself to go, renouncing without scruple a good situation, but gratified at the field of prospective usefulness which was so suddenly presented to him.

As we have already recorded, the workhouse boy had, nine years before, said in his Journal, 'I have even thought of plans to enable me to visit Asia and the ground consecrated by the steps of the Saviour. Even *now*, notwithstanding my deafnesss, it would not be impracticable, if some kind gentleman, on his travels, would permit me to be his (though not expert) faithful servant. After all, I fear it is a vain scheme, never to be realised.' And yet it was realised, and that far beyond expectation, for he went

out in the immediate character of tutor to the two little
boys of Mr Groves. The mission of Mr Groves was certainly peculiar in its origin and complexion, and as strange
was his selection of á deaf and self-taught tutor for his
children. But such an appointment proved, that whatever
others thought of Kitto, Mr Groves had not lost faith in
him ; neither in the reality of his talent, nor the genuineness of his piety ; neither in his honesty of purpose, nor in
his sincere desire to give the utmost satisfaction to those
above him, by his conscientious discharge of duty. Nor
was he so ill qualified for the responsible situation as one
might imagine. He was now in his twenty-fifth year, and
his acquirements, the result of such continuous labours and
vigils, were highly creditable to him. True, indeed, as he
confesses, he had to learn some branches, in order to teach.
But he instructed his pupils in Hebrew, Scripture, theology,
history, geography, writing, arithmetic, and English composition, and surmounted, by devices of his own, the disability of his deafness. Again had he risen—lately a
printer, now an educator—another step upward and onward
to his destiny. Thus the cloud was lifting, though he knew
it not; and the next four years of his life, spent in travel
and eastern residence, originated those Biblical works which
have immortalized his name. 'Darkness' was made 'light
before him,' though he but dimly perceived its dawn ; and
'crooked things straight,' though, from his angle of observation, he could scarcely measure the change. His journal
of travel to Bagdad is very full, but much of it presents no
topics of biographical interest or of characteristic detail ;
and we shall, therefore, make use only of such sections as
either afford a glimpse into his inner life, or present some
striking observation or amusing incident, or show how his
mind was fascinated by oriental scenery and manners, and
thus prepared to illustrate Holy Scripture.

L

CHAPTER VI.

JOURNEY TO THE EAST.

Mr Groves, who had already taken Kitto to Exeter, and who now engaged him to travel, was a man of marked peculiarity. He had latterly, and before leaving Dublin University, joined in such extra-ecclesiastical meetings for sacramental fellowship and prayer, as characterize the religious party now commonly known by the name of Plymouth Brethren. He abandoned a lucrative profession in order to become a missionary, and made no stipulation for maintenance when he went abroad, but relied solely on the voluntary aid of Christian friends, and 'on what his Master inclined the hearts of his brethren to furnish.' His notions of self-dedication were acted out by him with rigid fidelity. He was a 'good man,' and 'full of faith.' His labours in Persia did not by any means produce the anticipated fruits ; but his subsequent toils in India were largely blessed. He was one of those men who exercise an immediate and deep personal influence upon others. Mr Müller of Bristol, a near relative of Mr Groves, and the originator and promoter of that marvellous orphan-house on Ashley Down, says, in his interesting 'Narrative,' that the example of Brother Groves both excited and cheered him in his prolonged and arduous efforts—efforts which, sustained by no visible machinery, but resting solely on 'faith in God as to temporal things,' have realized £77,990, and which actually received in one year no less a sum than £15,000.

Mr Groves being himself in earnest, had strong force of character, and made his imperious will the law to all around him. So that various estimates were formed of him by those who came in contact, and those who came into collision with him ; by those who beheld his actions at a distance, and by those who were immediately under his control. Whatever he felt to be duty, no matter how he made the discovery, he would do it at all hazards, and every one in his sphere was expected to bend to his convictions. These convictions sometimes bordered on fanaticism. On one occasion, in Exeter, when the mind of Mrs Groves was in doubt as to a critical point of duty, she proposed that ' Kitto should search out the mind of the Lord from the New Testament, and say what he thought.' ' The result' of this oracular inquiry Mr Groves laments, ' was, as might be expected, seeing Kitto had no interest in the question ;' that is, Kitto's decision was contrary to that of Mr Groves himself, and he would not be bound by it. In various parts of his journal, he avows his belief that miracles might be still expected by the Church ; nay, he argues, ' that as miracles were designed for unbelievers, and not for the Church, we must expect to see them arise among missionaries to the heathen.' Might they not, therefore, be expected in his own position? Now, if one gift more than another was needed and coveted by him, it was the Pentecostal gift of Tongues ; and yet we find him again and again lamenting the fatiguing labour gone through, and the precious time spent in acquiring a new and eastern language, the pursuit of which ' disordered his soul greatly.'

He relates, in his second journal, published in 1832, that when Mr Newman[1] was sick, and ' at the worst, and

---

[1] Professor Newman, now of University College, London, who, in a fit of devotedness, joined Mr Groves at Bagdad, but whose early creed, springing to a large ex-

they had given up all hopes of him, they anointed him
with oil, according to James v. 14, and prayed over him,
and the Lord had mercy on them; yea, and on me also,
and restored him. It seems to me truly scriptural.' But
his unguarded notions were sometimes sharply corrected;
for when the plague did enter his dwelling, take away his
wife, and prostrate himself, he slowly admits that he did
not expect such a visitation, but rather thought he had
been secured against it, and that his 'error arose from
considering the temporal promises of the 91st psalm as
legitimate objects of faith.'

On being asked by Mr Burnard as to some points in Mr
Groves' Christian character, Kitto replied from Exeter,
after he had been a short time in his employment, 'Mr
Groves is not a Methodist, a Calvinist, a Lutheran, or a
Papist. What, then, is he? A Deist, a Unitarian, an
Antinomian? No. He is one of those rather singular
characters—a Bible Christian, and a disciple of the meek
and lowly Jesus; not nominally, but practically and really
such. A man so devotedly, so fervently attached to the
Scriptures, I never knew before.' Of his benignant influence on Kitto we have already spoken, and his young
friend, though he could not agree with him ultimately in
many of his peculiar views, never ceased to regard him
with esteem and affection.

The company that embarked with Mr Groves consisted
of seven persons. Those immediately connected with him
were his wife and sister, Miss Taylor, his two boys, and
Kitto. The Osprey, a vessel of forty-five tons, and belonging to the Royal Yacht Club, conveyed them, free of
expense, to St Petersburg; and its owner, Mr Puget,

tent out of a strange facility of impression from men and books, has gradually been
abandoned by him to the awful point of abjuring the teaching, challenging the
character, and impeaching the life and honesty of Jesus Christ.—See *Phases of
Faith*, etc., chap. vii. Fourth edition.

along with Mr Parnell, now Lord Congleton, accompanied them to the Russian capital. We can afford space for only a few sketches of the journey. Kitto wrote copious letters about some parts of it, and kept as copious journals of other parts of it. He was ever writing, that being of necessity his principal and almost only method of giving utterance to his thoughts. Most of us are fond of detailing what our impressions are in scenes of novelty. Kitto's method of record was not by the use of his tongue, but by the tracery of his pen ; and some of these papers were composed with a view to subsequent publication. Indeed, he often meditated a book of travels ; but the fruits of his journeys assumed a different form.

Mr Groves and his friends sailed from Gravesend on the 12th June 1829, and, after encountering a heavy storm in the Cattegat, cast anchor before the village of Wedbeck, in the vicinity of Copenhagen, on the 20th of the same month. The yacht had sustained some damage in the gale, and underwent the necessary repairs at the Danish capital. During almost the whole voyage, the Osprey's people had worship on deck morning and evening. The first notice of Kitto in Mr Groves' journal is under date, Sunday, June 14 :—'K—— is not quite well, complaining of headache.'[1] The second is Monday, June 22 :— ' K——'s connection with the dear little boys is most promising, and leads us to feel assured that he is really sent us by the Lord for that very end, and others important to the mission. He seems happy, and, I trust, is so, which comforts us greatly.'[2] The next allusion is still more characteristic. July 1 :—' I feel the expediency of forming a more regular plan with K—— about the little boys. May the Lord, in His great goodness, lead us to adopt a wise one, in the spirit of Christian wisdom. I perceive that

---

[1] Journal, p. 6, London, 1831. James Nisbet.   [2] Ibid., p. 12.

K—— has a deep sense of neglect, or apparent want of respect. May all things be so ordered, that he may not feel this. I feel his heart is worth winning even on natural grounds, for he has affections that are strong and true; but on spiritual grounds it is our duty, and may it be felt by us also to be our privilege.'[1]

The party stayed for some days at Wedbeck with the British Charge d'Affaires, and then sailed for St Petersburg. Prevailing light winds made the voyage longer than was anticipated. At Cronstadt, Kitto saw a portion of the Russian fleet, and, after the Thames, never beheld such a forest of masts. The Osprey was brought up the river nearly to the city, and then her passengers went ashore in a boat. A pilot had been hired for the difficult navigation; and this transaction set Kitto on thinking of Peter the Great, who often conducted vessels from Cronstadt, and uniformly demanded the usual wages. After three weeks' sailing, Kitto was glad to set his foot on land, and to 'lie down on a quiet bed;' but the pilot in the channel, and the scenes in England which had so grated on his spirit as to impel him to travel, were wrought into a dream, which he relates in impressive style :—

'Methought—you see I begin in the orthodox style— methought the scene was the same as that of the preceding day, only sublimed in the alembic of dreams. Rocks tremendous and awful, and dangerous shallows, were there, which the charts do not exhibit; and the city in the distance, to which we were approaching, seemed more glorious than Petersburg by far; more glorious than the cities of Arabian tales; than the hundred-gated Thebes, Nineveh, or Babylon. Rivers of peace—bowers of repose —and palaces, and walls, and gates refulgent with diamond and gold, in magnificent perspective, were laid out there.

Amidst these rocks and shallows, not knowing which way to take with safety, we lay to, and made signals for a pilot. One came off in a boat from the shore. He was the Great Peter himself. He had clouted shoes, and, excepting the band and hat, was dressed much like the peasants I had seen at Cronstadt. He seized the helm ; issued his orders as pilot with dignity ; and guided the vessel with the air of one who was fully confident that he could bring her, through all the difficulties by which we were surrounded, to the desired haven.

• I gazed on this extraordinary character with interest and emotion ; but a change suddenly came over the spirit of my dream ; a mist arose, which concealed the pilot from me. The mist dissipated, and the autocrat was no longer at the helm. His place was supplied by a tender and delicate woman—by H—— A—— herself. (I like to dream, but I would cease to dream for ever, rather than dream once more of her. Once she had made my waking dreams very happy, but now—Well! you know it all.) She was attired in the white vestments of a bride—which were also the vestments of her grave. There was nothing warm or vital in her appearance. She gave impulse to the helm indeed ; but her eyes were fixed on the deck, and, though open, there was no motion in them. I was not surprised. People are not generally surprised in dreams. I tried to speak, but I could not ; to move, but I could not. My first impulse was to haste and take the helm from her hand. She had made shipwreck of my heart and its best feelings once before—and should she again guide the helm? No. But I could not carry this conviction into effect. I sat down in desperate idolatry, and gazed upon her. Do what thou wilt ;—let me live—let me die—let me arrive in safety, or let the deep swallow me up.

'Once more the mist arose, and veiled one whom I had loved "not wisely, but too well." When it expanded, the helm was in the hand of the Master Himself. There was nothing terrible in the appearance. He was as in the days of His sojourning among men—meek, lowly, and kind. Yet I trembled. But He said to me, "Fear not, for I am with thee." Then I thought, What should I fear, if Thou art with me? and I ceased to be afraid. Oh! how happy I was then. I had no doubt. This was the Pilot who never yet made shipwreck of aught that He ever guided; and our safety now was assured. Happy he, the vessel of whose hopes and whose desires Thou steerest, O Lord.

'This was my dream. An interpretation occurs to me; but as I should like to compare notes with you on the subject, I shall expect to receive your interpretation in the first letter you send me after this comes to hand.'

Really, as to the interpretation, it is not very difficult. The dream, as any one may perceive, was but a reproduction of past sensations and agonies, cast into naval imagery by the recent passage through the shoals and intricacies, islands and lighthouses, of Cronstadt Channel. Ben Jonson sang—

'And phantasie, I tell you, has dreams that have wings,
And dreams that have honey, and dreams that have stings;
Dreams of the maker, and dreams of the teller;
Dreams of the kitchen, and dreams of the cellar.'

It requires not a soothsayer to tell under what class the preceding vision of the night should be placed. Kitto, it may be said in passing, had considerable faith in dreams, and, as his papers show, he again and again philosophised on their character and predictive power.[1]

[1] The phenomenon of dreaming has often engaged, and as often eluded, the researches of physiologists and metaphysicians. It is, however, in a different style that Kitto dwells upon it, and the following is a specimen of his lucubrations on the

During Kitto's stay at the northern Russian capital, many Christian friends showed him attention. He makes grateful mention of Mr Knill and of Miss Kilham, a lady who was patronised by Prince Galitzin and the imperial family in her excellent educational institution. In writing to Miss Hypatia Harvey from Bagdad, October 17, 1831, he thus records his reminiscences of this lady :—

'Did you never hear of *Mrs Hannah Kilham*, the Quaker lady, who has made so many voyages to Africa, with the view of benefiting the poor negroes? If not, the history of her most benevolent labours is worth inquiry. The lady I speak of is her daughter, who walks in the steps of

---

subject :—'My own conclusion is, that there is a prophetic principle in the soul, by which, with proper attention, our future path in life may be distinctly enough marked out. What is this principle? whence does it arise? These and such questions as these, cannot be more easily answered than the questions, What is mind itself, whence does it proceed, what are its principles? . . . I should rather think that there are three species of dreams quite distinct from each other. First, such as arise from repletion, from recent impressions, or from intoxication and the use of drugs, as opium. These are the "reasonable soul run mad." These are the most common dreams, and they are in general so gross, physical, and empty, that they have brought discredit on dreams altogether. These are the vagabonds, swindlers, and pickpockets in the society of dreams; but why should the whole society be counted disreputable for their sakes? Second—Dreams which seem to proceed from the immediate influence of a supernatural agent. I am sufficiently aware that this will be called fanatical. Be it so. I am inquiring after truth, and I will take it under whatever form it appears to me. Reason, Scripture, and experience teach, that there are dreams proceeding from such influence on the mind in sleep. Third—Under a third class may be arranged dreams which are prospective, future, and prophetic. Of these there is less distinct knowledge. There is no room for mystical interpretation in them. They picture out exactly the persons who shall be seen, and the circumstances which shall occur, but they seem unmeaning, because they have no relation to any previous experience, and are therefore not recognized as having any personal relationship to ourselves, till the persons are seen and the circumstances occur. I do not suppose these dreams at all peculiar to myself. Most people must have had dreams, which, in the same manner, exhibit in regular concatenation the history of their lives and their connections in life; but, in the intervening period, the bustle and hurry of daily circumstances, obliterate them from the mind, and prevent that recognition which might be otherwise obtained. . . . In conclusion, I think this general inference may fairly be deduced, that there are powers and principles in the soul hitherto hidden and unthought of, but which it is possible to discover, define, and apply to practical uses.' —From a long paper, the title of which has been lost.

her noble mother most entirely, and who has resided some years in Russia, promoting the work of female education, and superintending a school of Russian females, half of whom were slaves. I saw them. They were fine girls. So far as female education is at all an object of attention in Russia, French and dancing are its primary objects. Miss Kilham's institution has nothing to do with these studies. They are taught to read their native language— to write—cipher—sew—and, in general, the affairs of domestic life—to qualify them for useful wives—mothers —servants—and above all, to teach them their duty to God and man, which is done in a way beautifully simple and impressive. This is a sort of model school, and is, I hope, the germ of a most valuable system of education for the lower classes of females in Russia. Miss Kilham, with nothing outwardly on which the eye of man rests with pleasure, has that superior beauty of "*the king's daughter, all glorious within*" (Psalm xlv.), which, being combined with infinite humility, and a manner, unassuming, quiet, and unostentatious, conciliates the affection of many who do, and the respect of those who do not, understand the high principles on which her mind and character are formed. For myself, I count it among the best fruits of my travel, to have formed so inestimable a friendship.'

Kitto formed no high idea of the Russian people, or of their government: 'Their calendar is unreformed, the peculiar costume remains; the knout remains; slavery remains; ignorance remains.' 'There is little show of literature. The booksellers' shops are few, and those few about as well furnished as the bookstalls of London. Upon the whole, the exterior of Russian society is repulsive, notwithstanding the gloss, which the courtesy and politeness natural to all classes of the Russians throw upon it. The air of military despotism—the strut of office which meets you at every turn, and the abject worship which inferiors render to their superiors, are most disgusting. Government! government! There is nothing to be done or said without government. Government must control all your movements. Government would know the secrets of your chamber. With a feeling of much personal kindness to Russians as individual men, I detest such a system of minute rule and legislation.'

'The mass of the people are much more superstitious than I had expected; in this respect, there seems little to choose between this and a Popish country. But superstition is here of a less imposing character. Very pitiful pictures are placed about the city, before some of which lamps are continually burning, and which the people salute in passing, crossing themselves repeatedly and bowing. Statues are no objects of aversion in the Russian Church, and, though pictures are more frequent, I have seen the same homage paid to statues and to figures in alto and basso relievo. This species of idolatry is more common than I ever saw it in Malta, and if religion were measured by it, the Russians might be pronounced a very religious people. But this is all their religion. Their mode of crossing is considered heterodox by the Romish Church. I do not understand the difference; but I remember that at a grand religious procession at Malta, when a company of Russian sailors stood crossing and bowing after their fashion to every banner, statue, picture, and cross that passed by, they were grossly derided by the Catholic worshippers. Poor fellows! why in all the boasted improvements of their nation, has it not been endeavoured to teach them that "God is a Spirit, and they that worship Him, must worship Him in spirit and in truth." From this species of homage, men in the employ of government seem to consider themselves exempt. I never saw it rendered by a soldier ; and I do not recollect to have seen one man of the crowds who pour out from the admiralty, at eight o'clock in the evening, stop to cross himself at a famous crossing place near.'

Miss Groves was prevented by sickness from proceeding on the journey, but her brother was joined here by Mr Bathie, and Mrs Taylor and her suite, who had preceded him by way of Lubeck.[1] The company left St Petersburg on Thursday, the 16th of July, and arrived at Moscow on the 24th—a city which Kitto regarded as the most pleasant he had ever been in. On his first night's journey, he saw some fires, round which gipsies, as he fancied, were encamped. To show his prevailing thoughts at this time, we subjoin his reflection :— 'Is the conversion of gipsies impossible? If not, why, having them at our doors in England, have they been so much neglected there? Their former hardy and vagrant habits would admirably prepare them for some departments of missionary service. Most likely a gipsy missionary would ramble with peculiar pleasure in Cabool, Beloochistan, Bokhara, and Khorassan.' Still he was not very sure of his own ultimate position with Mr Groves ; for he uses such language as this—' As a Christian, I do not know if I may say, Missionary.' He went three times to inspect the Kremlin. ' There are others,' he writes, ' to measure columns, to paint scenery, and to describe churches and palaces ; to them I leave it.' He has given no description of Moscow. Somewhere he speaks of his intention of doing it, but confesses, that after leaving the city, he found that his impressions were not distinct enough to warrant an

[1] Mrs Taylor was an Armenian lady, the wife of Major Taylor, British resident at Bagdad. She had been staying for some time in England, and was returning to her husband. Mr Bathie was a young Scotchman that Mr Groves had met in Ireland and induced to join his mission

account of that strangely fated capital, which one of its own poets thus addresses :—

'Proud city ! sovereign mother thou
Of all Sclavonian cities now !
Work of seven ages !—beauty once
And glory were around thee spread ;
Toil-gathered riches blest thy sons,
And splendid temples crown'd thy head ;
Our monarchs in thy bosom lie
With sainted dust that cannot die !
Farewell ! farewell ! thy children's hands
Have seized the all-destroying brands,
To whelm in ashes all thy pride !
Blaze ! Blaze ! thy guilt in flames be lost;
And heaven and earth be satisfied
With thee, the nation's holocaust !
The foe of peace shall find in thee
The ruined tomb of victory.'[1]

Mr Groves' caravan left Moscow on the 28th July,[2] and reached Astrachan on the 15th of August—a distance of 1401 versts, or about a thousand miles. Kitto, in his Journal, makes the usual remarks of travellers, and instinctively compares the scenery through which he was passing, with the landscapes of his own country. The ordinary incidents occur: a landau sticking in the sand, and crowds gathering around the strangers, while Mrs Taylor's negro servant was absolutely mobbed. 'I believe all our heads ache : mine does.' In the churchyard of Ekiunouskoy, he witnessed a scene which prompted him not only to record his emotion, but to cluster around it a host of fancies and reflections :—

'As I passed through it, on my return from the river, I observed over a grave on which the grass had not yet

[1] Bowring—Russian Anthology.
[2] In Mr Groves' Journal (1857) it is said that he and his party did not leave Moscow till Monday, August 9. But on a following page, Sunday, August 9, is spoken of as a period when they were far on their journey.

grown, a group which affected me strongly. There was
one very aged woman kneeling, with her head on the
grave; another middle-aged woman kneeling also, with
her lips to the consecrated earth; and there were three
sweet children, the eldest of whom, a girl, lay flat along-
side the grave.

'It was easy to guess the story:—a son lay there, the
prop of his mother's age—a husband, taken in his prime
from the wife of his youth—a father, a beloved one, the
support of his children, their protector, their guide, their
friend. He lies there, in whom all this combination of
beautiful relations was bound—all dissolved now, and
broken, and lost.

'I looked on at a distance, for I had no mind to disturb
the sorrow of which I partook. How universal the true
feelings of nature! I was surprised to meet here such an
exhibition of those feelings; but why surprised? True,
they were poor—they were rude, and slaves, perhaps; but
had they not spirits, like me, to feel and suffer; had they
hearts less warm, feelings less acute, than mine? I was
ashamed of my surprise.

'Death, thought I, is a terrible thing after all that philo-
sophers have said, and written, and acted—terrible to the
dead, terrible to the living. It was intended to be terrible;
and I do not admire the philosophy which exhibits death
as an object of contempt. It is not contemptible. Is it
not terrible to close the eye for ever on the happy vales and
ancient mountains? Is it not terrible to hear no more the
voices which have been our music? to mingle no more in
the dear relations which, with all their burdens, are so
pleasant? Oh, it is terrible—very terrible to die! And
then, as to all the fine sayings about the independence of
the spirit on the body, and that the body not being part of
ourselves, we should think only of the better half—it is all

cant and rigmarole.   It is part of ourselves—an essential
part ; and if it were not, why does our holy religion teach
that these scattered elements shall be collected once more,
be once more married to their former companion.   If the
body be not part of ourselves, why would not rather the
unessential part be left to corruption and the grave?
Then, is it not terrible to feel that *that* part of ourselves, with
which all our pleasures, our feelings, our hopes, have been
identified, must, in a day or two, become a "kneaded clod?"

‘ And still more terrible it is to hang over the dead.
To wonder, in the midst of our sorrows, by what marvellous
process could thus become cold—cold—cold—that warm,
ardent, sentient being, which, but a little while ago, was
one of ourselves—went with us to and fro—talked with us,
felt with us, and loved us.   Indeed, I could never look upon
the dead with the conviction that there was nothing vital
left—no sense, no apprehension, in that which lay before
me.   Could I have realized this conviction, I should have
gone mad long ago.

‘ But were there no bright side to this picture, man were,
indeed, most miserable.   I believe the Bible, without doubt
or reservation, and though I find nothing there to tell me
that death is not terrible, I find there much consolation in
the article of death.   There is nothing to inculcate indifference to it, but much to strengthen under its infliction.
That combination of soul and body, which, separate from
all mysticism and metaphysical distinction, is properly and
truly ourselves, and out of which no idea of distinct personality can exist, has undergone no endless dissolution.
The spirit waits a happier union, in a happier place, where
He that sits upon the throne shall dwell among His redeemed.   In anticipation of this happy union, we may venture to meet him, whom even Scripture calls " the king of
terrors," undismayed.   And with these bright prospects

before us, there may be even moments in which, feeling the dissolution of these elements a necessary preliminary to full enjoyment, we may eagerly look forward to that hour —

" When this material
Shall have vanished like a cloud."

But, perhaps, the permanent realization of this feeling would not be either happy or wise.   It does very well in poetry, but nowhere else.

' As the poor people were returning home, I contrived to slip a small donation into the hand of one of the children, and as I could not speak their language, I contented myself with praying that God would be more than son, husband, father, to them.   In another half hour our carriage rolled away from Ekinnouskoy.'

The Moravian settlement of Sarepta was also visited, and found to be no longer a missionary station, but simply a colony of artificers.   Melons were sold at one copec each.   As the travellers approached Astrachan, Dr Glen met them, and during their brief sojourn in that city, showed them no little kindness.   He was then in connection with the Scottish Missionary Society, and was engaged in translating the Old Testament into Persian, having at this period proceeded as far as Ezekiel.   Many years afterwards, Kitto refers to this visit in the following glowing terms:—

' It was, in 1829, the privilege of the present writer to witness something of the progress of this great work.   He was then one of a large party which found themselves, for several days, the inmates of Dr Glen's primitive missionary establishment at Astrachan, and beheld, with admiration, the quiet way in which this good man, absorbed in his task, pursued his wonted course, undiverted for one hour by the engagements or excitement which the arrival of so large a body of Christian friends from home might have been expected to create. At his appointed hour he withdrew, and was to be seen no more until the labour of his day had ended. Yet this was made consistent with the most cordial hospitality, and the utmost attention to, and consideration for his visitors. We were reminded, by application, of the words of Nehemiah—"'I am doing a great work, so that I cannot come down : why should the work cease, whilst I leave it, and come down to you?"—Neh. vi. 3.'[1]

According to Kitto's Journal, they left Astrachan on Monday, August 25, and yet he dates the following Thursday as the 27th.[2] The routine and monotony of travel, one day so like another, seem to have made both Groves and Kitto somewhat oblivious of the Calendar. Under the last date, and at Koumskaia, he went to sleep on a cart, with some straw under him, and a saddle for a pillow. The hardness of this primitive couch did not prevent him from both ruminating on and dreaming of ' the dear objects which, desolate as he was, he had left behind him.' In the morning he became the subject of close inspection, and condescended, in his humour, to give the curious on-lookers a proof of his skill in the earliest craft he had learned.

' I was awakened by the efforts of a Tartar to withdraw the saddle, which was wanted, from under my head. He endeavoured to do it with a polite cautiousness, not always met with among more civilized people, but it awoke me, nevertheless. As I lay a few moments longer, to yawn and stretch myself, some other Tartars gathered

---

[1] The Court and People of Persia, by John Kitto, D.D. London: Religious Tract Society, 1848. Dr Glen, while engaged, in connection with the United Presbyterian Church, in circulating his own Persian version, and that of Henry Martyn, died suddenly at Tehran, January 1849.

[2] In the Memoir of Mr Groves, it is stated that they left it on the 23d, which would be a Saturday,—not a very likely day for Mr Groves to take his departure on. Mr Groves also thought very highly of Dr Glen, and speaks of ' the kindness and Christian love which had been manifested by the dear Glens.'

round the cart. They were most inquisitive. They examined the texture of the camlet cloak on which I lay, and of my trowsers which were of the same material, with peculiar minuteness. I amused myself and them by an exhibition of the articles I had about me. My pocket-book, lined with green silk, and containing a pair of scissors, knife with two blades, and tweezers, was an object of peculiar attention, and one Tartar must needs have some of his mustaches clipped with the scissors. The same man wanted to shave off the scanty hair on his face and chin with the penknife, till I explained to him its use, by cutting my pencil with it. Of this and the case containing it, their admiration was boundless, greater, I think, than at any other article I produced, and the ease with which I protruded the pencil and drew it in, occasioned nothing short of amazement. The one whose mustaches had been clipped, lifted up his hands with wonder, and I verily believe he began to doubt whether there might not be greater and wiser people than Tartars. I suffered him to take the pencil, and instructed him how to draw it in and out. He soon understood it, and I think his admiration was greater of the simple principle on which it acted, and accompanied with more pleasure, than it had been before. I have observed, on this and other occasions, that even the savage mind admires more that which it can understand than that which it cannot. The principle of the pocket compass I could not make this interesting man understand, further than that, though the needle was moveable, and did actually move, the magnetized point always settled so as to turn to the same point of the horizon. This seemed to be contemplated with more awe than admiration, and none were so anxious to touch this, as the other articles. My English knife, with three blades, one of them large, was completely admired, for though they did not seem to have seen one before, its utility was at once understood. My watch was an object of curiosity, but not of peculiar admiration, as they seem to have seen watches before. With my large clasp knife, the man before mentioned wished to withdraw and shave himself, promising to bring it back again. I had no doubt that he would return it, but whilst I explained to him that it would not do so, I promised to shave him myself. I then produced my dressing-case, to dress myself. The whole process was watched with intense interest by the same congregation. Every article of the case was examined in detail, with more or less admiration, but the brush, I think, had the largest portion. I unscrewed the top, and made them expect something was to come out. Every eye was fixed to see what, and when the brush came, every hand was lifted up in amazement. When I had done, the man anxiously reminded me of my promise. So seating him on the axle of a cart, and telling him to keep his head still, I shaved him. After this was done, no man ever strutted more in the dignity of a chin newly shaven. I had cut a pimple, which bled a little. On this I put a bit of court plaster; of the black patch, which he considered ornamental, he was infinitely proud.

'One article struck me as peculiar. It was shaped more like one of the vulgar circular horn lanterns than anything I can remember, moving on a pivot inserted through the centre. It was formed of hard dark wood, well carved, considering by whom it was wrought—chiefly Calmuc-Tartaric characters. On my requesting to know its use, an old man took off his cap, and, with much gravity, pulled a string, which made it revolve on its axis, pointing his hand upwards at the same time. This brought to my mind the praying machines of which I had read; this was doubtless one. I inquired if anything were inside, and received a negative reply.   The same old man, who seems the patriarch of the camp, produced a copy of the Evangelists in Calmuc-Tartaric.   It had been well read and thumbed, and some leaves were wanting.   He valued it so highly, as scarcely to trust it out of his own hands. He afterwards brought it up, and our Persian friend assured us he read it fluently.   Indeed, I could perceive, by signs which he used in speaking, that he was explaining one of the miracles of Christ.   May we not hope, that this book has been, or may be, a means of directing their views to the true object of devotion, and to the true salvation by Jesus Christ?   He says he got it from Petersburg.'

Beyond the Terek, they fell in with a large party, having a military escort.   Kitto, for a great part of the dusty journey, kept up on foot with the procession, and at night had 'a memorable fit of the headache.'   He slept on the roof of the stable ; but the lightning and rain were a sad discomfort, and he went into the house at Mr Groves' suggestion.   At Ardoon, an officer who had been wounded at Waterloo, and attended by an English surgeon, was very attentive to them, and a sentinel was placed over their carriages, robbers being daring and rife.

' The next day (Tuesday) we woke at beat of drum. About noon we stopped at a place called Archom.   The remainder of the stage was whiled away by amusing conversation, which was interrupted by our arrival at Kophkai.   Its church, with some good white houses, gives it a pretty effect in the distance, which is sadly lessened on a nearer approach.   We were quartered in a tolerable cottage ; and the knowledge that we should pay for our accommodations, procured also the use of a room in the next cottage, for some of the ladies to sleep in.   The woman of the cottage, on this occasion, made a very pretty display of some clothing, in the English style, which she

had.   She really made, *pro tempore*, a very tolerable Englishwoman.   In my various travels, I have found men vary
very much in their national characteristics; but women
are so much the same in all countries, that they are only
distinguishable by language and feature.   With this view,
when a friend has married, I seldom inquire what country-
woman he has married, as all essential knowledge is sufficiently implied in the significant and comprehensive desig-
nation, " *woman*." '

At length they came to the grand pass of the Caucasian
mountains; the valley narrow, and the road in part cut
out of the rock.   Between Lars and Dariel, they threaded
their way through the narrowest defile.

' We were very much struck by the tremendous precipices on either hand, and with the scene of wild and
savage magnificence presented to us.   The rapid motion
of the Terek, dashing and foaming along the base of the
right-hand precipices, was admirably in unison, and must
have been more so to those whose ears are not closed to
the music of nature.   Here, and on many other occasions
during our Caucasian journey, the inquiry spontaneously
arose—Who can paint like nature ?   Can imagination ?
The negative reply could not fail to be very decisive.'

The Calmuc tents at Dariel resembled English pig-
sties.   From Kobi they climbed up several sharp ascents
to the Mountain of the Cross—the monument of a Russian
victory.   On descending, Mrs Taylor's carriage upset, the
drag-chain having given way, and the horses darting down
the hill at their highest speed.   Providentially the carriage
was empty at the time.   Then they came to the most
' fearful pass of all the Caucasus'—a narrow defile, rich
and wooded heights overhanging it on all sides.

' The view was the most splendid I ever saw, or my
imagination ever pictured.   The snow-capped mountains

behind—the water falling in beautiful white cascades down the gullies—the finely wooded mountain before us, contrasted with the grassy mountains behind and the snowy ones beyond—the valley below, with a village and farm on either side of the Aragvi, diminished in the distance—the castle, surrounded with firs on the high projecting hill of basaltic rock, which stretched out its bold, nearly circular form, on the other side of the valley — the shepherds watching their snow-white flocks on the sides of the mountains—all, among other little details, combining to compose a scene, such as, having seen once, I will never expect to see again in any other place. At Kashaur we arrived about six in the evening, having been twelve hours in accomplishing a stage of as many English miles. It is situated in a cultivated valley, amongst a considerable number of native farms and villages.'

While Kitto's eye and imagination revelled in the picturesque so lavishly strewed round about him, we cannot suppose him insensible to the higher and holier influences which such scenery and travel are so fitted to produce. No doubt, his soul often retired into itself, or rose in rapture to the gates of heaven. Though, from his ' maimed sense,' he could not literally enjoy many of the sensational experiences depicted by the poet of ' The Christian Year,' yet he could, and we believe did, often and easily realize them. Nature spoke to ' reason's ear,' and he listened, understood, and was comforted.

> ' Where is thy favoured haunt, eternal Voice,
>   The region of Thy choice,
> Where, undisturbed by sin and earth, the soul
>   Owns Thy entire control?
> 'Tis on the mountain's summit, dark and high,
>   When storms are hurrying by ;
> 'Tis 'mid the strong foundations of the earth,
>   Where torrents have their birth.

'No sounds of worldly toil ascending there
  Mar the full burst of prayer ;
Lone nature feels that she may freely breathe,
  And round us and beneath
Are heard her sacred tones : the fitful sweep
  Of winds across the steep,
Through wither'd bents—romantic note and clear,
  Meet for a hermit's ear.

'The wheeling kite's wild solitary cry,
  And, scarcely heard so high,
The dashing waters, when the air is still,
  From many a torrent rill
That winds unseen beneath the shaggy fell,
  Track'd by the blue mist well ;
Such sounds as make deep silence in the heart,
  For thought to do her part.

.   .   .   .

'There lies thy cross ; beneath it meekly bow ;
  It fits thy stature now :
Who scornful pass it with averted eye,
  'Twill crush them by and by.

'Raise thy repining eyes, and take true measure
  Of thine eternal treasure,
The Father of Thy Lord can grudge thee nought,
  The world for thee was bought :
And as this landscape broad,—hill, field, and sky,—
  All centre in thine eye,
So all God does, if rightly understood,
  Shall work thy final good.'

The exit from the Caucasus was as beautiful and romantic as the entrance, though the descent was difficult.
They passed several stations or villages, in one of which
was a church dedicated to St Ahithophel—perhaps the
patron saint of Russian diplomacy. Opposite a place
called Ananour, Kitto saw a blasted tree, and at once, as
was his wont, thought of himself :—

' Just opposite, or rather below this place, I observed
what I never observed before, a tree rent asunder by lightning—the half which had fallen was withered and dried up,
but that which stood, though burnt also, spread forth its
leaves as if nothing were the matter.   I thought this something of a phenomenon.   In physical nature it may occur,
but rarely does it happen in our moral nature that he whose
better half of being—his fresh and pleasant hopes—has
been dried up, can himself, though standing, put forth his
green leaves and fruits again.'

' I omitted to mention in its place, that early this morning, I had expressed the pleasure I should feel in seeing a
white · thorn,—as a truly English shrub which I did not
remember to have seen since we left our own country.   The
wish had hardly been expressed half-an-hour, when a white
thorn actually occurred, and afterwards continued to be of
frequent occurrence.   The thorn seems to me to be to
England what the thistle is to Scotland, and the shamrock
to Ireland.   I do not know why the rose should be the
national plant.   It is more properly that of Persia and
other countries, where the " Gardens of Gul " bloom far
more beautifully than in our own isle; and roses, and thistles,
and all, have thorns.   We like nothing which has not a
thorn of some sort or other, although these may not always
be so palpable as in roses and thistles.'

Teflis was seen at a considerable distance before the
travellers reached it, and this first view of it did not raise
great expectations.   For thirteen nights before they reached
it, the party had not had their clothes off.   Teflis was found
to be a disagreeable place; but there was some relief in
intercourse with a curious colony of German settlers.   The
observant traveller says of the other sex :—

' I have been rather disappointed in the Georgian ladies.
To say nothing of their dreadful eyes and eye-brows, which

last are too remote from the eye and from each other, in-
dicating a character volatile, easily moved, and little enterprising, but withal open, warm, and of quick sensibilities;
their foreheads recede too much; their noses enormous;
teeth and mouth good, and often the chin; but the nether
part of the face is so much wider than the upper, as to
give a character of bluffness to the whole, which is quite
unpleasing. Their figures are, in general, large and awkward, and their hands and feet great clumsy things indeed.
Expression is not to be looked for in a Georgian face. I
never saw it in one.'

. At Teflis the mode of conveyance was changed. The
carriages were parted with, and German waggons without
springs substituted. The new vehicles distressed their inmates by their terrible jolting, and it was some time before
they became accustomed to the motion. On the road toward Shusha Kitto found some brambles, and remembered,
in a moment, his grandmother's excursions with him when
he was a child.

'Brambles begin to be frequent this stage, and at the
place where we stopped, there was almost a thicket of them,
interspersed with trees and shrubs. Being the season for
blackberries, they afforded an agreeable regale to some of
us. I have always relished this humble but pleasant fruit;
and although I have been in the countries of the fig-tree
and the vine, I continue to like it. I remember how often,
when a boy, I wandered far in search of them. Sometimes
I found none,—sometimes I did; and when I did, my hands
were lacerated and my clothes torn. How much is this
like many parts of my subsequent experience! How many
things have I wandered after which I have found, and which
were sweet to me, but there were briars and thorns in them
and with them, which tore my hands and my feet, and rent
my very heart asunder!'

Annafield, a colony of German Millennarians, was passed, and at another, called Helmsdorf, they spent the Sabbath. 'We here first,' he says, 'observed Persian women in the streets, walking about, muffled up in their long striped veils.'

'The people had heard of us before we came, and we experienced a kind and hearty reception. There is a free-masonry in Christianity, by which Christians, in all places, are known to each other, and sympathise with each other, without the intervention of human language. The people have, in this country, found a refuge from the persecutions to which they were subjected in their own country. Every man here sits, literally, under his own vine, and under his own fig-tree, and there are none to make him afraid. How far this peaceable state of things may have had the effect of subduing their ardent expectations of the second advent, I have yet to learn. During the late war with Persia, the people of this village were despoiled of some of their little property by the Persians, but no other harm was done. The Russian Government is very tolerant to all denominations whilst they continue in the profession of their fathers, but it looks with an evil eye on all conversions from one denomination to another, unless to the Greek Church.'

On their arrival at Shusha they met with a most ardent reception from the German missionaries. On the 29th of September they left this town, and Herr Zaremba, one of the missionaries, accompanied them to the Araxes, the river that here separates Russia from Persia, and had his horse stolen from him during the journey. Mr Pfander also joined them for the purpose of going to Bagdad. In seven days they reached Tabreez. On the last stage of the journey, Kitto's horse threw him; but as he had lost his cap the day before, and now wore a turban, its thick folds saved his skull from being crushed by the fall. 'Yes, my mother,' he writes in reference to this escape, 'God has not done with me yet; I have more yet to do in this world, and more to suffer.' At Tabreez, Mohammed Ali Khan, a Mohammedan married to an English lady, gave them accommodation. But their own countrymen, of whom there was a considerable number at Tabreez, had heard of the fanatical character of the strangers, and were not prepared to welcome them. Here the party was lessened in number. Mr Nisbet, of the East India Company's Service, married Miss Taylor, and as some compensation to Mr Groves for the loss of one of his assistants, the bridegroom gave him a handsome pecuniary subscription.

Miss Taylor's marriage must have confirmed Kitto in the views which he had already expressed. For in one of his letters from St Petersburg, composed a very few weeks previously, he discusses the question, whether unmarried ladies should go to the East as missionaries; and he is hostile to the idea, because so many of them fall away from missionary labour by accepting the offer of a husband. It is different, he admits, in other portions of the world, but in the East there are peculiar temptations. 'I always thought that the energy of the Christian principle of action was never more strongly exemplified than when a tender and delicate woman goes out to "the wilderness and solitary place," with no other arm than that of her God, without a husband's arm to lean upon for support, and without a husband's wing to protect her.' But after taking exception to single females coming out to the East, since, being brought into contact often with men from their own country, they listen to matrimonial overtures, and cause the 'adversary to speak reproachfully of missionary motive,' he adds, 'I except Quaker ladies, because they would be less tempted by such overtures, and I believe them less tempt-

able. Their independent character, their masculine understanding, their deliberate energy, give them great power
and intensity in the pursuit of those objects they understand and feel distinctly.'

At Tabreez Kitto met with Mr, now Sir John M'Neill,
and the meeting was to the lonely and eager inquirer of
immense benefit. Sir John's kindly manners overcame the
young man's modesty, and drew him into conversation.
He found him very intelligent, and having the 'utmost
avidity for information ;' and especially did he gratify him
with some illustrations of Biblical customs, which his own
experience in the East had made familiar to himself.
Kitto's mind was evidently occupying itself a little with
such ideas, but Sir John gave it new impulse and ardour,
and he referred the inquisitive student to ' Morier's Second
Journey through Persia.' The reader cannot but mark
with peculiar interest those conversations of such a stranger
with Kitto at this time ; for, in fact, they touched and
awoke a latent power, which, after years of development
and training, gave its possessor his merit and his fame.
To the results of Sir John M'Neill's sympathizing and
suggestive interviews with Kitto, we shall soon have occasion again to refer.

After the cavalcade left Tabreez, it came into Koordistan. The ferocious character of the inhabitants was at
once apparent, daggers being drawn on the slightest pro-
vocation. When the Mehmandar[1] of the party had shown
his usual tyranny to the people of the first village they
entered, they at once resented it—brandished their wea-

---

[1] Kitto defines the Mehmandar as 'a person who has great powers, and whose
duty it is to provide accommodation for us.' Mr Morier gives a more terse and
telling description: 'He acts at once as commissary, guard, and guide, and also
very much as Tissaphernes, who, in conducting the ten thousand Greeks through
Persia, besides providing markets for them, was also a watch upon them, and a reporter to the king of all their actions.'—Second Journey through Persia, etc. p. 46.
London, 18'8.

pons, and let loose their dogs, while even the old women thumped the travellers with clubs. Similar scenes occurred from time to time. They left Bannah, and reached Suleimaniyah over the most frightful roads they had seen. On November 30, they crossed the last and formidable pass, amidst agitation and alarm about robbers, and the people appeared to be more wretched than the Koords.[1] A month was spent in the journey between Tabreez and Bagdad, and they reached the latter city on the morning of Sunday the 6th December 1829, about six months after their departure from Gravesend. According to Mr Groves, the journey of three thousand miles from St Petersburg to Bagdad, cost about £38 for each person of his party, including the expense of living and travelling. Kitto writes :—

'On taking a mental review of this journey, I feel there is great cause to thank God for His many mercies towards us, and His gracious protection of us from many apparent and real evils. I do most truly believe in the doctrine of a *particular* providence, and I shall feel happy in the assurance that you do so. It is a doctrine from which I have, in the course of my life, derived much consolation and support, and I would not for a great deal, relinquish the satisfaction it is so capable of affording.

'We have been till now the guests of Major Taylor, the Resident, and live, and shall live, in a house connected with his. He is a man of much talent, and is very kind to us, being also fully disposed to assist our undertakings. He is of much authority here, and the Residency is a sanctuary. It is contemplated that Bagdad should be the head-quarters of the mission, whilst its members itinerate about in the

---

[1] Perhaps the only instance of humour in Mr Groves' first Journal occurs where he says of one of those Koords—'If this man be a specimen of the general state of clothing among these banditti, it would be difficult for a missionary to go clad, however simply, without at least, in this respect, furnishing an object of temptation.'—Pp. 109, 110.

surrounding countries. I have no locomotive talents, and
shall probably be a fixture here, writing books and tracts,
and bringing up the little boys.'

Bagdad was once renowned over all the East. The
'Old man' says of it to Thalaba,—

> 'It is a noble city that we seek ;
> Thou wilt behold magnificent palaces,
> And lofty obelisks, and high-domed mosques,
> And rich bazaars, whither from all the world
> Industrious merchants meet and market there
> The world's collected wealth.'

But now it had fallen far from its high estate. Literature
had decayed in the once famous capital of Haroun-al-
Raschid, and it was said that a perfect copy of the 'Arabian
Nights Entertainments' could not be found in a place that
figures so conspicuously on its merry pages. It has often
been besieged and pillaged by various armies. Though
built on the Tigris, the Euphrates is distant from it only
a six hours' march, and its surplus waters during an inundation are here discharged into the Tigris by means of
the canal of Isa. Mr Groves selected this city as the commencement of his mission, but left it in 1833 for India,
where he laboured in various schemes of benevolent enterprise during the remainder of his life. Failing health
obliged him to return home in 1852, and he died in peace
and hope at Bristol, May 20th of the following year.

It may be mentioned in passing, that, as the following letter indicates, Kitto identified himself with Mr
Groves' mission, though he was not formally engaged in
evangelical work.

Bagdad, April 30, 1830.

'.   .   .   We are now settled in a house of our own, in
the Christian quarter of the city, in which we have room
for an Armenian school, which is this day opened, and

which we hope it may please God to bless to His own glory, and the benefit of that highly interesting people, who have hitherto been so much neglected in missionary operations. We have thought it most expedient to begin with an Armenian school, as the Mohammedans here are very jealous, and this jealousy will be less provoked in the first instance by an Armenian school than an Arabic one ; but we hope before long to have that also. We anticipate less opposition from the natives than from the Catholic Bishop of Babylon. But he has thus far contented himself with forbidding his people to send us their children. From his flock, however, we meet with attention and kindness, and some of them have offered to send their children, provided we would teach them English.

'. . . You will be glad to hear that, though we are here, in the head-quarters of Islamism, we are subject to no personal molestation. A rude boy may call us *" dogs,"* as we pass the streets, but this rarely occurs, and this is all at present. There are many circumstances, however, which lead us to feel that we hold our lives on a very uncertain tenure, in a place where a man's head can hardly be considered as safe as his hat in England.

'. . . I have an undertaking in hand of a laborious character, which was suggested to me by Mr Groves himself. It is to combine, in one view, our own observations with those of various travellers and authors, to form a view of the sects and denominations of Asia and of Asiatic countries, for missionary purposes, rejecting all information but such as may be thought useful to a missionary.'

Kitto's residence in Bagdad was monotonous—the daily teaching of the boys, the solitary walk on the housetop, and the writing of letters and journals. But his observant eye noted much, and he has recorded many of his observations. Of the houses he says :—

'I will just mention, *en passant*, that the roofs of our houses, though not gardens, clearly illustrate the gardened roofs of Babylon. The internal aspect of the upper rooms is that of an arch, supported on pilasters ; these rest on an abutment, which runs round the middle of the room, and form very convenient recesses for books, etc. Sometimes, however, the ceiling is flat, and then the beams are occasionally seen, unless otherwise covered with ornamental wood-work. In both cases, the actual roof is supported by great beams, over which mats are laid, on which earth or clay, three or four feet deep, is heaped. This lies tolerably firm, and I have not known an instance in which rain water penetrated. There seems no reason at all, why, if the people wished it, or understood it, or it were to their taste, proper earths being used, gardens might not be formed on these terraces. They, however, prefer, perhaps wisely, to reserve them as bedrooms for summer. Rains would not much interfere with such an arrangement. It never, or very rarely, falls, but in winter, and then not in large quantities ; and I do not see that, in this respect, there is any difference between this place and Babylon. Such roofs would not do at Malta, where, from its insular situation, there is a good deal of rain. In that island, therefore, they spread the terraces with a composition, which hardens almost to the solidity of stone, and in which, I believe, lava from Sicily is a principal ingredient. In more rainy places hereabouts, where they use the same roofs, they seem obliged to *roll* their roofs after every rain, to give them consistence. At Suleimaniyah, which, being among the mountains, is rainy, I saw, after a shower, many persons drawing stone rollers over the roofs—this I never saw here.' Again,—'The houses here swarm with vermin ; mosquitoes all the year round, but most in summer. They are, however, not so abundant as in Malta, and in

the country between the Volga and the mountains. Fleas
swarm, even in the most cleanly houses, for a month or six
weeks about the commencement of summer; but we are
not made aware of their existence for the rest of the year.
'During that season, even English ladies are not ashamed
to complain of them. Scorpions are not numerous in the
houses. On removing some clothes from an open recess
in the wall one day, I found one—the first I had ever seen
—and not being sufficiently acquainted with verminology
to recognise it, I felt no alarm; but, not liking its appearance, I brushed it out with my hand, and crushed it under
my foot. Of rats and mice there are plenty.'

He describes the streets in no flattering terms:—

'The state of the streets after rain is such as would
disgrace the worst village in England. The causeways,
where there are any, are about a foot wide, and in as bad
a state as the road—a level of three feet it is impossible to
find, and the mud is ankle deep. The pedestrians either
wear great buskins of red leather over their usual slip-
pers, or else go barefoot on such occasions—the last most
generally—men, women, and all, holding up their clothes
higher than is quite decent—that is, the poor women, for
others either do not go out at all, or wear the great boots
aforesaid. I have often thought that the state of government is indicated by the state of the streets. In all the
countries I have been in, subsequent experience has confirmed the impression thus first obtained. Pavements are
bad, or none at all, where the government is bad. In
Russia, I have not seen a regularly paved street out of
Petersburg and Moscow. In Georgia, still worse; and in
Persia and Turkey, worst of all. Pavements bad in Spain
and Portugal—in England, very good. Verily, the principles of a government may be read in the dust of the
ground. I saw one woman, having a sort of clogs on her

naked feet, raised high, and fastened over the instep by a
band of leather, like a print in Calmet. I never saw it
before. There is nothing here like the system of mutual
accommodation and civility in street-walking which we
find in England. None give the wall, not even the poorest,
nor turn aside at your approach, but expect you to step
off the causeway, such as it is, into the muddiest mud.'

Nor has he forgotten to tell us of the social habits and
common occupations :—

' The people may be considered to have but one regular
meal, which is supper, at or a little after sunset. This is
generally a *pillau*, that is, mutton or fowls, with rice. The
poor seldom get animal food ; bread, dates, and fruit, are
their chief provisions. Mutton is the principal animal
food used. Beef is little esteemed, and wild buffaloes' and
camels' flesh is mostly eaten by the poor. The Christians
can procure pork without much difficulty—we do ; wild
hogs are common among the reeds down the river. A
Mohammedan considers it a defilement to touch a pig ; yet
a Moslem water-carrier, who serves the house with water,
brought a small live hog the other day as a *present*, for
which, however, he expected in return its full value. The
venison is very good ; we get it sometimes, though not so
often as pork. The wild gazelle is found about the river,
and I think the flesh superior to any I have tasted. Coffee
is drunk continually by those who can afford it, but only
regularly in the morning. The poor seldom get it. Coffee,
as made in England, is brown water ; here it is *coffee;* as
they make it and take it without milk or sugar, all its deli-
cious *aroma* is preserved. It is handed round in small cups
of delicate china, in cases of silver or even gold, to prevent
scalding the fingers. Each cup contains about a table-
spoonful, the contents as black as ink, but as they are the
very essence of a considerable quantity of coffee, I have

felt more refreshed after such a small cup, than after a pint of the washy stuff dispensed in the London coffeehouses.

'*February* 12.—I have been, at times this week, considering, with some amusement, the operations of the native carpenters. They uniformly work squatted on the ground, which a European carpenter would consider no very convenient posture. Work benches are things quite unknown in this country. Thus, in planing a plank, as a table-board, they sit down cross-legged upon it, and having planed the space before them, change their position, and perform the same operation on the space themselves had before occupied. Of course they ride upon the board, from the impulse of the plane, to some distance from the place where the board lay when they commenced; but when they change their position to plane the other portion, they ride back again! They make much use of their toe in holding their work. I am not aware that they have chisels, hatchets, or gimblets; the adze performs by far the greatest portion of their work. Holes they drill with a bow. They have saws, of course, but the teeth are indented in quite the reverse position to ours; they, therefore, are obliged to use the strongest exertion, not in pushing the saw from them, as with us, but in pulling it to them. Of this instrument they make, comparatively, but little use. They have much more idea of reducing the wood on which they labour to the required dimensions, by hewing with the adze, than by sawing. I believe a carpenter, working from sunrise to sunset, earns about sixpence sterling, which, considering the price of provisions, is about nine shillings a week; and considering the little work they do, this is no inadequate recompense. A good deal of their time is spent in smoking, which, as their pipes are long (a long stick inserted into an earthen bowl), prevents them from working and smoking too; sometimes, however, when they are pressed, they will take out the earthen bowl, which has a short stem, and smoke while they work.

' Most of the Mohammedans of this city, being of Arabian descent, wear beards. The Osmanlees wear simply mustaches. These are the only general rules. The rest of the people wear beards or mustaches indifferently, according to their fancy, but I think mustaches are most general among the Christians, though they often wear beards. Jews have more generally beards, though often mustaches. As you seldom see a head in these countries uncovered, it is not easy to know whether they are shaved or not ; but from those I have happened to see uncovered, I conclude they are not completely shaven—about half so, that is to say, about half the space between the ear and the crown is shaven quite round, leaving a semi-circle of hair on the top, where the hair is suffered to grow thick. This is commonly enough dyed red ; but beards are not dyed of this colour so frequently as in Persia. Occasionally, however, it is done, and a most disgusting and sometimes ludicrous effect it has. A northern eye, which is accustomed to see the natural red, is not for a moment deceived by the imposture, even so far as the colour is abstractly considered, as it has none of the glossy hue of the natural red hair ; and, accustomed as we are to associate this colour with a fair complexion, a red beard on a dark face seems to be a monstrous anomaly. Moreover it frequently happens, from the neglect of the proprietor of the red beard, that the part which has grown out since the operation, is of the original colour—black, grizzled, or venerable white, whilst all the rest is red, presenting, from the contrast of colours, a most curious and truly laughable appearance.

'' My barber, a tall Osmanlee, with a white turban, is the gravest barber, certainly, under whose hands I ever sat. He bends his tall figure over me with infinite solemnity, and proceeds slowly and deliberately at his work, taking, I think, half an hour to cut my hair, inflicting martyrdom upon me, and causing me to feel most acutely the excision of every particular hair.'

He thus describes the opinions of the people :—

' Here (speaking more particularly of Bagdad and its neighbourhood) the English are much better known than any other Franks, partly from the frequent intercourse with India, and the presence of many who have resided there many years, and partly from the highly respectable and respected Residents the East India Company has had here. Of the power, the wealth, the integrity, and justice of the English, they have very exalted ideas. Defective as the system of our Indian administration is, according to our English notions, the Asiatic, who can compare it only with Asiatic systems, has a better idea of it; and I am sure you will be gratified to learn that those who come here, after having resided there, generally eulogize so highly the comparative impartiality, justice, and liberality of the English administration in India, and the security of person and property they enjoyed under its protection, that there seems a general wish among the mercantile and other more intelligent classes, that the English would take Bagdad into their hands, and they calculate with satisfaction the possibilities that such an event may occur one day or other. Like most other foreigners, perhaps brother Jonathan only excepted, they seem to think Englishmen are made of gold. It puzzles me sometimes, when men, not ill-informed for Asiatics, occasionally inquire if England is as large as Bagdad, how they can suppose the land able to contain all the gold they think Englishmen derive from it. The Russians, though nearer neighbours, are *here* less distinctly known ; they seem to be regarded with much the same sort of feeling, as I regarded, and, I suppose, we have all re-

garded, when children—the Ogres, the fee-faw-fum men
of nursery tales.'

That Kitto, the deaf pauper boy, should find himself so
far from home as Bagdad, must have sometimes surprised
him. When he thought of himself as a little ragged
urchin running wild about the streets, or pictured his seat
of lowly and solitary toil in the Hospital—

> 'As one past hope, abandoned,
> And by himself given over '—

then, indeed, he must have felt that it was a watchful and
mysterious providence which had guided his steps by a
tardy and circuitous route from Plymouth, through Exeter,
Islington, and Malta, to the ' City of a hundred Mosques.'
In this spirit he writes to Mr Burnard, February 25,
1830 :—

' MY DEAR MR BURNARD, . . . Here I am, in this
city of enchantment and wonder, the renowned seat of an
empire which stretched its gigantic arms from the Indus
to the Mediterranean, and the great scene of Arabian tale
and romance. I am quite amazed to think, when I think
of it all, how different the actual scenes and circumstances
of my life have been from any I could previously have anticipated for myself, or others for me. At one time I had
no idea but that I should spend my days in the obscurities
of my humble vocation, and then, when this view was
altered, it seemed so much the tendency of my deafness
to make me a fixture in some chimney-corner, that I should
quite as soon, perhaps sooner, have thought of crossing the
rivers of the moon as the Neva, the Volga, the Terek, the
Araxes, or the Tigris. But here, in spite of a thousand
anti-locomotive habits and dispositions, and ten thousand
fireside attachments, I have been wandering about the
world by a way I have not known, and in which I had not

intended to walk; and, as I am now situated, I see no end
to my wanderings on this side of that bright city to which,
I trust, notwithstanding my weakness, my sin, my evil, I
belong, and to which I hasten, forgetting many things
which are behind, and pressing forward to them that are
before. So true it is, that "a man's heart deviseth his
way; but the Lord directeth his steps." None have had
cause to feel this more strongly than myself; and, with
my past experience, I am almost tired of devising anything at all, but am inclined to sit down quietly and take
whatever it pleases God to send me, whether it appear to
me good or evil, pleasant or painful. I know you are not
a predestinarian; it has been the tendency of many circumstances in my life to make me one; but I do not tell
you whether I am one or not. . .

'I have at present tolerable health and spirits. I find
myself upon the whole very congenially situated, and I am
not aware that I have at any time regretted the determi-
nations which have a second time brought me abroad. I
thank God for that faithful and tried friend, with whom I
am now again connected more closely and naturally than
before, and whose unexampled, and persevering, and un-
tired kindness to me, I am happy to be able in some poor
measure to repay, by undertaking, among my other employments, the education of his sons. May I thus be
enabled, in my humble way, to acknowledge, though I can
never adequately return, the many obligations he has at
different times laid me under.'

Kitto's language at this period betokens, not only that
he had felt the purification of sorrow, but that, apart from
the growth of religious principle, his own observation and
experience, stimulated by travel and enlarged by intercourse, had taught him the great truth unfolded by Spenser,
his beloved bard,—

> 'It is the mind that maketh good or ill,
> , That maketh wretch or happie, rich or poore;
> For some that hath abundance at his will,
>   Hath not enough, but wants in greater store;
>   And other that hath little, asks no more,
> But in that little is both rich and wise,
>   For wisdome is most riches; fooles, therefore,
> They are which fortunes do by vowes devize,
> Since each unto himself his life may fortunize.'

Presence of mind, trust in God, calmness of heart, self-denial, and unrepining adaptation as well to sudden evils as to expected trials, had been gradually acquiring strength within him. Very soon were they all put into requisition, so that, while their genuineness was tested, their power was at the same time developed, in the midst of pestilence, flood, famine, and siege.

CHAPTER VII.

By the month of April, the Pashalic of Bagdad was in agitation. The Pasha was out of favour with the Porte, and the Arabs were at war, both among themselves and with him. Several messengers had been sent from Constantinople for his head, but none of them had ever returned to report his success. In August, between twenty and thirty thousand Arabs encamped close upon the city ; but Daoud Pasha prudently made peace with them, and for the present they dispersed. The plot, however, was thickening, which ended in a siege. Meanwhile, the plague had reached Kerkook. It had already devastated Tabreez in the previous year, and now it came slowly and surely down upon Bagdad. Who could watch the stealthy approach of the foe that 'walketh in darkness,' without feeling either anxiety for himself, or deep commiseration for the helpless victims fluttering and trembling on all sides of him ? Kitto says :[1]—

'. . . But you will wish to know how we are personally affected in the prospect of plague and siege. I am sure Mr Groves feels no personal anxiety on this subject. While he laments the misery which the people have in prospect, he is fully persuaded (and I endeavour to get the same feeling, and do, *in limine*, concur with him) that we

[1] Letter to Mr Woollcombe, Bagdad, February 19, 1831

shall be safe; or if we are visited by the pestilence or the sword, it will be for some wise and useful purpose. He thinks it would be a very poor return for the protection we received from Almighty Providence during our long and perilous journey, particularly in the mountains of Koordistan, were we, in the prospect of new dangers, to distrust that care by which we have hitherto been preserved. The Resident, with his usual kindness, has offered him accommodation, during either the plague or the siege, or both, in the Residency. In the latter case, I know he is at present averse to accept the protection of armed men, which we should there have, for, besides his servants and retainers, the Major has a guard of thirty sepoys; but whether this repugnance extends also to the case of the plague, I have not yet asked him, and cannot do so at the moment. I think, on his principles, it would. Now, for myself, I am afraid that I think more precaution consistent with reliance on the Providence of God than he does. However, I am ashamed to feel any anxiety, which no one about me feels, and, in fact, I do not feel much; but what I may feel when the crisis arrives, I do not calculate upon. I hope to have within me all adequate support from above; and, at the worst, or that which would be thought the worst, I trust I have prospects of good beyond the grave, and life has not been altogether so pleasant a thing to me, to give an interest of much intensity to a question which, at most, involves no more than its possible loss. . . . I often think of the Library, and the first happy, very happy days of new life I spent there. The outward face of every book *then* there, and the inward contents of many, with the feelings and impressions with which they were perused, seem before me now. Many later things, and books more lately read, I do not so well remember.'

At length, in March 1831, the plague was officially declared to be in the city. Seven thousand perished in the first fortnight of the awful visitation, the population being probably about 75,000 ; so that 500 persons seem to have died in a day. The malady whetted its edge and widened its circle of operation, so that in April some days witnessed from 1000 to 1500 deaths. In two months, 50,000 are supposed to have been cut down. Nearer and nearer it came—entered the English Residency—took off some persons attached to Mr Groves' household—and seized Mrs Groves on the 7th of May. After a week's suffering, she died on the 14th. Kitto was deeply distressed by such a stroke. He kept the boys in his own room, and shared with the women the nursing of the baby.

When this melancholy bereavement threatened Mr Groves, Kitto again appears in his journal, thus :—

'Poor nature is bowed very, very low, when I look at my dear boys and little babe, and see only poor little Kitto to be left for their care for hundreds of miles around. . . . Dear little Kitto, I feel for his situation with all my heart. . . . Poor dear Kitto and the little boys are now become the sole nurses of the dear baby by day and by night.

'*May* 12.—Up to this day I am well, thank God; but, seeing the ways of the Lord are so marvellous, I have arranged all my little concerns, and put them into the hands of dear Kitto. But poor Kitto is so little able to provide even for himself.'[1]

The awful scene is described by Kitto in the following terms :—

'Mrs Groves was interred a few hours after her decease, and the things she had used were burned. It went very sharply to my heart, to see the corpse of so good a friend

[1] Journal, London, 1856, pp. 132, 137.

brought out, wound up in the way of the country, in a
sheet, without a coffin, and laid on a sort of grating made
of palm branches, which was fastened on horseback with
cords, by two strange men, who took it away for interment with little ceremony. No one followed her beloved
remains to the grave, and no funeral rites were performed
there—indeed, we know not the spot of her interment—
but our hearts followed her, not to the grave, but to the
throne of the heavenly King, where she appears certainly
not the least brilliant gem among the jewels of His kingdom.[1]

'My dear little pupils bore the news better than I expected, after the first impression. Indeed, if we did not
know the character of a child's mind, and the transient
tone of its impressions, this event seemed to visit them
much more lightly than I could wish. But there is so
little—I have myself felt it bitterly—*so very little strong and
permanent feeling among men and women*, that I know not
what right we have to expect it from children.

'Mr Groves himself, also, bore it much better than,
from the extent of his affection to his departed wife, and
her apparent importance to his happiness and comfort, I
should have expected. However, there were circumstances
to make this dispensation particularly mysterious to him.
. . . Since she came here, she had experienced a peace
and joy in Christ which she had not before known, and
her faith was remarkably strong and implicit; so that her

---

[1] 'Dead bodies were often tossed into the streets, and devoured by the lean and
hungry dogs. 'He did much, then, who took the dead of his household to the
river, and threw them in.' In a stable-yard, close on Kitto's dwelling, nearly a
hundred graves were opened and filled in the course of a day and a half. 'It was
a frightful thing to see the uncoffined dead brought on barrows, or on the backs of
asses, and laid upon the ground till the graves were ready for them.' 'Rich persons
took the precaution of buying their own winding-sheets, and the monopolist, who
sold them at prodigious prices, did not long enjoy the fruits of his greed. Little
orphans were running through the streets, crying in despair for father and mother;
and grandsires were sometimes left alone without a single surviving relative.'—
See Kitto in Penny Magazine for 1833, p. 458.

husband was led to cherish the idea, that the Lord was ripening her for usefulness, and to strengthen his hands in the work of the Lord. How short-sighted are the best of men, when they leave the proper sphere of faith in forming definite expectations for the future, beyond the general persuasion, that all things shall " work together for good" to the children of God. I know many other instances of similar miscalculation. When we see the children of God become more strongly built up in Christ, and more visibly grown, and strengthened, and fructified in Him, we have concluded them to be ripening for great usefulness in the Church, while, in fact (as in this case), they were all the while ripening for the garner of heaven, which we perceive when they are actually gathered in.

' . . . If it be one property of faith to believe *all* mysteries, and receive them, it is not in the abstruse points of theology that the difficulty lies—such as the Trinity, Freewill, etc. — but to believe and receive such great mysteries as this, that the stroke which separates us from the desire of our eyes, the companion of our way, the beloved of our youth, and lays the garden of our earthly hope a bare and desolate thing, is intended in kindness, and to work final good. Yet nothing is more certain than this great mystery. This we shall, in such cases, understand ere long—and this, they who are taken, understand already; and adore, and wonder that there is so much of mercy and of love in that which they once thought grievous and hard. I, too, my dear Marsh, have had losses, more personally my own than this, to sustain ; and I have felt it useful, at such times, to think of the feelings and points of view in which the liberated spirit probably saw the dispensation I mourned under ; or, in other words, to borrow the eye of the other world with which to look on the calamities of this.

'. . . I confess to you, I did not say a syllable to Mr Groves on the subject of this visitation for nearly two days after it occurred, because I did not know what I could say. To many other men I should have had a great deal to say; but I rather look to him, to profit by his words and example, than expect I could be of any use. Till, therefore, he spoke himself about it, I was content that he could see and feel how deeply I sympathised in the loss he had sustained.' Again :—

' Whilst the plague was in the house, the chief object of my anxiety was Mr Groves. I was indeed persuaded he would be spared, yet I could not but feel the possibility of his being taken; and when I considered how much he had been exposed to the contagion, it seemed he could hardly escape without a miracle. I have sat for hours watching him, with an anxiety which I cannot describe, and which unfitted me for reading or study of any kind. On the Monday following Mrs Groves' death, he seemed poorly in the morning, and at dinner took his meal apart, which he had not done the preceding day. In the afternoon he arose from his couch, and came, with rather a tottering gait, towards me, and said, "Have a firm and stedfast heart towards God, and be sure He does all things well: I feel the same symptoms coming upon me as my dear wife mentioned. It is the earnest desire of my heart to be where she is, but for the sake of the dear little ones, I thought it might be better to stay. But He knows best." I said something, with tears, as to the consolation I had felt in all these calamities, in the hope he would be spared. He said, " The Lord does wondrously." He then gave me some instructions in the event of anything having happened to Major Taylor, as the plague had been carried from hence to Bassorah, recommending me to write to England to his friends for money immediately, and to

Aleppo, and to wait here till I got answers. His only thought, he said, was for the children and me; yet he was quite sure the Lord would care for us, for His holy name's sake. The next day he was much better, and now seems quite well. There is no doubt, however, that it was really an attack of the plague, as the Worshabet's[1] attack, which occurred two days after, began with exactly the same symptoms, and which, therefore, no doubt, might have been fatal, but for the great mercy of God to the poor children and myself.'

Kitto himself escaped, but he knew not how soon he might be prostrated, and, at this critical moment, he addressed a farewell letter (May 1831) to his mother, from which we present a lengthy extract :—

'. . . So far as I consider myself a dying man, I am led to review my life a little. It has been a striking one, abounding in mercies, and also in troubles; and also in the elements of happiness: and yet my life, as a whole, has been unhappy; and, perhaps, this is one reason why I the less regret the prospect of its termination. How little would my grandmother have thought, or how little should I have thought myself, ten years ago, that I should have thus been led about the world to die in Irak Arabia. I am glad now that I am not married. When I put myself in dear Mr Groves' present case, and think what I should feel in his situation, supposing that he has the plague himself, and knowing that his beloved wife has— apprehending, also, that he shall have to leave three little orphans in a strange city, under the care of a deaf man,— when I think of this, I am afraid I could not bear it as he does, and I thank God I am not so tried. Yet, if I were,

---

[1] A Worshabet, or Wartablet, is an Armenian priest and teacher; a Moolah has usually some connection with a mosque; an Imaum is a higher spiritual head; and a Moonshee is an amanuensis or interpreter. Mr Groves was taught Arabic by an Imaum.

perhaps *He* would strengthen me, as He does Mr Groves, to bear all He might lay upon me. How easy it is, in comparison, for me to die! As to me, it seems of little consequence to any whether I die or live; but as to Mr Groves, it seems of much consequence to many, and to his own family, at least, that he should live. For myself, I only say, " Do with me as Thou wilt, only make Thy will mine." In case of my death, you will, my dear mother, perhaps, feel it as a little trial—if so, may that and every other trial be blessed to you, in bringing you nearer to Jesus Christ, who became Himself a man of sorrows and acquainted with grief, for our sake. That will be a blessed thing, whatever it be, which brings us nearer to Him, and carries you more frequently to your Bible. As for myself, I have nothing to boast of; no ground of consolation in the prospect of death, but in the free mercy of Christ. I have been a very great sinner—though not habitually indulging in external sin; but my besetting sins have been *within*, sins of the mind; I doubt if my heart were ever truly converted to God, till after I was at Plymouth the last time.

' My dearest mother, I hope you will earnestly seek after the salvation of God. I hope you will attend at Mr Hatchard's regularly. I know no minister at Plymouth who is so well acquainted with the way of life. Above all, do not neglect the Bible and private prayer.

' God bless you, my dear father, and put your *heart*, or keep it if it be there, in that true way which your *head* knows so well. Dear Betsy, dear Mary Ann, dear William, believe me that I love you all very tenderly, and would do anything I could have done for your welfare, whether spiritual or temporal. I hope you may all walk with Christ through the wilderness of this world, that by and by you may join your elder brother in that house not made with hands, eternal in the heavens, whither he goes before you. Take care of our parents. Think how much we owe them; you must do the more for them, now that Johnny can no longer share this pleasure with you. I had hoped to see you again, but God knew better than I what was good. I have a great many things I could say, but I have no room, and my head aches bitterly.

'My dear brother Tucker, as a legacy, I give you an article I highly value, my sister Betsy. It is the best thing, next my parents, belonging to me, and I hope you will regard it for my sake. God bless you both, and make you still more happy together than you have been. I would kiss little Jack Hickerthrift, if I could, but as I cannot, I hereby send him word that he must be a good boy. Tell him that his uncle John prays the Great King in heaven to bless him, and that uncle John wants him to learn the way to come and gather flowers with him in the gardens of Paradise.

'And now, my dearest father and mother, believe how sincerely I have ever been and am, till I put on my new being, and *then* too, perhaps, your affectionate son,

'J. KITTO.'

Kitto must have suffered not a few privations during this forced confinement, but he bore them all with patience, and at some of them he could smile :—

'After describing so much calamity, on a grand scale, it is a little awkward to descend to minor inconveniences. You would, however, have been surprised to see your friend performing, at least in his own apartment, the usual duties of housemaid, such as sweeping the floor, making the bed, and keeping things generally in order. But at the beginning of the plague, the Jew who did our errands left for Bassorah, and the man-servant, who was much ter-

o

rified at the plague, for Mosul; then only the two women remained, one of whom had enough to do in nursing the baby, and the other in cooking; and when the latter died, we had not only all our own things to do, but also to nurse the baby, whilst the nurse performed some of the duties of the deceased servant. Thus, also, no washing could be done—not at home, because water and hands were both wanted; not without, on account of the plague. Our stock of linen was, however, sufficient to prevent much annoyance from this cause, except the occasional necessity of washing a handkerchief or so for ourselves.

'Among these grievances, I should not, perhaps, mention, in my own case, that of being unsupplied with snuff. When the plague began, I was an inveterate snuff-taker. I, however, did not approve the habit in which I indulged, and had often thought of breaking it off; but the craving of the nasal organ was so intense, when its supplies were suspended, that I forgot all the arguments against the practice. I therefore was led to determine to make it a matter of compulsion. So, when the plague began, having enough of the titillating dust to last three weeks, I resolved to lay in no further supply. When that was exhausted, no further supply could be had, and, as I had foreseen, my appetite bitterly repented this determination, while my conscience approved it. So, after I had taken every grain that was to be found, in any hole or corner of box, shelf, or wrapper, I was obliged to sit down without, and, after a few uneasy days, my appetite was reconciled to its want, and, long before the plague was over, I had ceased to desire an article which seemed, two months before, to have assumed the character of an absolute necessary. There are many habits with which it is of no use to reason. They will not be talked down or argued down; they must be compelled; and however lightly some may

think of the exertion necessary to overcome a habit apparently so insignificant, I venture to believe, that the degree
of fortitude which a man must exert in overcoming or re-
sisting such a habit as opium-eating, snuff-taking, or
tobacco-smoking, would gain him a high name, if applied to
some public or prominent object. But mankind have not
learned to estimate *mind* by its own measure, but by its
modes of exhibition.'

But misfortunes did not come singly. The river over-
flowed its banks to an extent 'without recorded or tradi-
tional example,' and on the night of April 27th threw
down seven thousand houses, and fifteen thousand people,
the majority of them already stricken with the malady,
lost their lives. Hosts of fugitives from the doomed city
were caught by the waters and prevented from escaping.
Many of them died, and some gained the heights, on which,
though spared by the plague, they perished of want. The
house in which Kitto dwelt was exposed to the danger :—

' The house we live in is, perhaps, as strong as any
in Bagdad. The waters have not flowed into our street,
though they were only kept out at one end by an accidental
elevation of the ground. The water, however, soon found
its way into the *Sardaubs*, where it now stands to the depth
of nine feet, and though now stationary, has nearly attained
the level of the court-yard. Mr Groves, while dressing in
the morning, in the room which he and Mrs G. had usually
occupied, observed some dust fall down from a crack in the
wall, and at last it occurred to him to remove from the
room his things, which mostly lay there. All were employed in this business except myself (who held the baby),
and it had been finished but a quarter of an hour, when the
arch which supported the room gave way, and the floor of
earth and brick fell into the water with a horrid crash.
Blessed be the Hand that supported the arch till such pre-

cious lives were withdrawn from the danger! A few evenings
after, as I was sitting in my room, I felt the house shake,
and was almost suffocated by a cloud of dust, and, rushing
out, found, as soon as the dust had settled a little, that the
wall of the same room, which had separated it from another,
had fallen, and with it a great portion of the roof or terrace of the house, which it helped to support; and when,
after the dust had subsided, one stood on the house-top
and looked down into the very cellars from thence, and saw
a confused mass of earth, bricks, great beams, and water,
it was affecting to think of the Divine goodness which had
been exhibited in these transactions; for, in this last instance also, the servant, with the baby in her arms, had
but a few minutes before been in the room, which the fallen
wall divided from that of the floor which had already fallen.'

The reflecting journalist adverts to the proximate causes
of these terrific scenes of plague and mortality :—

Bagdad, July 3, 1831.

' We have not, I think, to seek for the cause of the terrible character it assumed, in anything inherent in the
plague : we may, then, inquire what collateral causes gave
it this destructive character. The answer is, *the inundation.*
In these countries people have no other resource than to
run away when the plague appears. In the present case,
however, this common resource was precluded by the inundation, as if the Agent of Destruction acted with design
(and did he not ?) in unbinding the rivers, that the waters
might confine his victims, as in a prison, awaiting execution. Now, within the walls of Bagdad, there is not much
room to spare. It is not a widely spaced town, and, of
course, in such a case, the danger is greater in proportion,
as the population, being thus confined, are more exposed
to the chance of contact, and the miasmatic corpuscles are
more condensed, longer held in suspension, and more

slowly dissipated in the purer air; and not only, it appears, will the smaller mass of air be more strongly impregnated by the greater quantity of miasma, but the air will be, on the same account, additionally loaded by the foul effluvia of a crowded population, as well as from the decomposition of animal substances left in the streets, including, in our own case, bodies unburied, as well, perhaps, as the thousands buried within the walls, slightly under ground, in which the miasma of the plague will not readily dissolve. And to these causes may be added, the probable generation of bad air by the action of the sun on the waters, which so widely surrounded the city—all circumstances concurring to give a peculiarly noxious character to the pestilential miasma in this case. And when the full operation of all these proximate circumstances was effected, by the destruction of such a great number of houses by the eruption of the waters, which obliged the survivors to crowd together, thirty or forty in a house in the uninundated parts, the wonder, physically speaking, seems to be, not that five out of seven have died, but that the remaining two escaped.'[1]

The horrors of a siege followed the havoc of plague and flood. After various feints on the part of Daoud Pasha, the Arab Pashas of Mosul and Aleppo advanced against him. They had been waiting at Mosul till the pestilence

[1] It may be added, that the heat at Bagdad is sometimes so excessive, that the birds sit on the palm trees gasping for air. At the time referred to, in consequence of the inundation, the inhabitants could not retire into the sardaubs or sardebs—subterranean apartments, where the atmosphere is several degrees cooler than in the higher rooms of the house. Various devices of funnels and chimneys are employed to send a current of air down into the apartments of a Persian house, as in the allusion in ' Lalla Rookh:'—

' If Zephyrs come, so light they come,
    Nor leaf is stirred, nor wave is driven;
The wind-tower on the Emir's dome
    Can hardly win a breath from heaven.'

The embankments of the river are now made more secure, for a few years since the water rose 22½ feet, considerably higher than in 1831, and yet no damage was done.

and the waters should subside. Robbers took the advantage, and began to plunder the city ; entered Mr Groves'
dwelling, in their lawlessness, firing a shot through the door;
but a civil answer and some money, about a pound sterling,
pacified them. The Georgian defenders of the reigning
Pasha having fallen before the plague, no resistance could
be offered to the invaders. The Pasha was taken prisoner,
and Kitto saw him carried past the door under a strong
guard. Yet the crafty governor contrived to re-establish
his authority for a season at Bagdad, and held the uncertain reins of power till September; the Pasha of Mosul,
who had taken his place, being, in the interval, condemned
and put to death. Such a daring act could not be pardoned,
and the Pasha of Aleppo finally gathered his forces for a
regular blockade. The city, knowing the insecurity of its
ruler, was full of disorder, and on the night of the 28th
of August, the house of Mr Groves was broken into and
partially plundered. The loss fell most heavily on him
who could not hear the robbers' intrusion, and he thus re-
counts it :—

'*August* 29, Monday.—I was surprised this morning, on
arising and coming down from the roof of the house,
where, like other people, we sleep in summer, to find some
of the contènts of my clothes-box scattered about in the
adjoining room and the verandah. My first idea was,
that thieves had visited us ; but the servant-maid, who
had risen just before, and, on observing the same, had
gone to ascertain that the door was safe, as no other
means of access to the house occurred to her, was looking
on with some terror, being afraid to touch the things which
lay here and there, in the persuasion that the devil had
been busy about them ; for here they assign the same
paltry and mischievous employment to the Prince of Darkness as in enlightened England.

'We soon ascertained, however, that, whether men or devils, they had not left us empty-handed, and that they had obtained access by wresting out the wooden frame-work of a window, in a neglected room, which looked into that same yard where so many of the dead were buried during the plague, and which, though high up in the wall, they had probably ascended without a ladder (a ladder is here a ponderous pair of steps), the people here being expert in climbing, from their habit of clambering up high date trees. Now, we had no idea that thieves, though we expected them, would come otherwise than openly and forcibly by day; or else that the house was impregnable against silent robbery; hence our doors were all unlocked, and the robbery was so silently managed, that neither we, nor the man-servant, who slept on the same floor with the rooms robbed, and quite opposite to them, knew anything of it. I say *we*, though, as far as *hearing* goes, they might have pulled the house down for me. Yet I was not undisturbed, for I dreamt of seeing a man hung outside Newgate, probably at the very time that the robbery was going on, illustrating the peculiarity of my dreams, which I have before had occasion to consider.

'On examination, it was found that their principal de-predations were committed on poor me. They seem to have visited the rooms in the order of march; from the first they took bread, but omitted to take the silver spoons, which lay there quite exposed. It is plain that they had no light with them; and as the room was dark, not admitting the beams of the moon, the spoons escaped their notice. In the next room, that of the little boys, they found nothing to their purpose; and in the next, which is an open room, between mine and theirs, there was nothing to steal.

'The next room was mine. The contents of my box

(chiefly of the things in actual wear, for what was not so I had, some weeks before, put away in a secret place) they seem to have taken out to the moonlight to see what was most worth taking; hence the things in the adjoining open room and the verandah. All my clean shirts, about a dozen, they took, leaving only two coarse ones; also my hose, sheets, pillow-cases, towels, handkerchiefs, and some flannel articles. The last loss is irreparable, as also that of shirts, which no one now in Bagdad knows how to make. There was one little parcel also, which I had made up the preceding day, and intended to *bury* on this, and which contained some little articles belonging to my lost one. This they opened, and, taking thence some small valued trinkets of silver and gold, left the other articles strewed about. That they had left any of the contents of this dear parcel I thank them, whilst my heart quarrelled with them for having taken that which they did. A bundle, containing old rags, etc., they also took, and another, containing Persian and other worsted hose, together with a quantity of linen cloth. This was the extent of their depredations on me; my money was hid away; and, happily, they did not look farther than my box, else they would have found razors and other cutlery, the loss of which would have been irreparable here. I think, indeed, they took alarm when they had done examining my box; and hence had no leisure to examine the room fully, or the next, that of Mr Groves. They went there, indeed, and brought out some of his clothes to the light; but they stole nothing, nor seemed to have examined more than one box, though the others contained property much more valuable than they could find with me. For several hours we thought that I had been the only loser, but it was found then, that from another room they had taken two fine Persian carpet rugs, worth about L.6. Mine, however, is the greater loss, consisting of various articles of use, and some of that adventitious value, which things derive from having belonged to friends now in heaven. If there were an Englishwoman, a wife, or a sister here, such losses as these I mention would not signify, but one feels it, in present circumstances, a little vexatious; and then one is the more vexed to think that such things should have the power of vexing at all. My books, which I value most, will not tempt them —my money, and more valuable things, are concealed among the ruins of the fallen arches and roofs, and of that which remains they have taken that which pleased them best; so really there is some comfort in having been robbed; and, to be a little more serious, I trust I may say that I am enabled to take "joyfully the spoiling" of my goods, knowing of better goods in possession and prospect, which man did not give to me, and cannot take from me.'

The siege was continued with all its usual fruits, and the Pasha was reduced to the last extremity; the population in the town proving as dangerous to him as the beleaguering foe beyond its walls. Kitto's quaint observations are tinged with sadness :—

' *September* 11.—The siege has now been going on for several months. In such circumstances, my deafness is no small benefit to me. I am not disturbed by the noise of artillery and musketry, and of other commotions around; and I do not, except sometimes through Mr Groves, hear the reports which are so heart-sickening. Upon the whole, if not told, I should hardly know what was going on, as I do not go out of doors, and life passes with me as it was wont, were it not that we are now straitened in several articles of provisions to which we have been accustomed; and if, when I walk in the cool of the evening on the house-top, I did not perceive the flash of mortars, cannons, and muskets, and observe the ascent and fall of bombs. The besieging party regularly begin to bombard the city about three quarters of an hour after sunset, when, in this country, it is dark, though it would not be so in England so shortly after the sun had set. If not for the feeling of their being destructive, the flight of the bombs so high, and their frequent explosion in the air, would have a very fine effect. Most of them do burst in the air. We have to be thankful that we are so near the middle of the city, where the bombs do not often fall; yet one did fall on the top of a house not far from ours, and, by its explosion, killed three persons who slept there. But, upon the whole, I have not understood that their bombs have done much harm to the city or people; and altogether, it seems the city has much better and more artillery than the enemy. We often pick up musket balls in the court and on the terrace. The enemy seems to be straitened for metal. The balls, both for cannon and musket, are often of *clay*,—the application of which to such a purpose is quite a new thing to me. Such balls, however, have quite force enough to kill a man, it seems; though that they have made a breach I have not yet learned. I know not what stronger evidence we could have of the misery of man, and the ruined state of the world, than what we have seen and heard in Bagdad in the course of the year 1831. In Europe, particularly in England, the world is presented under so many disguises, and in features so externally attractive, that it requires no ordinary discernment to perceive the utter worthlessness, vanity, and hopelessness of all it can offer. She is here naked, and the heart sickens at the deformity which sin has made in her once excellent form of character; and in the depth of its abhorrence and disgust at all it looks on, is tempted to cry, perhaps too impatiently, "O that I had wings like a dove, for then would I fly away and be at rest!" May all we have felt and suffered be made useful to our spirits. And I think it cannot fail to be so. We have known and seen what can never be forgotten, and which, while we remember, we cannot easily fall into the error, which most do, of mistaking earth for heaven; and in its legitimate effects on our minds, must lead us to feel as strangers and sojourners in it more strongly than we have ever done.'

The Pasha, to raise funds, sold his dagger studded with diamonds, and the jewels of his wives. The roofs of the bazaars were torn down and sold for fuel, and a drunken rabble did as it pleased with property and life. Provisions had risen in price, and there were all the horrors of a famine. The favourite pigeons of Kitto's pupils had to be killed, and the goats on which the motherless baby depended for milk could not be spared. On September 15th, Daoud Pasha fled, and he of Aleppo prepared to take possession. As in Samaria in the days of Elisha, the aspect of things suddenly changed, and, as Groves states, ' wheat, that sold on Wednesday for 250 piastres, sold on Thursday for forty, and other things in proportion.' After five months' close confinement in the house, from pestilence, inundation, and blockade, Kitto ventured out, and the appalling spectacle deeply affected him. The old Hebrew sovereign was, in the day of Divine anger, offered his choice among God's ' sore judgments '—dearth, sword, and pestilence—and he humbly and wisely replied, ' Let me now fall into the hand of the Lord ;' but Bagdad suffered from all these scourges, either simultaneously or in rapid succession. While the angel of death might be seen standing over the city with his drawn sword, the Tigris was collecting its furious torrent among the hills, and the 'hand of man' was mailing itself to join in the devastation,—the camp-fires of the Arabs gleaming in the distance. The combined results of this resistless agency, acting on a crowded, perverse, fatalistic, and misgoverned city, cannot be easily imagined, and Kitto's narrative is not by any means overcharged :—

' *October* 1.—I went out this afternoon for the first time these five months, in order to get myself a book or two from Major Taylor's library, to which I understood there was still access, notwithstanding his absence. The contrast between the aspect of the streets *now*, and when I was last in them, was very striking, and greater than I expected to find, after the accession of strangers which the place has received, and the distance of the plague. The streets I had to pass through are among the most populous of the city ; but I doubt if I met more than fifteen persons in going and returning, except in one part of the way which lay through the bazaar. This desolation was very affecting, when its cause struck the mind ; when it occurred to one's thoughts, that of the busy and anxious population which went through the streets a few months back in their many-hued and multiform array, plotting and scheming for years to come, three-fourths now lay buried beneath the soil they then trod. I looked round for the accustomed faces which, from frequent passing, had become familiar, but they were all gone. Most I meet now seem to be strangers. The former frequenters of the streets were, at last, accustomed generally to our European dresses, and ceased to stare much at us ; but those I meet now eye me with the wondering gaze of strangers, and such, indeed, their dress betrays many of them to be. All the time I have been in Bagdad before, I think I never saw a real Turkish dress, except on Captain Chesney, a traveller, who assumed it ; but now, many of the persons I meet have that dress, which, though a nearer approximation to ours than the long flowing attire of the Arabians, is far

less gratifying to a European taste ; and the simple red
cap, without a folding around, which the common Turks
wear, has an unpleasant effect, compared with the striking
and stately head-dresses which all, except the poorer
Jews, delighted to wear ; these often contented themselves
with a little coloured handkerchief twisted round the red
cap, which, however, was better than nothing. The red
cap, though it forms a pleasing *part* of the proper head-
dress, is a contemptible thing of itself. In Greece, however, and the Western Arabic Provinces, it is often worn
alone,—here, never till now, the Bagdadians being most
rigid turbanites ; a predilection which does credit to their
taste, for, after having seen almost every variety of masculine head-dress, I venture to pronounce that none are more
graceful, imposing, or useful, perhaps, in a hot country.
The shops also in the bazaar, or leading to it, were nearly
all closed, to as large an extent as in England on a Sunday.   Often, I do not think more than one was open.
The men who used to sit there cross-legged, with their
stores around them, and smoking their pipes, are all
dead.   How terrible, how very terrible, these things
are to a European, and, of all Europeans, to an English
mind !

'I was surprised, also, to see the number of houses
which had been thrown down by the inundation. I had
thought that the consequences of that calamity had been
confined to one part of the city ; but here I saw houses
fallen, and others partly fallen, among those which remained entire.   Some had simply their fronts fallen, whilst
the rest remained entire, exposing to view the best and
well decorated apartments of many houses.   Nothing can
present a more striking contrast than the gloomy outside
to the gay, and even splendid interior, of the houses in
Bagdad. Many of the internal decorations seem in very

good taste, however little of it the Turks exhibit in other
respects.   It is usual to report these people as wanting in
taste.   I know not on what this imputation is founded,
except in the difference of their taste from ours.   As to
dress, I venture to think our European dresses exquisitely
absurd, and can excuse my Arabic friends for thinking so;
but what European ever thought the Arabian, the Al-
banian, or the Persian dress absurd ?   And, in building,
I know no structure more effective, more finely propor-
tioned, and delicately turned, than the minars I see around
me.   If they make no display of taste or skill in their
houses or palaces externally, the reasons are pretty well
known; but when we come *within*, I will say with confidence, that in the cities of Turkey and Persia, and particularly Bagdad—though I know this is not by any means
the finest, or one of the finest, cities—there is a *greater
proportion* of houses, elaborately finished and tastefully
ornamented within, than in any cities in Europe, not excepting Italy, where such processes are confined to the
palaces.   Of this assertion, the gracefully arched ceiling
of the room I write in is a proof and illustration.   It is
true, the style of embellishment is different generally from
ours, except as in this room, which is a Gothic chapel in
miniature.   The common style, however, is more light and
gay, more of both, indeed, than at the first glance would
be thought very compatible with the apparently sombre
and heavy genius of the Turks.   Yet, I don't know, either.
The tame Arabs, who form the basis of the population,
are far enough from anything that is sombre and heavy
As I looked around, from the top of Major Taylor's house,
the city seemed in a great measure laid open, from the
falling down of garden and other walls, and I did not, in
any one instance, perceive that the least attempt was making to build up that which was fallen.   Indeed, I doubt

very much if the city will ever regain its former footing,
low as that was compared with its ancient fame.'

These weary and eventful months taught Kitto many a
salutary lesson, and deepened within him a spirit of calm
resignation. The crisis had again and again brought him
face to face with death. The firmness of Mr Groves,
under the trying circumstances, was not lost upon him.
There must have been 'great searchings of heart' until
unwavering confidence in God was established in his soul:
' Thou wilt keep him in perfect peace whose mind is stayed
on Thee.' In October, Mr Groves had an attack of typhus
fever, and Kitto again felt no ordinary responsibility. But
he persevered and fainted not, committing all to Him who
has a Father's heart to pity, and a Father's arm to guard
and bless.

On recovering, Mr Groves contemplated a journey to
Aleppo, to confer with some friends there. The design,
however, was immediately abandoned. But towards the
beginning of next year, the monotony of Kitto's sojourn at
Bagdad was varied by an unexpected trip down the Tigris,
in company with Sir John M'Neill, who was on his way
to Bushire, to another political post. Kitto had suffered
much in body and mind during the five months of disaster
and evil tidings; but no sooner did he meet Sir John
M'Neill again, than the ruling passion revived, and he
recurred to the old topics of conversation at Tabreez,—
the illustration of the Bible through Oriental manners and
legislation. It had by this time become a subject of settled
study, and he was desirous above all things of increasing
his acquaintance with it.

The party sailed down the river in a species of barge,
and not, as is often done, on rafts resting on inflated skins.[1]

---

[1] These inflated skins are still used for navigation, as they have been for many
ages past. Kitto refers to Herodotus and Xenophon as having mentioned them, or

Kitto, never very sure in his footing, fell into the water the first day, and having, as might have been anticipated, a load of books in his pockets, he sank at once to the bottom. But he playfully adds:—'I fortunately pulled a Persian groom of Mr M'Neill's *in* with me, in return for which he had the good nature to pull me *out*. This was a transaction which the light-hearted Irancé always thought of afterwards when he saw me, and never thought of without "roars of laughter," as they say in the House of Commons' reports ; and this, at last, to my no small annoyance, as my perception became too obtuse to perceive where the joke lay which amused him so highly.'

On one occasion Kitto strayed from the party, and when the boat was about to sail, he could not be found. To shout to him or fire a shot was needless. Sir John M'Neill started in pursuit, and commenced naturally to call after him, ere he recollected that he was only wasting his breath. 'After a sharp run,' he says, 'I came up with him, but as he could not hear my approach, he was completely taken by surprise, and when I seized him by the collar of his coat, supposing himself in the hands of some Arab robber, he turned on me a face of such agony, that, ludicrous as the circumstances were, I could hardly laugh.'[1] On another occasion, during night, or rather towards morning, the party was attacked by some Arabs, and shots were exchanged, ' without injury to any of the fleet,' though Kitto supposed, from their yelling, after a volley had been fired at them, that some of the invaders had been wounded.

at least, he says, Major Taylor so translated Herodotus. But in the passage probably referred to, I. 194, the historian speaks simply of hides stretched on ribs of willow, and calls such vessels, πάντα σκύτινα—'wholly of leather.' Xenophon. however, in his Anabasis, 1-5, 10, speaks of skins stuffed with hay being employed in the construction of rafts. Layard describes the building of those referred to by Kitto.—*Nineveh*, Vol. II., p. 96.

[1] Communication from Sir John M'Neill to Mr Ryland. *Memoirs of Dr Kitto*, second edition, p. 351.

'The cries of the women,' he mentions, 'were very conspicuous on this occasion, and indeed they are always active participators in such affrays. This I was about to mention as a peculiar disgrace to the "womankind" of this country, but I have just read the account of the Bristol riots[1] in the Courier.'

At Zechigyah, Major Taylor met them with the information that the pestilence was raging at Bassorah, and that Mr M'Neill's appointment at Bushire had been cancelled. They had no alternative but to return to Bagdad, and be again shut up during a second threatened visitation of the plague. Kitto felt more anxiety about this second exposure to the malady than about the first. Of the kindness of Sir John M'Neill and of the Resident, he speaks in the highest terms. He kept, as he describes it, a 'terribly copious journal' of this brief voyage. 'Mr Groves himself has written a very good journal. . . . I find on comparing our journals, that my attention has been directed to many things with interest, which Mr Groves did not at all observe, or did not think it worth while to mention. Moreover, I have been by far the most *minute* observer of the two, as is, indeed, natural for a *little* man to be. . . . In England, the notes I have been in the habit of making, and shall make during our future journeys, if it pleases God to prolong my life, will afford me, I hope, interesting materials for communications to my friends ; though I am not ignorant that the ideal value the mind gives to what comes from afar, would make the same facts and observations, which I may then relate, of much

[1] These riots, unparalleled in the modern history of England, occurred in the last week of October 1831. The bishop's palace, the prisons, the excise office, and nigh fifty private dwellings were set fire to, and some hundreds of individuals were killed or wounded. Tho disturbances arose in connection with some procedure of Sir Charles Wetherell, the recorder of the city, who was exceedingly unpopular, from his hostility to the Reform Bill.

greater interest, if they came from Bagdad, in letters
smoked and dried, like a neat's tongue, and stabbed through
and through, as I suppose mine are.'[1]

Kitto's journal, chiefly scrolled in pencil, is certainly
minute and topographical, though there is not much in it
of special interest, beyond an account of the banks of the
river, the scenery within view, the ruins and villages passed,
the interviews with the Arabs, and some scattered remarks
on their character and condition.   On returning to Bagdad,
the family were shut up in Major Taylor's house, the plague
having broken out, but not with the severity of the preceding year.   The city, however, was so deserted, that the
very women walked through the streets unveiled.

By midsummer, Kitto's thoughts were turned toward
England.   He felt that he was becoming of less and less
service to Mr Groves.   Mr Newman, who had recently
come out to Bagdad, was doing the work of a tutor, and
Kitto was not permitted to exercise any of the functions
of a missionary.   But the object of his journey to the East
had been served, though he was not himself aware of it.
His mind had been storing itself with the knowledge of
Oriental customs, laws, and other peculiarities, and he had
seen the importance of these for the illustration of Scripture.
The first awakening of his attention to this point was the
critical moment of his life, and it is recorded in his journal
under date August 3, 1829.

'The different modes of raising water in Russia may
not be unworthy of notice, particularly as one of them
seems to illustrate a passage of Holy Writ. I do not know
what mode obtained, till about half-way between Petersburg and Moscow; but there, a very long pole serves the
purpose, which is balanced from a beam, placed over the
well, by the bucket at one end and a block of wood at the

[1] Precautions used by the post-office with regard to letters from infected countries.

other. The weight of the bucket causes it to descend, when a strong exertion of manual strength is applied, and in the same manner to ascend when strongly pulled, by the assistance of the balance at the other end. A large number of these poles, stretching out their long arms, form very curious and conspicuous objects in Russian scenery. The other mode of raising water is by means of a wheel, from six to eight feet in circumference, which, being turned round in one direction, carries the bucket down to the depth requisite to fill it, and then brings it up again. It depends, in a great measure, on the weight of the bucket and balance, but I have tried very few of these wheels which I could turn with ease. As it is a very simple plan, it is also a very ancient one most likely, and I agree with Dr Henderson in thinking it sufficiently illustrates " the wheel broken at the cistern," in Eccles. xii. 6. In some places pumps are used, but I have not much recollection of having seen a windlass.'

The next instance occurred at Teflis, where he saw the oxen treading out the corn; and the third is mentioned as having struck him at Shusha :—

' Two women were there, occupied in baking bread. The elder of these made me understand, by signs, that the whole establishment, including the threshing-floor adjoining, belonged to her. The baking process is very simple, and I am inclined to suppose it, from the rapidity of the work and coincidence of circumstances, to be the scriptural method of baking cakes. A convex plate of iron is supported on three stones. Under this a fire is kindled, and the dough, spread out into very thin cakes, is placed upon it. Each cake is dressed in a minute or two. Cakes are thus made more or less thin. At Shusha, where I write, they are our common bread. The cakes are as thin as brown wrapping paper, and more flexible, and, as is well

known, the Persians use them for napkins at table, and
then eat them.   They are really very palatable.   The nature of the process renders turning necessary, which reminds
one of the passage, " Ephraim is a cake not turned." '—
Hosea vii. 8.

In Bagdad he alludes to another point :—

' When you look at the higher class of buildings, you
have an idea of their solidity, which is by no means correct.
You see walls three or four feet thick, but they are merely
loosely faced with bricks, and the rest is filled up with dust
and rubbish.   They are, in short, entirely adapted to a
climate where it seldom rains.   In an inundation of the
river, even when the streets are not flooded, the cool cellars
already mentioned, lying below the then level of the water,
are soon filled, and, in a few days, sap the foundations of
the arches which support the rooms above, which then fall
in.   How easily, then, are such buildings swept away when
exposed to the full tide of waters, and how much more, the
habitations of the poor, who, as in Job's time, " dwell in
houses of clay." '

Before coming to Tabreez his attention had been point-
edly turned to this subject, for he speaks of a person clad
in a certain costume as resembling ' one of the prints in Calmet's Dictionary.'   At length his mind became full of it, and
he seized on information wherever he could procure it.   His
interviews with Sir John M'Neill at Tabreez and Bagdad,
and in the brief voyage on the Tigris, were exciting and
beneficial to him, and powerfully contributed to give his
mind that tendency which ultimately carried him to the
great work of his life.   Kitto was very sensible of Sir
John's kindness, felt at home in his company, and was thankful for the varied information which he was so frank in com-
municating.   Great credit is due to him for the sympathy
he felt with the little deaf querist, for the pains he took

with him, for his appreciation of his talents and acquirements in spite of numerous drawbacks, and for his readiness in at once gratifying his curiosity, and stimulating his
mind to future and deeper inquiry.

Kitto was now ready to come back to England, though
he knew not what spheres of labour might be opened to
him. What he should do on his return was an object of
great anxiety, and the subject had been repeatedly talked
of with Mr Groves and Major Taylor. 'At Mr Groves'
desire,' he writes to Mr Lampen,[1] 'I have opened to him
my views and feelings, and he has entered into them with
greater kindness and consideration than I have been accustomed to even from him.' Still Mr Groves thought
that he was becoming low in his aims—that mere literature
was a sinking of the missionary character, which he had so
decidedly preferred. He lamented over such defection, and
suspected that his nine years' connection with Kitto had
produced little or no spiritual fruit. Another tutorship
was out of the question, for no one would be likely to employ him, and his deafness would be held to be an insuperable barrier. Not hearing the conversations of his pupils,
he could not check any froward word or unguarded expression, and was, therefore, incapacitated for one special function of the office. Kitto makes this admission himself, adding, however, 'it seems, upon the whole, the least repug-
nant to my habits of the things I have hitherto tried.' But
he was rarely troubled with doubts of his fitness, when any
end was to be gained, and his mind turned to periodical
literature and an editorship. He was wishful that such a
situation, in the first instance at least, might be found for
him about his native town.

'If Plymouth has its Roscoe, I will hasten to wipe his
shoes. Meanwhile, I have a most exaggerated notion of

[1] Bagdad, April 6, 1832.

the influence of a newspaper, if the editor of a well-sup-
ported print, keeping this object steadily in view, might
not, in this respect, be of some use. A magazine might
do more in the end ; but a magazine does not seem the
thing to *begin* with. There seems no spirit for so spirited
a thing, as, otherwise, I think I could lay my finger on
the names of several persons who, among them, might
construct a very able periodical. . . When I was at
Plymouth, poets seemed as thick as blackberries. Besides
four known ones, I remember a lady sent me a poetical
invitation to dinner, and an artizan wrote a very tolerable
acrostic on my poor name. Prose writers are not so common, unless it be taken for granted that a good poet must
also necessarily be a good prose writer, which I doubt.

'As to my own competency for this same editorship,
there is not a single *if* or *but* in Mr Groves and Major
Taylor's admission of it. You will see, by my letter to
Mr Harvey, what spirits they have put me into by their
saying, that they have now *no doubt* that I shall be able
to get a comfortable living in some of the departments of
literary employment. This admission from them seemed
the slow and tardy recompense for all my retired, unen-
couraged, uncheered, and often *opposed* exertions in the
improvement of my own mind. I shall, perhaps, surprise
you by declaring that,.excepting the year in the Library,
and excepting that I have had greater facilities in procur-
ing books, my opportunities for study have been fewer
since I left the workhouse than while in it. I have had
less time from my stated employments. Even now, for
instance, I write this nearer to one than twelve at night,
when every one else has been three hours in bed ; by day
I have no time. My employments, indeed, are more
pleasant to me than before, but they do not inform my
mind. If I were asked, whether, in my secret mind, I

think myself equal to such an employment, I, who never pretended to more humility than sixpence would cover, would answer instantly *I do*. And now, at this period, I think I may venture to mention a bit of a secret. My simple love of knowledge, and habits of attachment to pursuits which I venture to call *literary*, would, I think, have failed under the discouragements I have met with, but the admixture of another feeling urged me on. Then, I know perfectly well, that many thought you and my other earliest friends not justified in their original kindness to me, by any actual possession or future promise I held out. What is more, I soon began to think so too myself. But I thought then, and think to this day, that all the fine stories we hear about *natural ability*, etc. etc., are mere rigmarole, and that every man may, according to his *opportunities and industry*, render himself almost anything he wishes to become. I proposed it, therefore, as an object to myself, to make such attainments—to possess myself of such qualifications as might justify my friends to themselves and others, for their early kindness, and the mode of its exhibition. I think that, small as my opportunities, upon the whole, have been, I can now do this, and shall hereafter be able to do it better; for I should grieve to think that every day will not be with me a day of some improvement, till the last of my existence—an existence which I should desire to be prolonged to that period when the faculties of improvement must fall into " the sear, the yellow leaf." I am now near thirty, a period at which it is surely high time for a man to enter upon his plans of life—to endeavour to get into that path in which he desires and intends to walk; and no one can be more deeply sensible than myself, of the danger of postponing, from year to year, such designs, till postponement becomes a habit—till no strength or vigour remains for enterprise

—for the effort necessary to carry these designs into effect. If, therefore, it be my lot to spend the remaining period of my existence in the class of employments I desire, and which are now admitted to be best for me, it is certainly high time to make the effort, and encounter the risk necessary; and I think my mind is now wound up to make every possible effort necessary, before I can be led to relinquish these designs; and if, at last, I must do so, the relinquishment will then probably be final. That I have no "small certainties" in *other* things, will, perhaps, at this juncture, be an advantage to me. I have long been in the habit, according to a suggestion of Lord Bacon, of noting down the idea of any paper or work which occurred to me. Among the mass of such ideas, there are enough which my mature judgment would approve, to occupy, in their accomplishment, a longer life than I wish mine to be; and new ideas are continually occurring, so that a dearth of matter is the thing which I shall at any time least dread.

'What reception I am likely to meet with on my return, I cannot tell. I shall need encouragement from my friends, but, I confess, there are some at whose hands I do not very sanguinely expect it; and this misgiving arises from circumstances which occurred when I was in England last. However, I hope the best; for I can see no reason why I should not be kindly welcomed to my native land once more. I return under no imputation of blame, under no suspicion of having merged my duty in my own inclinations. If I had any *duty* that required my stay here, it was the tuition of Mr Groves' sons. I always contemplated to return when this duty should be fulfilled, and now, accordingly, I am retired from it and left disengaged; the rather, as Mr Groves himself admits, that my deafness precludes me from any occupation that can be called *missionary;* and, I confess, I see not how any one, free from the obligations of detaining duties, could prefer to live in this miserable land. Thus, clear from any just ground of censure in returning, and with a mind improved, I trust, by travel, and stored with images it had not before, I do apprehend I shall occupy a much more advantageous position in returning this time than the last.'[1]

'I thank God,' he had already written to Mr Lampen,[2] 'with all my heart, that I have been able to give satisfaction to somebody, particularly when it is one whose satisfaction circumstances have taught me to rate at no common value.'

There was, as his repeated language implies, one impression which Kitto wished most especially to make on his friends, in the prospect of his return to England, and that was, that he came back with no imputation of blame, and under no suspicion of having merged his 'duty in his own inclinations.' He remembered the crisis in Islington, when he renounced his connection with the Missionary Society, and he had not forgotten the emotions which preyed upon him when he returned from Malta, or the cold reception he met with on his last visit to Plymouth. Now, his anxiety was to let it be known that no such misunderstandings or objections had prompted him to leave Bagdad. He knew what he had suffered already, and he was careful to warn all his correspondents that he was not dismissed from any dissatisfaction with him, and that he had not sullenly thrown up his situation, but that the object of his engagement being accomplished, he was at liberty to come home, there being no further prospects for him in the East. And thus he opens his mind to Miss Puget—an intimate friend of Mr Groves—on September 8, 1832 :—

[1] Letter to Mr Woollcombe, Bagdad, July 21, 1832. [2] Bagdad, April 6, 1832.

'My return is not so difficult to account for, or so unpleasant to think of, as it assuredly would have been, if
I could have allowed myself to think, or if I had been
allowed to think, that I had any *missionary* business here.
But as it was admitted on all hands that I had none, and
as the only thing I could regard as an imperative and
detaining duty, was the charge of the dear little boys
which devolved upon me, so when Mr Groves contemplated
taking them to England, I had no idea of returning again
from thence.   This intention of Mr Groves first suggested
the idea of return ; and when that intention was altered,
in consequence of letters from the friends at Aleppo, who
have now so happily joined us, purposing to take the dear
little fellows under their charge, the question of my return
remained as it was—since *they* (the boys) would then be so
very much better provided for in the matter of their instruction than was in my power.   A letter I received from
Mr Newman, about the same time, on the subject of my
[Missionary] Gazetteer, expressed his impression, that
things of that nature had much better be done in England
than here, from the difficulty and delay in obtaining the
necessary books ; and as things of that nature are the only
things in which I could hope to be even indirectly useful
to the missionary cause, my way, upon the whole, seemed
clear enough to return.   I am sure Mr Groves, if he mentions the subject to you, will say it does not arise from
any misunderstanding or unkind feeling in any sense, and
I am equally sure his prayers and good wishes will follow
me home.   It will, therefore, appear to you, and other
friends who may have felt some interest about me, in consequence of my connection with Mr Groves, that my
return does not imply that I have turned back from the
class of feelings which led me into missionary connections,
or that I have relinquished any principle my heart ever

held. I shall ever count the day happy in which I came,
for, I hope, I have been enabled to learn much which
before I either knew not at all, or very imperfectly. . .
However, I have no desire to magnify my attainments, my
feelings, my character, my motives; and if any think badly
of my return, let it be so. If I have gained anything
more of the true riches than I brought out, may the praise
be the Great Giver's, who has forced upon my heart, in
hard and bitter ways—truths, lessons, gifts, which, but for
its hardness, might have been sent gently down upon it,
"like rain on the mown grass." The man does not live,
who thinks, or can think, so low of me, as I do think myself low in all high things.'

Kitto had become aware, at a very early point of his
career, that his letters were freely handed about by his
friends as literary curiosities. His knowledge of this
publicity naturally prompted him to give them more of a
general than of a personal interest. The influence of this
motive remained with him; and, therefore, many of his
letters to his Plymouth friends indulge in dissertation, and
are a species of colloquial essay, wanting that inimitable
charm which belongs to those of Cowper. But the following epistle is a remarkable exception—the affectionate
unbaring of a son's distressed heart to his mother. It
reveals some of his secret griefs and fears in connection
with one whose vice had brought shame upon his child
even in its tender years. As he thought that he might get
employment in Plymouth or the west of England, he was
anxious to pave the way for his future peace by such a
preliminary statement :—

'*Bagdad, Sept.* 2, 1832.

'MY DEAREST MOTHER,—. . . . It was my earnest
desire to be able to live at Plymouth; but since I got your
letter, I feel this desire much weakened; for it seems to me

I am not likely to find much comfort in living where father
is.   Vexation and trouble is only likely to arise from my
connection with him.   My poor father!   God knows how
gladly I would do all which might be in my power to help
him, if he were disposed to lead a quiet and sober life ; but
as it is, if I did not know the mighty power of God, I
should be altogether without hope for him; and I do not
see, even if it be in my power, what it will be possible to
do with him.   I think I can only hold myself ready to
help him in sickness ; but while he is well, leave him to
himself, unless it pleases God to work a change in his
heart.   I never trusted to his religious-looking letters,
while he talked of his *misfortunes* and sufferings, instead of
speaking as a repentant *sinner*—as one who mourned deeply
before God over his own pitiable state,—a state to which
he was brought, not by *misfortune*, but by *sin*.   He has not
been an *unfortunate* man.   The Kittos have been very fortunate men.   God put many blessings in their hands, and
they were in a fair way of living with their families in
respectability and peace.   But they threw His gifts from
them, and both John and William, and Dick too, not only
ruined themselves, but brought poverty, misery, and shame
on their families also.   Yet they call themselves *unfortunate*
men!   I most earnestly desire my dear father's welfare,
and I would do anything to promote it ; and notwithstanding the shame he has brought and will bring yet, I fear,
upon me and the rest of his family, I have no harsh or
unkind feeling towards him ; but whilst he goes on thus,
and continues in health, I have made up my mind that he
shall never touch a farthing of my money, however the
Lord may prosper my own undertakings.   The Lord has
enabled me thus far to make my way through all my *misfortunes* (for mine have been real ones) and difficulties, and
I trust He will continue to do so ; but I shall never feel it

my duty to let the money I may hardly and honestly earn
be spent in public-houses. This is my resolution, which,
the Lord helping me, I will keep, let people say what they
will; but still holding myself in readiness to help him when
any real calamity or distress falls upon him, and even then
I shall endeavour to benefit him without trusting him with
money. With yourself, my dearest mother, the case is
very different indeed. I am sure you will believe there is
nothing I will not do for you which may be in my power;
and as you are now alone, it will be the easier to manage.
I hope I shall be enabled to be both a husband and son to
you. Wherever I live, it will be my desire to get an
apartment, and have you to live with me to manage things
for me, and I have no doubt we shall live very happily and
comfortably together. But when I come home, and have
found out what I shall be able to do for myself, I shall be
able to see more distinctly the course which had better be
taken. That I shall be able to obtain a decent provision
in some way or other, neither Mr Groves nor I doubt,
though I may find at first some difficulty. . . . Billy's
account of the doings at the King's coronation amused
me. The "most splendid arches" he mentions, I hope to
see when I come to Plymouth, unless the children have
eaten away all the gingerbread they were made of. That
the dear fellow is in the way of doing for himself, and
getting his livelihood by an honest trade, is a great comfort to my heart, for I have had many anxieties about
him. Now they are over, and God grant I may never
have to hear of anything to make me ashamed of him, as
I have been of many other of my relatives. I think I
never shall. I pray God bless him, and guide him in all
that is good and right and honest all his life. I only remember him as a boy, but suppose he has got a beard
by this time. I hope he will take great care in the choice

of his companions. Much of his happiness or misery in
this life, if not in the other, may depend on his choice
of company. I hope he does not think of marrying yet.
One piece of advice I may now give him, which is, never
to get a bird till he has a cage to put it in. I have waited
for my cage till the season for catching birds is over. I
hope now to get a cage soon; but you, my mother, are
the bird for my cage, and you shall sing me there all your
old songs over again. Give my love to Billy, Betsy,
Mary Ann, Tucker, Aunt Mary, and all my friends, and
remember me kindly to Mr and Mrs Burnard.—My dearest
mother, I am your very affectionate son,

'J. KITTO.'

His connection with Mr Groves had been of signal
benefit to Kitto, and it was now about to be terminated.
In the private notes of Mr Groves to him, there is much
plain speaking, and no doubt it was occasionally needful.
Many faults, which resulted from defective training, had
to be rectified, and Mr Groves did speak to him with
fidelity, if not always with tenderness. He could not bear
what he thought Kitto's self-sufficiency, though that self-
sufficiency referred not to spiritual matters, but to the
ordinary business of life. Nor had he patience with his
continuous anxiety to rise, since himself had voluntarily
descended, and left all for Christ's sake. One ambitious
peculiarity in his character he saw and rebuked, to wit,
that any situation he had obtained was usually held merely
as a stepping-stone to another, and that the duties of the
first were sometimes overlooked in preparation for the next.
During their residence at Bagdad, Kitto gave him satisfaction in regard to his boys, and Mr Groves often alludes
to it. But it could scarcely be supposed that persons of
temperaments so different, as were Mr Groves and the

teacher of his boys, could be at one on all points. Correspondence by written documents must also have often been
very unsatisfactory, for what is written is written, and it
wants those numerous and indefinable modifications which
tone or countenance might give it. An epithet has a distinctness on paper which it might not convey when spoken.
Kitto's notes to Mr Groves did sometimes so irritate him,
that on one occasion he replies,—'You cannot forget the
expression contained in your last letter to me during the
last time we had any misunderstanding; if you have, I
never can, though I have not, relative to it, the slightest
unkind feeling.' The fact is, that Kitto was beginning to
despond again, and to reckon any longer residence in Bagdad as so much lost time; and he wished Mr Groves to
carve out some new path for him. Mr Groves, however,
refused to interfere, for he was afraid that his decision would
not be in harmony with Kitto's own views. Both men, indeed, were akin in mental constitution. Mr Groves was
of a nature that would maintain its own course, and in
this respect his tutor closely resembled him. He was a
reserved man, too, living much in his thoughts, and among
his own griefs and disappointments; and the deafness of
his younger friend naturally tended to lessen the amount
of communication between them. In a letter written a
short period after Kitto left him, he confesses[1]—'I cannot
tell you how I lament over my own folly, in not discharging
my Christian service to you, and leaving all results to God.
Had I so done, instead of living years with you without
confidence or affection, I might have had you given me of
the God of grace, to have comforted me in my sorrows,
and it might never have come to a separation.' He then
commends to him his fellow-traveller, Mr Newman, of whom
he says—'I love him as my soul, for the faithfulness and

[1] Bagdad, September 23.

truth which the God of grace has given him.'[1]   Kitto, on his part, complained that Mr Groves sometimes made arrangements, 'without thinking it necessary in the least to consult him;' and he adds, in his journal, about the beginning of 1832—'I am persuaded no one can live happily with Mr Groves *in a dependent situation.* . . . I am willing to suppose the fault is in myself, as no doubt partly it is.   Yet, I doubt not, he might live happily with *friends and equals;* and from my inmost soul do I honour and love him, while I feel most intensely (and the more fully, since I am not singular) the extreme difficulty of living with him happily in a *dependent* character.   Yet it is still good for me to be with him now, and thus far certainly.'   On the 19th of September 1832, Kitto, in company with Mr Newman, left Bagdad for England.

[1] Did not Mr Groves live to ' lament'—' Alas! my brother ?'

CHAPTER VIII.

RETURN FROM THE EAST.

THE homeward route of Kitto and Newman was to Trebizond, and thence by the Black Sea to Constantinople. In
prospect of going to Aleppo at the beginning of the year,
Kitto had prepared a journal, and composed a preface, in
which he enters somewhat into the philosophy of journalism,
and makes the just remark—'that to travel usefully, one
must carry information with him, and the information obtained will be in exact proportion to the weight of information carried.' At that period he did not care much about
going home, his reason being—'I do not yet feel qualified
to enter on the path of action and life I contemplate there.'
But his opinion had changed in a few months, and he accordingly bade adieu to Bagdad, 'accompanied into the
open country by Mr Groves and the other dear friends,
where we took leave of them with tears.' The journey was
on horseback, in eastern style, the animal carrying all
necessary equipments, and its rider, who had again cultivated a mustache, dressed in a dark cap of Persian lamb-
skin, a Turkish gown, and an Arabian black cloak—presenting rather a grotesque spectacle. He soon felt what
thirst was, and yet, though his throat was parched, he
passed the river Dialah, but was afraid to dismount, lest
he should not manage to climb up to his horse's back again.
His 'bones ached miserably,' and his face and hands were

Q

scorched and blistered with the sun.   The travellers soon
joined a caravan of some size—'200 mules, 100 asses, and
50 horses.'   The native Christians of the party were kept
at a distance by the haughty Mohammedans.   About a
week after his departure, he records, with evident satisfaction, that a messenger brought him 'memorials from all the
dear little boys.'

He was obliged to have recourse to various shifts for
comfort :—

'I also found this day the use of cording my trowsers
tight round my legs, drawing a pair of long English hose
over these, and over the feet of these placing a pair of
Persian worsted socks, which are inserted into a pair of red
Turkish shoes with peaked toes.   For want of some precautions of this kind last time, my legs were much ex-
coriated.   As for the shoes, they are much too large, and
thus, also, require to be filled up.   When I complained to
the man of their capacity, he said they would hold six pair
of stockings besides my feet, and six pair of stockings I
should find it necessary to use when I got among the mountains.'

He notes carefully the villages through which they
passed, and the caravanserais at which they halted; but
one day's journey very much resembled another—mosques,
tombs, ruins, and water-courses.   One Mohammedan gentleman was very kind to him, and did everything but eat
with him and take a pinch out of his box.   How they ate
with those who would eat with them is thus portrayed to
the life :—

'The men tucked up their sleeves as if going to slay a
sheep.   We did the same ; and water having been poured
on our hands—each man's handkerchief serving him for a
towel—we fell to with our fingers, having been supplied
with part of a cake of bread each.   This we introduced

into the stew, taking up as much with it as we could. For
the rice, N. and I were accommodated with a wooden
spoon, one for both. We were made very welcome, and
ate a hearty supper, which concluded with bread and cheese.
After supper we washed again with *soap*. Upon the whole,
the Oriental mode of feeding seems much more disgusting
in theory than in practice. People may have felt disgust
in hearing the process described, but few, I apprehend, in
seeing the thing practised.'

The nights were spent by the travellers as best they
might, though Kitto sometimes complains of his fellows—
one man's feet poking him in the ribs, and another claiming
more than half his pillows, which were merely portions of
his horse's furniture. They were occasionally taken for
Russians, and sometimes for Georgians. The Mohammedan
gentleman referred to knew them to be English, but thought
England and India the same country. The encampment
was usually well watched at night, each man sleeping with
his weapon by his side; for the thieves would have made
no scruple to steal the bed on which the sleepers reposed,
—nay, now and then succeeded in similar daring attempts.
Kitto prudently put away his watch, 'lest,' as he owns,
'its display should get me robbed.' He and his companion
did not carry arms, and the people imagined that they had
no property but books—' a very safe conclusion for us, as
it may save us from pillage.' One person seemed greatly
taken with his companion :—

' This man seemed so much pleased with Mr Newman,
that he told me by signs he was a good man, but I—
imitating my stoop and other infirmities—I was a little,
crooked, deaf, dumb, good-for-nothing fellow, an opinion
to which I nodded assent ; but afterwards, when I had
given him a pinch of snuff—the first Mohammedan in the
caravan who has accepted it—he signified that I was good

also, at which I smiled, but shook my head in dissent. I
see in Mr N.'s glass that I really cut a curious figure now.
To say nothing of my beard, the skin of my face, neck, and
hands hangs in tatters about me, the sun having burnt it
up. Whether my new skin will be sun-proof I cannot tell,
but I hope so.'

He complains with some show of justice :—

' I do not ride at all comfortably. The men are very
impertinent, perhaps the more from our being unarmed.
Sometimes they strike my mule behind, which makes him
start forward so suddenly as almost to unseat me, not seldom getting entangled among the back horses, or crushing
against some who may be before. One man, whom we
crushed slightly, drew his scimitar, and held it close up to
my throat : a joke perhaps, but a joke they would not take
with an armed man.'

An occasional squabble diversified the scene :—

' Soon after a grand dispute arose between some of our
caravan men and the Persians of the village, in which this
young man most hastily mingled. There were most loud
language, vehement gestures, pushes, pulls, and some few
knocks on both sides. In the heat of the fray, the Seid
came down briskly, and acted as arbitrator and pacificator,
speaking vehemently also—an advocate, it seems, on the
side of the party he took, which was that of the caravan
men. Both sides seem to look on a Seid as a very fitting
umpire and judge, a character which I did not before know
at times devolved upon them. We exerted ourselves a
great deal; and one of the most violent disputants, a respectable Turk, he laid hold of by the shoulders, and pushed
him away, following him in that manner. The occasion of
the dispute was the attempt of the Persian Governor of the
village to extort a tax on some bags of dates imported by
our caravan. This exaction was resisted, and finally not

paid by our people. Before we lay down, Mr N. conversed with me about pronunciation and metre. He thinks I speak better than could be expected in one deaf so long; but, among other faults, he endeavoured this evening to teach me to enunciate the final *L* distinctly. When initial, he says I can do it well enough. I am afraid, however, that in this case the best theoretical instruction will have little influence on my practice. Mr N. conjectures that we are about 2000 feet above the level of the sea, and that a mountain, the remotest of three ridges lying not very distant, is about 2000 above our present level.'

' *Thursday*, 27.—I have, since I became a traveller, some occasion to regret my ignorance of botany and geology. Perhaps I shall begin these studies in England. Study also is vanity! We learn many things we think we may have a use for, but never find that use; and in the use of life we discover we have left many things unlearnt, which we set about acquiring when the occasion of their use is past, and will not return.

' Mr N. relates, that I am a great object of interest to the people of the places we have passed through. I can, upon the whole, readily . apprehend that a people who have, like the Persians, an exquisite sense of the ridiculous, must find something exquisitely exciting to that sense in our many oddities, as talking on the fingers, etc. Their impression of the ridiculous is in this case, however, apparently softened to a milder feeling, by the consideration, that the oddest of these circumstances arises from a misfortune—my deafness. As it is, I suspect that they will frequently, in time to come, relate among their odd and curious recollections what they saw of *Numa* (Mr Newman), as they call him, and poor me. Be it so. I shall have also something to say of them. It seems they take us for spies.'

They reached Kermanshah on the 30th of the month—
' the first great stage of the journey.' Kitto gives this
month—September—thirty-one days in his journal, writing
down *Sunday* as the 31st, but corrects himself by calling
Monday, October 2. ' The city made but a poor appearance.' Kitto went out to see the sights, and surveyed the
bazaar with some attention.

' In eastern towns, life can be best studied in the bazaars.
The artizans seem very industrious. Several seemed to
feel it irksome to have their labour interrupted by serving
a customer. I went through all the bazaar, in all its parts,
as well for the purpose just stated as to make purchases.
Notwithstanding my Turkish dress, which is common
enough here, they seemed easily to detect that I was not a
Turk or Persian. Several accosted me, to whom I replied
in English, feeling it much better than to make signs. In
the latter case they laugh ; in the former they turn quietly
away, finding they could not understand. I should wonder if they did, for not many Englishmen understand me
till accustomed to my manner of speech.[1] But when I
wanted to deal, I signified plainly that I was deaf, and
managed the matter by signs. . . .

' Snuff-boxes are here, but no snuff. Wherever I inquired, and made the sign of taking a pinch, they produced
spices and perfumes; and when I showed the small quan-

---

[1] The following is Sir John M'Neill's description of his voice: ' It is pitched in a
far deeper bass tone than is natural to men who have their hearing. There is in it
a certain contraction of the throat, analogous to wheezing; and, altogether, it is
eminently *guttural*. It may be suspected that this is attributable to the fact, that
his deafness came on in boyhood, before the voice had assumed its masculine depth.
The transition having taken place without the guidance of the ear, was made at
random, and without any pains bestowed upon it by those who could hear and
correct it. His pronunciation is generally accurate enough as regards all such
words as young boys are likely to be familiar with, and as to others which closely
follow their analogy, but is naturally defective in respect to words of later acquirement. In spite of the too great guttural action, his articulation of every English
consonant and vowel, considered in isolation, is perfect.'—*Lost Senses, Deafness*,
p. 22.

tity I had left, they thought I wanted to sell it; others, that I wished to get it scented. At last one old man, after groping about in a box, found a small quantity in a paper, for which he charged me so highly, that I must at this rate make my present stock serve till we get to Europe, small though it be.'

Impertinent queries were often showered upon the foreign pilgrims. Mr Newman parried them as best he could, and Kitto was often annoyed by such teasing investigations.

' I have now regularly adopted the plan of conversing in English when accosted in a way I either do not like, or do not wish to reply to in the more intelligible way of signs. So to-day, when I went to fetch a jug of water, I was accosted by half-a-dozen men, whose countenances seemed to me impertinently curious; so I replied something as Benjamin Franklin to his American landlord,— My name is John Kitto of England; I am from Bagdad, and going to England, at which I hope soon to arrive, by way of Tehran! They seemed wonderfully edified by this communication, and then, as I observed, seeming to repeat the words " Bagdad " and " Tehran," ceased to molest me with any more questions.'

Kitto reached Hamadan on the 5th of October, and visited the bazaars, as was his wont, but did not go to the so-called Tomb of Esther, because he could ill afford the present usually paid to the sacred edifice. Before he left the city, he relates—

' Last night I was amused by dreams of home—England, I should say; for I am not one of those who have a home in any land to go to. One of the most pleasant exhibited me as finding at an old book-stall a copy of a book I read in my boyhood, and of which I have often sought a copy in vain. May I find it indeed, and if I dream, may I

find there all my waking and sleeping dreams tell me of ;
but this my not over-sanguine mind often questions. Well,
I have equally weighed, I trust, the results of both success
and disappointment, and have a mind prepared to look either
quietly in the face.'

Sometimes, on the journey toward Tehran, Kitto was the
caterer for the party :—

' Mr N. was of opinion that I, even I, poor Pilgarlick,
was a better marketer than Kerian.   He is of opinion that
my dress and Oriental countenance impose so far upon
them, that, though they perceive I am a foreigner, they do
not suspect me for a Frank ; and my deafness preventing
questions, they, unless I tell them I talk English, suppose
I am dumb also—all which readily accounts for my peculiarities without supposing me a Frank, or exposing me to
exorbitant charges.   My being deaf, and perhaps, in their
view, dumb, i.e. a mute, and it may be a dwarf to boot,
facilitates my entrance into their houses, which would not
be allowed to any other stranger than one under some
physical incapacity, which, in their view, is calculated to
preclude harm, or which they are accustomed to consider
as removing reserve.   I therefore volunteered, with these
qualifications, to go in quest of fruit to the village.'

They reached Tehran, the present capital of Persia, on
the 14th of October.   So Kitto's journal intimates ; but
he calls it the 13th, in a letter to Mr Woollcombe.   They
were at once kindly received by the Elchee or ambassador,
Captain Campbell.   Kitto was joked by the ambassador and
by Sir John M'Neill upon his sun-burnt and hirsute appearance, his beard being nearly of a month's growth.   No
sooner was he in Sir John's company again, than he set to
his old work.   ' I have given him,' says the restless inquirer, ' a paper of queries, which he has promised to
answer me, and which will much extend my little stock of

information.' And he gratefully acknowledges, before he left Tehran—' Mr M'Neill has given me satisfactory answers to my twenty queries, and has promised to do the same to seven more I have proposed to him.' Various incidents of his stay in Tehran may be grouped together.

' Yesterday I was chiefly employed in writing to my friends at Bagdad. After breakfast, I noted the English servants congregating with their Prayer-books and Bibles ; and soon after, Mr M'N. called me into the dining-room where all the English were assembled, to whom Captain M'Donald read the prayers and lessons for the day. I confess I entered into much of the service with great satisfaction, after having been so long precluded from services in which I could not, from my deafness, have any actual participation. I feel very comfortable here, after the fatigues and privations of the journey. A journey is like life—an alternation of repose and labour, of progression and rest, of good and evil. The pleasure now of having English faces around us, and to me still more of faces I knew before, is a satisfaction which, in the route pointed out, we cannot easily expect again to experience. . . They are all here very kind to me, and put to shame my proud doubt of whether I ought to come when not *by name* invited in the letter sent by the Gholam, and my proud question, whether they would admit poor Pilgarlick to their table or not. I meant the Elchee, for I had before been a guest at Mr M'Neill's. However, having been freely entertained, both at the Resident's in Bagdad, and the Elchee's in Tehran, I hope to have my foolish thought on that foolish subject at rest in time to come—satisfied that, if I have not yet found a place in general society, I shall one day do so. I shall ! I shall !'

Kitto and Newman were both taken ill at Tehran, and

in Mr M'Neill's absence.   Kitto's malady was supposed to
be the ague.

    ' The friends here, and Dr Daoud Khan, the Shah's
physician, were disposed to set it down for the ague, which
I did not myself think it was ; and they adduced as a proof,
the shaking of my right foot, which proof I overthrew by
the assurance that my grandmother, my mother, and myself, had shaken our right feet all our lives long, under
the pressure of mental or bodily pain.   I myself had more
confidence in Captain M'Donald, nephew of the late Elchee,
than in the Shah's physician; and, indeed, the kindness
and care which this gentleman manifested towards us, and
the trouble he took, have left on my heart an impression
not easily to be effaced.   At length, in the height of our
malady, Captain Burnes, a gentleman who had come from
India on an exploratory tour, saw us in bed, and pronounced our case *bilious fever;* and without more ado, or
consulting the doctor, he went away for a barber, who bled
Mr N. ; but my bleeding, much against the wish of this
warm-hearted and decisive man, was postponed out of regard to the Khan, who had expressed a particular opinion
on the subject.   When he came, however, he agreed to my
being bled in the evening, though he assured me I " had
no symptom to be bled."   Accordingly, in the evening, an
old barber with a red beard came ; and, strapping up my
arm with a leathern thong, produced a rude-pointed instrument, and performed the operation with no small dexterity.   From that time we both grew better, and now the
only thing we want is *strength.*   This we now seem gathering, and I trust we shall soon be on the road again.   I
thought, not once nor twice, that my journey would end
at Tehran; but it has pleased God otherwise, and I do
thank Him for it—for though I trust I am enabled to look
at death as quietly as most men, yet there are times when

death seems a very terrible thing. Miserably wet and wearisome seems the journey before us; but after this sickness, the spirit seems as it would go forth mad as a March hare, rejoicing in all things it can find under the open heaven.

'Our arrival at this place, and kind reception, were very reviving after the privations and fatigues to which we had been exposed during the journey; nor, for my own part, was I at all insensible to the good cheer which the Elchee's table supplied to me, who had been living so long on nothing but bread and fruits. The party, we found, consisted of the Elchee, "one of that numerous division of the human species," to quote the author of Adam Blair, "answering to the name of Captain Campbell," a remarkably handsome gentleman, with black bushy mustaches, meeting his equally black and bushy whiskers—a conjunction which has a very imposing effect; Mr M'Neill, our old friend with whom we voyaged on the Tigris, a gentleman of much oriental and occidental knowledge, and who has supplied me with a good deal of information on points of which I desired to be informed. *He*, I suspect, is the spirit of the Mission, though not, nominally, its head. Then there is Captain M'Donald, the nephew of the late Sir John M'Donald, and whose kindness and attention to us during our illness, I have already had occasion to mention. All these are remarkably fine men, and, perhaps, if such were an object, few could be selected calculated to give a people who judge so much by externals as the Persians, a better impression of our countrymen. There are also the ladies of the Elchee and Mr M'Neill, both fine women, and after so long an exclusion from the society of Englishwomen, it was very pleasant to look upon their faces. Mrs M'N. is the sister of Professor Wilson, otherwise Christopher North, the Editor of Blackwood's Magazine. With this lady I have enjoyed more conversation, on the whole, than with any other member of the party, having known her before on the Tigris. She contemplates that I may turn my travels to account in the end. This I do not at present know, nor to what account I could turn them. I regret more and more every day that we came at this season of the year. I hate winter altogether, and I hate travelling in winter more than I hate winter itself. All that I may see between I would gladly forego, to be set down quietly in England at once. My desire to be there becomes hourly more intense; and whilst I am not blind to the difficulties I may meet with, and entertain no vast expectations, the spirit with which I do anticipate obtaining, in some way or other, a decent subsistence and a settled home, has not yet failed me, and I trust will not while I need its support. It is wonderful to me what a staid and sober old fellow I find myself becoming, and I am sure you would wonder too, if you could see my little plans of *life* (not *literature*) as they are chalked out in my mind.'

Of Mrs, now Lady M'Neill, Kitto formed a very high and just estimate :—

'On Friday I went to their house, and looked at her books. On showing me "Adam Blair," she mentioned its being written by Mr Lockhart. I remarked, it seemed of the same class with the "Lights and Shadows of Scottish Life;" to which she assented, and added, that the latter work was written by her brother. I then had an opportunity of stating that it was not till the preceding day I knew her relationship to Professor Wilson, at which she seemed surprised. She showed me her brother's poems; and I regretted I had not time to read more than a few passages of "The City of the Plague," a subject on which I feel interested, from having been in the midst of the city of a plague more horrible than that of London. I was

pleased to obtain "Adam Blair" and a volume of Blackwood to amuse my frequent comparative idleness.'

His mind, recovering from the lassitude of an exhausting
sickness, was in doubt, as it often was, as to the future and
its results.

'*November* 1.—Where shall we go now? I do not know.
Travelling, wearisome and irksome though it be, seems
paradise when compared with the miseries of a sick-bed.
O England, pray God I may soon be set down in thee, and
walk in thee again! Oh! oh! I wish with all my heart I
could plump into London at once!'

On Monday, the 4th November, the travellers left
Tehran for Tabreez. The route had all the novelties and
all the usual discomforts. Kitto's busy pen narrates somewhat jocosely:—

'N. tells me that, from the habit of talking to me spelling each word on his fingers, he finds himself spelling the
words in which he thinks; and when he repeats to himself a passage of Scripture, he generally spells it through.
I expressed a hope that he would not spell audibly in
company in England. . . I am fully persuaded that
N. thinks his talk on his fingers audible to me; he often
talks to me when my back is towards him, and admits he
has often been discouraged, after having been telling me
some long story, to find that I have not been observing
him.' Yet Kitto hints that his companion sometimes complained of the fatigue and irksomeness of talking so much
and so often to him on the fingers. It must, indeed, have
been no easy task to be speaking in this form every minute
to one so curious to know all that was passing, and so
prone to put crowds of questions about anything or everything that either came into his head, or happened to arrest
his attention.

Tabreez was reached on the 23d of November. Mr

Nisbet, who, as narrated on a previous page, had married Miss Taylor, received the travellers with abundant hospitality, and his lady and he had, with praiseworthy consideration, fitted up a room in their house called the ' Missionaries' Room,' perhaps in imitation of the prophet's chamber in the dwelling of the Shunammite.   Mr Newman here left Kitto, and proceeded overland to Constantinople.   Kitto, however, consoled himself for his friend's departure as any one that knew him would have anticipated :—' Doubtless, I shall be more *independent* without him ; notwithstanding his peculiarities, I love him, and find the prospect of going without him more painful than I would have thought.' But at this place he unexpectedly got a new companion, with whom his own subsequent history was strangely bound up, and about whom his first notice is :—

' Mr Shepherd I have just seen, and, to my surprise, find him an Indo-Briton—nothing the worse for that, however.   I am led to expect that we have no principle in common, but that his obliging disposition will prevent our coming into collision on any point.'

It may be added, that Mr Shepherd had been attached to the Persian Political Mission, and was now returning to England to enter into business, and with the prospect of marrying a lady in London, to whom he had been for a considerable period engaged.

On the first of December the new associates left Tabreez. The weather, being exceedingly cold and frosty, caused them no small discomfort, but Kitto several times eulogises Mr Shepherd as a travelling companion.

His own birth-day came round, and he moralised—

' *Wednesday*, *Dec.* 4.—My birth-day !   Are there any who remember to-day that it is my birth-day ?   I know not, but hardly think so.   Before my next I must be something that now I am not ; but what, time must disclose.   I know not by what it has been distinguished more than my feeling, for the first time, seriously about my cough. It is now nearly three weeks since I took the cold that brought it on, and, according to the usual process of my colds, it ought to have gone long since. I apprehend its ending in consumption; and what that ends in every one knows. I was a fool to slight it so far as not to apply to Dr Cormick about it. If it lasts to Stamboul, I hope the physician of the Embassy will do something for me. On the whole, I have felt this a very uncomfortable day, both as to health and travel.'

On the sixth of the month, Kitto obtained the first view of Ararat, and revelled in the spectacle. 'Its grandeur surpasses all description. I made my neck ache in turning my head to look at it, till I felt it was firmly fixed in my mind's eye. . . Great Ararat is of irregular shape, and its top has not that appearance of unsullied white which I have seen in points of inferior elevation. It has a black and white appearance, the hollows being full of snow, whilst the more prominent parts appear in dark contrast. Its blunt and irregular appearance is strikingly different from the regular and pointed cone of Demavend. My feelings, as I rode beside these solitary mountains, were more excited, or rather impressed, than I have at any former time during this journey experienced.

' . . . Close by Diadin flows a small stream of beautiful clear water, shallow and easily stepped over. This is the *Euphrates*. I stood astride it a moment, and then passed over. I was never before so near the source of a mighty and famous river; and my thoughts were many, and to me interesting, though, perhaps, to others they would seem commonplace enough. The water seems to me more pleasant than any I have ever tasted, and I have drunk a great deal of it. It is something to have seen Ararat and the Euphrates in one day! At the fountain there were the maidens of the village drawing water in vessels of truly classical form.'

What a glorious eyeful for one day—the Euphrates and Ararat!

At the monastery of Utch Kilissa, Kitto's spirit was stirred within him at the gross superstitions which met his view.

' I have said the body of the church is a cross, with two side aisles, or which may be considered as divided into three compartments in breadth, by the square pillars, or rather congeries of pillars, which support the arches. Of these three, the eastern, of course, includes the altar. It is laid with carpets, and hung with pictures; while the altar itself, in a recess, with a curtain before it, which was withdrawn for us, is adorned with a small picture of the Virgin and Child. I felt disgusted with this tawdry, childish array, the more so, as contrasted with the simplicity of the naked walls of the church itself. We were permitted to enter this most holy precinct, and I felt some interest in examining the pictures, most miserable daubs, the execution of which would disgrace a country sign in England. Of Scripture subjects, I recognised but two, the Crucifixion and the Ascension; the rest were portraits of saints, monks, and bishops, with historical and legendary subjects. Of the legends, I recognised George and the Dragon, and that of the miraculous picture of the handkerchief with which Christ wiped His face, and which a king holds in his hands. One of the principal pictures represents Gregory baptizing: the converts kneel in grand procession; a king foremost, with his crown at the saint's feet, behind whom are men, bearded black and brown, and women, among whom is a queen. Above, on a cloud supported by little cherubs, sit the Father and the Son, the last with a circular, and the first with a triangular glory,' which is black or brown. The Holy Ghost, in the form of a dove, also with a transparent glory, is between them, and held as it were by both, which describes, I suppose, their belief in the equal procession of the Holy Ghost from the Father and the Son. Another represents a jolly-looking angel standing on a dead body, apparently of a king, and holding a little child, or, to speak from the picture, a fairy, in his left hand, whilst his right holds a drawn sword, which appears to have done fearful execution. In the upper corner stands the Devil, with his European tail and horns, and black complexion, and goatish extremities. He appears in the act of tearing some papers, which angels are snatching from him. One is in the act of doing this, while another is flying away with the paper preserved. What this means, I know not.'

On the 18th of December Kitto arrived at Erzeroum, the chief town of Armenia, where he was kindly received by M. Zohrab, the vice-consul, who had been educated in England.

' *December* 21.—M. Zohrab was one morning asking me about the Breakwater,[1] understanding I was a native of Plymouth. I could tell him some things, but not about measures of length, depth, breadth, etc. He inquired, good-humouredly, how it ·was that I was so imperfectly acquainted with so noble an undertaking at my native place, and was yet so anxious to collect information everywhere abroad; " but so," said he, " it always is." I replied that, while residing at Plymouth, I was a boy ; and unless for a short visit or two, I had not been there for ten years.

---

[1] The Breakwater at Plymouth, about which the vice-consul inquired at Kitto, is at low water a mile long. It is forty-five feet broad at the top, and two feet, in some places three feet, above the high water of spring-tides. 3,500,000 tons of stones have been employed in its formation ; many of those in the original mass, flung into the sea, being from a ton to ten tons in weight. The expense to the present time has been about a million and a half sterling.

" A difficult question very well retorted," he replied, and then related the following anecdote:—As a Turk was quietly smoking his pipe in the presence of an Englishman, he asked how many times he might fill his pipe from an *oke* of tobacco; the Briton, after some consideration, said, "four hundred." Soon after the Turk saw the Englishman writing very quickly, and said, " Since you could answer the question that had no connection with your own habits, you will doubtless find it easier to answer another that has. How many sheets of paper will you fill with an oke of ink?" " Really," said the Englishman, " I cannot tell; you ask a puzzling question."

' *Dec.* 21, *Saturday.*—We ate, at dinner yesterday, a fish from the Euphrates, near Erzeroum, not unlike a herring in size and taste. Fish is somewhat of a rarity to me since I left England, except at Astrachan, where I ate plenty of sturgeon, which, I think, among the best fish I ever tasted. Since leaving Bagdad, I only got fish at the Elchee's table. Somewhat of a grievance this to a decided *Ichthyophagist.*

' It is agreed, in consideration of Mr Shepherd's state, helpless from rheumatic pains, that we will go in the kind of litter called *cajavas*, which hang, like panniers, on the mule's back, but are high and arched, and covered with felt. The prospect of such a comfortable mode of journeying makes me more willing to set out. They are short, so that one cannot lie down, but may recline or sit upright, and sleep or perhaps read; this, is the way in which women and invalids commonly travel.

' *Dec.* 27.—Still at Erzeroum. We were to have gone to-day, but it was found that the litters wanted some improvement, and the carpenter was sick, and another, who promised to come in the evening, did not. Now, however, they are at it; yet, to-morrow being Friday, we shall not be able to go, as the Moslems do not begin a journey on that day. . . I feel more and more every day that it will never do for me to mix in company. At the best, a deaf man must always cut an awkward figure in it; and, from the peculiarity of his situation, he will find it difficult to preserve to himself that consideration to which he thinks himself entitled. It is manifest to me that I can only comfortably mingle in society when I have a right to make myself a place in gentlemanly society; in all other a deaf man must suffer much. May I be enabled to establish my claim to such a place. My stay here has been for the benefit of my correspondents. The want of books, and anything to do, has driven me to write to them largely; and now that I have written all my writing, read all my reading, mended all my mending, and bought all my buyings, it is high time for us to go. I shall be glad enough altogether when we get off, as I am equally weary of vulgarity on the one hand, and of the consequential condescensions of patronage on the other. I am tired to death of everything now, myself included. . .

'*Dec.* 30, *Sunday.*—The muleteer, with whom we have stood some days engaged, refuses to go, on the ground that he cannot get lading for all his horses. However, another set of less respectable looking men came with him, with whom we have engaged, and we are still, it seems, to go to-morrow. Our litters look very comfortable, being lined with thick felt within, and covered with it without. Only they look too *high*, not less than four and a half feet, I think, and I am in fear of their capsizing, which would be a fearful job in any of the terrible mountain passes of which Mr S. speaks. . . I am also afraid I shall see little during this journey, thus shut up; but, in fact, what did I see but snow during the last part of our pilgrimage. However, I shall endeavour to see all that is to be seen, which is not much, unless some fine scenery, which the snow will, at this season of the year, have much marred.

'*Dec.* 31, *Monday.*—Rose in high spirits for the journey. We were somewhat startled this morning to receive a bill of fifteen ducats, for necessaries during our stay, and in preparation for the journey, and more so to find, among the items, a charge of more than £1 for firing, and another charge for porter *drunk at the table of our host.* The men were a long time getting our things ready for departure, and, at one time, they came to declare the impossibility of the horse carrying the cages. This arose, however, from their inexpertness in adapting the vehicle to the back of the horse, and, it seems, their ignorance of it altogether; for, from the crowd assembled in the street to look at them, and partly perhaps at us, I inferred this mode of conveyance not to be common in these parts. Indeed, except at Teflis, I do not recollect such another exhibition of curiosity as was manifested on this occasion. At last, about one o'clock, we got fairly into these machines. It was then found, as I suspected, that Mr S., though himself a light man, far outweighed me, and that it was necessary to adjust the balance. This was done by the men tying their horse-bags, etc., to my side of the litter. I had myself with me, in the litter, a pair of little saddle-bags containing books, etc. At last this was adjusted too, and on we went. I found the cage much smaller than I expected; within, about four feet high, three and a half feet long, and two wide. Its narrowness prevented me from sitting in the most convenient posture, cross-legged—most convenient, not only from its occupying the smallest space of any posture, but also from keeping the feet warm, which I found no easy matter as it was. However, I wore boots, which, even under other circumstances, would have prevented my sitting cross-legged. Another inconvenience

is, that we ride backward, and the door being before
us (open if you please), you have no view of what is ahead
of you, and you come upon everything, and everything
comes upon you, unexpectedly. The convenience, however, is very great. First, being lined with thick felt
within and without, it is warm comparatively, and I felt
the convenience very sensibly, when contrasted with the
frozen beards and mustachios of those without, who
were also exposed to the snow and sleet which fell about
through the ride. And though the motion, under certain
paces of the horse, was inconvenient, lumping one's head
about, yet, on the whole, it was not worse than that of a
coach on an English road; indeed, shutting the eyes, one
might almost fancy oneself in a coach. Lastly, the comparative *repose* of such a mode of riding is a very important circumstance, reclining or sitting being assuredly a
more convenient posture than sitting astride. If one be
dozing, also, he may indulge the propensity if he can,
without the fear of a fall. . . With the power of seeing fully behind, and through a hole on one side, I do not
expect to lose much as to seeing. In consequence of this
riding with the face to the tail of the horse, seeing nothing
but the caravan, the servant who rode behind us, and the
tail of our own horse, when he frisked it about, Erzeroum
was fully in sight till the usual evening mist arose, and
first obscured and then concealed the view. . . In the
muhaffy I was soon settled so cosily and snugly, that it
was some time before I could make up my mind to exert
myself so far as to take a pinch of snuff; and when I
had made up my mind, I found myself so confined, that it
was with much trouble I got at the snuff-box, and then,
from the motion of the cage, it was no easy matter to take
one pinch without spilling half-a-dozen; hence I was
obliged to wait my opportunity of momentary pauses, and

actually succeeded in taking no less then three pinches.
I had also purposed to amuse myself by reading, but for
this, also, it was a good while before I got heart, and then
I found it from the same cause impossible to read. This
I had anticipated, and, therefore, looking out those passages in Spenser which I had marked as memorable, I
proceeded to decipher a line now and then, and learn it
by heart. At this rate I hope to have stored my mind
with some pleasing, beautiful, and striking images, by the
time we reach Trebizond. This, with my snuff-box, and
compass to mark the direction of the road, will amuse the
time well enough. To-day, the road W.N.W., sometimes
due W. . . How full Spenser is of beautiful images,
fine sentiments, and striking passages! It is a pity he is
so little known but by name. I shall not think my time
unemployed in endeavouring to know him intimately.
This few do, because to do so is a work of labour; yet
there is enough of the beautiful and pleasing even on his
surface, richly to reward those who will not think it worth
their trouble to cultivate an intimate acquaintance with
him. Where, in all poetry, is anything more lovely than
the lay which some one chanted in the Bower of Bliss—
evil as its object was? I am anxious to see what Todd[1] has
done with him. It is one of the first books which I shall
inquire after. If I am not satisfied, I may possibly, though
most unequal, attempt something myself, less elaborate,
but more illustrative, than I expect to find in that commentator. If Shakspere has found work for a thousand
and one commentators, surely there is enough in Spenser
for two. Spenser is the only poet I have a wish to deal
with in a literary way. A slighting word of Spenser and
his Faery Queen goes to my heart.'

<hr/>

[1] The allusion seems to be to Archdeacon Todd's edition of Spenser, eight volumes
8vo. 1805.

In January 1833, Kitto passed the village of Gunnish-Khora, and, from the nature of the road, was obliged to pursue his journey on horseback, entering Trebizond on the 11th of the same month. And he thus describes the prospect :—

' On ascending the difficult mountain behind Trebizond, we had a full view of the Black Sea, extending boundlessly in front, but rather bounded by Cape Vona on the left, and Cape Kereli on the right. Being accustomed to look upon the sea with delight from a child, and viewing it now as the termination of the more arduous part of our journey, I can hardly describe the emotion with which I gazed on the great blue expanse before me.'

He made his usual visit to all the public places, enjoying the company of the consul and his partner, and lamenting, however, this drawback, that ' there were no ladies.' He witnessed the absurd ceremony of ' blessing the water,' the archbishop who performed it having been ' a woman's tailor formerly ;' ' hypocrisy and roguery' being, in one of his friends' estimation, ' the only talents necessary to an archbishop more than a tailor.'

' We, however, saw the archbishop stand forth, and lifting up his hands, throw a cross, as far as he could, into the water, and, after a short interval, another. There were two men swimming about in the water with their drawers on, this very cold morning, and when the cross was thrown, there was a competition between them who should get it ; he who got it threw it farther into the sea than the bishop had been able. Then the procession left the rock and proceeded to the church, to which we did not follow them. I am not aware that any particular blessing is expected to come to the waters from this ceremony. The Black Sea looked neither the blacker nor whiter for it; nor, in the expectation of less rough seas after the ceremony, do we felicitate ourselves that our voyage has not taken place before it. To use an expression of the consul, nothing but drunkenness comes of it.'

Kitto did not sail from Trebizond till the first of March, and before he left it he had prepared himself for enjoying the voyage to Stamboul, by reading the Argonautics of Apollonius Rhodius, in Fawkes' translation.[1] The assistance got from reading such a version of such an original, must have been of very little service, for the poem is noted for its mere mediocrity,[2] and is full to excess of mythological episodes, and very sparing and indistinct in its topical allusions. The fabulous voyage of the Argonauts to possess themselves of the 'golden fleece,' presents no lists of places like a descriptive chart, save in a very few instances, and can by no means give such aid and interest to the traveller as the 'Lord of the Isles' does to any one sailing up the Sound of Mull. The poem is in imitation of the Homeric verse, but at an immeasurable distance, though a few lines here and there have some fire and power. On board Kitto amused himself in studying the character of the motley group of his fellow-passengers, in reading Spenser, and in identifying scenes of actual or legendary interest on the shore. After a brief voyage, the ship entered the Bosphorus on the evening of the 7th. When Kitto got up next morning, the scene entranced him.

'When I first came on deck in the morning, a scene was presented which I had often heard described, but of which description had conveyed to me no adequate idea. It seemed as if Europe, at the point where Asia looks upon her, had put on all her garments of beauty, and Asia had

---

[1] London: J. Dodsley in Pall Mall. 1780.

[2] Æquali quadam mediocritate. Quintilian. Instit. Orat. Lib. x. i. One of the most spirited portions of the poem is the description of Prometheus chained to the rocks of the Caucasus, the eagle that preyed upon his vitals first wheeling, with heavy oar-like pinions, round the ship, then rushing up to his prey, and again, when gorged, sailing slowly down the side of the mountain.

made herself pleasant to her eyes in return. He who has not seen Stamboul may be said to want a sense—a feeling of the beautiful, which no other object can convey. . . The shipping in the harbour are much more numerous than I had been led to expect; I suppose not less than a hundred merchant vessels. In this enumeration of the objects presented to view, I must not omit the numerous canoe-shaped boats, having low beaks, scudding about on the water. They are very neat, ornamented with much carving, and without any water in the bottom, as is common in English boats; they are admirably adapted to easy and rapid progress, but easily overset, being very narrow, and having little depth in the water. The house of Leander is no very classical object, notwithstanding its name. It stands on a low rock between Constantinople and Scutari, but nearest the latter, and looks like a mosque or chapel, gaily painted and enclosed by a low battlemented wall. Such were some of the objects which drew my attention ; but a panoramic exhibition only could convey a clear notion of the glorious and beautiful whole. It was not simply the object, as it lay before me, which interested, but the geographical, the political, the historical interest connected with it, and which the more interested me, from my previously studying in Gibbon the account of the last days of the Greek empire, which enabled me to trace out the scenes of that most interesting contest, though I suppose the city presents a very different aspect now from what it did in the time of the Eastern empire.'

The American missionaries, Dwight and Goodell,[1] received him very kindly. With Mr Goodell he had been

[1] Dr Goodell is known by his version of the Armeno-Turkish Scriptures; Mr Schauffler by his Spanish-Hebrew Bible; Mr Dwight, by ' Researches in Armenia, 1833.' Kitto was also acquainted with Dr Eli Smith, who was subsequently the companion and philological coadjutor of Dr Robinson in his travels, and recently died, while engaged in a most admirable Arabic translation of the Old Testament.

acquainted in Malta, and here, too, he met Mr Schauffler and his old friend Mr Hullock.　His journal is full of re-marks suggested by the kindness of the missionary family. Bnt his fellow-traveller, Mr Shepherd, was confined by sickness at Pera.　During Kitto's stay in Constantinople, as he rambled about the city and suburbs, two rather amusing incidents befell him, in consequence of his want of hearing.　First his umbrella got him into danger :—

‘ Arriving at Constantinople, from countries farther to the East, and having learnt to regard the umbrella as a mark of high distinction, I was much astonished to find it in very common use there in rainy weather.　I should imagine that the example of the Europeans, established in the suburb of Pera, brought it into nse, and much oppo-sition to the innovation was not to be expected from the present reforming Sultan.　However, I had soon occasion to learn that traces still remained of the distinction, so usually throughout the East associated with that article. I resided principally at Orta Khoi, a village on the Bos-phorus, about three miles above Constantinople ; and hav-ing urgent occasion, one wet day, to go down to Pera, I set out, umbrella in hand.　On arriving at the waterside, none of the boats that usually ply between the village and the Golden Horn remained, and I was therefore under the necessity of walking all the way along the road, behind the row of buildings that face the Bosphorus.　One of these buildings is a favourite palace of the Sultan, in which he was then residing.　As I approached the gate of this mansion, with my umbrella over my head, I observed that one of the sentinels stationed there accosted me in a com-manding manner ; but not comprehending what he said, I went on.　Upon which the soldier ran towards me with his fixed bayonet levelled, and without any indication of a friendly intention towards my person.　That I took it safely that day to the great city, was probably owing to the good nature of a Turk, who was walking close behind me at the moment, and who, on observing the advance of the soldier upon me, snatched my umbrella with violence from my hand, and thrust me forward, partially interposing himself between me and the assailant, who then returned to his station, and allowed me to proceed in peace. The friendly Turk, in returning my umbrella, endeavoured to explain a fact which, I afterwards ascertained more distinctly, that it was incumbent on every one to take down his umbrella in passing the actual residence of the Sultan. I had, indeed, observed, with some surprise, that persons walking before me had lowered their umbrellas as they approached the palace, and again elevated them when they had passed, notwithstanding the heavy rain ; but without imagining that this was a matter of obligation. Now that my attention was directed to the circumstance, I failed not to observe, on subsequent occasions, that persons passing on the Bosphorus in boats never omitted to take down their umbrellas as they approached in front of the mansion, which " the brother of the sun and moon" honoured with his presence.'[1] The other jeopardy was more formidable :—

'I was detained in Pera longer than I expected ; and darkness had set in by the time the wherry in which I returned reached Orta Khoi. After I had paid the fare, and was walking up the beach, the boatmen followed, and endeavoured to impress something upon me, with much emphasis of manner, but without disrespect. My impression was, that they wanted to exact more than their fare ; and as I knew that I had given the right sum, I, with John Bullish hatred at imposition, buckled up my mind against giving one para more. Presently the contest between us brought over some Nizam soldiers from the guard-

house, who took the same side with the boatmen; for,
when I attempted to make my way on, they refused to
allow me to proceed.   Here I was in a regular dilemma,
and was beginning to suspect that there was something
more than the fare in question; when a Turk, of apparently
high authority, came up, and, after a few words had been
exchanged between him and the soldier, I was suffered to
proceed.   As I went on, up the principal street of the
village, I was greatly startled to perceive a heavy earthen
vessel, which had fallen with great force from above, dashed
in pieces on the pavement at my feet.   Presently such
vessels descended, thick as hail, as I passed along, and
were broken to shreds on every side of me.   It is a marvel
how I escaped having my brains dashed out; but I got off
with only a smart blow between the shoulders.   A rain of
cats and dogs is a thing of which we have some knowledge; but a rain of potter's vessels was very much beyond
the limits of European experience.   On reaching the hos-
pitable roof which was then my shelter, I learned that this
was the night which the Armenians, by whom the place
was chiefly inhabited, devoted to the expurgation of their
houses from evil spirits, which act they accompanied or
testified by throwing earthen vessels out of their windows,
with certain cries, which served as warnings to the passengers : but that the streets were, notwithstanding, still so
dangerous, that scarcely any one ventured out while the
operation was in progress.   From not hearing these cries,
my danger was of course twofold, and my escape seemed
something more than remarkable : and I must confess, that
I was of the same opinion, when the next morning dis-
closed the vast quantities of broken pottery with which the
streets were strewed.   It seems probable that the adventure on the beach had originated in the kind wish of the
boatmen and soldiers to prevent me from exposing myself

to this danger. But there was also a regulation preventing any one from being on the streets at night without a lantern; and the intention may possibly have been to enforce this observance, especially as a lantern would this night have been a safeguard to me, by apprising the pot-breakers of my presence in the street.'[1]

On the 14th of April Kitto set sail for England, having parted from his missionary friends at Orta Khoi, with regret; feeling, as he confesses, 'miserable and irritable, and with few prospects of happiness before him.' So sunken was he in heart, that, unlike himself, he was disposed to repress the caresses of a little dog that fawned upon him. But his kinder nature triumphed.

'I thought better, and caressed him, poor fellow! I wished myself in his place; bowed down by a load of cares, as I felt, and felt how gladly I would have changed mine for any animate or inanimate condition—a tree, to grow in the blest sunshine, and bear my fruit; a dog, to frisk about, and know no care; anything but what I was. But there was no condition I so much envied as that of the missionaries, particularly Dwight, married, having children—his blest Madonna-like wife—his useful, respectable, quiet, and happy life, and his happier feelings, with heaven here and heaven hereafter. . . . Kind people! God bless them abundantly, for all their kindness to one ready to perish. It tore my heart to part with them, more than the hearts of others were torn, though I saw they were affected, and tears were in the eyes of some; mine flowed. Dwight vexed me by saying his little boy would not be able to hold me long in remembrance. I would not that anything I love should forget me. They kindly gave me memorials of their regard, which I hold above all price.'

Ere he left he kissed the little ones all round; and

Messrs Goodell, Dwight, and Hullock, accompanied Newman and Kitto to the beach; the first-named gentleman
going on board and dining with them. Mr Shepherd,
whose strength had been exhausted by the long journey,
and by severe and protracted rheumatism, was carried to
the vessel 'on a kind of wheelbarrow.' When the captain
joined them, he saluted Kitto with nautical freedom, told
him 'how highly he regarded him, and that he looked quite
a different person in his European dress.' 'I replied,' says
Kitto, 'that I believed I was much the same for all that.
He said he believed so too. As he thought well of me
before, doubtless this was intended for a compliment. I
confess I did not feel it as such. He also told Mr Shepherd,
that if he did not get better I should take his sweetheart.
I told him that my heart was too sour to be sweetened
even by a sweetheart, and that, at all events, the lady
would prefer Shepherd sick to Kitto well.' The captain's
blunt humour was ominous, though no one at the time
gave any thought to his prediction. Certainly not Kitto,
for he heaves a sigh and adds, 'Now then, "once more
upon the waters," God speed us! I confess that I have a
fancy running about in my head for several days, that I
shall never land in England.' The captain told his passengers some exaggerated stories about pirates, which so
greatly frightened the harmless Kitto, that he jots down
in his journal, 'If a skirmish arises and any one is killed,
I think it will be myself, and I never cared less about such
a result.' The dark sensations of an earlier period were
returning, for he was coming home without any cheering
anticipations of literary employment and reward. But
reading and conversation with Mr Newman beguiled the
weary hours on the billow. 'I am,' he records, 'annoyed
by the short tacks in traversing the Hellespont. Soon
after I fix myself in the sun, the new tack puts me under

the shadow of the sails, and obliges me to shift my position.   I love the sunshine, and whatever man may deny of
the world's sunshine, of God's man cannot deprive the
poorest and the humblest.'

The journal of the voyage to London is filled with reports of Mr Newman's sayings and criticisms, not forgetting the ordinary incidents of weather and sailing, and
the capture on one occasion of three turtles,—'a glorious
day's sport.'   The vessel passed near to Malta, the scene
of his former painful residence ; yet he says, ' I should feel
less pleasure in reaching London than in touching at
Valetta.   In the last place I have many friends ; in the
former few indeed, if any.   God bless them for all their
kindness to me while I remained among them.'   ' A beautiful sunshiny day, notwithstanding the high wind.   I wonder how it is that Sunday is generally the sunniest day in
the week, in every country I have been in, and every sea I
have been on.'

The vessel skirted the Spanish shore, and by the middle
of May the snowy mountains of Granada appeared in sight.
But the spectacle, like everything else at this period, only
tended to depress him, by recalling previous emotions, and
he writes as if in bitterness :—

' They are the same as when I first saw them ; but oh !
how changed am I, and all things in my retrospections of
the past, and my hopes of the future.   When I first beheld them, they were the first high, the first snowy mountains I had seen, and my heart was open entirely to their
beauty.   I have seen others since, more high, more beautiful, more grand ; and they now interest more, from the
recollection of what I formerly.felt than what I feel now.
When I saw them first, I thought, too, that other eyes
than mine would soon look upon them and admire, but
those eyes never saw them, and are now shut up in the

darkness of the grave, and left my own only open to see the desolation of all my hopes and blessings.'

The captain, mate, and some of the crew, pleased Kitto immensely by their literary taste—their anxious perusal of Shakspere and particularly of Spenser.

'*May* 28.—I was interested yesterday, and on former occasions, to see one of the sailors engaged in reading one of the cheap editions of Shakspere, which belongs to himself. I perceived that the last time he was reading *All's Well that Ends Well.* Verily, it is something to talk of, when our common mariners find pleasure in such books as Shakspere and the Faery Queen. My edition of the latter is in two volumes, and I can hardly keep one for my own use, so anxious is every one to read in it. The mate has read both volumes once through, and yet snatches up a volume whenever I lay it down on deck. The captain has got through the first, and now begins the second. The same man who reads Shakspere borrowed the second volume of me, which, when he had done, I lent him the first; but the captain, who wished to read it, made him give it back again. I am really afraid, in dispensing the loan of my Spenser, of giving offence, by my partiality. Now the first volume is vacant, the captain having done with it, yet I am rather afraid of giving it back to the man from whom it was taken, lest I should offend the mate. I trust my Spenser will not generate a mutiny.'

On June 2, the cliffs of England were hailed, but 'only *pro forma*' by Kitto, and 'with no very impetuous emotions :'—

'*June* 4.—Close by land; two miles perhaps. We saw a white cliff, which, said the mate, was Beachy Head, with Hastings beyond; but which turned out to be the Culver Cliff of the Isle of Wight, so that we are actually gone a good way back with the current since I went to bed. Lovely England! who can view thy beautiful shores, and think of what they enclose, and what thou art, and what thou mightest be, without being proud that he is an Englishman? I cannot, and would not. And, albeit my heart has gathered sterner stuff around it than it once had, it cannot but feel deeply and strongly in looking on these shores once more, that I had not hoped to see so soon.'

Still later, and when the shores of England were smiling before him, he inserts in his journal:—'How happy should I be now, were it not for the uncertainty that hangs over my future prospects.' Then nerving himself, he subjoins, in pithy terms:—'God help me: the struggle—a death struggle—comes.'

The coasts of Sussex and Kent interested him :—

'Oh, when I look thus intently on the verdant fields, velvet greens, fine trees, and pleasant villages of my own land, the beauties and excellencies of all others fade before me, and I say to myself, what I have often said, "Who that can live *in* England, would live *out* of it?" I return to the land I have loved, and I see few possible inducements before me to make me leave it again. I have already wandered more than nine hundred and ninety men in a thousand, and am content to think I have wandered enough; but if it be not so, let me for the future wander from one of her own pleasant scenes to another, and from one of her bright cities to another.

'Passing Dungeness, with its conspicuous high red lighthouse, and a place which does not seem more than a village to a spectator from the sea, and Hythe and Folkestone, we came to *Shakspere's Cliff*, below the town of Dover. It is probably a unique circumstance that a place should be called after the name of a poet who had described it. Dover Castle is a very fine object; as fine as any of the Turkish castles on the Bosphorus and Dardanelles, and finer.'

The ship, being laden with silk, was obliged to lie under the law of quarantine in Stangate Creek. Mr Shepherd had gradually sunk during the voyage; and though he was immediately and kindly taken into the physician's own vessel for better treatment, he died on the evening after his removal. Kitto had been charged by him, in the prospect of his death, with some tender messages, tokens, and farewells to the lady to whom he had been engaged, and whom he was coming home to wed. He sets down in his minute record, that there came to the doctor's ship, at Mr Shepherd's decease, the father and brother of Miss F., his intended bride. The elder of the two was a 'venerable gentleman;' and the latter he thus sketches:—'I recognised the younger as the brother of poor Shepherd's betrothed from his resemblance to the portrait which S. had of the lady. I did not,' he quietly concludes, 'introduce myself to them, but when relieved from quarantine shall do so, in compliance with the wishes to that effect expressed by poor S.' How he discharged this melancholy task, and with what romantic result, will be seen in the sequel.

It was on Friday, June 12, 1829, that Kitto left Gravesend for the East, and four years all but a day after—that is, on June 11, 1833—Mr Shepherd's funeral took place. The body, enclosed in ' a coffin without a plate, and with pieces of rope for handles,' was taken on shore by the sailors, and buried close to the water's edge, the other two vessels in quarantine, the Nymph and the Leander, wearing their colours half-mast high, while the doctor's servant read a portion of the burial service. The piece of ground selected for interment had its *uses* indicated by what the captain called ' *wooden tombstones*,' there being only two of them, and both dated 1832. One is tempted to ask if the captain now remembered his prediction, made when his ship was weighing anchor at Constantinople? The outburst of his hilarity may have been forgotten by himself, but as it rose to the memory of John Kitto, he imagined and pondered.

By the end of June the vessel was dismissed from quarantine, and Kitto once more rejoiced in being at home in England. His sensations at this period were afterwards touchingly portrayed by himself :—

' Only those who have spent years in distant lands can tell the yearning of the heart for one's native country—the craving, increasing in intensity as time passes, to return to its loved shores—to live there a few more years before life closes, and at last to die in our own nest.

> " 'Tis distance lends enchantment to the view."

Distance of either place or time lends this enchantment to the view which the mind takes of the far-off or long-forsaken home; and not less to the returned exile than to the man long sick, when he " breathes and walks again"—

> " The common sun, the air, the skies,
>   To him are opening paradise."

But the feeling is more enduring ; for if one is at length privileged to return to his own land, he finds that land has acquired an interest in his eyes which age cannot wither nor use exhaust. This is not speculation, but experience ; for the writer can declare that, after some years of absence in the far-off lands of the morning, with little thought or intention of ever returning, and after the first agonizing rapture of greeting once more his natal soil had subsided, he has not ceased, during nineteen years, to feel it as a joy and a privilege, which has in its measure been a balm to many sorrows, to dwell in this land; and he has experienced a constant intensity of enjoyment in the mere fact of existence in it, which had not formerly been imagined, and 'which only the facts of privation and comparison can enable one thoroughly to realize.'[1]

He narrates to Mr Woolleombe[2] his first experiences on returning :—

'My poor mother will have it to be a miracle that I have at last returned in safety. I would not say so; but, believing in a special Providence, as I think you do, I do feel that I owe my life to its protection under all the varieties of danger to which I have been exposed since I left my native land. I desire to be enabled, by my future life, to express the thankfulness I ought to feel for the most undeserved mercies which I have received. I will only just mention, that the first event which happened within a quarter of an hour after my landing, was to have my pocket picked of a silk pocket-handkerchief.'

He also tells this correspondent how, as the result of his eastern life, he felt amazed at first on seeing women walking unveiled, and averted his eyes when a lady passed; but archly adds, ' this is nearly off already, and I run into the other extreme, of looking at every one that passes ; and, verily, in walking from Barnsbury Park to the turnpike gate, I see more lovely countenances than in all the four years of my second absence, and in all my wanderings from Dan to Beersheba.'

His residence in an eastern climate had somewhat darkened his face :—

' Those who do not know me often take me for a foreigner, and to this mistake, perhaps, my complexion, browned by the various suns of the East, not a little conduces.'[3]

Somewhat later he writes to Lady M'Neill at Tehran :—

[1] Daily Bible Illustrations, vol. vi., p. 256.
[2] Upper John Street, Islington, July 8, 1833.
[3] Deaf Traveller, I.—Penny Magazine, vol. ii., p. 310.

'I had understood that the world had been turned up-side down while I had been out of it in the East; but when I came back, no other tokens of change were at once visible to the naked eye, than new churches, bridges, and streets; and of the Reform Bill itself, no other indication was immediately apparent besides "*Reform*" inns, coffee-houses, coaches, and shaving-shops. In whatever else the people of all classes differ, in one thing they all agree, that *the times are bad*. I am sure I believe so; for ever since I can remember, I never heard any one say that they were good; and I question if the Wandering Jew himself, in all the ages he has lived, and all the countries he has travelled, ever once heard that they were. Maybe some simple lads and lasses, during some hours of their wedding-day, may have thought so; but even they soon found out that the times were bad—as bad as they could be, and worse than they ever were.'

Toward the beginning of July, as if by a fascination which he could not resist, he had established himself in lodgings at Islington. The era of preparation was over, and that of active labour was about to commence. He had little doubt of being able to secure a maintenance if any engagement should be opened to him. It mattered not to him what toil it should cost, for he had braced himself

'To scorn delights and live laborious days.'

He had already advised his friends in Plymouth of his return, asking their assistance in securing for him some remunerative employment, and Mr Lampen and Mr Woollcombe at once responded to the earnest appeal of the returned wanderer.

CHAPTER IX.

AND what had Kitto gained by those travels, from which he was now resting?

At an early period in his career, and when he was dreaming of the future, rather than earnestly training himself for it, he had freely expressed his opinion as to the theoretic advantages of travel. He hoped to visit the continent and some 'interesting parts of the island,' in company with some person who would not think him an incumbrance. 'Important advantage would accrue to me from travel,' he remarks, 'viz., it will enable me to write with the confidence of personal observation, of the characters and natural and artificial productions of other parts of Britain and Europe.'[1] This was but a modest desire, for he had then only a limited object in view. Any one who had seen him a few months before he made this statement, within the walls of the workhouse, and plying his trade with undisturbed assiduity, would have thought him as firmly fixed to Plymouth for life, as the limpets to the rocks on its shores. He never travelled, indeed, as he originally contemplated, for he passed through various foreign countries, not to see them, but only to reach a distant point

[1] Letter to Mr Harvey, Public Library, Plymouth, August 7, 1823.

beyond them. He never was a traveller in the same sense in which Robinson and Livingstone are travellers—men who make a journey with an avowed and definite geographical purpose. He sailed and rode to the East in order to get to Bagdad, and he rode and sailed to the West in order to get to London. But his experiences of travelling cooled his earlier ardour. Though he prized the results, he did not relish the process of obtaining them. ' *To have travelled* is a very fine thing, but it is not a very fine thing *to travel* '—is his language to Mr Harvey.[1] Three months afterwards he declares to Mr Burnard[2] more emphatically :—' I hate action, I hate travel, unless, indeed, I must travel ; and by and by I must.' Yet, on his progress homeward, he makes another revelation to Mr Woolleombe :—' As to travelling, it will be borne in mind, that I am not travelling as a traveller ; and in the way I have travelled, I never would travel, except on business, again. If I do not marry, it by no means appears to me that I may not travel again. But my ideas of future travel are vague and remote, and at all events will in a great measure depend, in their consequences, on the direction given to the current of my life on reaching England.'[3]

Though a dark hour sometimes passed over him, as toward the end of his residence in Bagdad, the moral influence of his travels was certainly healthful. His own acknowledgment in his Journal, under March 12, 1831, is—

' I assured Mr Pfander that, though there were some circumstances that did not quite satisfy me in coming abroad, I rejoiced, upon the whole, in having done so ; for this one reason among others, that my love of mankind has been more extended than under any other circum-

---

[1] Bagdad, September 25, 1831.   [2] Bagdad, December, 1831.
[3] Tehran, October 30, 1832.

stances it probably would have been.   When I left England, I had a general disgust, if not contempt, toward
mankind, fully including myself; I despised men for being
what I thought they were, and I hated myself for being
like them.   My personal associations, even with religious
people, had not been happy, nor had much tended to raise
my respect and love for their character.   But the many
truly excellent and amiable individuals I have become
acquainted with since I left England, have brought round
my feeling to a more healthy tone.'

Kitto had also made no little intellectual gain by his
journeyings and residence in the East.   The extracts from
his Letters and Journals, which fill so much of the three
preceding chapters, sufficiently attest his powers of observation, and his habits of reflection.   Whatever he saw interested him; whatever befell him excited inquiry.   His
eye was ever busy, and was never 'satisfied with seeing;'
nay, it had acquired a special dexterity in taking in a
large panorama, and photographing an indelible image of
it on the memory.   Customs and habits so different from
those of England arrested his attention, and led him to
study humanity under 'new aspects of society and forms
of life.'   His mind was enlarged, and his stock of information greatly increased.   'Facts and images' were laid up,
and he distinctly knew 'some things which the untravelled
can only conceive.'[1]   In spite of his deafness, he had made
himself acquainted with all he wished to know.   Indeed,
the appetite of his youth retained its eagerness in his maturer years, for he thus limns himself in a miniature portrait of his boyhood.

' At a very early period of life, and in the midst of un-
toward circumstances, and of occupations which left me
the least possible leisure, I was a diligent collector of all

¹ Letter to Mr Woollcombe, Bagdad, December 15, 1831.

the odds and ends of knowledge that fell in my way. I read all the bills that were posted on dead walls and empty houses. I studied all the title-pages and open leaves that appeared in the windows of booksellers' shops; joyfully hailing the day when the windows of a particular shop were cleaned, and a change of books and pictures introduced. Sometimes, also, when I was allowed a little leisure, I brushed myself up as smart as possible, and ventured so far on the respectability of my appearance as to make the tour of the book-stalls, pausing at each; and, after dallying a little " about it and about it," taking up some humble looking volume, and devouring so much as was possible of the information it afforded, with the utmost intensity of appetite, and all the excitement that attends a stolen enjoyment. In process of time, I knew well the state of every book-stall, and could tell at a glance what books had been sold, and what additions had been made since my last visit; and many severer troubles in my subsequent life have made my heart ache less than sometimes to find a book gone, from which I had calculated on gleaning more information on a second occasion than my first spell at it had enabled me to obtain. I knew perfectly the dispositions of every proprietor of a stall in the three towns of Plymouth, Devonport, and Stonehouse, and could tell to a minute how long I might dabble at his books before he would look sour; and in process of time, most of the stall-men, on their part, became habituated to me, and came to regard me as a tolerated nuisance, or as one of the customary inconveniences incident to the trade.'[1]

What the youth had been, the man was still, but the curious boy had become the inquisitive traveller; gratifying the same desires on a larger scale, and with proportionate results. He had 'laid up in store against the time to come,' and that time was now at hand. He had also been qualifying himself for literary labour, for his pen had not been idle at Bagdad. He tells Mr Harvey, 25th September 1831, that he was 'preparing an account of the cities, towns, etc., between the Mediterranean and the Indus, which claim the attention of a missionary,' and that, for this purpose, he was in correspondence with missionaries in Armenia and Syria, having, at the same time, collected nearly all the information which Major Taylor's library could supply, and being also in daily expectation of books from England. Hosts of Essays, Tales, Dialogues, Disquisitions, Allegories, and Sketches, had also been thrown off by him.[1] Shut out from human intercourse, he was necessitated to give shape to his ideas, and body forth his imaginings, so that by the time he returned to England, he had acquired great facility of composition, and found it a comparatively easy matter to give expression to his teeming thoughts and reminiscences.

On being settled down in London, Kitto, as in time past, displayed uncommon ingenuity in devising plans for himself, though, as was usual with him, he was apt to overlook their feasibility. What appeared most plausible to his own mind, sometimes failed to commend itself to the judgment of others. But if one scheme failed, he had no hesitation in proposing or adopting another. Anything rather than rely on bounty, or be abandoned to total idleness. 'Language would fail to describe all the anxieties I felt on

---

[1] The following are the titles of some of his compositions, which range over a great variety of topics—The Seals of the Kaliphs; On the Mendicant Orders; the Astrologer; Calligraphy; Mahomet Ali Khan; The Principle; Maria Bell; The Modern Student; Ancient Student; Sights and Insights; the Silver Spoon; The Chrystal; The Angel of the Ruby; Hot-Cross Buns; Recollections and Collections about Malta; Language; On a Future State of Being; Chosrou; Plague of Bagdad; Childhood; Hubert and Eleanora; The Stars; Geographical Queries; Lella; Bastan; London in 2417; the Young Astrologer; Blindness; Persia; Farewell to Malta, a Poem; Lylan; Hebrew names of God, etc. etc.

my return about a temporal provision. Many dear plans of my own were in a short time blown to atoms, and I was sinking down into despondency."[1] But he was, sooner than he expected, relieved from his distress, and he entered at once on that career which grew in brightness as it extended in usefulness, till the gloom of the sepulchre was suddenly thrown over it.

Through the influence of his friends, Kitto was brought under the notice of the Society for the Diffusion of Useful Knowledge, of which Lord Brougham, then Lord Chancellor, was president, Sir Henry Parnell, and afterwards Lord John Russell, vice-president, with a large committee of high and honoured names in London and throughout the provinces. In July, Mr Woollcombe gave him a note of introduction to Mr Coates, the secretary, recommending him for employment. On the 18th of that month, he waited on Mr Coates, and handed him a written proposal to give a brief account of his travels, in the shape of weekly numbers, like the Penny Magazine, or of volumes in the Library of Entertaining Knowledge. Mr Coates told him that the latter alternative could not be adopted, but referred him to Mr Charles Knight, the editor and publisher of these popular serials. On the 19th he wrote to Mr Knight, stating his willingness to make up papers from his journals for the Penny Magazine, and on the 20th he had a personal interview. After the exchange of a few letters, and the presentation of a few approved specimens of his composition, he became a regular contributor to the Penny Magazine,—a rich collection of miscellanies, read, it was supposed, by a million of people in England, besides being reprinted in America, and translated into French, German, and Dutch.

The rate of remuneration was a guinea and a half per

[1] Letter to Lady M'Neill, Tehran. London, August 12, 1833.

page, but he was limited to two or three columns weekly.
His first two contributions appeared in the same number
for the 10th of August—one a collection of Arabian proverbs, and the other a paper introductory to his travels. Its
title is 'The Deaf Traveller,' and it is headed with the
following editorial explanation :—' We have much pleasure
in placing before our readers the first of a series of papers,
which, we think, will be found highly interesting, not only
from their intrinsic merit, but from the peculiar circumstances of the writer. These circumstances he has described in the following introductory account of himself.
We have only to add, that the writer has been introduced
to the notice of the Society by a valuable member of one
of the local committees, who is fully aware of his singular
history.' Some interest attaches to this paper as the
first-born of so many successors in various walks of literature. Kitto gives in it a succinct account of his previous
life. ' There are circumstances in my condition which
would exonerate me from censure, had I nothing at all to
say, or less than I really have. It is not yet a month
since I returned to my native shores. I made a pause
at the first book-shop, and the Penny Magazine attracted
my gaze. . . Some of the papers I had purchased at
the shop I skimmed over on my way home, cutting open
the leaves with my forefinger for want of a knife ; and
before I reached my lodgings, I felt that I should like
to have to do with some of these publications, particularly the Penny Magazine, in which I felt an espe-
cial interest.[1] . . I have certainly in the course of my
life been in very remarkable and interesting situations,
but I remember few more interesting than that in which

---

[1] On his return from Malta in 1829, the first place he stopped at was a bookshop,
but his eye fell on the following title-page, 'A Treatise on the Art of Tying the
Cravat.'

I am now placed, whilst talking to a million of people about myself.' Referring to his past days, he makes this further disclosure :—' Though, with a painful effort, I *could* speak, I seldom uttered five words in the course of a week for several years. I always said the little I had to say in writing, and I know not whether it be not to this circumstance I owe that habit of composition which now enables me to address the readers of the Penny Magazine. . . . I have endeavoured to keep one object steadily in view—the acquirement of such information and general knowledge as I found open to me in the midst of much occupation, and of difficulties which, though considerably different from those of my earlier life, have often been very great.'

He was now fairly harnessed for work, and began to reap the fruit of his toils and travels, his consistent behaviour, and his honest perseverance. Writing from Bagdad to Mr Woollcombe, July 21, 1832, he expressed his gratitude, and gave as the reason : 'For you have waited so patiently and so long to see whether the wild and rude plant you assisted to transplant and water, would at last become fruitful.' His introduction, through this same friend, to the Useful Knowledge Society, had now produced at least promising first-fruits. His contributions being so acceptable, and his month of virtual probation being successfully passed, Mr Knight offered him a general engagement at a salary which Kitto thankfully accepted, saying, 'the terms offered would be sufficient, not only for my present, but for my prospective wants.' What occurred during the interview which led to this arrangement, is artlessly told by himself.

'Mr Knight said, "I am perfectly satisfied with what you have done, and only fear you may feel such employment dull ; but I trust its usefulness will in time make it

pleasant to you." I also spoke on the subject of my independent contributions to the Penny Magazine, as The
Deaf Traveller, etc. You have perceived that my papers
have been few and far between; and as I thought this
might be from fear of tiring the readers, by the frequent
recurrence of the same subject, I expressed the satisfaction
I should feel in being permitted to fill up with other subjects
the intervals between the various papers of The Deaf
Traveller. Mr Knight said he would be glad if I did so;
but the reason The Deaf Traveller had not come in more
frequently, was the fear that I had not exactly hit his
meaning in preparing the papers. I had better take some
one subject, and bring my collected information to bear
upon it, rather than carry the readers on from stage to
stage, as in a book of travels. "I do not say, don't write
a book," Mr Knight remarked, "for that is a different
matter, but don't write a book for the Penny Magazine."
I am now preparing the papers on this principle.'

Kitto was also to take a certain charge of the Penny
Cyclopædia, suggesting new words or additions, looking
through German, French, and Italian books of reference,
and answering letters of contributors. He was somewhat
dismayed by the prospect, but Mr Knight very kindly
encouraged him, and told him, that 'his zeal would overcome all difficulties.' This task necessitated his personal
attendance for seven hours daily in Ludgate Street. 'I
sit,' he boasts to Mr Harvey,[1] 'in Mr Knight's room,
with plenty of books about me, and more below. Whatever spare time the Penny Magazine does not require is
spent in perfecting my knowledge of French and Italian,
and in acquiring German.' Though he entered on his
labours with some anxiety, he was soon enabled to go
through them with credit. No one knew better than Mr

[1] August 18, 1833.

Knight what contributions were adapted to such periodical literature as that which he was issuing, and Kitto was therefore under a kind and able monitor.   Mr Knight gently checked his strong propensity to dwell on a subject, and work it out to a disproportionate length.[1]   Kitto was now as busy as he could desire, doing whatever was required of him—abridging, compiling, translating, as well as composing original articles.   The Penny Magazine was largely indebted to his pen, and the Penny Cyclopædia to his care.   His pecuniary income was considerable, and had every appearance of steadiness and increase.   He had climbed long and bravely, and he was now but a few steps from the summit.

When the vessel which had brought him from Constantinople was easting anchor in Stangate Creek, he concluded a section of his journal with this racy soliloquy :—' Give me a little house, a little wife, a little child, and a little money in England, and I will seek no more, and wander no more.'

In a few days after, this aspiration assumed a practical aspect, and in a manner quite as peculiar and striking as had been the previous steps of his life.   Bitter disappointment with a bride who had deserted him, wedded another, and then died in sorrow and remorse, sent him to the East; and now, when he had returned, the mysterious hand of death brought him into connection with the betrothed of a fellow-passenger, who had sickened on the journey, and expired within sight of the shores of England.   For Mr Shepherd, who had died when the vessel was lying in quarantine, had charged .Kitto with several bequests and memorials for Miss Fenwick, the lady to whom he had been long engaged.   Mr Newman and Kitto made their

---

[1] Thus, at a later period, the Cyclopædia of Biblical Literature, and the Daily Readings, grew to double the size originally agreed on.

first visit together to express their condolence—the former
relating to the lady all the painful circumstances, while, according to her own description, Kitto 'sat all the time
mute, the very image of sympathy.' Such an interview did
not suffice for Kitto, for he had private matters, both of
Mr Shepherd's and of his own, to talk about. The whole
circumstances of the drama, so touching and so strange,
had impressed Kitto very deeply, and disposed him to fore-
cast 'whereunto this would grow.' For attachment was
springing out of the melancholy adventure; and he had
learned to love her,

> ' .   .   . Though her thoughts are straying
> To one who sleeps the dreamless sleep
> Of death; though midst her sighs are playing
> The hopes o'er which her visions weep.'

Again he called upon her, and again, and found her, as he
describes the result of his interviews to his friend, Lady
M'Neill, to be 'a very interesting person, with much information and more understanding. The loss she takes more
sadly than I should have expected, and, of course, she will
henceforth " wither on the virgin thorn for ever." So she
thinks—not I, knowing, as I do, that no intense feeling can
be lasting, or any resolutions permanent, which are formed
under their influence. I believe our minds are wisely and
well thus constituted. I remember the time when I had
firmly made up my mind to die an old bachelor, but now,
if I find any one who will have me, nothing is further from
my intention.'

He knew by the time he wrote these words that there
was one not averse to him, nay, that he had found one
who was willing to have him. 'My sympathy,' he says to
Mr Lampen, in reference to his first errand, 'made my
company pleasant to her; and though I did not for some
time think of her in any particular way, she won upon me

by her modes of thinking, her correct feeling, and strong and accomplished mind. She was ultimately led to think that she might find happiness with me.' The wooing— the success of which he owed to some extent to his innate persistence—had all but accomplished its object, when he felt that it behoved him to try to learn the probable amount, and especially to ascertain the certainty of his future income. There was only one way of coming to a satisfactory conclusion on the delicate subject, and that was by sounding his employer. Accordingly, on the 13th of September, he wrote a confidential letter to Mr Knight, freely stating his position, and his anxiety to be assured about his prospects of work and pay. The main question was thus put—' Whether my engagement with you is one which *you* wish me to retain? . . . I should say, there is nothing I desire more than to remain.' Mr Knight returned a satisfactory answer, and Kitto's heart was rejoiced beyond measure. Every impediment was thus easily removed, and the charge of imprudence could not be urged against the step which he was about to take. What he had so intensely longed for—a hearth and home of his own —was now to be attained. The cup had been dashed from his lips before, but again it was filled to overflowing. The happy day was at length fixed, and accordingly, on the 21st of September, and at Christ's Church, Newgate Street, was solemnized the marriage of John Kitto and Annabella Fenwick. The church was under repairs at the time, and the workmen being obliged to suspend their noisy operations during the ceremony, became its amused spectators. The bridegroom afforded them some merriment which they were scarcely able to conceal, for more than once, from his deafness, he got before the officiating clergyman, and had to be recalled to the actual duty which the course of the service devolved upon him. The day of his marriage was

T

the famous St Matthew's day, and as the civic dignitaries
of London were on their annual visit of ceremony to Christ's
Hospital 'next door,' there was no small stir in the neighbourhood.   The bridegroom wondered much at the bustle,
especially at the Lord Mayor's ' fine coach' waiting without, but could not at the time divine the reason.   Yet the
lively scene was not forgotten, and many years afterwards
he referred to it on occasion of the admission of one of his
boys to the great educational institution, jocularly remark-
ing, that the time, place, and circumstances of their father's
marriage seemed to give them some claim upon it.

   This new connection added unspeakably to Kitto's happiness, and contributed in no ordinary degree to his usefulness.   At the termination of the honey-moon, he rejoices
to proclaim, ' she now thinks she has found happiness, and
I hope to give her no cause to think otherwise.   I have
now a fireside of my own to sit down by, and on the other
side is my wife darning stockings.'   But she was not allowed
to keep long by such domestic employment, for her time,
during some years, was largely occupied in gathering literary materials for her busy husband.   She daily visited the
British Museum with him, and each, in that ample repository, pursued a separate path, he plying his immediate task,
and she amassing materials for other meditated productions.
She was the lion's provider, and was obliged to cater
liberally among all sorts of authors, living and dead; for,
as his den was a scene of uncommon voracity, his daily prey
required a skilful and diligent purveyor.

   If the previous pages indicate that Kitto was` alive to
female charms, other portions of his writings show his high
appreciation of the sex, on which he has pronounced many
noble and graceful eulogies.   He has recorded his sentiments more than once, and that towards the last years of
his life.   For example, the history of Samson suggests

to him, that 'reliance upon the tenderness and truth of woman's nature is not in itself a bad quality; nay, it is a fine, manly, and heroic quality—and we may be allowed to regret that Samson fell into hands which rendered it a snare, a danger, and a death to him.'[1]

Or, again, he has thrown out this striking sentiment:—

'But not to dwell further on particular instances, it may be well worth our while to note one great matter that deserves to be mentioned to their praise, and to be kept in everlasting remembrance. We have read of men once held in high esteem, who became apostates—Demas, Alexander, Philetus, and others; but never, by name, in all the New Testament, of a woman who had once been reckoned among the saints. This is great honour. But not only have women been thus honoured with extraordinary gifts; they have been otherwise favoured with special marks of attention from the Lord. To whom but unto women did Christ first appear after His resurrection? Of what act did He ever so speak as to render it everlastingly memorable, save that woman's, who poured upon His feet her alabaster box of precious ointment; and to whom He promised that, wherever, in the whole world, His Gospel should be preached, there should her work of faith be held in remembrance?'[2]

Or, still further, in vindication of Job's wife, and against the opinions which some commentators have formed of her words, translated in the English version, 'Curse God and die,' he protests right cheerily:—

'It was telling him that death was his best friend; that it was better for him to die than to live a life like this. Such a life was a continual death; and it were better to die at once than to die daily. Now, as many ladies are among our readers, we will at once ask them, if this is a true or probable explanation? We will feel assured that

[1] Daily Bible Illustrations, vol. ii., p. 413.   [2] Ibid., vol. iii., p. 12.

they will at once say it is not ; that this is not the language
which any true-hearted wife would hold to her afflicted
husband, and that the advice is not " wholesome," as this
explanation supposes.   It is the ingenious speculation of
dry old scholars, shut up among their books, and not of
men knowing anything about the hearts of wives.' [1]

Kitto's work with Mr Knight was somewhat multifarious,
but he was pleased with it.   For a time, indeed, he walked
'fearfully and tremblingly,' but he gradually gained confidence and courage.   Toward the close of this eventful
year, on December 9, 1833, he gives some recital of his
experience to Mr Woollcombe.

'52, St John's Road, Islington.

'. . . With me things have gone on as smoothly as
I could reasonably expect. . . I have to bring into
admissible form the contributions of correspondents, whose
letters I also answer.   In this last employment I have great
occasion to feel how much I owe to your kind recommen-
dation, as I have often to write for Mr Knight, declining
offers of assistance, which I cannot sometimes help thinking, would be more efficient than my own.   I am happy to
hope that I have not altogether discredited your recom-
mendation, and I trust that I shall not.   I find my employments so very congenial, and my facilities in them increase so rapidly, that I think often that I have at last
been enabled, through your kindness, to find my proper
place and level. . .   There is a letter of Mr Groves in
the Record newspaper of last Thursday.   I am sorry to
say that no letter from him has yet come into my hands.
I have been poorly lately.'

The next year, 1834, was passed in similar industry, his

[1] Daily Bible Illustrations, vol. v., p. 95.

remuneration being L.18 a month. Still, as his work grew familiar to him, he contemplated some other and future tasks ; nay, as labours multiplied upon him he ' sang in his heart.' At length more than half the Magazine was of his preparing, and he avers, with some exultation, ' all the papers I write now are printed.' Books for children held a prominent place in his projected authorship, of which Uncle Oliver's Travels in Persia is a favourable specimen. His articles being printed anonymously, he was saved from the imputation of inordinately thirsting for a name. He was all the while acquiring practice for higher achievements, for he was training himself to harmonise compactness with detail. The brief and uniform limits of the Magazine constrained him to proportion the space he occupied, to the differential value of his topics. The hardest lesson he had to learn was that of literary perspective, and he never thoroughly mastered it ; nay, he almost complains, that ' the readers of the Penny Magazine are so accustomed to condensation, that they cannot bear details.'

During this year was born his eldest child, Annabella Shireen—the second name being a reminiscence of his Persian travels. She was a source of new joy to him, and he had a thousand happy ways of delighting and amusing her in her infancy. When the little lady gave any sign of being gratified, he would at once turn to her mother and say (with what a tone!) ' Does she make a noise? Pray tell me what kind of noise it makes.' The tear starts in the eye on reading these touching words. He complains seldom, but ah! he utters a deep and mournful sigh as he thinks of ' children's voices, and the sweet peculiarities of infantile speech,' and then points to his daily sorrow and privation as he sat among his darlings, being doomed 'to *see* their blessed lips in motion, and to *hear* them not.'

The materials to be employed in Biblical illustration, had for a period been stored up in Kitto's mind; but as yet no outlet had been found for them. He had, however, some notion of their value, and of their adaptation to general purposes. But his plans had been overruled. Yet the germ of the Pictorial Bible lies in the following statement :—'I am to undertake the description of remarkable things and customs in foreign countries, beginning with those in which I have actually travelled. It was the very thing I wanted to do when I first came home.' This idea, which was still uppermost, only received a special direction when the Pictorial Bible was edited. The light which would have been scattered on a variety of points, grew brighter and steadier by its concentration on . Scripture. At a later epoch, after he had acquired ' celebrity,' and when ' black mail' was freely levied upon him, though not to the extent he sometimes imagined, he indicated the peculiar source of his superiority and power by the avowal, ' Nothing in fine saves me from being smothered by my own children, but the certainty of *actual knowledge* which my residence and travels in the East confer.'[1] This ' actual knowledge' was his tower of strength. For the description of a veritable eye-witness differs usually from that of a mere compiler, as much as a green garland from a faded chaplet. He who has seen the animal killed and cooked by one continuous process, and has partaken himself of the feast, diving into the pillau of rice or barley with his naked hand, and fetching up his morsel, can paint the festive scene with a few vivid touches, as he illustrates Abraham's hospitality, or give an edge to Solomon's proverb about the slothful man's hiding his hand in the dish, that is, not using his three fingers, as is generally done, but so filling his whole palm at once, and loading it, as to

[1] Letter to Mr Oliphant, October 30, 1851.

save such repeated motion.[1] The flesh of animals is in
the East more a luxury than an article of daily food, and
men are cautioned in Scripture against being 'riotous
eaters' of it. The Arab, as often as he can, does feed
himself to satiety, but the spectator can add his own
humorous touch :—

'We have often had occasion to witness a meal of meat
indulged in under such circumstances, to a degree of in-
conceivable intemperance, and enjoyed with a degree of
hilarity very much like that which attends the consumption of strong drink in our northern climates. We have
the Arabs more especially, but not exclusively, in view ;
for it is in connection with this·people that the present
expression, " riotous eaters of flesh," has been brought most
forcibly to our mind, on beholding the strong and irrepres-
sible satisfaction with which a party of them would receive
the present of a live sheep, and on witnessing the haste
with which it was slaughtered and dressed, the voracity
with which it was devoured, and the high glee, not unattended with dance and song, which seasoned the feast.
We are almost afraid to say how much an unrestricted
Arab will eat when an opportunity is given. It is commonly considered that an Arab can dispose of the entire
quarter of a sheep without inconvenience ; and we have
certainly seen half-a-dozen of them pick the bones of a large
sheep very clean.'[2]

The rider who has carried at his saddle the skin filled
with water or wine, or the guest who has been cognisant
of the Persian fashion of debauch, which begins at sunrise
or before it, can give point to an exposition either of the
trick of the Gibeonites, or of the prophet's denunciation,
' Woe unto them that rise up early in the morning, that

---

[1] The allusion is based upon a peculiar interpretation of Prov. xxvi. 15.
[2] Daily Bible Illustrations, vol. v., p. 343.

they may follow strong drink.'   The invalid who has been unfortunately under the hands of Oriental physicians, can speak from experience of their thirst for bleeding their patients with a dull lancet, or a knife rudely made into the shape of one, or of their fondness for the actual cautery with a common iron nail, or a piece of wire.'

The 'publicans' of the New Testament, or officers of inland revenue, were specially detested. · Why?   Let Kitto's experience declare :—

'It has not been our lot to be acquainted with any country, the inhabitants of which are so alive to their obligations to the State, as to receive with pleasure and regard with respect the collectors of the revenue, under whatever name they may come, whether tax-gatherers, rate-collectors, excisemen, customhouse-officers, or tollmen. The popular dislike to this class of public servants has always existed everywhere; and in an eminent degree it has always existed, and does exist, in the East, where the antipathy to anything like a regular and periodical exaction for government objects goes far beyond the dogged churlishness, with which the drilled nations of the West meet the more complicated demands upon them. This may, among other causes, be owing to the fact, that the eastern tax-gatherer feels quite at liberty to use his stick freely upon the person of a tardy, inadequate, or too reluctant tax-payer.'[1]

Speaking of the erroneous application of western forms and ideas to eastern usages, and that in reference to the scene of the Saviour's birth, so inaccurately handled by poets and painters, the pilgrim can affirm from observation :—

'The explanation we give of this incident, is founded upon actual observation, made while ourselves, more than

[1] Daily Bible Illustrations, vol. vii., p. 272.

once, were constrained to lodge in the stable, because there was " no room in the inn ;" and was, in fact, suggested in a place that led us to say, " In such a stable as this was Jesus born ; here might have been an excellent retreat for the Virgin; here she would be completely screened from observation at the time it was needed ; and here in this very ' manger' she might have found no unsuitable cot for her first-born son."'[1]

The student who, one afternoon at Bagdad, had been startled from his book by a sudden obscuration of the sky, as if the sun had been eclipsed, and had ascertained the cause to be a cloud of locusts, black from its very thickness, and covering the city 'like a pall,' could not fail to be picturesque in his comment on the first and second chapters of Joel.

As to the character and effect of eastern salutations, one who had often made and returned them with all their picturesque formality, is warranted to say :—

' The servile demeanour of the poor in this country is hateful to every well-ordered mind. It has grown out of circumstances which there has been too little effort to resist ; and we may go to the East to learn how the poor may be treated with courtesy, and be continually reminded, in every passing form of speech, of their natural and religious brotherhood, without being thereby encouraged to disrespect or insubordination, but with the effect of a cheerful and willing character being thereby imparted to obedience.'[2]

The gaze that had frequently wandered over Asiatic fields, entitled the expositor to show the immense loss, which the foxes let loose by Samson, did to the harvest—thus :—

---

[1] Daily Bible Illustrations, vol. vii., p. 62.

[2] Ibid., vol. iii., p. 27. Dr Kitto might have noticed, that our own common forms of salutation had once a religious significance. Adieu, is a commendation to God and Good b'ye, is God be with thee.

'The reader must recollect that the cultivated lands are not separated by hedgerows into fields as with us, but are aid out in one vast expanse, the different properties in which are distinguished by certain landmarks, known to the owners, but not usually obvious to a stranger. Thus, as the time of harvest approaches, the standing corn is often seen to extend as far as the eye can reach, in one vast unbroken spread of waving corn. Hence the flames, once kindled, would spread without check till all the corn of the locality was consumed; and we are further to remember, that there were fifty pairs let off, doubtless in different parts.'[1]

The oratory at Philippi was by the river side, and the sojourner in remote Russia can quote an apposite illustration :—

'It is rare at the present time to witness worship by a number of persons under such circumstances, as they usually find other means for ablution; but it happened to us, that the first act of Moslem worship we ever witnessed, was thus performed. This was nearly a quarter of a century ago, in the Caucasian mountains, at a time when many Turkish prisoners of war were kept there by the Russians. Bodies of these were conducted, at the hours of prayer, under a guard of soldiers, to any open place traversed by a river, near the military stations, and after performing their ablutions at the stream, they prostrated themselves upon the green sward, and went through the several acts of their remarkably demonstrative worship.'[2]

But not to multiply examples. Almost every one is aware how unlike an Oriental dwelling is to one among ourselves. But the wayfarer who has lived in both, can give a striking picture of the difference, and invest it, too, with an architectural interest.

[1] Daily Bible Illustrations, vol. ii., p. 416.   [2] Ibid., vol. viii., p. 340.

'The probability is, that the majority of the houses of Nineveh, like those of many eastern cities of the present day, consisted but of one storey, spread therefore over a large extent of ground. We have always observed the Orientals to be exceedingly averse to ascending stairs: and where ground is not an object, as it seldom is, they consider it absurd to build habitations in which they must be continually going up stairs and down, when they are at liberty to spread out their dwellings over the ground as widely as they like. Hence the accommodation which we secure by piling storey upon storey, they think they realize with much more advantage, by placing these storeys separately upon the ground, connecting them by doors, galleries, courts, and passages. This is their idea of comfort, and we must confess to being considerably of their opinion. The result is, however, that the house of an eastern gentleman in a town will generally occupy four or five times as much ground as that of an Englishman in the corresponding condition of life.'[1]

These extracts are only a specimen of that full and exact illustration which one can adduce who 'testifies what he has seen.' Though they are taken from Dr Kitto's last work, they show what stores he had at command for his earliest Biblical exposition. Sir John M'Neill gave him, when he met him at Tabreez, a peculiar illustration of the territorial meaning wrapt up in the phrase, 'Jacob digged a well,' by informing him, that in Persia the law enacted, that he who digs a well in the desert, is entitled to all the land which it will irrigate. Morier's 'Second Journey through Persia,' also recommended to him by the same authority, contains numerous elucidations of customs and sayings in the Old Testament, some of them ambiguous, indeed, and others based on misconception, but the majority of them

---

[1] Daily Bible Illustrations, vol. vi. p. 407.

singularly perspicuous and happy, and many of them veri-
fied by the deaf yet sharp-eyed wanderer himself. It is
true, indeed, that Kitto did not travel in Palestine; but
the East has an unvarying type among its Shemite races,
and especially among those of the Syro-Arabian dialects.
Manners are in many things the same on the banks of the
Tigris as on those of the Jordan—the same among the
children of Elam as among the children of Eber. What
are often called Jewish customs, are, apart from religion,
not confined to Abraham's progeny through Isaac, but belong equally to his descendants through Ishmael. Dr
Asahel Grant forgot this truth in one part of his argument, when he endeavoured to prove that the Nestorian
Christians are the remains of the Ten Tribes, from certain
customs and ceremonies, which, so far from being distinctive
of Israel, are common to all the provinces of Western Asia.[1]

While Kitto wrought heartily on the Penny Magazine
and other periodicals, he had not yet found his appropriate
function. Still he was but a common literateur, and in
that 'line of things' would scarcely ever have been known
beyond the immediate circle in which he moved. But
when the hour came the man was ready. Exploring his
dim and uncertain way towards his right sphere, he had
been frequently and partially baffled, though he was constantly nearing it.

> 'The cygnet finds the water, but the man
> Is born in ignorance of his element,
> And feels out blind at first.'

At this juncture, the active and enterprising mind of Mr
Knight, suggested the idea of an annotated Bible, and he
thought that his man of all work was well qualified to
write that portion of the notes which related to Oriental

[1] The Nestorians, or the Lost Tribes. By Asahel Grant, M.D., chap. xviii.
London, 1841.

manners and life, and which his travels might help him to furnish. The plan at once rivetted Kitto's attention as something peculiarly fitted for him, and in which he could excel. He prepared a specimen, with which Mr Knight was so pleased, that he resolved to gratify Kitto's earnest solicitation, and intrust him with the execution of the entire work. This decision was a wise one on the part of the publisher, and a happy one for the editor. Kitto thankfully owned Mr Knight's kindness, as one 'qualified beyond most men to judge of another's fitness,' and he eulogizes his 'generous confidence in intrusting to my untried hands a great and noble task, which others would have deemed to need the influence of some great name in literature.'

This new experiment brought him at once into the field which he had been long preparing to occupy, and for the occupation of which much of his previous training and travels had really qualified him. Prior to that objective preparation which his eastern journey had given him, and along with it, there had been another and a superior discipline. The Bible had become to him the Book of Life. Before his fall from the house-top, he had regarded the Bible 'as a book especially appointed to be read on Sundays,' and had not 'ventured to look into it on any other day. It seemed a sort of profanation to handle the Sacred Book with work-day fingers.' But, as he lay on that bed of slow convalescence, the exhaustion of his slender literary resources drove him to it, and then he read it 'quite through, Apocrypha and all.' His studies from this period took a marked direction towards Theology. Works of a religious kind were found and devoured by him, such as Foxe's Martyrs, Josephus, Hervey's Meditations, Bunyan, Drelincourt, Baxter's Saint's Rest, Sturm's Reflections, and Watts' World to Come. In course of time, indeed, he extended his reading to a more miscellaneous class of

books, and especially in the public library did he give himself to Metaphysics; yet he hints, that 'amidst all this,
the theological bias given by my earlier reading and associations remained.'[1]   But it was at Exeter that the 'day-
spring' for which he had long prayed arose upon him.
Up to that time the Bible, he confesses, had been 'a sealed
book' to him, for the 'instructing influences of the Holy
Spirit did not attend' his reading of it, and he did not
come to it 'with the humble and teachable spirit of a
little child.'   Now, and for some years, the inspired Word
had been the food of his soul—the daily theme of that devout and earnest meditation which, 'comparing spiritual
things with spiritual,' makes 'wise unto salvation through
faith which is in Christ Jesus.'[2]   So that, when in due time,
he came to illustrate Scripture, he did it in the right spirit,
and never forgot the divinity of the volume on whose
pages he was lavishing so many literary and pictorial
illustrations.   Spiritual qualification guarded and hallowed
scholastic equipment.

The work, commencing in the end of 1835, was published in monthly parts, and completed in May 1838.   During its progress Kitto 'received L.250 a-year, and when
it was finished he was presented with an additional sum,
which seemed to him a little fortune.'[3]

The Pictorial Bible rose at once into high popularity.
It was his first work in that department, and it led the
way to all his subsequent productions.   No sooner had he
entered on this form of labour than—

> 'Almost thence his nature was subdued
> To that it worked in, like the dyer's hand.'

Little, indeed, had been previously done in this neglected
province of illustration.   There had been huge commen-

[1] Lost Senses—Deafness, p. 14.   [2] Ibid., p. 16.
[3] Article Kitto, in Knight's English Cyclopædia—Biography. Vol. III.

taries, and good ones too—the quaint and pithy Henry, the solid and judicious Scott, and the more erudite and ambitious volumes of Patrick, Lowth, Whitby, and Adam Clarke. These authors, however, had, to a great extent, treated Scripture in one aspect. But the Bible, like the Redeemer whom it reveals, has two sides of view—divine and human. The former had been principally thought of by earlier expositors. They regarded more the truth of Scripture than the mode in which it had been conveyed. Their attention was given rather to the sound of the trumpet, than to the shape of the instrument, or the music of the peal. They busied themselves more with what history said, than with the style of recital; more with what the ritual taught, than with the scenes and ceremonies of the pageant itself; more with what poetry had sung, than with the lyre, drapery, and attitude of the Hebrew muse; more with what prophecy revealed, than with the allusions and colouring of its oracles. So that, with all the important service which they rendered, they had left a wide field unoccupied. For the Bible, though a Divine revelation, is also a human composition; and though 'given by inspiration,' it is essentially an Asiatic or Oriental book—the product of Hebrew mind, and laden with the riches of Hebrew imagination.

Various illustrations of manners and customs had been already collected, such as the treatises of Harmer, Burder, and Paxton; the travels of Sandy, Purchas, Maundrell, Shaw, Niebuhr, and Burckhardt, were not unknown; and every scholar was acquainted with such writers on antiquities, geography, and natural history, as Bochart, Reland, D'Herbelot, Pococke, Celsius, Forskal, Harris, Jennings, Jahn, and Roberts. Many of the more prominent features of the eastern world had also been distinctly apprehended. It was perfectly well understood that houses in the East

had flat roofs, that the so-called bottles were of skin, and
that sheep followed the shepherd, and were not gathered
or driven by dogs. But Dr Kitto's merit lay, not so much
in discovery as in application. He brought the public
mind into vivid contact with Oriental scenery and life, by
moulding them into the form of a continuous commentary
on the Old and New Testaments. His readers are so ini-
tiated, that they are placed under the eastern sky, with its
bright days and starry nights, and are so privileged, that
they may gaze on the glory of Lebanon, the beauty of
Carmel, and the rugged sublimity of Sinai; throw the net
with the fishermen on the Lake of Galilee; raise the 'shout'
of the vintage on the slopes of Eshcol; recline by the 'still
waters' with the shepherd, when the 'pastures are clothed
with flocks;' work and sing with the reaper when the
'valleys are covered over with corn;' go up at the great
festivals to 'the testimony of Israel,' with 'the tribes of
the Lord;' or march with the accoutred yeomen of the
land, to fight for hearth and altar against Moab or Philistia,
Ammon or Syria, the foes of the old theocracy. The Pictorial Bible gave glow and reality to ancient scenes and
customs, and threw a wondrous light on what is external
or Oriental in the drapery of Scripture.

Striking and appropriate illustration is borrowed from
the Egyptian monuments. Witsius and others had
laboured hard to disprove any religious connection between Israel and Egypt. Their arguments were, however,
more of a theological than of an artistic and antiquarian
nature, and there is no doubt that Marsham and Spencer
carried their opposite speculations to an unwarranted extent. But it is natural to suppose that no small portion
of Hebrew custom and art was learned in Egypt, so famed
for its ' wisdom.' Therefore the figures on the monuments,
so various in their allusions, and portraying so much both

of the religious and common life of the nation, are a fertile source of illustration for the Pentateuch—the law and the history of the chosen people, just after it had migrated from the shores of the Nile.   And thus, in the notes and woodcuts, you have Egypt everywhere—its wheat and its bulrushes, its flax and its frogs, its gods and its mummies, its priests and its ark, its feasts and its funerals—all of them verifying and explaining the Mosaic annals and legislation.   The same felicity is displayed in the references to Oriental usage, which is so brought before the reader with pen and pencil that he lives in it.   Distinctness is given to his conceptions, for every intelligent reader of scenes, travels, battles, and manners, must form a mental picture to himself as he proceeds, and Kitto sets before him the exact similitude, copies from nature both to be 'seen and read.'   Some of the curious and difficult points of Hebrew jurisprudence are well illustrated by apposite examples and analogies, some of them better than those which Michaelis has collected.   We need not allude to the many engravings taken from Petra, Persia, and Babylon, and so profusely scattered through the exposition of the prophetical books.   The introductions prefixed to the various sections, though brief and unpretending, are full of good sense, and convey useful information.

We need not wonder, therefore, at the immediate popularity of the Pictorial Bible.   It was a new idea successfully carried out.   It brought down to the people what had lain on the shelves of students, or been stored away in the treasures of the British Museum.   It gave an impulse to this species of biblical study, familiarised the ordinary readers of Scripture with its geography and antiquities, and showed. that research, no matter how far or in what direction it was carried, served to confirm the truth, authenticate the history, develop the beauty, and promote

U

a fresher and fuller understanding of the Book of God. It was at first objected that the comment wanted the evangelical element; but the author's purpose must be kept in view, and as he professed to deal with neither exegesis nor theology, he must be judged by the aim which he sought to realise.

What are called 'Illustrations from the Old Masters,' are usually of little value. Nay, they often mislead. Those of them, for instance, which are found even in the first volume of the Pictorial Bible are of this nature. In the one which forms the frontispiece, the artist has paid no attention to Egyptian features, dress, or custom. In the plate representing Laban's covenant with his son-in-law, Jacob is pictured as still a young man, whereas he could not have been far from threescore years and ten. But it was the special superiority of the Pictorial Bible, that it discarded such fanciful illustrations, except as mere occasional ornament, and that it figured actual animals, plants, garments, and scenes, so as to give to the reader's eye the zoology, botany, costume, geography, and ethnography of Scripture. Many objectionable plates in the first edition were excluded from the fourth, for they were often inaccurate as exponents of history, and imperfect as representations of manners and dress. The first edition, completed in 1838, formed three large imperial octavo volumes, and from the stereotype plates of it various large impressions were taken.

The book was published anonymously. Its reception not only gratified Kitto immensely, but decided what was to be the labour of his subsequent years. For the reviews were very favourable. One of them spoke of the *men* employed in the publication 'as fully competent to their anxious undertaking;' and the *one* man who did the entire work, secretly and heartily enjoyed the plural reference.

The approbation of the public was not only a reward to him for his toils and anxiety, but he took it as the index of Providence pointing out what he now rightly regarded as the work to which he had been called, and for which so many years of study and travel, and growing religious faith, had so admirably disciplined him. The 'almost unprecedented favour' with which the book was received, was therefore owing to its real worth, and not to any fame of its author—for his name was concealed—nor to any sympathy with the workhouse boy, who had wandered from Plymouth to Bagdad, and plodded his way back again to London. Kitto could not but record his high satisfaction with the result—' The degree of attention with which my labours have been favoured, has not arisen out of any sympathies for, or had reference to, my peculiar condition : for my greatest and most successful labour was placed before the public without any name ; and although the author's name has been attached to later works, it has not been accompanied by any information concerning the circumstances which have now been described. As, therefore, the public has had no materials on which to form a sympathising, and therefore partial, estimate of my services, and has yet received them with signal favour, I may venture to regard the object which I had proposed to myself as in some sort achieved. And since it is at length permitted me to feel that I have passed the danger of being mixed up with the toe-writers and the learned pigs of literature, I have now the greater freedom in reporting my real condition.'[1]

He stated also to Professor Robinson of New York,[2] then in London, that 'through incidental notices and allusions in periodical publications, the public had got some notice of his history,' but that even then (1840) he was not

[1] Lost Senses—Deafness, p. 83.   [2] September 28, 1840.

extensively known as the editor of the Pictorial Bible. Not
that there had been any studious concealment, but, he declares, ‘it has rather been my wish that I should not seem
to owe any part of the success I might attain as an author
to the sympathies which my sufficiently singular personal
history might be likely to produce.’ Indeed, he affirms,
more unreservedly, and with some degree of warmth, that
at an early period he had found little encouragement from
others, even from those who ultimately favoured him with
their notice; that when he spoke of literature, he had been
kindly pointed away to other means of occupation and usefulness; that his literary predilections had usually obtained
no encouragement, but had rather been opposed as an un-
reasonable infatuation; and that therefore he had ‘determined, at whatever risk, to act upon his own soul-felt conclusions, and to stand by the truth or fall by the error of
ineradicable convictions.’[1]   So completely unknown was
he in Scotland, that when we first heard that the Pictorial
Bible was edited by ‘John Kitto,’ we thought that the
brief and uncommon name must surely be a *nom de plume*.

In a fragmentary Journal, July 4, 1837, we find this
characteristic paragraph:—

‘Newman writes me,—“I have taken in the Pictorial
Bible. Parnell tells me that you were the editor. I said,
perhaps of the later portions. Is it true that you were
the editor of the Pentateuch part?” Bah! I answered,
rather shortly, yes—and did not altogether omit the opportunity of slightly girding at the discouragements I had
received, and the calamities which were foretold me from
my adherence to my literary predilections; to which adherence I owe all the benefits I now enjoy. I said just
enough to let him see that I did feel something of triumph,
to have it thus established that I was right in my obsti-

[1] Lost Senses—Deafness, p. 90.

nacy. These old college folks, I fancy, cannot like the successes of parvenus, self-educated men like myself.'

In short, though Kitto rejoiced in doing all manner of service for the Penny Magazine, and other useful and popular periodicals, he felt, for the first time, that he was in his true element when he commenced his studies for the Pictorial Bible. His benefactors, in their kindness, had assigned him different forms of labour, from the making of shoes to the setting of Persic types, from the teasing of oakum to the manufacture of artificial teeth, and in all of them he did his best, but in none of them was he contented. Each was but a resting-place—his heart still said, Excelsior! and he arose and climbed again. Various spheres of work were opened up to him, but he could not find a home at Plymouth or Exeter, Malta or Bagdad, when Providence at length set him down in Ludgate Hill, and yoked him to the great business of his life. And then he felt that he had been slowly training for his high vocation, and that what had disabled him for the physical toils under which his soft sinews had first bent, had but set him apart to higher and more exhausting labours. Then, too, he learned that no phase of his life had been without its advantages—that his love of lore now enabled him to pay his tribute of veneration to the Book of books, and that his journey to the Tigris yielded fruits to be afterwards reaped on the Thames. And thus he waxed 'strong in faith, giving glory to God.'

During the progress of this first and great labour he tells Mr Knight, in the fulness of his heart—

'I cannot begin any observations respecting the Pictorial Bible, without stating how highly I have been gratified and interested in the occupation it has afforded. It has been of infinite advantage as an exercise to my own mind. It has afforded me an opportunity of bringing nearly all

my resources into play ; my old Biblical studies, the observations of travel, and even the very miscellaneous character
of my reading, have all been highly useful to me in this
undertaking.   The venerable character of the work on
which I have laboured, the responsibility of annotation,
and the extent in which such labour is likely to have influence, are also circumstances which have greatly gratified,
in a very definite manner, that desire of usefulness, which
has, I may say, been a strong principle of action with me,
and which owes its origin, I think, to the desire I was early
led to entertain of finding whether the most adverse circumstances (including the privation of intellectual nourish-
ment) must necessarily operate in excluding me from the
hope of filling a useful place in society.   The question was,
whether I should hang a dead weight upon society, or take
a place among its active men.   I have struggled for the
latter alternative, and it will be a proud thing for me if I
am enabled to realise it.   I venture to hope that I shall :
and to *you* I am, in the most eminent degree, indebted, for
the opportunities, assistance, and encouragement, you have
always afforded me in my endeavours after this object.'

Sir John M'Neill and Mr Knight were, each in his time
and place, of essential service to Kitto ; the one in the
East had greatly and opportunely helped to store his mind,
and the other in London devised the plan which brought out
his knowledge into popular and practical form.   The one
encouraged him to gather the ore, and, after its fusion, the
other shaped the mould, and there ' came out' the Pictorial
Bible.   During the years in which it was in process of
publication, his toil was incessant, though he was never far
ahead of the press ; so that he complained of the time lost
by going in search of books, especially to the British
Museum, and wished a few serviceable volumes to be procured for himself.   Matters connected with the work, over

and above the writing of the notes, took np, he affirms, ' a
fourth of his time, and more than half of his anxiety.' And
he ends his request with the memorable declaration, ' The
Musenm day is bnt *six* hours long, whereas mine is sixteen.'

It may be added, that the Pictorial Bible was reprinted
in four quarto volumes, in 1838, but not stereotyped ; that
in 1840 the notes and some of the illustrations, without
the text, were published in five small octavos ; and' that
in 1847 was commenced what may be called the standard
edition, completed in 1849, in four volumes imperial octavo.
Kitto bestowed special pains npon this edition, and ' received
upwards of £600 for his labour.'[1]   Not only did it excel its
predecessors in better paper, larger page, choicer woodcnts,
and more tasteful printing, but it possessed other and higher
improvements.   The editor, who was best qualified to speak
of it, for he knew the labour it had cost him, says himself :—

' The final resnlts appear in a considerable body of fresh
matter, exhibited in some thousands of new notes, and in
additions to and improvements of a large number of the
notes contained in the original work.   Space for this has
been provided by an actual increase of the letterpress, by
the omission of one class of woodcuts, by the careful excision from the original work of such matters as might,
it was judged, be spared, not only withont loss but with
advantage, and by the pruning and condensation of many
notes which remain without essential alteration.   The effect
of all this may be seen in the fact that, in the Pentatcuch
alone, besides introductions occupying several pages, between four and five hundred new notes have been introduced without the sacrifice of any valuable matter contained
in the original work, and with the addition of a large
nnmber of really illustrative engravings, which did not
appear in that publication.

[1] Article ' Kitto,' in Knight's English Cyclopaedia.

' The general result may be thus stated: that the matter of the original work has undergone a most careful and elaborate revision; that nothing of interest or value in the original work is wanting in the new edition; and that large additions have been made, equal altogether to above one-third of the whole work, of the same kinds of useful information which have secured for the Pictorial Bible the high consideration with which it has been favoured.'[1]

In this edition, there was prefixed to each book a list of commentators upon it, and the editor regarded this as a ' new feature.'   Certainly it was; but he adds, ' A complete list is scarcely possible.'   His lists are fuller than any we have seen extending to all the various books of Scripture; but we have met with much fuller lists on separate books.   He has omitted, especially in the New Testament, several good expositors, both on the Gospels and Epistles.   Some that he has put in his lists are mere curiosities; but it was impossible for him to assign their several value to books which he had never seen, and their respective merits to authors whom he had never consulted. There is this benefit, however, that ' even the thoughtful general reader may find some matter for suggestive meditation in these lists.   They will enable him to see what are the books which have been chiefly attractive for separate exposition; he will perceive how much more attention has, until of late years, been given to the separate consideration of particular sacred books abroad, than in this country; and he may trace the periods in which this department of biblical literature was most cultivated.'[2]

[1] Journal of Sacred Literature, vol. iv., 1849, pp. 162-165.

[2] The stereotype plates of this last and improved edition belong now to the Messrs Chambers of Edinburgh, who have issued an elegant reprint, with useful and interesting appendices to the first three volumes, by a qualified contributor, referring to books of research not published in 1843.

It is stated in the preface to Dr Chalmers' Daily Scripture Readings, that what he called his ' Biblical Library,' consisted of the Pictorial Bible, a Concordance, Poole's Synopsis, Henry's Commentary, and Robinson's Researches in Palestine. In another place, Dr Chalmers says to his grandson :—' Perhaps when I am mouldering in my coffin, the eye of my dear Tommy may light upon this paper ; and it is possible that his recollection may accord with my fervent anticipations of the effect that his delight in the " Pictorial Bible " may have, in endearing still more to him the holy Word of God.'

The labour of the last three years had been so incessant, that Kitto had no time to fill much space in his diary. Twelve months elapse between some of the entries. But a few scattered notes of some interest occur :—

' *June* 20, 1837.—This day the king died, and this day I put the last hand to the second volume of the Pictorial Bible. *Mem.*—I am, it would seem, a dab at presentiments. At the beginning of the year, I had a presentiment that the king would die this year. Mentioned it at the time to Bell (Mrs Kitto), who recollects it. Would I had been a false prophet ! Who is not sorry that the king is dead ? I am sure I am.

' *Same day.*—Very anxious about baby—indeed miserable. A lump on her head. Doctor says she has no bone on the left side of her head, and showed Bell, in the skull of a dead child, the very bone which the living one wanted. A case of great ultimate danger, probably fatal. She has good health now ; and it is awful to see the dear little thing crawling about, laughing, and affecting to address me on her fingers, and to know that the sentence of death is upon her. I have not often—never—been more distressed ; for I do love the dear little article most entirely.

'*June* 21.—Sent her to Sir Astley Cooper. After a very slight examination, he said that the bump contained extravasated blood, probably arising from a fall; doubtless, the fearful fall she received about two or three months back; nothing could be done but rub it with vinegar. No danger whatever. When told about the *bone*, he said "Pho! Then you may tell the medical man, from me, whoever he is, that he is mistaken." Now, blessed be Sir Astley Cooper! I receive the dear little creature as one given me back from the grave. May she live a thousand years! Bless her little eyes!'

The humour which the next excerpt contains was native to him, as the reader must have frequently perceived in the course of the narrative:—

'*June* 30.—Was much amused by the piscatory propensities of the juvenile cockneys about the New River, which are well worth an extended notice; *e.g.*, one boy, with a basket, rod, line of black worsted, and bent pin, proceeding, with great importance, river-ward, between two other boys, proud of being parties in the affair, and dying with envy at the luck of their companion, and the dignity· to which he had attained. Some respectable-looking boobies, approaching manhood, groping the poor river with very complete and costly apparatus. Others of all sorts, returning fishless home, their blank looks admirably contrasted with the animation and glad expectation of those proceeding river-ward. Coming home by the green, met with a capital practical satire on this—at the butcher's, a boy about four, infected with the piscatory mania, was fishing out of the window into the road with one of his father's flesh-hooks.'

Mr Groves paid a visit to England, on his return from India, in 1835; and though Kitto and he had parted in the manner already described, yet they rejoiced to see one another in their native land. Kitto tells Mr Woollcombe (April 12), 'Your letter conveyed to me the first impression that Mr Groves was in England. I heard nothing further of him until, on returning from Mr Knight's to dinner, about a month since, I found he had called in my absence, and left word that he was about to start for the Continent, but should be in Chancery Lane till four o'clock (it was then three), if I could call upon him there. I did so, and had the greatest satisfaction in seeing him once more.' Two months afterwards, June 10th, he informs Mr Lampen—

'I have had the pleasure of seeing Mr Groves several times since his return to this country, and I was gratified to learn that he had an opportunity of seeing you at Plymouth. I confess to you that there are many of his views in which I do not concur nearly so much as I seemed to myself to do, while I was under that strong personal influence, which I think he exerts over those who are in near connection with him, through the warmth and energy which, more than any man I ever knew, he throws into his opinions. Whether the difference between *now* and *then*, in my mode of considering the subjects to which my attention, while with him, was so forcibly drawn, results from a more dispassionate and uninfluenced view of the same subjects, or merely from the greater ascendancy of worldly influences in my mind, I cannot venture to determine. I fear Mr Groves might be disposed to consider the latter the most probable account; while *you*, perhaps, might be willing to allow the former cause as sufficient to produce the effect.'

CHAPTER X.

AFTER the Pictorial Bible was completed, Kitto and his family paid a friendly visit to Plymouth, and were received in a manner which must have been highly gratifying to him. How different his condition now from that in which he had visited his birth-place on his arrival from Malta! Then appearances, to say the least of it, were against him; now realities were for him. He had achieved celebrity; and every friend who had ever given him a kind word might greet him as a man of note, and claim an interest in his success. Many must have reversed their previous opinion, and perhaps affirmed that, after all, they had uniformly believed, and had indeed so predicted, that John Kitto would make a figure. Some of humbler rank might remember the deaf and ragged boy, who had devoured so many books; or the poor and pitied youth, who had drudged so contentedly in the workhouse. We wonder whether Mr Bowden, whose tyranny had brought the smart youngster into notice, lived to see or hear of the editor of the Pictorial Bible.

Kitto tells one friend that he often 'mused on his inner history,' but his outer life also presented many topics of reflection. As, therefore, he walked through Plymouth, and visited Seven Stars Lane, the place of his birth, or surveyed the grim walls of the hospital, or shook hands with some one whose friendly countenance he might not recognise, he must have wondered at the changes in his history; his memory must have suddenly leapt back to days gone by, and brought them into immediate contrast with present scenes and enjoyments. Once it was night— poverty, rags, hunger, toil, and loneliness without a home: now the day had dawned—competence, study, fame, and usefulness, with a smiling and a growing household. He was designedly taking his own picture when he grouped and arranged the opposite elements of such an experience as the following :—

' Afflictions and trials are often allowed to accumulate, one after another, without rest or pause for a certain time, until a point of such accumulated wretchedness is reached, that it seems as if the last point to which even human endurance can stretch—the utmost pitch to which even heavenly sustainments can uphold this earthly es- sence, has been attained, and that it needs but one atom more added to the agglomerated burden of these troubles to break the spirit on which it has been piled up. Then, at what seems to us the last moment, He who knoweth our frame, and remembereth that we are dust—He who will never suffer us to be tempted beyond what we are able to bear—appears as a deliverer. With His strong hand He lifts the burden from the shoulder, and casts it afar off; tenderly does He anoint and bind up the deep sores it has worn in the flesh, and pour in the oil and the wine ; and graciously does He lead us forth into the fresh and green pastures, where we may lie down at ease under the warm sunshine of His countenance, till all the frightful past becomes as a half-remembered dream—a tale that is told.' [1]

After a sojourn of three weeks in Plymouth, Kitto returned to his daily toils. 'Uncle Oliver,'[1] on which he
had been long working, was published during the year.
The devotion of so much of his time to the Pictorial Bible
had greatly retarded its completion. The book is a description of Persian scenery, with an account of plants,
animals, villages, houses, habits, markets, domestic customs,
and religion. Uncle Oliver is an old gentleman who has
travelled in Persia, and who doles out his information
night after night to two nephews and a niece, while Mr
Dillon, tutor to the two boys, vouchsafes occasional explanations. Uncle Oliver has, of course, almost all the
talk to himself, the boys and girl putting in a word only at
intervals ; but his descriptions are simple, and, being those
of an eye-witness, they are interesting and well adapted
to the young. The style is professedly in 'the manner of
Peter Parley.' It does not seem to have excited much
sensation on its appearance, nor did its author seemingly
care much about it.

Kitto's next great work, after the Pictorial Bible, was
the 'Pictorial History of Palestine and the Holy Land, including a complete history of the Jews.' Nine months
were spent in laborious preparation—'collecting books,
examining authorities, and digesting materials.' The want
of books was still felt by him, for many of those he coveted
were of an exorbitant price. He had, however, been
fortunate in gaining some valuable tomes, many of which
had once been in Mr Heber's collection, 'containing Travels
and Descriptions of Palestine,' extending from the fifteenth
century to the present time. But he experienced great
difficulty in getting authentic information as to the natural

---

[1] Uncle Oliver's Travels in Persia, giving a complete picture of Eastern manners,
customs, arts, sciences, and history, adapted to the capacity of youth, in the manner of Peter Parley. Illustrated with twenty-four woodcuts. 2 Vols. 18mo.

history of the country. 'The work,' he says to Lieuten-
ant-Colonel Smith, 'is, therefore, in this part, one of original
research sufficiently laborious and difficult.' The first
volume, with a considerable portion of the second, contains
the national history of the Jews, commencing with the
patriarchs, descending through the times of the Old Testament, filling up the interval between the Restoration and
the birth of Christ, and concluding with the capture of
Jerusalem and the ultimate dispersion. The physical
history occupies by no means so large a space, and was,
perhaps, curtailed, to keep the work within certain fixed
dimensions. He opens this section with a brief sketch of
various writers on the subject—beginning with that store-
house, the Hierozoicon of Bochart; glancing at the Ar-
boretum Biblicum of Ursinus, and the Hierophyticon of
Hiller; eulogising, as it deserves, the Hierobotanicon of
Olaus Celsius, the patron of Linnæus,—not forgetting, at
the same time, Paxton, Harris, Calmet, and Taylor; and
describing some strange and valueless peculiarities in the
engravings which so profusely embellish the Physica Sacra
of the Swiss physician Scheuchzer. The very full list of
travellers is arranged, to some extent, according to the
countries to which they belonged—those being specially
referred to who have added to our stock of information on
the natural history of the Holy Land. He next discusses,
under separate heads, mountains, geology, valleys, lakes,
and rivers, history of the months, and zoology,—the animals
being arranged according to the order of Cuvier's Règne
Animal.

The Pictorial History of Palestine and the Holy Land
never reached the popularity of the Pictorial Bible, and
probably has never been fully appreciated. It seemed to
be supposed that the mass of its information had already
been anticipated in its predecessor. The supposition is

so far correct in reference to the Bible history, and that
has always formed the special object of interest.   Many of
the illustrations also are repeated from the previous work.
Nor do general readers care to find Sacred Narrative done
into other words—recomposed in another style, which, as it
mingles up illustration and paraphrase, and is broken by
explanatory references, wants the simplicity and terseness
of the inspired original.   The book, however, contains
much that is valuable, and, of course, treats of portions of
Jewish history which are not found in Scripture.   Nine
months of incessant and conscientious preparation for the
task could not be without some proportionate fruit.

The part which contains the physical history is deficient
in arrangement.   To describe all the hills and rivers col-
lectively and in separate sections may make up good dis-
sertations, but it fails to give the reader a full and correct
notion of geography—that is, of the features and character
of the country as they really present themselves.   It would
have been better to have constructed an ideal pilgrimage
through the land, bringing out scene after scene as they
actually occur.   The imaginary tour might have begun in
the peninsula of Sinai and advanced northward, or it might
have followed the poet's order, and commenced its survey
where

> 'Hoar Lebanon! majestic to the winds,
>   Chief of a hundred hills, his summit rears
>   Unshrouded ; thence by Jordan south,
>   Whate'er the desert's yellow arms embrace—
>   Rich Gilead, Idumea's palmy plain,
>   And Judah's olive hills ; thence on to those
>   Cliff-guarded eyries, desert bound, whose height
>   Mocked the proud eagles of rapacious Rome—
>   The famed Petraean citadels—till, last,
>   Rise the lone peaks, by Heaven's own glory crowned,
>   Sinai on Horeb piled.'

Such a method, while it would have imparted more variety and interest, would have also taken away from the work its detached and miscellaneous appearance.   One prefers to see Palestine as it is, rather than to have it dislocated into fragments : one of these built up of all its mountains, and another overflowing with all its waters.   The same objection partly applies to the history of the months, arranged after Buhle and Walch.   That portion is replete with useful facts, but of such a kind, that the reader would never think of consulting the section for them.   The author pleads for his arrangement, that by it the largest information might be thrown into the smallest space.   True. The argument is good for those who may read through the 'Economical Calendar,' as Charles Taylor calls his translation of Buhle ; but it is forgotten that many a one buys such a book for reference, and that its value is in proportion to the facility with which he finds at once what he wants.   Who, without some previous knowledge, would search for almonds under January, or hennah under May— sycamores under August, or agricultural operations under October ?   Had Kitto, with his subsequent experience, handled the work for a second edition, he would have turned out almost a new production.   Having been paid for this work ' according to the highest scale of literary remuneration,' and having laboured on it so long and diligently, he was greatly disappointed at its slow sale, and. thus explains himself to Mr Knight—May 28, 1840 :—

'   .   .   .   I was deeply disappointed to learn that the success of the Pictorial Palestine is so much below your expectations.   I feel assured in my mind that it deserves to succeed, and will still hope that it may afford an adequate remuneration to you, when it comes to be sold in a completed form.   If I have misgivings, they arise from the fact, that the work will not be completed to the extent which was promised. . . . It is quite true that the Scriptural narrative was too diffuse at the beginning, arising partly from the difficulty of calculation, and partly from my wish to bring out characteristic customs and ideas. . . . I am, on the whole, well satisfied that, as it will stand, the Pictorial Palestine will do no discredit to the editor of the Pictorial Bible. It is, in fact, a much superior work, though, as it happens, it would seem to be less adapted to attract attention " in the market of literature." I know nothing that could mortify me more than to hear you say that the Physical History would not sell by itself. It is a pocket question to me ; for most of the time spent by me in preparation, before the work went to press, was occupied in forming collections for this very portion. With the other portion, by which I gain as much, and which will be more profitable to you, I could have gone to press at once, and furnished a part month by month. It seems possible to make books *too good* for the great world ; and if so, you can neither afford to publish nor I to write good things that will not sell.'

Thus will authors complacently misjudge the comparative merits of their productions. Yet he admits that Professor Robinson of New York, then in London, had pointed out several inaccuracies in the plates of some of the most beautiful of the landscapes ; and it is plain, from a tedious correspondence, that there was considerable misunderstanding between publisher and author about the size and proportions of the work. He had also expressed distrust of Professor Robinson's view as to the scene of the passage through the Red Sea,[1] stating, in his usual tone of unqualified firmness, that the traveller could scarcely be unbiassed in his judgment, and would see nothing to disturb his ' foregone conclusions,' as he had previously

[1] Pictorial History of Palestine, vol. L, p. 189.

published the same opinion in an American periodical. Professor Robinson then wrote him, calmly denying the imputation,[1] and Kitto replied[2] in a long letter, conveying his full appreciation of the traveller's successes, and his hearty thanks for the unparalleled service he had rendered to biblical geography. Many points, too, on which Kitto gives a decided judgment, such as the identification of Sinai, are yet unsettled—points on which Lepsius, Ritter, Robinson, Stanley, Stewart, and others well qualified to judge, are by no means agreed, and further research is still indispensable to a just conclusion.

The question may now be naturally asked, how did Kitto find leisure to get through those multifarious employments—how did he so divide and occupy his hours as to bring so much labour within the limits of human capability? His plans necessitated no ordinary industry, and twelve hours were not sufficient for his day. From early life he had taught himself to be a miser in the use of every moment, and he was so disciplined as to content himself with a very small amount of sleep. His quiet and retiring habits, formed before his marriage, were not altered by it. He would still sit at breakfast with a book in his hand, as if he had forgotten that he had ceased to be a bachelor. At tea, however, he made it a point to offer compensation for the morning's monopoly, by reading aloud to his wife, but the deep and unvarying bass of his guttural tones, prolonged for hours, often set 'his sole auditor' asleep. So innocent was he in his own opinion, that, when gently spoken to as to his persistence in the practice, he could not at first understand what possible cause of complaint he had given. He had imagined that what had so interested himself as to induce him to try his vocal organs

---

[1] Letter to Mr Kitto—Regent Square, London, October 12, 1840.
[2] October 19, 1840.

upon it, could not fail to interest his wife. But the practice, he admits, 'brought to light new and previously
unknown talents in him.' 'Were I again in Persia,' he
merrily exclaims, 'it would be in my power to realise a
handsome income by the exercise of a gift, which is only
there well appreciated. It throws into the shade all the
boasted wonders of the mesmeric trance, to behold the
gradual subsidence of my victim under the sleep-com-
pelling influences of my voice, in spite of all her super-
human struggles to avert the inevitable doom!'[1] In many
ways did Mrs Kitto feel at first those strange peculiarities
which his habits and labours had created or fostered; for
while he coveted the seclusion of a hermit for his work,
he had the intense relish of a husband for domestic and
social enjoyment.   Indeed, his wife had to undergo a
willing process of assimilation, and soon became not only
so reconciled to his modes of life, but so much at one with
him, in admiration of his abilities, and in sympathy with
all his pursuits, as to be able herself to put on proud record that 'during the twenty-one years of our married
life, I may say, in perfect truth, that ten hours have not
been spent separate from him in visiting.' His toil was
incessant, and many a day his only walk was from his
study to his parlour, and from his parlour to his study.
To overtake his many tasks, he began to sit up during
night, but soon abandoned such a dangerous method, for
nature would assert its claims, and he insensibly dropped
asleep before midnight among his books and papers.
Suddenly starting from slumber, he would resume his pen,
and by the third watch of the morning would be found
eager and busy at his allotted duty.   His lamp, however,
did not always shade its flame, when he nodded; and more
than once there was the risk of a conflagration.   Then

[1] Lost Senses—Deafness, p 28.

he betook himself to a far better and healthier plan, that of early rising—the alarum-clock employed for the purpose first rousing his partner, who could hear it, and she touching him. A bell, which could be rung by the watchman, was next substituted for the alarum; but still he must have depended on the faithful ears of another, and his wife was often obliged, sorely against her will, to wake him from a slumber which his exhausted frame so much required. Getting up at the first summons, usually at four, he at one period repaired directly to his study, prepared himself a cup of tea by means of a spirit-lamp, and then sat down and laboured till the hour of breakfast. After breakfast a few turns were occasionally taken in his garden, and having dressed, he went to his workroom, and remained till he was called to dinner at one. The writing of letters, the correcting of proofs, and other miscellaneous duties, occupied him till tea at five; then he returned to his desk, writing till toward ten, and reading till eleven. This was a work-day of sixteen hours, and of incessant application. All the socialities of out-door life were completely set aside. His wife was enlisted in his service, and so well did she drill herself, that, so far from being a cypher, as she at first thought, he used jocularly to call her his ' hodman.' She never allowed him to be checked or interrupted in his labours by any domestic hinderances; so that no visitor ever found him, like Melancthon, Hooker, and Thomas Scott, holding a book in one hand, and rocking the cradle with the other. So essential did she become to him, that he could never bear her absence from home. Her activity blended so admirably with his sedentary habits, that he delighted in his own humorous image, ' What with my centripetal and her centrifugal force, we move in a very harmonious orbit.'

When he was employed in Mr Knight's office, he commonly went and came with book in hand, for the noise around could cause him no distraction. Then and afterwards he ran no little risk in the streets of London. His load of books in his pockets had nearly drowned him in the Tigris; and the volume on which he poured, amid the crowded thoroughfares of the metropolis, frequently brought him into jeopardy of life and limb. And even when he had no book to fill his eye and occupy his attention, he sometimes saw the people staring as if at some novelty, and could not divine what or who it was, till a whip laid smartly across his shoulders, told him that himself in imminent peril had been the unconscious object of curiosity and alarm. At other times, the excited gestures of a policeman warned him to look behind, just as the hot breath of a horse blew into his face, and its uplifted hoof was about to tread him to the ground. But he was mercifully preserved; and the coarse epithets of cab-drivers and waggoners, and the more sympathising badinage of orange-women, as the one cursed, or the other commiserated his stupidity, were all happily lost upon him.

While his daily toils left him little leisure, he yet delighted to relax for a brief period with his children. He took them, as soon as they were able, to assist him in his gardening operations, and they were delighted at the symbols of approbation, whenever they received them. Rejoicing in their little joys, he partook of their gambols, and each, on its birth-day, was sure to receive an appropriate present. But while they enjoyed themselves to the utmost in their pastimes, and could range their home without restraint, to one room they were debarred access. The library was a sacred place; and if they did cross the awful threshold, they were solemnly interdicted from touching anything in it. They must have often looked on its litter with curious wonder—its piles of letters and bundles of papers—books shut and open huddled together on the table, and volumes as large as themselves strewed in heaps on the floor. Shireen was at length allowed the high and envied privilege of occasionally touching some of the papers, and arranging a few of the books. But she was bound in her procedure by a strict and formal stipulation, to all the articles of which she promised a rigid adherence. The formidable document ran as follows :—

'Plan, Programme, Protocol, Synopsis, and Conspectus, for clearing Dr Kitto's Table.

'1. Make one pile of religious books. 2. Another of books not religious. 3. Another of letters. 4. Another of written papers other than letters. 5. Another of printed papers. 6. Put these piles upon the floor. 7. The table being now clear, dust, scrub, rub, and scour the table till you sweat ; and when you have sweated half a gallon, give over, and put the piles upon the table, leaving to Dr K. the final distribution.—Signed, sealed, and delivered, this 28th day of May, in the year of our Lord 1852.

'Witness, HOLOFERNES PIPS. 🕸 JOHN KITTO.'

His home, in short, with all its monotonous and incessant toil, was to him a source of perpetual delight. His previous life had prepared him to relish it. He who had so often been a guest under others' roofs, and so long 'a stranger in a strange land,' felt his own hearth and household to be an unspeakable pleasure. We have been with him in the height of his fame, and when his family were round him. How heartily he was one with them! He was a happy and playful father, and his young ones were full of innocent freedom in his presence, each anxious to say a word to him—that is, to present it in visible form to the paternal eye—even the infant imitating in its own way, and with 'infinite seriousness,' the finger-talk going on so busily round about it, and crowing in ecstasy at its

success in obtaining a nod or a smile. 'It was quite a
treat,' says one of his visitors,[1] ' to see him out of his study,
especially at family devotion, conducted with so much
solemnity by your dear husband, surrounded by his little
family. The dear little one, too, brought in for its morning kiss by his aged mother, and then herself receiving the
same token of affection. I think I have never seen so
much love and reverence manifested by children for a
father—indeed, all was love and harmony; and that *look*
of affection (over his glasses) so often bestowed on them,
impressed my mind more deeply than words could have
done, that he tenderly loved them.' Again and again, had
he intimated, in his journals and letters, his desire to provide for his mother, who had seen so much of the shady
side of life; and now, in the evening of her days, she was
an honoured inmate of his dwelling; and so much was she
bound up in him and his family, that when his failing health
obliged him to go to Germany and leave her behind, she
was so grieved and stunned by the separation, that she
seldom spoke afterward, but sunk into a melancholy which
continued till her death at the end of last year.[2]

His children, all of whom had acute ears, and tongues
of rattling eloquence, were each of them, as they grew up,
at a loss for a time to understand their father's infirmity.
They could not comprehend why a word or a call should
not at once tell upon him as upon their mother. They
were unable to divine why, at their cry of ' Papa,' he did
not lift his head from a book, or lay down his pen for a
moment; while the cry of ' Mamma' brought her at once to
their side, no matter in what business she might happen to
be engaged. From mere imitation, they began the finger-
talk before they could speak, and resorted to it when other

---

[1] Mrs Hullock, in a letter to Mrs Kitto—Plainfield, Massachusetts, Nov. 5, 1855.
[2] 1856.

infantine signals failed. ' If the little creatures are so placed as to be unable to engage my attention by touching me, they call to me, and on finding that also unavailing, blow to me, and if that also fails, stamp upon the floor ; and when they have, by one or other of these methods, attracted my eyes, begin their pretty talk upon the fingers. One of the least patient of them used to stamp and cry herself into a vast rage in the vain effort to engage my attention. It is very singular that these practices should have been taken up by all of them in succession, like natural instincts, without having learned them from one another.'[1]

His modes of recreation were, at this period, like himself, somewhat peculiar. It was not exercise he coveted, but rather a ride in an omnibus, and a walk home afterwards. The flowers in Covent Garden in summer, and the glory of the shops in winter, greatly delighted him. But scarcely more than once a week could he afford such an indulgence. ' If I failed,' such is his own record, ' to secure this recreation, from press of editorial or other literary business, during the early portion of the week, I seldom missed it on Saturday night. This was because, as an observer of character, I took much interest in seeing the working people abroad with their wives, laying out the money which their week's labour had produced ; and in witnessing the activity which this circumstance gave to many streets, and inspecting the commodities there exposed for sale in the open air. I felt that I could enter with interest into the feelings of the various parties pausing, hesitating, or purchasing, at the various shops and stalls, materials for the hiss of universal fry, which on Saturday night ascends from fifty thousand hearths, or for the scarcely more enjoyed bake of the Sunday dinner. It was something to be able to enter into these matters, and to follow a hundred of

[1] Lost Senses—Deafness, p. 98.

these parties home, to assist in blowing the fire, to turn out
before the eyes of the bigger children the treasures of the
basket, to pacify the young ones, now all alive in bed, with
an apple or other nicety, to watch the spit and sputter
and hubbub of the frying-pan, and at length to share its
steaming contents with all. What a multitudinous host of
beggars are then abroad, whom one sees not at any other
time! Their faith in their own class—always willing, but
then only able to assist them—their assurance of the warm
sympathies of those who have dominion over Saturday
night, more than in the cold charities, or colder uncharities,
of gentlefolks who have rule over the rest of the week, are
the influences which that night may draw forth into the
streets, from their wretched nooks, hundreds of miserable
creatures, who, but for the gleams of sympathy and kindness which, on that one evening, shine upon their hearts,
would perhaps cast themselves down in helpless despair to
curse God and die. Then, also, the music is all abroad.
Barrel-organs we have at all times; but on Saturday nights
bands of fine instruments are about in all directions, as well
as songsters and solitary fiddlers. This is not without
enjoyment to me. I like to stand a few paces aloof from
a party of Saturday night people gathered round the
musicians. I watch the impression it makes upon them.
I sympathize in their attention, and by identifying myself
with them, derive real enjoyment from the music through
them, and drop my dole into the plate with as much cheer-
fulness as if the whole concourse of sweet sounds had rushed
into my own ears.'[1]

She who had the best experience of his social qualities
has thus described them:—

'I desire to give some idea of my dear husband's habits
with friends, but I find the task somewhat difficult. No

[1] Lost Senses—Deafness, p. 153.

one who ever saw that noble brow, and that eye lighted up with intelligence, could doubt his social powers. That bright thoughts were ever passing within, might be inferred from the glowing expression of his features, even when unuttered by the lips. In ordinary company he was far from comfortable, and could only take refuge in a book. Most of his friends, though they might enjoy hearing him talk—that is, the few who could understand him, had themselves so little to say, or were so discouraged by the slow process of finger-talk, and the still more cumbrous resource of pen and paper, that they seldom or never made the effort to speak. Thus he was generally left to himself reading, or while watching an opportunity to speak, perhaps incurring the mortification of finding that he had interrupted some one. When he met with literary characters, or men of real information, he kept them continually writing, often catching, with his quick eye, the meaning of their answers before they were fully written. He had one friend who was capable of keeping him in a state of continued excitement. Though I could execute the finger-talk with great rapidity, I could never read it; so that I could only guess at what had been said by other persons from the tenor of my husband's remarks. I was always aware when the company was irksome to him. Husbands are not clever at hiding their feelings from their wives; and I could easily discern his, which often made me quite as miserable as himself. I felt that he ought not to be made to feel his infirmity, which was always the case when he was out of his library. We therefore mutually agreed, that the reception of friends was not suited to our condition, and learned to live alone. But there was one dear family of children, whose growing intelligence he had watched from their infancy, on his visits to their parents. Them he delighted to visit, or to be visited by. They had all been

drawn to him in love during their childhood, and had
learned to talk on their fingers, and could as freely ask
and reply to questions as any of his own family. He
always kept these young people in full talk, and, while in
his company, there was no reprieve for their poor fingers.
Sometimes he insisted on their playing on the piano the
Battle of Prague, and he sat with his fingers placed on
the sounding-board, seeming to derive pleasure from the
vibrations he felt. His entire helplessness in all matters
extraneous to his library, rendered him quite dependent on
me; whilst I felt it a privilege thus to guard and keep in
quiet one whose time was devoted to such noble ends.
But the cares of a large family quite destroyed, of late
years, the close union of the early period, and I may say,
quite separated us, except at meal-times; for it rendered
such exactions of labour necessary on his part that he
had no spare time—but of this he never complained. He
would say, " My work is my pleasure also, and, if it
please God to give me strength, I have only to work a
little harder." '

Of the ' Christian Traveller,' a periodical publication
which Kitto had thought of for fifteen years, and which
was now commenced, he formed the highest expectations
—' a work devoted to a cause for which the public gives
half a million a year out of its pocket,' must, he argued,
' be received with favour.'   The object of the papers was
to give sketches of the missionary enterprise in various
parts of the world. He was anxious, for several reasons,
to do all the work himself, as he rightly thought that the
editing of what he did not himself compose, would take
up very much of his valuable time, and if he should ask
for contributions, he shuddered to ' think of the showers
of twaddle by which he should be inundated.' He felt
that he was competent to the task, for he could now do

before breakfast what he should once have considered a
good day's work; and one personal reason for the undertaking is honestly stated by himself. It was not simply
that he wished to get all the credit, but this—' I have to
build up the provisions for my family from the foundations,
and under any possible contingency, there is not one on
earth from whom those that God has given to me can expect
a crust of other bread than such as I may be enabled to
provide for them.'

Only three parts of the periodical were published, when
it was stopped by the pecuniary embarrassment of Mr
Knight's publishing house. Kitto, so suddenly severed
from remunerating labour, was soon reduced to straits.
He had been able to earn only a little more than daily
bread by hard exertion; and when occupation could not
be found, difficulties at once enveloped him, and so grew
upon him, that he was obliged to sell his house at a
considerable loss, leave London, and remove to Woking
in Surrey.[1] Fits of his early melancholy sometimes recurred; and no wonder—a wife and four children were
now dependent on him.

His own explanation is, 'In 1841, the only publishing
house with which, up to that time, I had been connected,
fell into difficulties, and was obliged to bring to an abrupt
close an engagement with me, which had promised a fair
income for some years. I thus became out of employment
at a time when the general difficulties of the trade for a
long time indisposed booksellers to enter upon new undertakings. At first I lived upon the little I had saved; then
upon the sale of my books, helped out by a little credit for
the necessaries of life to a large family.' At a later period,

---

[1] A few pages of what he calls Village Memoranda have been preserved, but
they contain nothing of note. 'I begin to perceive,' he says, 'how people in the
country can appear as grandees on an income which would barely enable them to
support the appearance of respectability in London.'

he states more fully to Mr Groves, that between the ending of one task and beginning of another, he had no employment for twelve months, and that he had made an arrangement to pay what he owed by instalments in three years. ' This,' he adds, in 1848, ' has been done to the uttermost farthing.'

But during such domestic eclipses, he could conceal his own discomfort, and charm away that of others with a little touch of gaiety. On one occasion, when the more solid portion of the family dinner depended on the sale of some books, which necessity had compelled him to part with, and when she who had gone on the melancholy errand returned without having converted the volumes into money, he surveyed first his children's faces of anxiety and disappointment, and then, moving towards the window, exclaimed, ' Well, we must *look* at the butcher's shop opposite to get the right relish for our bread.'

Let it then be understood, that Kitto's straits arose, not from inadequate compensation, but from want of employment. Had he enjoyed constant work, he would have lived in comfort. His books were not of a nature to bring him or his publishers very large profits, yet they had an excellent circulation. They could not, like the works of Dickens, realise a magnificent revenue, but they would have insured him a sufficient income. His great helplessness lay in the precariousness of his means. His torment was not a surplus, but a want of work. ' Leave to toil ' was his prayer, for he knew that abundant fruit would follow. ' There are ten thousand things in the world that I fear more than work,' he says ; and he might have added, ' What I dread above all things is the want of work.' He states to his friend, Mr Tracy,[1] ' The position which I have attained is not without its anxieties. I see, for instance, a large

[1] Woking, Jan. 20, 1847.

family growing around me, and entirely dependent upon the labours of my pen, which, *in the line I have chosen*, are much more productive of honours than emoluments.' Lest a want of economy, or some other folly, should be laid to his charge, he explains, a month afterwards, to the same friend—'I heard, last week, that there is a general impression in the city of my being a very rich man. I accept this as an acknowledgment, that one whose works have been so well received by the public *ought* to be so. So I might have been, probably, if I had commenced my career with any capital to enable me to retain the copyright of my own works.' This statement speaks for itself. He could never command property in his books, but was obliged to compose them for daily support, so that, when the work was finished, the salary ceased. He never was able to finish a work, and then sell it. He simply presented his plan, made his bargain, and was paid in proportion as the work advanced. But the possession of literary property was still his hope, though he never could manage to secure it. Accordingly, two years afterwards, in offering to Mr Oliphant the Daily Bible Illustrations, he declares, 'It was my wish to undertake this intended set of books on my own account, but circumstances have arisen to render it more expedient to pursue, at least for a time, the plan upon which all my works have hitherto been produced, viz., *by making arrangements for them, before I get to work seriously upon them.*' But we have been anticipating.

Previously to his removal from London to a rural retreat, his anxious mind had been devising many forms of literary industry. Not a few prospectuses were penned by him, and sent abroad in various directions. He proposed to the Religious Tract Society to write for them either a Biblical Cyclopædia or a Life of Christ, entering at length into an explanation of his views; but the Society

do not seem to have entertained the offer. The project
of a new Cyclopædia of Biblical Literature, sent to Messrs
Black of Edinburgh, engaged their attention ; and they
entered into a correspondence with him, the issue of which
was the publication, in the first place, of a 'History of
Palestine, from the Patriarchal Age to the Present Time,'
12mo, pp. 378, Edinburgh 1843. This was a brief school
history ; and while it put a little into the author's pocket,
it added nothing to his fame. Some months elapsed before the Cyclopædia could appear—months in which his
household suffered the pinch and pressure of want. The
'Thoughts among Flowers'[1] was published in 1843, by
the Religious Tract Society. The little volume shows
the author's love of flowers, and how he could moralise
among them, and indicates what snatches of poetry lay in
the stores of his memory. The reflections are occasionally
far-fetched, and are not the natural scent of the blossoms,
but rather a borrowed fragrance. Between 1841 and
1843, he prepared for Mr Fisher the letter-press of the
'Gallery of Scripture Engravings,' in three volumes quarto.
The letter-press is simply to explain the engravings, and,
except as a show-book, the volumes are of no great utility.
In 1845 he prepared for Mr Knight 'The Pictorial Sunday
Book, with 1300 engravings, and an appendix on the
Geography of the Holy Land.'[2] This volume was in
folio, and a portion of it was published separately, under
the title of the 'Pictorial History of our Saviour.' 'The
publication,' it is stated in the preface, 'now submitted to
Christian families, is intended to present, at the very
cheapest rate, a series of engravings illustrative of the
Bible history, the prophecies, the psalms, the life of our
Saviour, and the Acts of the Apostles, exhibiting the
scenes of the great events recorded in Scripture, the

32mo, pp. 156.					[2] Charles Knight and Co., 1845.

customs of the Jews, the natural history of the Holy Land, and the antiquities which throw a light upon the Sacred Writings.   With these are united some of the more striking and impressive compositions of the great painters and original designs.   These pictorial illustrations are connected with a course of Sunday reading, which, avoiding all matters of controversy, endeavours to present, in the. most instructive and engaging form, a body of Scriptural narrative and explanation.'   There is nothing new in the volume—it is but a classified re-exhibition of plates and wood-cuts employed in previous publications of various kinds, both secular and biblical, with pages of letter-press between.   The physical geography annexed is a reprint, with a few changes, of the similar portion of the Pictorial History of Palestine.   Yet, apart from its immediate value in relation to Scripture, and that value is not great, the volume contains such a number and variety of engravings, both from nature, the Egyptian monuments, and the masters of all schools and countries, that it is an amusing and informing production, and was certainly of marvellous cheapness at its first appearance.

In the meantime the 'Cyclopædia of Biblical Literature,' published by the Messrs Black of Edinburgh, had been commenced.   The idea was his own, and he had much correspondence about the details of the plan.   In the multitude of opinions proposed to him, he held in the main to his own original view, but was obliged to depart from his first resolution to do the whole work himself.   He knew what had been achieved in this department, and what remained to be done.   Nor was he confined to British assistance in the enterprise—he laid his hands also on several German contributors.   The book, as it proceeded, grew to a size not originally contemplated,—a circumstance not unusual with its editor.   But the allotment of articles

Y

to respective writers was a responsible task, and it needed
some tact to get the contributions in time from his numerous assistants. Swarms of suggestions poured in upon
him as the publication went on, and he sometimes felt that
the multitude of counsellors endangered safety. Objections, too, were started, and there was ground for some of
them. He replies, in his own portion of the preface, 'that
he felt that he could not find forty independent thinkers,
among whom there should be no visible diversities of sentiment;' observes that ' it did not become him to dictate to
them the views they were to take of the subjects intrusted
to them;' and confesses that some of them exhibit opinions
in which he is not able to concur, though he regards them
as not less competent than himself to arrive at just conclusions. He claims, however, and that justly, that the book
be judged not by particular articles, but by its general
character; and he adds, that his 'physical privation,'
placing him in complete isolation from many external influences, ' had enabled him to realise more extensive co-
operation in this undertaking, than under any pastoral or
official connection with any religious denomination he could
expect to have obtained.' ' The work owes its origin to
the editor's conviction of the existence of a great body of
untouched materials applicable to such a purpose, which
the activity of modern research and the labours of modern
criticism have accumulated, and which lay invitingly ready
for the use of those who might know how to avail themselves of such resources.' The book was at once felt to
meet a want of the age. Nothing of a like nature existed
in the English language. Previous dictionaries were defective both in scholarship and materials. Calmet had
been done into English, and overlaid with learned fancies;
while Winer could not bear translation at all. Other works
of less pretension were also in circulation. But Dr Kitto

had concluded an enterprise which embraced the ripest scholarship, and took in the most recent researches. The Cyclopædia, therefore, rose at once to a lofty position, and, as we have elsewhere said, ' can be excelled only by itself in a new and corrected edition.' It is beyond our present business to offer any criticism on the unequal merits of the various articles, written by so many contributors. Only, we may say, that Dr Kitto did not appear to full advantage as an editor. Though his own religious views were fixed, yet his catholicity of temper unfitted him for doing the harder work, and pronouncing the sterner decisions of the editorial chair. He received a thousand pounds as editor, and more than double that sum was expended on contributions and illustrations. We regret that he was not spared to superintend a second edition, for he was well aware that a second edition would require to be, in many respects, a new book.

When the great work was at length brought nigh to its termination, and its toils and dangers were past, we find its indefatigable editor relaxing, and recording thus,—

' *July* 13, 1845.—Put the last hand to the regular work of the B. C. ; that is, did the last article in Z that was upon my list. A day to be remembered on many accounts besides.

' *July* 14.—Cleared my table of the books that have lain on it for three years—placed them on the shelves, not long to slumber there perhaps.'

On the title-page of the Biblical Cyclopædia, when published in two volumes, the editor's name stands no longer in naked simplicity. It is now John Kitto, D.D., F.S.A. —a very different addition from that which he assumed in his early dream of authorship. It was then ' John Kitto, shoemaker, pauper, etc.,' the inmate of a workhouse ; but now, it is John Kitto, Doctor of Divinity, Fellow of the Society of Antiquaries—a double elevation

to which he had never aspired in his wildest reveries.
To be a missionary, sometimes appeared to him a probable occurrence—to be a clergyman, was scarce within
the range of possibility; but now he had received a theological title, and was the first, and we suppose the only
English layman, who ever possessed such an honour. In
1844, the University of Giessen, through his friend Professor Credner, sent him the diploma of Doctor of Divinity.
And had he not earned it by his literary works?—the
works of a man who had passed through such a boyhood
of privation and suffering, and had spent such a youth of
desultory and unsatisfactory pursuits. Among Kitto's
papers there are preserved two documents, that stand out
in startling contrast: the one his indenture to Bowden,
the shoemaker, somewhat ragged and torn, with its many
' seals and signatures;' and the other his diploma from the
University of Giessen. They mark the two opposite poles
of his life. In 1845, Dr Kitto became a fellow of the
' Royal Society of Antiquaries, and this body honoured
themselves in thus honouring him. We have occasionally
seen the epithet ' reverend ' prefixed to his name. The
error arose, no doubt, from the idea that a theological
title implies a clerical status. But degrees are simply
academical, not ecclesiastical distinctions. In Germany,
as Dr Kitto explains, they are sometimes conferred on
scholars who are not ' in orders,' as very recently on the
Chevalier Bunsen; and in such a case, if one, who has
already obtained the title of Doctor in Divinity, ' desires
to undertake the pastoral office, he is ordained without
the examinations which all others must undergo.' ' Thus
Tholuck was Doctor in Divinity and Professor of Theology before his ordination to the ministry, which, conse-
quently, took place without the usual examinations.' [1]

! Daily Bible Illustrations, vol. viii., p. 121.

In 1845 Dr Kitto made two contributions to Mr Knight's Weekly Volume. Both are named the ' Lost Senses ;' the first part having the special title ' Deafness,' and the second ' Blindness.' The first is a charming little book—in fact, an autobiography—a revelation of his life and history, as they were modified or developed by his deafness. ' His condition,' he admits, ' is not new; but that it has never hitherto been described, may be owing to the fact, that a morning of life, subject to such crushing calamity, has seldom, if ever, been followed by a day of such self-culture.' He was a D.D. when he penned these words. In this brief volume he first traces the growth of his mind with great distinctness, and shows clearly under what awful disadvantages he laboured. The books in common circulation in his young days were far inferior to those now produced; but he had triumphed over such a drawback. After his deafness he became more and more loath to speak, till his friends, during his voyage to Malta, forced him ; and through life he used no superfluous terms —' avoiding all remarks about the weather, all expletives, adjuncts, complimentary phrases,' and even terms of endearment ; so much so, that one of his boys was startled when his father, for the first time, called him ' *dear.*' There is a chapter of great interest on ' percussions.' The loudest thunder-storm was perfectly inaudible to him, though once, a peal having shaken the house, he supposed it was a servant moving the table in an adjoining room. He could not hear the throb or music of a set of bells ; but when he was placed in contact with the tower in which they were ranged, he was conscious of a dull percussion overhead, as if blows had been hitting the wall above him. The great clock of St Paul's struck when he happened once to be examining it with a friend, and the sensation was that of heavy blows upon the fabric on which he stood, communicated to his feet, and diffused over his body. When a cannon was fired near him, he heard no sound, but felt as if a fist, covered with a boxing-glove, had knocked him on the head. The drawing of furniture, slapping of doors, or falling of books upon the floor, produced a vibration that often distressed him, though he could not determine precisely whence the disturbance proceeded. A knock at the street door he could not hear, but the shutting of it, affecting the entire edifice, was 'painfully distinct.' The lightest footfall upon the floor of his room would sometimes rouse him from sleep. He *felt* the sound of vehicles in Fleet Street only when they were on the same side of the pavement, and opposite to him, but this 'sense of sound' did not affect him in the house. When the points of his finger-nails rested on the board over which the wires of a piano are stretched, he could make out the higher notes, in such a stormy piece of music as the 'Battle of Prague.' In corroboration of what he has said in the 'Lost Senses,' we may add another of his subsequent experiences. He witnessed, from the apartments of the Society of Antiquaries, in Somerset House, the great procession of the Duke of Wellington's funeral. But he says, 'Not the shadow of a sound, or the faintest vibration, struck upon the paralysed organ from the great military bands that passed below, though a person, I have been in the habit of supposing as deaf as myself, told me he could not only distinguish the sound, but follow the notes with considerable distinctness.'[1]

Yet there were some compensations. He had developed within himself a keen sense of the beautiful, and a passionate love for it. He could not bear what was ugly. He loved to gaze on the moon 'walking in brightness;' and 'high mountains were a feeling.' 'The slaughtering of a tree

[1] Letter to Mr Oliphant, Nov. 20, 1852.

affects me more sensibly than that of an animal.' He was fond of colours, and, when a boy, knew every print in every window of Plymouth by heart. He travelled over every countenance distinctly within his view, as a florist would inspect a bed of tulips, and often performed the same experiment upon character as he walked from St Paul's to Charing Cross, or from the top of Tottenham Court Road to the Post-office. He hated to sit in twilight. Dr Kitto then paints some of those disqualifications which deafness produces, and how he rose above the trials of his earlier years; how the craving to be honourably known grew upon him, and how this was refined into a passion to be useful. He felt that deafness, while it aided the amount of work done, had many drawbacks; for it prevented explanation, retarded business, and the making of bargains. This defect had more than once annoyed him in his transactions and literary covenants. 'Men of business have a feeling that affairs can be transacted much better by personal interview than writing. In fact, there is no concealing it, that the deaf man is likely to be regarded as a bore. Sensitively alive to this danger, he will perhaps depart, leaving his business unfinished.' 'The deaf man,' he repeats, 'is confined to the solid bones, the dry bread, the hard wood, the substantial fibre of life, and gets but little of the grace, the emotion, the gilding, and the flowers, which are to be found precisely in those small things which are "not worth" reporting on the fingers.'

He has a very playful chapter on the shifts to which deaf people resort to catch the talk of a general company, and how they are usually far behind in their enjoyments of clever and witty sayings, beginning to smile at one piece of humour, while those around them are concluding their laughter over another which has superseded it. He might have added, that the epithet 'absurd' has its origin and

meaning from the common misappropriateness in time or
subject of a deaf man's answer.　Strange to say, he was
six years deaf before he knew that there was any mode of
communication by means of the fingers.

Dr Kitto then enters at some length into the philosophy
of teaching deaf mutes, and diverges into an account of
some famous institutions for their education.　He used to
attend public meetings at Exeter Hall, and the most animated speakers pleased him most.　When the audience
'broke into loud cheers,' he became keenly alive to his
privation.　In the House of Commons he was more amused
than awestruck—was shocked by the 'want of solemnity ;
and he says, 'My far too entire sense of the ridiculous
almost overcame me, when the very remarkable sergeant-at-
arms shouldered his mace, with the air of a musketeer,
and escorted up to the table two masters in Chancery, who
brought down a bill from the Lords, and who, in retiring,
walked backwards the whole length of the floor, stopping
at regulated intervals in their retrogressive move, to bow
very low to the Chair.'　Toward the conclusion of the book,
Kitto hazards a conjecture as to the origin and significa-
tion of his name.　The English would have it to be Cato,
the Spaniards Quito, the Italians Chetto.　Himself gives
it a Phœnician source, Κιττώ in Dioscorides meaning a
species of cassia, pronounced in Hebrew קדה, and he avows
that the Phœnicians, in their early intercourse for tin
in Cornwall, probably planted the name in that southern
province.　The likelihood is, that it is simply a miner's*
contraction of an older and longer Cornish name.　The
Cornish and Celtic are closely allied ; the epithet ciotach, in
Irish, means 'left-handed,' and this Celtic term is not unknown in a more Anglicised form.　The reader will remember
Colkitto as the epithet of the royalist chieftain Macdonnell
in Milton's eleventh sonnet.　The original spelling Kittoe,

is also so far fatal to the eastern derivation. Cato or Catto is a common name in Aberdeenshire, and may be only our northern Doric form of the English word. This small autobiography is Kitto's record of his first difficulties and subsequent progress, of his physical disability and its results —a record made at a period when he was able to take a patient survey of his inner life and its outer course.

The second volume, 'Blindness,' has not the charm of the former, chiefly because it does not contain the results of self-analysis and experience. It describes many cases of blindness, and shows what high excellence in various departments of art and science the blind have attained. For the roll of the blind includes many illustrious names, far more than that of the deaf mutes. The deprivation is, in fact, less than that of hearing, for the want of hearing necessitates the want of language. Among blind poets, we have Homer and Milton, and at a great distance Blacklock, who was also a clergyman; Euler and Saunderson, among mathematicians; and Huber among naturalists. Many have been musicians; and Handel was blind in the last years of his life. Lieutenant Holman, blind from his twenty-fifth year, had travelled round the world, being at one time sent out of Russia as a spy; and in 1834 he published his travels, in four volumes. James Wilson was the blind biographer of the blind. Dr Kitto adduces many instances of persons whose touch was a kind of second sight—who could distinguish colours by smell or touch— or who were able to comprehend locality in a marvellous degree, such as Tom Wilson of Dumfries, not only an ingenious mechanic, but one who often was seen, on a Saturday evening, conducting a 'groggy neighbour' home to his wife and children. We ourselves knew as remarkable a case as any that Dr Kitto has mentioned—that of blind Alick of Stirling, who, as he twirled his key in his hand, would repeat the words of any portion of Scripture, if you simply named its chapter and verse, and who, if you recited any passage, would, in a moment and as easily, tell you the chapter and verse where it occurred. We heard, in our boyhood, of a blind tailor, too, in the same town, who was famous for his taste and accuracy in sewing tartan dresses, distinguishing the various colours by the sense of touch. Dr Kitto dwells with special tenderness on the sad condition of those who are at once blind and deaf and dumb, creatures in perfect isolation; the most remarkable cases being those of James Mitchell, in the north of Scotland,[1] and the well known Laura Bridgman of America. In fact, Laura Bridgman is the most awful example on record— totally blind, deaf, and dumb, with no power of smell, and almost none of taste. Touch alone remains; and her education is a surprising instance of ingenuity and perseverance.[2] The volume, however, notwithstanding its

[1] We saw James Mitchell at Nairn last summer (1857). He is certainly a strange creature; yet contrives to walk about, feeling on all sides of him, and has great pleasure in ascertaining, in his own way, the progress of any new buildings in the town.

[2] The following incident in the history of Laura Bridgman, her first interview with her mother after eighteen months' absence in the Institution, is one of the most touching ever recorded in any language:—

'The mother stood some time, gazing with overflowing eyes upon her unfortunate child, who, all unconscious of her presence, was playing about the room. Presently Laura ran against her, and at once began feeling her hands, examining her dress, and trying to find out if she knew her; but not succeeding in this, she turned away as from a stranger, and the poor woman could not conceal the pang she felt that her beloved child did not know her. She then gave Laura a string of beads which she used to wear at home, which were recognised by the child at once, who, with much joy, put them around her neck, and sought me eagerly, to say she understood the string was from her home. The mother now tried to caress her, but poor Laura repelled her, preferring to be with her acquaintances. Another article from home was now given her, and she began to look much interested. She examined the stranger much closer, and gave me to understand she knew that she came from Hanover; she even endured her caresses, but would leave her with indifference at the slightest signal. The distress of the mother was now painful to behold; for, although she had feared that she should not be recognised, the painful reality of being treated with cold indifference by a darling child, was too much for a woman's nature to bear. After a while, on the mother taking hold of her again, a vague idea seemed to flit across Laura's mind that this could not be a stranger! She

interesting statements, never did, and never could, obtain the popularity of its predecessor.

Between 1846 and 1849 Dr Kitto composed, for the Tract Society's Monthly Volume, 'Ancient and Modern Jerusalem,' two parts; 'the Court and People of Persia,' two parts; and the 'Tahtar Tribes.' These little books, when not dealing in extracts from accredited authors, are very interesting, and put into plain language and brief compass, the result of former researches and previous publications. 'The Tabernacle and its Furniture' was published in a thin quarto in 1849, and is well worth reading.

By the time that the Cyclopædia was nearly concluded, Dr Kitto had fallen again into pecuniary difficulties, which preyed upon him for some years to come. He could not readily find employment of a kind to support him, and his

therefore felt her hands very eagerly, while her countenance assumed an expression of intense interest; she became very pale, and then suddenly red. Hope seemed struggling with doubt and anxiety, and never were contending emotions more strongly depicted upon the human face. At this moment of painful uncertainty, the mother drew her close to her side, and kissed her fondly; when at once the truth flashed upon the child, and all mistrust and anxiety disappeared from her face. as, with an expression of exceeding joy, she eagerly nestled to the bosom of her parent, and yielded to her fond embraces. After this, the beads were all unheeded, the playthings which were offered to her were utterly disregarded; her playmates, for whom but a moment before she gladly left the stranger, now vainly strove to pull her from her mother, and though she yielded her usual instantaneous obedience to any signal to follow me, it was evidently with painful reluctance. She clung close to me, as if bewildered and fearful; and when, after a moment, I took her to her mother, she sprang to her arms and clung to her with eager joy. The subsequent parting between them showed alike the affection, the intelligence, and the resolution of the child. Laura accompanied her mother to the door, clinging close to her all the way, until they arrived at the threshold, where she paused and felt around to ascertain who was near her. Perceiving the matron, of whom she is very fond, she grasped her with one hand, holding on convulsively to her mother with the other; and thus she stood for a moment. Then she dropped her mother's hand, put her handkerchief to her eyes, and turning round, clung, sobbing, to the matron, while her mother departed with emotions as deep as those of her child.'—The preceding description is by Dr Howe, her teacher.

. Another very remarkable instance of the pursuit of knowledge under difficulties, will be found in a volume called—The Rifle, Axe, and Saddlebags. By William Henry Milburn, the Blind Preacher. Reprinted from the American edition, with a Preface by the Rev. Thomas Binney. London: S. Low and Son, 1857.

sources of income were scanty and precarious. The composition of the small works we have referred to was of little
value in money. The new edition of the Pictorial Bible
took up more time than he expected, and for what he called
'surplus time' he obtained no remuneration. His friends,
however, stood forward to assist him, and His Royal High-
ness the Prince Consort was a generous contributor.

At this period he projected the 'Journal of Sacred
Literature.' His object was noble, but the circulation
never repaid him for toil and effort. The prospectus was
of considerable size, and embraced a great variety of topics.
The editor represents that there are many excellent religious periodicals, and much valuable matter locked up in
them, but they are little read save by adherents of the
ecclesiastical bodies to which they belong as organs. Very
much more is equally lost in languages which few general
readers know, and not many scholars understand. His
inference is, that there is, therefore, an undoubted want of
'a publication which, being established on a wider basis,
should not be regarded as the organ of any one religious
denomination, or of any one country; but should be the
means of enabling different denominations and different
countries to impart to one another whatever they know,
which is likely to advance the general interests of biblical
literature.' There is truth in this statement, but much is
taken for granted. Denominational predilections, though
certainly weaker in this branch of sacred learning than any
other, are not wholly without antagonistic influence. The
editor adds :—' It will also appear that the current theological literature of this country, and especially its religious periodical literature, is too exclusively formed out of
materials arising among ourselves, and in our own language.
We have the apostolical assurance, that " they who measure
themselves by themselves, and compare themselves among

themselves, are not wise ;" and yet, for nearly two hundred years, we have done little else.   There were of old " giants" of biblical literature in our land, who, in their lifetime, kept up a profitable intercourse with the scholars of the Continent, and whose names are even now cited with respect by eminent foreign writers, who have but little acquaintance with our more modern labours in sacred literature.   We therefore want a publication which shall keep us acquainted with all that is sound and valuable in the labours of biblical scholars of the European Continent and of North America, and in whose pages such of them as now live may interchange the results of their researches with our own writers.

' All these wants, and more than these, it is the object of the present publication to satisfy; and those, who are apt to discern "the signs of the times," are strongly sensible that the time is come in which the demand for such a work is most urgent, and in which it may, with the greatest advantage, be produced.'

' The editor was induced to think of this publication by the frequent representations, to the above effect, which he has been in the habit of receiving from various quarters ; and already the private notification of his intention to venture on the undertaking has excited much interest both in this country and abroad.   It is only, indeed, in consequence of the extensive literary co-operation which ·he was enabled to organize for the purposes of another publication (the Cyclopædia of Biblical Literature), that he has been induced to think seriously of this work in the form which it bears in the present prospectus : but with the like, and even more extensive co-operation, applicable to the existing undertaking, he finds no reason to distrust his means of producing a publication adequate to the supply of the wants which have been indicated.'

Nobody will question Dr Kitto's desire to promote

biblical scholarship, but he regarded the working of the machine as too easy a matter. He forgot that many persons had not his promptitude in pouring forth the ripened results of their research and judgment; that it is one thing to induce a scholar to write an article for the Cyclopædia—a work of permanent value, and quite another thing to prevail upon him to send an elaborate contribution to a periodical, the interest of which too often passes away with the current number. The conspectus, as first published, embraces a wide range— Original Essays on Biblical History, Geography, Natural History, Antiquities, Biography, Bibliography, with Reviews, Notices, and Quarterly Lists of New Publications, Expository Passages, Philological Essays, Ecclesiastical History, Translations and Reprints, Oriental Literature, Correspondence and Intelligence. Dr Kitto thought that his previous success secured a basis of prosperity to his new undertaking. 'Every writer,' he tells us, ' does, in the course of time, gather around him a public who understand him better, and sympathise with him more than the rest of the world. Such a public, consisting chiefly of the possessors of his former publications, the editor of the Journal of Sacred Literature may venture to suppose that he, after many long years of well accepted labour, has brought around him; and though the present publication is of much wider range than any of his former productions, singly taken, and a proportionate increase of readers may be expected for it, he naturally looks to his old friends as the chief and most earnest supporters of an undertaking, to which the matured plans and the most cherished hopes of usefulness are now irrevocably committed, and in connection with which he has assumed responsibilities more anxious than he ever before ventured to incur.'

Dr Kitto, in forming such an estimate, evidently forgot to distinguish between scientific and popular literature. Thousands of the readers of the Pictorial Bible, who were delighted and benefited with the work, set no value whatever on biblical criticism or Oriental literature; and many of those who purchased the Cyclopædia, did so because, from its compacted form and its learned treasures, it could be easily aud profitably consulted. When they opened it, they could turn at once to the article they wanted. Whereas, in subscribing for a periodical, they did not know what they might get to read, or what peculiar subjects or texts might be handled. The notes of the Pictorial Bible, if scattered through the volumes of a Quarterly Review, would never have attracted hosts of readers—their charm lay in being so compendious, and in being found so readily in connection with the text of the Sacred Volume.

Dr Kitto sadly miscalculated when he thought of finding so large a circle of subscribers to his Journal. The very prospectus warned away hundreds who had rejoiced in his previous labours, and who might wish him success in a path in which they had neither inclination nor ability to follow him. Yet who cannot sympathise with the editor when he thus winds up his address?—'If it tends to advance the glory of God by promoting the better understanding of His word and His ways, if it contributes in any useful degree to the advancement of sacred literature in this country, and if, by the sympathies of common labour, and by the development of common interests, it becomes a uniting tie among all those to whom those objects are dear, then may God bestow His blessing upon it, that it may prosper; but if it does none of these things,' it is useless, it is not wanted : let it perish.' The objects sought are noble, and it will be a happy day for the various churches when they can be reached; when sanctified scholarship shall have lost all sectarian bias; and when ministers of the Gospel shall seek their mental nutriment in biblical science, and be active in its advancement. At present, however, a Review, if it maintain its scientific character, must address itself to a select circle even of clerical readers, and can rarely have a large and compensating circulation. A better period is commencing. Erudition is rising above denominational influence, and assuming a true catholicism both in commentaries and in the higher forms of periodical literature. Still it must be admitted, that while a religious journal, in order to succeed, must have its party to appeal to, and fall back upon for support, Dr Kitto failed, for other reasons, to realise his own purpose. In his delicacy toward his allies, no small amount of inferior matter was introduced by him, and contributions were subjected to no rigid scrutiny, either as to sentiment or erudition. What may be a very instructive paper for a popular magazine, may be wholly out of place in a journal of biblical science. It should be explained, however, that Dr Kitto felt fettered in rejecting or altering articles, from being almost solely dependent on the voluntary assistance of his friends, since the profits of the publication did not admit of the usual honorarium. In his letters to Mr Blackader, publisher of the second series of the Journal, and one who, from his literary and biblical tastes and acquirements, ably seconded the exertions of the editor, he alludes now and again to his being so hampered by the want of funds, that only a very few of his contributors received any pecuniary recognition. His hope was, that his 'friends would aid him for the sake of the good cause till better times came round. This has been the answer of some who have stood by me in all my

struggles, but it is not to be expected from all.'[1] His
heart, however, was set upon his Journal, and he laboured
anxiously for it.   His notes to the publisher show his continuous anxiety about all points connected with it—adver-
tisements as well as papers, postages as well as contributions.   He strove to offend nobody in any way, and was
sadly perplexed on falling into a dilemma, either when
some one complained of delay in the insertion of an article,
or a book was sent him with a request or virtual stipulation that the critique might be favourable, or two of his
friends happened to forward a contribution on the same
subject, or wished to review the same volume.   There
seemed to be a nervousness in all this business, quite unlike his usual firmness and composure.   But the Journal,
neither in its first nor second series, came up to his
own idea ; and, though it improved in several aspects, it
never took that high place which his name and fame were
expected to give it.   The first number appeared on the
first of January 1848 ; and, after anxiously watching over
it for several years, till eleven volumes had been printed, he
was obliged to give it up.   But he made some stipulations
as to its future character.   Though sorrowing to take
leave of it, he wished it still to retain its original impress,
and thus wrote :—'I have secured effectual guarantees
that it shall be always conducted on the essential principles
on which it was founded—that it shall retain its comprehensive and catholic character—that it shall be orthodox
—and that it shall not be sectarian.'[2]   It did not at first
'pay print and paper.'   'I hope the best,' he wrote to Mr
Tracy. . .   'I have little misgiving,—less now, indeed,
than ever ;'—but this was in November 1847.   'The
Journal is getting up nearly to one thousand copies,'
writes he to the same friend in March 1848.   What disap-

[1] Letter to Mr Blackader, Oct. 7, 1852.   [2] Ibid., Aug. 11, 1853.

pointment he must have felt! His plan had not succeeded; his anticipations were blasted. He should have begun with a large reserve fund, which might have been easily raised for the purpose, and not involved his own means and the bread of his family in the undertaking. Other and onerous duties pressed upon him, his health had also given way, and in 1853 he reluctantly handed over the Journal to Dr Burgess, its present able and indefatigable editor.

Dr Kitto had now lived some years at Woking; but he felt that while such a rural residence might enable him to economise, it was exceedingly inconvenient for his literary pursuits. Accordingly, in March 1849, he returned to London, and took up his abode first at 21 High Street, Camden-town, removing the following year to 1 Great Camden Street, where he remained till his final departure for Germany in August 1854.

CHAPTER XI.

DR KITTO had so often felt his way toward employ-ment, that he knew somewhat of the tastes of each pub-lisher, and the characteristic wares of each publishing house. To the enterprising publishers of the Encyclopædia Britannica he addressed the project of a Biblical Cyclo-pædia; and to the Messrs Oliphant of Edinburgh, so well known for their issue of many practical religious books fitted for general circulation and enjoying it, he sent, in June 1849, a long letter, out of which sprang, in a brief period, his last work—the 'Daily Bible Illustrations.' The plan which he sketched himself was different from that ulti-mately adopted. In his delineation of it, he premises that 'he primarily looked to an extended measure of useful-ness in that which seemed to have become his proper vocation.' 'The general title I purpose to be that of *Bible Evenings*; and as I incline to think that the book of Ruth affords an appropriate theme for the first portion, the full title of the volume we commence with would be—*Bible Evenings—the History of Ruth Conversationally explained and illustrated* by J. K., etc.; or perhaps, "Conversations on the History of Ruth" would be as well for the second title. The attraction in subjects of this sort is known to be very great; but it is my hope to enhance this attrac-tion by the manner of treatment. It is meant that the interlocutors shall be, not *sticks* but *characters*, and that the progress shall be enlivened and diversified by such scenes, incidents, and circumstances, as might naturally arise among such persons. The leading idea is, that a family in the middle educated class, devotes two evenings in the week to conversations on the Bible. Of the persons, one may be a biblical scholar, supposed to be able to explain everything that is not assigned to the other characters; another will be a traveller, who has seen everything, and been everywhere, and who is, therefore, able to supply a lively description of places and products, and to point out the analogous manners, customs, and ideas of the *Modern* East; a third may suggest practical improvements; and by so doing, he will give the key note to one more, who has a wonderful memory for all kinds of ancient and modern anecdotes, which appear to him to illustrate or bear upon the principles developed, or the conduct followed; and there may be another yet, apt to remember or to fabricate all kinds of poetry and snatches of verse, having some kind of connection with the matter in hand. All this is to be produced, not in the stiff A B C style of interlocution, but with all the animating turns and incidents of natural conversation.

'The result, as I conceive, would be a most instructive and entertaining book, for which there could not fail to be a large demand. The elements of success, in such undertakings as this, have been most carefully considered, and the work will be expressly formed to embrace them all. It is not designed to be ostensibly a book for children, but care will be taken that there shall be nothing beyond the range of intelligent young people of ordinary education; and the volume would, without doubt, be seen to be well suited to them, and would be largely used in presents to them.'

The sketch is ingenious, and such a colloquy would
have been interesting ; but it would have been very difficult to execute the plan, so as to give each scene a living
and natural aspect, apportion his remarks to each speaker
with natural propriety, and prevent the whole from becoming an artificial and tiresome set of little discourses.   The
true dramatic presentation cannot be elaborated by effort.
Dr Kitto had a vigorous imagination ; but such a work
would have taxed his powers to the utmost in forecasting
the various dialogues, and giving to every character its
harmonious utterance.   Indeed, Uncle Oliver is a failure,
so far as dramatic ease and fitness are concerned.   The
scheme adopted was far better.   It cost him less labour,
was far more natural, and it has been eminently acceptable.   Mr Oliphant suggested a series of papers for every
day in the year, each paper being on a separate topic,
and the whole of them, in order, forming volumes of conse-
cutive reading and comment.   Dr Kitto acquiesced in the
plan, for it was not new to him, having been one of his
multitudinous projects, which he purposed to call ' Bible
Readings for every day in the year,' or else the ' Daily
Scripture Reader.'   The Sunday papers were to be on
themes in unison with the sacred day, and the treatment
of them was to be in harmony.   Dr Kitto's own mind was
growing in spirituality, and he preferred to write these last
papers himself, rightly refusing some assistance which had
been offered to him.   ' I shall be glad,' is his argument to
the publisher, ' of the opportunity of refreshing my mind
by some spiritual writing ; and, besides, I am partial to
this kind of writing, and have had considerable experience
in it, though the general tendency of my undertakings has
been to drive me out of it.'

He entered upon his work in a spirit that could not fail
to insure success :—

'Since I wrote last, I have been enabled to look more closely into our new enterprise, and I cannot but say that the more I grapple it as a practical matter, the better I like it. I feel that the task which thus devolves on me is one which I shall execute with real zest and pleasure. I see that the execution of the design affords a fair opportunity of *usefulness*, which has always been a consideration with me, while it presents me with an occasion, not always to be found, of producing an agreeable and popular book. This encourages me; for, although I have produced books of the class, I began to dread getting too much entangled in books heavy with scholarship and the solidities of knowledge. I therefore enter upon this work with the determination that I will, and with the conviction that I can, produce a book which shall be read—and this not by being superficial, but by exhibiting, in an attractive manner, all the information that can be fitly produced, and the best of all such thoughts as my meditations may suggest.' Again, and after having succeeded, he states, in one of his prefaces, that his object had been 'to make the new familiar, and to make the familiar new.'

The first volume was produced a few days after the stipulated period; and he confidently says to the publisher, 'I never put a book out of my hands, of the success of which I have felt so sure as this.' And his confidence was fully justified. He pledged himself to punctuality in the publication of the volumes; and gave as his ground, 'that his working day was of twice the usual length, from 4 A.M. to 9 P.M., with little interruption.' His first work each morning was the paper for the day, though he felt such continuous labour to be occasionally a 'hard job.' The volumes were to be published quarterly. The first volume, 'The Antediluvians and Patriarchs,' is dated December 1849, and takes in the first three months of the year; the second,

'Moses and the Judges,' is dated April 1850, and is meant for April, May, and June. In the preface to this volume, the author avows his thankfulness 'for the warm favour with which the first volume was received,' and feels himself encouraged to 'hope for a blessing upon his labours in the direction which has now been given to them.' The third volume, for the months July, August, and September, brought Dr Kitto to his usual explanation, that the limits originally fixed for the work were too small, and that his plan must not be 'crushed in the attempt to force the substantial matter of two volumes into one.' Half the volume is occupied with the Life of David, and this portion is of great interest. The King of Israel is portrayed truthfully, without any attempt to palliate his sins, or tone down the darker traits of his character; yet how unlike he appears to the picture of him in Bayle, or to that in the article 'David' in Kitto's own 'Cyclopædia.' In fact, we have always been charmed by the papers on David: so much is brought out incidentally, and so many of the secret links of his court and policy are unfolded, by a reference often to a single clause of the inspired history; so just an appreciation of Joab and the other notable men about him is interwoven, and there is so striking an estimate both of his weakness and of his strength, of his sins and of his sorrows, of the raptures and the tears of his lyrical muse. 'David,' he says, 'was always great in affliction.' 'The bird which once rose to heights unattained before by mortal wing, filling the air with its joyful songs, now lies with maimed wing upon the ground, pouring forth its doleful cries to God.' The volume which completes the year is named 'Solomon and the Kings'—the characters of principal interest in it being the wise monarch and the prophet Elijah.

The publication of this last volume had been retarded four

or five months by subordinate engagements. He completed a work for Mr Bohn, named 'Scripture Lands Described in a series of Historical, Geographical, and Topographical Sketches.'—London, 1850. These sketches are simply a memoir to accompany and explain a beautiful biblical atlas of twenty-four maps, and are 'not wholly a reproduction of materials previously used by the same writer,' but contain the results of recent researches, though not to any large extent. There is, however, a very full and useful index, exhibiting the ancient and modern names of scriptural places, with their latitude and longitude, and other important information, in a tabular form. This excellent volume forms one of Bohn's Illustrated Library, and is, like others in the same series, handsomely got up. The other production, which occupied a portion of Kitto's time, was a book which had been written two years before for the Tract Society, but the printing of which had been delayed for want of requisite illustrations. 'The Land of Promise' is a re-exhibition of a great deal that he had said before, though in form and arrangement it differs much from 'Scripture Lands,' and one special object of it was to describe every place or site of interest 'as it now appears.'

At a personal interview between Mr Oliphant and Dr Kitto in London, in 1850, the second series of Daily Bible Illustrations was virtually agreed on, and in September of the same year, the publisher had suggested the dedication of the work to the Queen, when it should be completed. Kitto at first objected, inasmuch as such dedications are 'usually prefixed to works which cannot stand alone, and a royal dedication has come to be almost considered as a sign of intrinsic weakness. There seems, also, to my mind, in this case, a sense of disproportion, like mounting Great Tom of Oxford on a village church. One would think this distinction would better suit some great work, such as I may hope hereafter to produce. Yet, on the other hand, this is not absolutely a small work as to size, nor, if I may believe half that I read in the notices you send me, is it altogether unimportant or valueless in its contents. It is not unlikely that it might interest her Majesty more than any work I have yet produced. Upon the whole, perhaps, I should rather like it, if it can be shown to be a proper thing to do ; and I do see one point very clearly, that if the pension should be granted, it would be a very proper and graceful thing for me to take the *first* opportunity that subsequently offers, of thus expressing my grateful acknowledgments. Nothing can be clearer than that. Then, again, if this benefit should not be realised in October, such a dedication might advance the matter somewhat ; but of this I am not able to judge. It is well to wait, to see what October brings forth.'

The allusions in these last sentences lead us to state, that it had been deemed advisable by Dr Kitto's friends to make a united and hearty effort to obtain a grant for him from the Civil List. Memorials and letters were forwarded to the Prime Minister from all religious parties in the kingdom, including peers, bishops, clergy, civilians, and literary and theological professors. The application was at length successful ; and on the 17th of December Lord John Russell conveyed the brief but gratifying intimation, 'the Queen has directed that a grant of £100 a-year should be made to you from her Majesty's Civil List, on account of your useful and meritorious literary works.'

By February in the following year, Dr Kitto had got permission to inscribe his volumes to her Majesty, and he was somewhat at a loss to know in what words to frame the dedication. Nor was he sure whether it might not be necessary for him to go to court, adding—' I may take it into my head to go after all, especially if I can get hold of some one to help me through it.' He would have presented his volumes in person, if it had been deemed necessary; still, such an appearance would have been a trial to one of ' his nervous retiredness of temper,' and who had abstained from all public assemblies. 'It may be,' he consoles himself, 'that the feeling which thus holds me prisoner is but a protective instinct, guarding me from the circumstances which might press *too painfully* upon me the consciousness of my condition.' On the 24th June, the four volumes, with a copy of the Lost Senses, handsomely bound, were sent to Colonel Phipps, at Buckingham Palace, who acknowledged the receipt of them—adding besides, ' I have not failed to present these books to her Majesty the Queen, by whom they have been very graciously accepted.'

Before Dr Kitto had finished the first series, and at the beginning of 1851, there were decided indications of approaching cerebral debility. The pain in the back of his head, which he had often felt before, had become too intense to allow of mental toil. He was compelled to moderate his labour and shorten his hours. Rising at four or five in the morning was totally out of the question. To stoop his head to write created excruciating agony. He had vomited blood annually for a long period, but not during the last two years ; and the cessation of this self-relieving process may have burdened his brain. But the hemorrhage returned in the crisis, and á medical friend having bled him copiously besides, the neuralgia abated. These warnings were so far slighted by him, that he did not adopt decided measures to maintain his health and prolong his working powers. It was in this weakened state that he wrought upon the Evening Series, the first volume of which was published in December 1851, and the last in January 1854

—more than double the time that was fixed on for the production of the Morning Series.

We need not characterise at length the Evening Series,
which is quite equal to the Morning Series. The first
volume was ' Job and the Poetical Books'—to wit, Psalms.
Proverbs, Ecclesiastes, and the Song of Songs—and has
' more of a literary cast' than any of its predecessors. The
second volume, ' Isaiah and the Prophets,' is rather miscellaneous in its nature—giving some prominence to the
person and exploits of Cyrus, as well as the local fulfilment
of prophecy, and containing a digest of the results of those
researches which Botta and Layard had prosecuted at
Nineveh. The third is the ' Life and Death of our Lord ;'.
and the last is the ' Apostles and the Early Church.' The
Life of Christ is presented synoptically, and therefore the
various chapters are closely connected ; while the sketch
of the Apostles inweaves the historical intimations contained in the Epistles.

This work, to the eight volumes of which we have so
briefly alluded, has obtained, as it merits, a wide popularity. The topics are selected with admirable skill, and
are usually founded on some striking scene or novel adventure, some fact or sentiment, some attractive feature of
character or remarkable incident in eastern life and enterprise. Thus, in the first volume, you pass from the simplicity of the tent to the bravery of the camp, from the fire
on the hearth to the flame of the altar ; and whether the
paper be on a marriage or a funeral, a sacrifice or a scene
of revelry, whether the theme be Abel's death, Lamech's
polygamy, Jubal's harp, Enoch's piety, Noah's ark, Sarah's
veil, Hagar's flight, Lot's escape, Jacob's pillar, Joseph's
bondage, or Pharaoh's signet, each is told with a charming simplicity, surrounded with numerous and beautiful
illustrations, and interspersed or closed with pointed and

just reflections. Dr Kitto throws light, throughout the series, on many obscure allusions, says many tender and many startling things, opens his heart to the reader, as he unfolds the stores of his learning—all his utterances being in harmony with his avowed design, to make this work ' really interesting as a reading book to the family circle, for which it is primarily intended.' It is not easy to characterise the volumes ; and the author seems to have felt this difficulty himself, when he says, in the preface to the second of them, this work is ' not a history—not a commentary—not a book of critical and antiquarian research—not one of popular illustration, nor of practical reflection—but it is something of all these.' He admits that ' it would have been easy to have written a more learned work ;' but he carefully avoided the 'forms and processes of scholarship' on the one hand ; and, on the other hand, he made no pretension of 'writing down' to any class of readers. He aimed ' to put the whole into brisker language than is needful in heavier works.' ' I am amused,' he says, as the work was proceeding, ' to see what a hankering there is. among the noticers, that I should make these papers "*practical,*" etc.—that is, turn them into little sermons. This would be to spoil the thing altogether. It would be, to abstain from my own line, in which, from peculiar circumstances, studies, tastes, and travels, I can do better than many others, to attempt that of which there is already a superabundance, and which thousands could execute as well as, or better than, myself. This tone of remark is, however, natural for those who do not sufficiently consider my peculiar vocation. I do, however, try to give a religious turn to matters where I have a fair opportunity of doing so ; and, upon the whole, this is probably the most religious work I have yet written.' The papers are each independent and complete—a parable for the day, or a

meditation for the night. The interest never flags, dry
detail is avoided, and the themes for the Lord's Day are
in exquisite keeping with its sacred character. These
eight volumes are, in fact, the cream of all that Dr Kitto
had previously written. There is a special charm about
them, and a vein of serious instruction runs through them.
A rich and racy humour now and then shines out, not
indeed so frequent as in Matthew Henry, nor so salient and
picturesque as in Thomas Fuller. Nothing like a morbid
spiritualism is found in them—it is open-faced godliness.
They are suggestive, too, in their nature ; many things are
placed in a novel light, and many of the remarks made are
so new, and yet so much in point, that you wonder they
never struck you before. Difficulties are honestly met, and
are never set aside by any rationalising process. The
author has availed himself of all his former labours, as if
'anxious to disburden his full soul' of its treasures. He
writes, too, with earnestness and living power ; and the
results of his travels, experience, and research suffer no
deterioration from being moulded anew in the fire of a
devout soul, and set in the framework of an ingenuous and
healthful piety.

In the autumn of 1852, Dr Kitto was again and more
seriously endangered. The pain was more intense and
alarming, and he could no longer fight against it. Medical
advice was resorted to, and he was enjoined to do less
work and take more exercise. At least two hours a-day
was he enjoined to walk in the open air. But he complains, September 7, to his publisher, of such consumption
of time :—

'I have not got well so rapidly as I expected, and am
still under active medical treatment. The last week was
nearly a blank for practical purposes, and the anxiety thus
occasioned has probably retarded my recovery. I am,

however, gathering strength, and am undoubtedly better.
The excruciating pains are less violent, and I can venture
to sit longer at my desk without bringing them on. Thus,
I am beginning to return to my usual habits, although,
for the present, on a reduced scale as to time. The new
habit of *walking* has been so seriously impressed upon me,
that I hope to cultivate it as a matter of duty. The want
of a *definite* object is the difficulty : care for one's health
seems too vague an inducement for a practice so adverse
to one's habits, and, in its immediate aspect, a serious loss
of precious time. I suppose, however, that some one or
other will always be dragging me out now ; and Mrs Kitto
will probably look to it, as the doctor has enjoined her to
turn me out daily, and not to let me in again till my time
is up. I felicitated myself at first, that he only stated how
long I was to walk, not how *fast*, or how much, so that, as
I thought, I might manage to make the business entertaining, by sauntering about among the book-stalls ; but
the doctor is now too sharp for me, and talks of six miles
a-day. Think of that for a man who has almost lost
the power of putting one leg before another ! However,
seeing that there are so many little ones whose immediate
welfare seems to have been made dependent upon my
existence, and that I have set before me many labours
which I should be loath to leave unexecuted, I hope to be
enabled to adapt myself to this new condition of affairs.
It may be the Lord's method of strengthening and preserving me for such work as He means me to do. In this
point of view, the death of one whom I knew, Mr Porter
of the Board of Trade, "from want of exercise"—a cause
I never before saw assigned in an obituary notice—has
made considerable impression on my mind.'

Certainly the death of Mr Porter, and from such a
cause, should have checked his exhausting industry ; but

yet, when we think of the numerous family supported by his daily labours—a family of five sons and five daughters —we must not judge him harshly. Still his disease was of such a nature, that it was not to be tampered with; for the organ attacked was his only implement of labour and source of income. Weakness or injury to it would sadly diminish the supplies, or stop them altogether. He was visited with another relapse, ere September expired, in which the head-pains were continuous. On his being cupped, and on the application of other means, he revived, and, by the constant exercise to which he had been forced, his ' too solid flesh ' was somewhat ' melted off.' He could well spare some. Mrs Hullock, an old Malta friend, who had accidentally discovered him through means of ' The Lost Senses,' was surprised, on visiting him, to see ' the little *slender* man become so great in *person* and name.' He was very thankful for recruited strength, and in October was tolerably well, but complaining of the *immediate* loss of time which his daily walk occasioned. He should have remembered that Milton, one of the poets of his earliest admiration, used to walk daily after dinner in his garden, three and four hours at a time. Even the Exhibition in 1851 had small enticements for him. Fleet Street and the Strand were greater to him than the Crystal Palace, but he did not very often frequent them. Occasionally he sauntered down Oxford Street, Regent Street, the Strand, and Holborn, 'looking for bargains and curious things at the bookshops;' and even this lounging was better than no recreation at all. He, however, did visit the Great Exhibition, and saw it at its close; and though the noise made not the least impression upon him, 'the scene was striking—even to grandeur.' But he sighs and says, ' I certainly do not feel that I lost a day, but my work did.' This perpetual toil was fast wearing him out, and still he grudged the slightest relaxation. Yet one is glad to find that, on September 30, being the last of his boys' Michaelmas holidays, he went with them ' a-nutting to Epping Forest,' 'not sorry to have so good an excuse for a run.' He found relief at this period from Pulvermacher's hydro-electric chain, which threw a 'sensible continuous current of electric fluid through the part affected.'

Anxious to have some stable means of support, when the Daily Bible Illustrations should be concluded, he was induced to edit a weekly religious periodical—'Sunday Reading for Christian families.'[1] It did not succeed, and, after three months, was abandoned, though it deserved a better fate. The capital papers which its editor wrote for it, were not sufficient to ensure its success. Though warned that the project would be a failure, he was resolved to try, and the trial satisfied him. Thus he delivers himself:—' The case is this—For many years I have been desirous of finding a fixed basis of occupation and usefulness in the conduct of a periodical publication, which, by affording me a salary, would make regular and determinate a portion of the income I require, leaving me comparatively free for the book-work, which would be needful to complete that income, and relieving me from the perils of an entire dependence thereon.'[2]

But his malady soon returned in still more awful violence. The electric chain in which he had so fondly trusted, could not charm the pain away ; and, while he was in this state of prostration, he was visited with another trial. His youngest child, Henry Austin, died. This was the first entrance of death into his dwelling ; and every parent knows the pang of a first bereavement. Aye, though it be an infant that is taken away when yet unable

[1] London: Needham, 1853.   [2] Letter to Mr Blackader, March 3, 1853.

to prattle, the new sorrow pierces and lacerates the parental heart. Kitto's softened spirit bowed to the chastisement. He loved his children dearly, and never, with all his solitary study and toil, 'hid his face from his own flesh.'

This little child had wound itself round his heart. His earliest intimation to Mr Oliphant is (April 12) :—

'This is the first letter I have written for a week, and the first time I have taken up my pen for any purpose since Saturday. There has been much besides my ill health : a beloved child of mine has been dying, and now it lies here dead. God took it from us on Monday morning, and while I bow in submission to this stroke, knowing it is from my Father's hand, my heart is very sore. During the years that I have had a home of my own, death has not been permitted to enter, and its presence is, from its strangeness, the more grim and terrible. During that long time, I have indeed been tried with many griefs ; but *this* form of trial, the hardest of all to bear, has been spared to me. Now, this also has come, and finds my heart very weak. May the Lord strengthen it for me, and enable me in due time to learn what lesson it is that He means to teach me by this new stroke of His rod !'

The Rev. Dr Brown of Edinburgh, whose wide sympathies extend to every 'companion in tribulation,' sent him one of his useful and solacing little books—'Comfortable Words for Christian Parents bereaved of Little Children.' 'It touched him much.' Mrs Kitto also felt that it fulfilled the promise in its title, and as its balm dropped into her heart, she did not refuse to be comforted. The father was thankful for the 'seasonable memorial,' and in his own way tells how dear this babe had become from its very weaknesses, and how the only land he possessed had been purchased for a burial-place—a sacred spot with a precious deposit :—

'It was but a little child, thirteen months old. He was from the first difficult to rear, and required the constant care of his mother; and this brought his infancy, with its numerous little ways, more under my own notice than that of any other of the children; and the great solicitude with which he had needed to be watched over and prayed for, endeared him greatly to us. At length all difficulty seemed to be overcome, and he waxed fair and strong, and his mother ventured to trust him partially from her own constant care. Then he caught cold, and after a few weeks of suffering, heart-rending to witness, he died. His mother, with many tears, reproaches herself, that if she had never trusted him from her own care, but had continued to nurse him in her own arms, he would yet have lived. It is difficult to realise the idea that, nevertheless, he has not fallen without the will of God. It is hard to learn, but she is learning it, and so am I, and I feel that all real comfort, under a trial like this, must be rooted in that conviction. I am now become, for the first time, the owner of a grave—all the land in this wide world that I possess. This afternoon I shall be constrained to consign to it the remains—still beautiful in death—of this dear little child, into whose bright eyes I have for so many months been daily looking for matter of hope or fear. May the Lord strengthen in the hour now near, and make realities to my own heart the comforts I have sometimes endeavoured to impart to others!'

Those comforts which he had dispensed to other mourners, had been no mere commonplaces, no trite courtesies, no empty or unavailing regrets. He did not only throw his flower on the sepulchral urn, but he touched and stayed the bleeding heart with his 'bundle of myrrh.' 'When,' he writes in reference to the death of the widow of Zarephath's only son, 'we behold that a child so dear—

. . "Like a flower crusht with a blast is dead,
  And ere full time hangs down his smiling head,"

how many sweet interests in life, how many hopes for the
time to come, go down to the dust with him ! The purest
and most heart-felt enjoyment which life offers to a mother
in the society of her little child, is cut off for ever. The
hope—the mother's hope, of great and good things to
come from this her son, is lost for her. " The live coal that
was left," and which she had reckoned that time would
raise to a cheerful flame, to warm her home, and to preserve and illustrate the name and memory of his dead
father, is gone out—is quenched in darkness. The arms
which so often clung caressingly around her, and whose
future strength promised to be as a staff to her old age,
are stiff in death. The eyes which glistened so lovingly
when she came near, now know her not. The little
tongue, whose guileless prattle had made the long days of
her bereavement short, is now silent as that of the "mute
dove." Alas! alas! that it should ever be a mother's lot
to close in death the eyes of one whose pious duty, if
spared, should be in future years to press down her own
eyelids. This is one of the great mysteries of life, to be
solved only thoroughly, only fully to our satisfaction, in
that day when, passing ourselves the gates of light, we
behold all our lost ones gather around our feet.'[1]

Thus his afflictions were multiplying, for the process of
refinement was to be severe, because it was not to be long.
He who ' sits as a purifier,' gave special intensity to the
' refiner's fire,' as its action was not to be of continued dur-
ation. Beautifully had the mourner expressed himself
already as to the results of discipline :—

' It is only by the grafting of our will into His that we
can bear much fruit—any fruit ; and no branch was ever

[1] Daily Bible Illustrations, vol. iv., p. 228.

yet grafted without being cut to the quick.   In what He
allows us, or in what He takes from us, in His dealings
with us, or in His action upon us through others, the same
object is always kept in view, of teaching us our dependence upon Him; and it is well with us—very well, then
only well—when our will so works with His, that in all we
see, or hear, or enjoy, or suffer, we strive to realise for
ourselves that which He strives to teach—to see His will,
and to have no will but His.'[1]

At this period of sorrow he became worse himself, and
found no relief from any of his previous appliances.   The
late Dr Golding Bird was then consulted, who, refusing at
first to entertain the case of a deaf patient as it consumed
so much of his valuable time, no sooner learned who the
applicant was, than, in characteristic terms, he expressed
the warmest interest in him, and afterwards received his
fortnightly visits with the greatest cordiality, refusing, at
the same time, the customary fees.   He said to the sufferer,
'If you mean to live, you must work less, and take more
exercise.'   But, at the expiry of a few months, he declared
Dr Kitto incurable, because the intractable patient had
systematically counterworked his physician's skill and pre-
scriptions.   His brain wanted rest.   Dr Bird had tried to
subdue the cerebral irritation; but Dr Kitto persisted in
thinking and writing, and nullifying all his medical adviser's
kindness and efforts.   It was pressed upon him, that he
must cease from labour for a period; but he replied, 'No;
I must finish the work for which I have had the money,
and if I knew I should die with the pen in my hand, I will
go on as long as the Lord permits.'   So that he virtually
sealed his own doom.   In August he went down to Rams-
gate, and though 'he spent much of his time in the open
air, his head became rather worse than better.'   To induce

---

[1] Daily Bible Illustrations, vol. iv., p. 318.

him to prolong his stay, a box of books was sent for ; but 'the books spoiled the holiday, and the holiday spoiled the books.' His general health was, however, materially improved, and so little apprehensive was he of any serious ailment clinging to him, that he amused himself with projecting a plan of travel in Egypt and Palestine, '*mainly for the purpose of biblical illustration*,' which might be produced after his return 'in the shape of, perhaps, two 8vo volumes.' But he came back to London 'in *one* respect not sensibly better ;' and believing that, nevertheless, some 'salutary influence' had been received, he resolved to 'run about as much as time and circumstances would allow.' It was at this period that, as already stated, he resigned the Journal of Sacred Literature into the hands of Dr Burgess. But his hours of study were greatly curtailed, and his labours on his closing work greatly abridged. He was forbidden to rise at four or five in the morning, as he had done for fifteen years, and enjoined to walk in the forenoon, 'one of the prime portions of his time.' These and similar explanations he made to his Edinburgh publisher, confessing 'his fretting anxiety at his inability not to get on faster.' He had decided, at all hazards, to finish the book on hand ; and had for it and other pressing labours been tempted to neglect Dr Bird's keen and honest warnings.

It would be wrong, however, to suppose that the Daily Bible Illustrations, though professedly his main work, were either the heaviest or most exhausting element of his labours. It was his anxiety about his other engagements that fretted and fatigued him. He took too much in hand, and, in his haste to keep all his appointments, he overtasked himself. What he had been doing for Bohn's Library and for the Tract Society, his new enterprise in connection with the Sunday Reading for Families, and his uneasy feelings and unrelaxing tension of soul about his Journal—this combination of effort and vigilance was far more damaging to him than any study or writing necessary for the Daily Bible Illustrations.[1]   The series of chapters required for this work cost him little labour in comparison, many of them being subjective in their nature—the welling out of his own spontaneous reflections, and the others which exhibit research, being upon topics long familiar to him, and on which he had already delivered his thoughts. Though the Daily Bible Illustrations were, at this time, his largest, they were, on the whole, his easiest work, for he had ceased to compose a paper a day, and the toil had become a pleasure to him, as well as oftentimes a relief to his burdened spirit.   Nor did he die, as he had protested, with the pen in his hand, and his labour unfinished.   The angel of death calmly waited for him till he had laid it down.

He carried out his resolve as to the eighth volume of the Daily Bible Illustrations, amidst much weakness and delay, and at length concluded his task.   His wife and he together blessed God when the last sentence was written, and felt that they had abundant and pressing reason to ' offer thanksgiving.'   This closing composition of a closing life has for its subject the Catacombs at Rome, and the striking picture of early Christianity furnished by them. And his last words are, ' In these solemn recesses we meet with " none but Christ."   It is the unobscured light of His countenance, as of the sun shining in its strength, that irradiates the gloom of these solitudes.   He is the Alpha, the Omega, of all around.   All is of Him—

"HIM FIRST, HIM LAST, HIM MIDST, HIM WITHOUT END."'

---

[1] A tract which he wrote in 1852 for the Working Men's Educational Union, on Eastern Habitations,' needs scarcely be referred to.

It was in the frame of mind indicated by these glowing words, that he gave thanks to Him who had guarded and blessed him in his last great labour upon earth, and had carried him to its termination, though sickness and sorrow had often threatened interruption.

And the work was not finished a day too soon. The last day of regular toil was succeeded by the first day of his final illness; for next morning, as he attempted to rise, he felt a strange powerlessness, and said, in sad and hurried tones, to his wife, 'O, Bell! I am numb all down my side.' The effects of this stroke of paralysis continued for a considerable period, yet he gave what time he could afford to the revision of the Biblical Cyclopædia for a new edition. This work being stereotyped, the corrections could not be very many, though some of them were very important. Nor did he go over a large portion of the book, for the malady soon returned in a more intense and alarming shape. On the morning of the 4th of February, he was seized with a fit, which lasted till he was bled by Dr Tunaley, his medical attendant. Consciousness was quite restored, but violent and agonising headache, the result of congestion of the brain, still remained. That rest which he had been so unwilling to take, was now forced upon him by extreme debility. He was worn out by continuous and unrelieved labour. Still Dr Bird had thought and said that a year's rest might yet restore him. The farmer allows his field to lie fallow, and he believes that he loses nothing by a year's unproductiveness. But the powerless and moneyless author had, in the meantime, his household to support, and without work there was no income, save the small pension from her Majesty. Mrs Kitto consulted Mr Oliphant, and a plan was proposed to raise such a sum as might secure the overdone labourer two years' release. But before the idea was wrought out, he was seized again, and more severely; so that a larger and more permanent form of assistance was projected.   Committees for the purpose were formed in London and in Scotland, presided over respectively by John Labouchere, Esq., a generous philanthropist in the metropolis, and by his old and valued friend, Sir John M'Neill.   Sir John took the chair at a meeting in Edinburgh, and delivered, in his opening address, a just and eulogistic criticism on Dr Kitto's biblical labours.   When the plan was brought into operation, contributions were received not only from admirers at home, but from New York, Nova Scotia, and South Australia. The final result did not, however, come up to expectation, the sum received being only L.1800.[1]   Had the particulars of Dr Kitto's early life been extensively known—his hardships and privations, his fortitude and triumphs—much more, we believe, would have been promptly contributed.

For many weeks, Dr Kitto was utterly prostrated; but he was in no small degree gratified by the public interest shown in his behalf.   It was not, however, till the month of June, that he was able to pen a note, though he had made several attempts; and he wrote, on the 20th of that month, to Mr Oliphant, under great depression and feebleness :—

'At the present time, my head is, upon the whole, considerably better, and I have, on most days, intervals of comparative ease; but, at best, it is exceedingly tender, and any little movement or effort brings on *acute* pain.   I am led out now and then by Mrs Kitto, or one of the elder children, for a short crawl; but I generally return in great distress, the movement, however gentle, having disturbed my head, and the lower limbs being still very

---

[1] Of this sum, there remains about L.1200, which has been invested in the names of Trustees for the benefit of Dr Kitto's widow and family.

feeble, from the effects of the repeated seizures, though
the more obviously distressing results of these seizures
have most materially abated. · I rejoice to learn, that my
medical adviser is of opinion, that, in the state to which I
have been brought by diet and medical treatment, there is
little probability of further attacks of this nature. Still,
however, the original slight numbness along the whole left
side, which I was, if I remember rightly, describing to you
in the letter I left unfinished, and which was forwarded
to you after the dreadful attack of the 4th of February—
this has remained all through, though less sensibly felt at
some times than at others. The doctor is, however, persuaded that this also will be displaced, under a change
of air. This change has been retarded by various circumstances, with which you are acquainted ; and now,
lastly, by my wife's illness, which added much to my
other distresses. But, through the Lord's mercy, she
seems much better to-day, though far from well ; and I
entertain the hope, that the change, when it does take
place, will re-establish her health, which has been much
shaken of late.

'I cannot write more now ; but I cannot close this, my
first and necessarily short letter, without expressing how
deeply I have been affected by the kind interest which,
under these most trying circumstances, you have manifested on my behalf, and the zealous exertions you have
made to ameliorate the evils of this condition. God has
been very gracious to me, not only in keeping my heart
from sinking in the evil day, but in raising up many friends
to testify their effectual sympathy for me and mine. This
is most cheering ; and, if it should please Him to remove
the cloud which now hangs over my tabernacle, I shall
hope to be enabled to evince my gratitude by more entire
devotement to that service in which alone perfect freedom

is found—in actual labour, if that be possible, or, if not, in patient waiting for Him.'

Labour, indeed, was denied him, and 'patient waiting' was henceforth to be his duty. 'Wait' had been his motto, — 'only wait, only believe' had been his shield against despondency. In these seasons of trial, the Master had been saying to him, 'I come quickly;' and his response was, 'Amen, even so come.'

A journey to the Continent, which had been meditated for some time, was postponed for the purpose of trying the benefit of further medical skill in London. The experiment, alas! did not succeed. His daughter Shireen had gone down to Edinburgh, on her way out to Canada; but failing health obliged her to return to London. Her father, in this dark hour, writes in July to the same correspondent :—

'Shireen returned from Edinburgh on Saturday, without much exhaustion. Her return was a mixed pain and pleasure to me—pain, that her meritorious hopes and endeavours should be frustrated, and pleasure, to be reunited to one who had seemed lost to us. Under all, I thank God, however—and it is much to be thankful for—that I have been enabled to rest in the full and satisfying persuasion, that all things will assuredly work together for good, *vital* good to myself, and to those whom God has given me. I have no ground to expect—I never have expected, that the Lord should establish on my behalf an exemption from all trouble; but I believe and know that all must be for *eventual* good, though it may be by ways I should not prefer, or by ways that I might even wish to avoid. I am very unable to express the sense I entertain of the munificent kindness and delicate consideration which you have evinced towards me, both before and since this present emergency and trial. The *last* instance is peculiarly gratifying to me, and will occupy a pleasant place in my recollections of this time.'

The next letter has some faint scintillations of his former humour :—

'*July* 31. . . . It seems that we are to go on Wednesday se'nnight, and that in a day or two we leave this house, in which I thought I had made my life's nest, for furnished lodgings, as a preparatory step, having let the house. Changes so radical have become hard to me ; but the Lord's will be done, and I think that I seek only to know what His will is. At Shireen's supplication, I sat to the sun for my portrait on Saturday. Till I saw it, I had no idea how grand I look ; it seems the concentrated essence of twenty aldermen and ten bishops, all in one. Mrs K. sat also ; but, womanlike, she spoke in the very crisis of the operation, and so spoiled the likeness. I amused myself much with the idea, that the sun, who has hitherto lived like a gentleman, is now obliged to work for his living.'

As originally contemplated, Dr Kitto left for Germany on the 9th of August, with his wife and seven of his children, the other two remaining for the sake of their education in England, one of whom had in 1850, to his father's great delight, received a presentation to Christ's Hospital, through the influence of his old friend Mr Tracy. They were accompanied by a sympathising friend, the Rev. Cornelius Hart, incumbent of Old St Pancras. Landing at Rotterdam, the party proceeded up the Rhine by Mayence and Mannheim, and thence to Stuttgart. There Dr Kitto became greatly worse again, and Dr Ludwig, the king's physician, was brought to him. On his visit, he repeated what the medical men had said in London, and the certainty of speedy dissolution seems, from this time, to have become a conviction with Dr Kitto: A dream, as at the beginning of his life, pictured out his waking thoughts, and he saw, in sleep, his wife a widow and his

children fatherless. The telling of this sad vision next
morning filled his eyes with tears, for he believed that the
presentiment would soon be realised. Stuttgart was found
to be very hot, and the invalid next took up his residence
at Cannstatt on the Neckar. The mineral waters at this
place are much resorted to, but Dr Kitto found from them
no great benefit.

The 'beginning of the end' had arrived. First his
youngest child, Henry Harlowe, aged ten months, was
taken from him on the 21st of September. The infant had
been always delicate. 'His mother spent the days and
nights in walking to and fro with him, for so only would he
be quiet, shedding many tears over her once beautiful baby,
now so wasted, and so soon to be taken from her. For
me, I could only spend my hours in prayer to God, that
He would be gracious to her and me, and spare us, if it
were possible, this heavy stroke of His hand. Indeed, I
felt emboldened to pray with great importunity for the life
of this child. I ventured to ask it as a token for good, as
an encouragement to my faith; and I promised to receive
it back as a trust and a gift—a double gift, from the womb
and from the grave—and as such (should my life be spared),
to watch his steps with daily solicitude, and give my best
time and earnest endeavours to the task of bringing him up
for the Lord, in the ways of holiness. I allow myself to
think this prayer was heard and accepted. Certain it is,
that at his next visit the doctor began to express hopes,
and the child has since been reviving, and although still
very feeble, he is now so much better, that even my poor
Rachel refuses not to be comforted.

'I have written this by short instalments; my head has
been easier during the two nights which have intervened
since I began it. . . .

'*P.S.—Sept.* 22.—I was mistaken. Our dear child was

taken from us yesterday—Henry Harlowe Kitto, aged ten months. Our hearts are very sore. May He who does not afflict willingly, strengthen us to bear this new grief; but these are the things I find it hardest to bear, and the most difficult to understand. My poor wife suffers, greatly, for her heart was strongly set on this child. Please ask Dr Brown if he will write to her.'[1]

Dr Brown did not and could not refuse such an appeal. Nay, such an appeal was not required to elicit his sympathies, and bring out his genial words of comfort.

But the shadow of death was settling down on his household in thicker gloom. His first-born, unable to proceed to Canada, as she intended, had returned to London in declining health; and her removal to Germany, with its change of air, had effected no improvement on her. The watchful eye of her father saw her real condition, and it smote him to the heart.

' I have yet to grieve that I am obliged to report less favourably of our dear Shireen; she seems gradually sinking under her disease; and although there is perhaps no *immediate* danger, the hope of her ultimate recovery is very faint. It is sad to a parent's heart to see one so promising—his first-born—laid thus low, and I trust that the prayers of my friends will not be wanting to strengthen ours on her behalf.'[2]

Her disease was a complicated form of dropsy; and when the little Henry died, she was confined to bed from extreme debility, and never again arose from it. During the last twelve days of her life, her father seldom left her bedside, but strengthened and comforted the dying girl, though his own condition and her weakness made the necessary finger-talk very exhausting to both. Her eldest brother John was summoned from England, but before he could reach

[1] Letter to Mr Oliphant, Cannstatt, Sept. 18, 1854.   [2] Ibid.

Cannstatt, his sister had expired. Her mother tells the
sad tale :—

'We had both been desirous that she should feel that
her change was near, but how were we to tell her? I felt
I could not. Her dear father read and talked to her, and
gave some gentle hints that the doctors would not be
answerable for the results, and indeed, that they thought
it a critical case. Whilst we were hesitating thus to communicate with her, the Lord Himself showed His inten-
tions towards her. One morning, as I was attending to
her, she said, "Mamma, I dreamt last night that the dean
of the place came and told me I was only to live a fortnight." I took advantage of the opportunity as well as I
was able, and said to her, " Well, my dear, the Lord speaks
in various ways, and perhaps this is His message to you."
" Yes," she said, "I think it is, for certainly I cannot live
long thus." After that she became quite resigned and
composed, and daily talked very sweetly on the subject of
her decease, both with her dear father and myself. She
died exactly at the end of the fortnight, as her dream had
told her.'

Her spirit had been gradually ripened for the great
change, and the evident preparation for it gave her father
unspeakable joy in the midst of his distress. After her
decease, he writes to Mr Oliphant :—

Cannstatt, Oct. 18, 1854.

'It has pleased God to withdraw from us the bodily
presence of our dear daughter Shireen, our first-born thus
following in just three weeks our last-born to the tomb.
I blessed God in the midst of my distress for allowing me
the comfort of finding that she not only submitted to the
Divine appointment concerning her, but accepted it with
a cheerful spirit, and was enabled to move on, day by day,

consciously nearing the unseen world with an unshaken countenance, strong in the assured belief that to depart and to be with Christ was far better for her than aught which life could have in store. I thanked God with all my heart for this high grace granted to her; and while our affections have been deeply smitten by the loss of one so dear and so highly gifted, we refuse not the comfort which the contemplation of a death so serene and cheerful is calculated to afford to those who know that hopeless sorrow is a sin.'

His sensations at this period of bereavement were such as himself had already portrayed, though he knew not then how soon the case described was, in God's mysterious providence, to be his own. As he bent over the corpse of his lovely and accomplished daughter, his first-born and joy, did he not remember what he had once said with such truth and tenderness?

'With this instance in view [that of the Prince Abijah], we can find the parallels of lives, full of hope and promise, prematurely taken, and that in mercy, as we can judge, to those who depart. The heavenly Husbandman often gathers for His garner the fruit that early ripens, without suffering it to hang needlessly long, beaten by storms, upon the tree. Oh, how often, as many a grieved heart can tell, do the Lord's best beloved die betimes— taken from the evil to come; while the unripe, the evil, the injurious, live long for mischief to themselves and others! Roses and lilies wither far sooner than thorns and thistles.'[1]

The corpse, being that of a young and unmarried woman, was, according to the custom of the country, crowned with a wreath of myrtle blossoms, and the father was moved to tears at the spectacle. His deep sorrow

[1] Daily Bible Illustrations, vol. iv., p. 159.

had not as yet ventured to express itself in words. It wa
a double trial in a land of strangers,—himself expecting
soon to be joined to both his children, and anxious to
have a place secured for his own grave, by the side of that
of Shireen.

'The circumstances of this great loss, following so soon
upon the other, awakened much sympathy among the
kind-hearted Germans, and the myrtle-crowned corpse
was followed to the tomb by a large train of spontaneous mourners, composed *mostly* of persons unknown to
us, and who are not likely to be known. I was not
among them; for although I had seen her die, the doctor
and our friends here prevailed upon me to abstain from
attending her to the grave. But neither the bier nor the
tomb is here invested with the dismal incidents and ideas
which prevail in England. All is here made significant of
cheerful hope, as among the early. Christians. All the
symbols and inscriptions in the churchyard are of this
character, and the yard itself is called the "peace-yard"
(*Friedhof*), a sense which is probably local, as I find it not
in dictionaries. I forbear to tell you of the many things
this dear child was to do for me, and with me, "when she
got well;" and I am not yet strong enough to dwell upon
the close affinities of mind and character, and the ever
ready and quick apprehension on her part, which drew her
very near to me, and rendered my intercourse with her a.
delight. But all this is over. Year after year, week after
week, I am bereaved of my children; and other trials—
frustrated purposes, loss of health, loss of means, expatria-
tion from the land I love—all these, though heavy, seem
light in comparison. God help me—and I assuredly know
and believe that, even with this large addition to my afflictions, He *does* and will help me, and that His help is sufficient for me in all things.

'My head has suffered considerably from these trials, which necessarily involved the suspension of my usual exercise. But my poor wife, in addition to these wounds to her maternal affections, has had great personal fatigues, and nights of watching to undergo; and these together have left her in a state of much disturbed health, from which I trust that rest may restore her. She and I, with our son, have been this day to visit the grave of our two children (for they allowed the little one to be taken up and deposited with his sister), and we found it overspread with very beautiful garlands—free-will offerings of the good people here.'

Dr Kitto's last letter but one has a peculiar interest attaching to it. Mr Davis, once a publisher in London, but latterly a very prosperous settler in South Australia, having seen, in a London newspaper, some account of the benevolent exertions making for Dr Kitto, generously transmitted a subscription; and to him, as an acknowledgment in return, was sent the following note, so ripe in Christian feeling and hope :—

Cannstatt, Wurtemberg, Oct. 27, 1854.

'DEAR SIR,—Mr Oliphant has forwarded to me your kind letter, with its enclosure, and I beg you to accept my earnest thanks for both. In the midst of the trials which have been sent me, and by which I am laid aside from the labours in which I took much delight, I have been greatly comforted and encouraged by the strong interest for me which has been expressed by many who have known me only by those labours, and which has been evinced in warm and hearty endeavours to ameliorate the relievable evils of the condition to which I am reduced. Of these kind voices, none have reached me from so distant a quarter, nor have any been more encouraging than yours. To.

know that any of the writings which I have been enabled
to produce have been useful, under the circumstances you
indicate, in the land most distant from our own, is a
satisfaction very dear to my heart; and the accompany-
ing expressions of kind sympathy towards me will not be
the less precious to me, as coming from one whose name
is familiar to my remembrance, from its presence on the
titles of many publications which I used to see in former
times.

' The refreshment of your very friendly communication
comes most seasonably to me; for, in the short time since
I have been in this place—for benefit of health and economy
of living—my cup has been filled very high, in the loss of
my eldest daughter and youngest son, whom, within three
short weeks, I have laid in one grave. But though heart-
smitten, I have not been allowed to sorrow as having no
hope; and I begin to perceive, that, by these variously
afflictive dispensations, my Lord is calling me " up hither"
to the higher room in which He sits, that I may see more
of His grace, and that I may more clearly understand the
inner mysteries of His kingdom. What more awaits me,
I guess not. But the Lord's will be done.—I am, dear
sir, with affectionate regard, most truly yours,

' JOHN KITTO.'

On the same day, Dr Kitto wrote his last letter to his
friend and publisher. It breathes a spirit of deep composure; for the writer was now, as himself says of David,
' past all danger, for he knew he was to die.' ' We are
still most sorrowful; but, not being " forsaken," we try to
gather strength from the belief, that He whose love has
been so often proved, would not willingly lay upon us one
stroke more than is needed for our essential welfare, and
for the final welfare of those whom He has taken. My

dear wife was greatly cheered by Dr Brown's most kind
and considerate letter.   I may mention that, upon our first
loss here, we read his "Comfortable Words" all through
together (that is, I read it to her), and were indeed greatly
comforted by it.   We, more than once, exclaimed with
Mr Sherman, "God bless John Brown for writing this
book!"[1]

The time had now come when he 'must die.'   His work
was over, and he was calmly waiting to be called up.   He
was neither impatient to depart nor anxious to remain, for,
by God's grace, he was enabled to say, 'My times are in
Thy hand.'   The last weeks of his life were spent in quiet
meditation; and as soon as Shireen was buried, he selected
as his favourite chamber the room in which she had died,
whom he was so soon to follow.   He was soothed by
looking 'on the same scenes she had last looked on.'   His
spirit must have often pondered on the strange path by
which Providence had led him — a ragged boy, toiling
beyond his strength, till a terrible calamity disabled him
—a miserable stripling, forced into an almshouse—an apprentice to an ingenious form of surgical art—a printer
on a Mediterranean isle—a stranger in a far-off city of the
plague—a literary workman in the metropolis—a famed
illustrator of Scripture — and now a worn-out invalid,
about to enter upon his final rest and reward.   Thoughts,
too deep for utterance, and too sacred for publicity, must
have often sprung from such a retrospect.   He had sur-
vived an accident all but fatal; had outlived his own
purpose to die; had stood unscathed when thousands fell
before the 'burning pestilence' on all sides of him; and
now he understood the reason why Divine benignity had

[1] Mr Sherman said so in a letter of sympathy to the Rev. Dr M'Farlane of
Glasgow, prefacing the benediction by these words:—'If you have not seen his
sweet book, read it; if you have, read it again.' See Dr M'Farlane's touching
and consolatory little work, 'Why Weepest Thou?' pp. 74, 75. London: Nisbet.

uniformly spared him. The dreams of his youth had been more than realised, for—

       'Dreams grow realities to earnest men.'

But he had been informed long ago, by the Angel Zared, that 'the period of his sojourn on earth would not be, at furthest, very many years.' Of this ideal warning he had been reminded by the alarming illnesses which had so often seized him, and which had proved themselves to be seated beyond the power of dislodgment in that vital organ, which, though it had been so materially injured in early life, had still, by the forced abundance of its fruits, provided food and raiment for him and his. For many years of his earlier manhood, there had been little to attach him to life. Then he felt himself to be all but useless, and he was to a great extent dependent on others. But the later portion of his career had been signally successful; and, in the midst of his fame and usefulness, these premonitions of decease gathered thickly around him. The idea that he had fallen into a second state of dependence and uselessness, deeply affected him; yet he repined not; and, though he might wonder at the mysterious dispensation, he strove to profit by it. Two mornings before he died, he said, among other things, to his wife— 'Somehow I begin to feel a sad distaste of life. I am now in a useless state, with little hope, that I can see, of ever being useful again.' He added, 'I, who have all my life been in the habit of referring everything to God, naturally sit and ask myself what all these things mean, and endeavour, if possible, to find out what His mind towards me is; and, unless it be to draw me to Himself, I confess I am at a loss.'

His conclusion was just, and it was consoling too, as his experience had told him; for, since to-morrow was to be his last day on earth, there had been special kindness in

weaning him from life, and filling him with the consciousness, that every step towards and along the 'dark valley'
was a step nearer glory and God. She who had so deep
an interest in it, has herself described that solemn scene,
which left her a widow and her children fatherless :—

'In the evening he read to me Thackeray's Lecture on
Goldsmith, and said, that was the right spirit in which to
view literature, and expressed how much more happily and
respectably he had spent his life in that pursuit than he
could have done in any other occupation. He sat reading
till eleven o'clock, and seemed quite pleased that I had
been able to rest so long listening to him. He then retired
for the night. About three o'clock in the morning, I was
awakened by his step in the room. I immediately sprang
up, and inquired what was the matter. He said, "Unless I can be sick, I feel I shall be very ill." I applied
some remedies, which had the desired effect, and wished
to send for Dr Burckhardt, his medical attendant, but he
would not allow me, saying, "it would pass off." I did
not feel any particular alarm, and he went again to bed,
and slept till about seven, when I inquired how he was.
He said he felt better, and asked for his *sauerwasser*. He
then rose and dressed himself, but said he would defer the
more laborious process of shaving and washing till he had
·taken his breakfast. He sat at the table with the children
and myself. As soon as they had gone to school, he said,
"Well, after all, I think I must have a very strong constitution to stand what I have gone through. I never felt
so conscious as last night of the approach of a fit, and had
I not been sick I am sure I should have had one." Then,
making two or three circles with his finger, to signify
giddiness, he added, almost in the same breath, "Look
sharp, Bell!" I saw he was greatly affected, and caught
hold of him, calling loudly to the servants, whom I hurried

off to fetch Dr Burckhardt, and our kind friend Mr Hirsch, who had shown himself throughout most anxious to render every assistance in his power. Dear Kitto seeing I was greatly agitated, waved his hand gently up and down, signifying to me to be composed. His chest heaved violently, and continued doing so at intervals of about half an hour. Between the paroxysms, he kept trying his eyes, his fingers, and his tongue, and said, " My impression is I shall die." Medicine was given, but it could not be retained. He sat on his chair, with his feet in a mustard bath, and leeches on his temples, and, after an interval of some hours, he was bled in the foot. There seemed, however, no signs of amendment. About two o'clock in the day he was removed to bed. But the chest kept constantly heaving, and the head was swollen, and the face very red. Stertorous breathing commenced, and it became very difficult to understand him ; all told too plainly that, in a few hours, we should be left desolate. In the early part of the evening he said, "I am being choked. Is it death ?" I spoke with my fingers, but I saw that he could not make out what I said. I then, with my head, signified that it was. He added, " Pray God to take me soon." These were his last words. He continued for some hours in this agony, which no human power could alleviate. Mr Hirsch, and other kind friends, offered to sit with us during the· night, but all help of man was vain. Towards five o'clock, the convulsive struggle became too agonising to witness, and Dr Burckhardt, who had been sent for, insisted upon my retiring, and would not suffer me again to return. I never saw him afterwards. About seven o'clock I was told that all was over, and that my beloved husband had entered into the rest prepared for the people of God.'

Yes, rest had been prescribed for him by physicians, and urged upon him by friends, and he had gone to Cannstatt in search of it; but, on the morning of the 25th of November, he passed into that repose which the brave and the true enjoy, through the merits and mediation of the Exalted Redeemer.

'Spirit! thy labour is o'er!
Thy term of probation is run:
Thy steps are now bound for the untrodden shore,
And the joy of immortals begun.

'Spirit! look not on the strife,
Or the pleasures of earth with regret—
Pause not on the threshold of limitless life,
To mourn for the day that is set.

'Spirit! no fetters can bind,
No troubles have power to molest:
There the worn out like thee—the weary shall find
A haven, a mansion of rest.

'Spirit! how bright is the road
For which thou art now on the wing!
Thy home it will be, with thy Saviour and God,
The loud hallelujah to sing.'

The funeral, according to German usage, took place two days after his death. Dr Gleissberg the dean officiated, and the service began and concluded with praise and prayer. A sketch of Dr Kitto's life and labours was also given, and followed up with such impressive lessons as the scene suggested. The English residents, and a large concourse of the native population, followed to their resting-place the remains of the illustrious stranger, whose brief abode among them had been checkered with such trials. To be buried at Plymouth ' in New Churchyard beside Granny,' was his boyish prayer, but he sleeps with his two children in the cemetery of Cannstatt; and a handsome monument, erected by the publisher of his last work, marks and adorns the hallowed spot. The monogram, surrounded by a chaplet and winged with palm leaves, which is carved on the upper part of the stone, is taken from a slab in the Roman catacombs, and was the print selected by him for the concluding paper of his Daily Bible Illustrations, and appropriately symbolises his own warfare and his victory—ay, more than victory—through Christ.

The monument, with its inscription, is here presented:—

In Memoriam
IOANNIS KITTO, D.D., ANGLI,

INGENIO, DOCTRINA, PIETATE CLARISSIMI,

QUI ETSI MULTIS FORTUNÆ IMPEDIMENTIS OBSTRICTUS,

ATQUE JAM PUER CASU CAPTUS FUIT AURIBUS,

TAMEN LEGENDO ET PEREGRINANDO

MAGNAM VARIAMQUE SIBI CUMULAVIT ERUDITIONEM,

QUAM PERMULTIS LIBRIS,

IMPRIMIS SCRIPTURAS SACRAS ILLUSTRANTIBUS,

EXPOSUIT.

STUDIIS CONFECTUS IN GERMANIAM SE CONTULIT

UT VALETUDINEM DEBILITATAM RESTAURARET,

IBIQUE VITAM SEMPITERNAM IN CHRISTO INVENIT.

NATUS PLYMOUTHLÆ DIE IV MENS. DECEMB. AN. MDCCCIV,

MORTUUS EST CANNSTADIÆ DIE XXV MENS. NOVEMB. AN. MDCCCLIV.

ANNABELLA SHIREEN, FILIA EJUS PRIMOGENITA, MORTEM OBIIT XIII OCTOB. MDCCCLIV., ANNO ÆTATIS VICESIMO PRIMO;

HENRICUS HARLOWE, FILIUS NATU MINIMUS, XXI SEPTEMB. EJUSDEM ANNI, VIX DECEM MENSES NATUS.

CHAPTER XII.

MANY authors are remembered, not for their lives, but for their works. Their personality is lost, and they are known by what they have achieved, not by what they have been.

'Not myself, but the truth that in life I have spoken ;
Not myself, but the seed that in life I have sown,
Shall pass on to ages, all about me forgotten,
Save the words I have written, the deeds I have done.'

But this silent separation of the author from his works cannot happen in the case of Dr Kitto, whose name is now immortally associated with biblical study and literature. For the measure of his success is not more amazing in its amount than in the means by which he reached it. His life is as instructive as are his labours ; and the two combined, present an unequalled picture of triumph over obstacles which have been very rarely so surmounted, and ever circumstances which few have ventured to encounter, and which fewer still have mastered to such advantage. He did not merely neutralise the adverse position of his earlier years, but he wrung from it the lessons and habits which slowly built up his fame, as they prepared him for his ultimate achievements. Truly has he realised the riddle of Samson—'Out of the eater came forth meat, and out of the strong came forth sweetness.' What a contrast

between the deaf and pauper boy of 1819, wheedled into
a workhouse to keep him from 'hunger and fasting, cold
and nakedness,' and the John Kitto of 1854, doctor of
Divinity though a layman, member of the Society of Antiquaries, Editor of the Pictorial Bible and the Cyclopædia
of Biblical Literature, and author of the Daily Bible
Illustrations. The interval between the two extremes was
long, and sometimes very gloomy; yet he bore bravely up,
with earnest resolution and strong faith in God, often
murmuring to himself—

> 'Be still, sad heart! and cease repining,
> Behind the clouds the sun is shining.'

We have already characterised, in the preceding pages,
those numerous literary and biblical productions which
occupied the last twenty years of Dr Kitto's life. Suffice
it now to say of them generally, that they work principally
on the outer aspects of Scripture, and seldom touch the
deeper difficulties that lie beneath. Such labours have,
however, their own value; for, though they do not inter-
pret, they may conduct to the interpretation. They break
the husk, though they do not bring out the kernel. Many
of the topical descriptions so lavishly given in the quartos
of Conybeare and Howson, contribute not a whit to a just
exposition; but they wonderfully freshen our conceptions
of the toil and travels of the great apostle. On the other
hand, Smith's expository description of Paul's voyage[1] is
true to the life; the nautical language—ropes, anchors,
sails — is dexterously unravelled; the positions of the
labouring ship, day after day, are laid down with a sea-
man's precision; and the wreck and the scene of it are
delineated with such fulness and accuracy, that at once he
sketches a picture and completes an exegesis.

---

[1] 'The Voyage and Shipwreck of St Paul,' etc. By James Smith, Esq. of Jor-
danhill, F.R.S. London, 1848.

Sometimes Dr Kitto's illustrations are too ingenious, and sometimes, though rarely, they are beside the mark. Thus, in the Pictorial Bible and in the Daily Bible Illustrations, he holds up Ephron the Hittite as utterly supple and dishonest in his transaction with Abraham about the cave of Machpelah, and denies him all generosity, if not integrity—a mode of representation unwarranted by the narrative, and which errs in interpreting the ancient and simple manners of Canaan by the ingenious flatteries and lying courtesies of modern Persia. In writing under Acts xix. 2, of the question which, properly rendered, is, ' Did ye receive the Holy Ghost when ye believed ?' and of the answer, ' We did not so much as hear whether there be any Holy Ghost,' he understands the language as referring to the existence or person of the Spirit; whereas the context makes it obvious that it is to the gift, or rather the extraordinary endowments of the Spirit, that the querist and his twelve respondents refer—for when they were baptized, ' the Holy Ghost came on them, and they spake with tongues and prophesied.' In his remarks upon the rapid increase of Israel in Egypt, he declares—' After all the learned and sagacious talk about the laws of population and of human increase, there is really no law of increase in any population but the will of God.' No one doubts this great truth, yet surely the will of God neither acts without law nor by miracle, but according to certain physiological principles, which may be detected and explained. Under Ezekiel xiii. 10, 11, he has a curious dissertation on 'cob-walls'—a species of rude buildings formed of mud, and found in the south-west of England. But he jumps at once to the conclusion, that the process had been carried, like his own name, from Phœnicia to Devonshire, from Canaan to Cornwall. But the same methods of clay-masonry are found in Scotland and else-

where, and need not be traced to any other origin than
poverty and necessity. Mr Urquhart and he are puzzled
much about the syllable 'cob,' which certainly has a variety
of meanings in compounded forms, and they regard 'cob-
web' as meaning the wall and the web; whereas the first
syllable in *cob*web is simply the last of the early name of
the insect, called attercop still in Denmark, and in many
parts of Scotland and England.

The late Hugh Miller, an immortal example of the successful pursuit of science under difficulties, which to the
majority of men would have been insuperable, has, in his
last work, 'The Testimony of the Rocks,' taken Dr Kitto
as the exponent of the popular view of the universality of
the Noachic deluge. In our opinion, his direct refutation
of Dr Kitto fails on some points, turning the edge of the
weapon without breaking it, and is greatly inferior in
cogency and conclusiveness to the positive and very striking argument for his own hypothesis. Another recent
author has taken up and rebuked both Dr Kitto and ourselves upon a point on which he possesses practical skill
and experience.[1] The matter in dispute is the demolition
of the golden calf by Moses. The conjecture may be un-
tenable, that Moses dissolved the calf in some chemical
fluid, and mixed the nauseous potion with the water which
he compelled the Israelites to drink, though certainly a
solvent sufficient for the purpose might easily be fixed upon,
and might be known to Egyptian chemistry. The words
of Moses are, 'he burned it in the fire, and ground it to
powder, and strewed it upon the water,'—' he stamped it

[1] The Ancient Workers and Artificers in Metal, from References in the Old Testament and other Ancient Writings. By James Napier, F.C.S. 1856. This interesting and informing little work loses much of its value to the student, because,
with the exception of quotations from Scripture, it does not note the sources of its
extracts. It is, besides, far more profuse about modern than ancient metallurgy,
and ingeniously misinterprets several passages of the Bible, by giving them a
chemical allusion rather than a popular sense.

and ground it very small, even until it was small as dust.'
The text implies that the 'burning' in the fire was not
fusion, as our opponent supposes, for surely burning is not
melting, but some unknown process that prepared the
metal for being 'stamped' and then 'ground' to powder—a
process which Mr Napier, though he meditated a book on
'the Chemistry of the Bible,' has certainly not discovered,
but has been obliged to leave unexplained.

Dr Kitto's life was one of heroic daring and perseverance.
With a dissipated father and a broken-hearted mother,
afflicted with a deafness which a sad accident had brought
upon him, left pretty much to himself, and prone to wander about the fields, or lie among the rocks, the lad might
have grown up to lead a vagabond life, without settled
aim or occupation. But the waif, tossed about on the
billows, and in danger of being carried out to sea, was
floated into the haven of the old Plymouth workhouse.
And what was to be done with him there? In kindness,
the overseer set him to shoemaking, and probably his
relations thought him now provided for during life, and
reckoned the use of awl and pincers a fitting occupation
for a jobbing mason's disabled apprentice. And had
it not been for his mental elasticity, he would certainly
have been a poor labourer all his days. By and by he is
leased out to a brutal tyrant, who made the poor boy so
utterly wretched, that he cherished to familiarity the idea
of suicide. He 'tried hard to be happy, but it would not
do,' and at length he longed

> ' to be hurled
> Anywhere, anywhere, out of the world.'

Ah! little did Mr Bowden know, when he was so cruelly
cuffing his helpless drudge, and dashing a tobacco-pipe or
a shoe in his face, that the object of his contumely was
faithfully committing to record, in his Journal, the whole

of the brutal procedure, to be turned up thirty years after
wards to the gaze and reprobation of the world. The indenture must be cancelled, and the magistrates mercifully
sent him back to the almshouse: but he did not sink into
apathy, nor did his spirit prey upon itself, and become the
nursery or the victim of dark and vengeful passions.
Many, alas! in more propitious circumstances than his,
have yielded to such temptation. Byron's lameness was
an evil incomparably less than Kitto's deafness, and yet it
so soured his Lordship's temper, that he could not endure an unwitting allusion to his halt. It could be borne
that his mother called him a brat, but that she called him
'a lame brat,' was ever a plague-spot on his memory.
Shut out from intercourse with society, Kitto never learned
to hate it—cheerless and homeless, a butt to the wilder
boys, sometimes pitied and sometimes slighted, he maintained a calm and firm temper; and, at length, he could
speak and write of his infirmity with the analytical precision of a physiologist, and the quiet resignation of a child
of God, to whom all things 'work together for good.' It
was, indeed, a rough training to which he had been subjected. But it was not without its benefits; for though he
was not what he has himself called a 'mother-bred youth,'
yet a good deal of his earliest days would have badly 'fitted
him to endure the sharp air and gusty winds of practical
life.' 'The *hardening* of such a character is the most distressing moral process to which life is subject. Tender to
touch as the mimosa, morbidly sensitive to every influence
from without, even the kindness of *men* seems rough, while
neglect wounds and unkindness kills. Apt to see offence
where love is meant, mortified to be no longer the *first* object of thought and solicitude to all around,—such a young
man, in his first adventure from home, cannot possibly
find any society in which his self-esteem will not be deeply.

wounded.'[1]   The distinctness of this picture shows that it
was a sketch of himself, and the reminiscence is as sore as
if the wounds had scarcely been healed.

And that terrible fall was a prime means of his elevation.
But for this accident, the Cornish miner's grandson might
have been a decent tradesman, superior to his class in intelligence and moral worth, an active member of a Mechanics'
Institute, or a leading spirit in the committee of a public
library.   Men might have said, that the younger Kitto had
retrieved the good name which his father had lost.   The
boy had always a fondness for books; but his deafness,
shutting him out of the world, forced him, by an irresistible
instinct, to hold converse with himself and others upon
paper.   There was in him a yearning for interchange of
thought, and therefore, as he had few friends, he wrote
letters to himself, and communed with himself through his
' Journal.'   Had he been born a deaf mute, the same result
and tendency would not have been so strongly felt.   But
twelve years of boy-life, formed an experience not easily
forgotten.   Through that mysterious and instinctive necessity which exists between thoughts and language, what he
had been accustomed to put into words, he longed to put
into words still.   As he could not hear his own words, so
he compensated himself with seeing them, and the eye became the natural substitute for the ear.   In the meanwhile,
his spirit was sustained by such nutriment and solace; and
literature, of the humblest sort, was a welcome luxury.
The native vigour of his mind achieved for him a good
self-education.   Kind friends noticed him, and took him
out of the Workhouse—' O happy hour!'[2]   But few of
them guessed what was in him.   They could not see what
fire was in the flint, for it had not been struck.   He was at

[1] Daily Bible Illustrations, vol. viii., p. 271.
[2] Letter to Mr Harvey, July 20, 1823.

this period not unlike Beattie's Minstrel, the object of most
opposite opinions—

'   Silent when glad—affectionate, though shy;
    And now his look was most demurely sad;
    And now he laughed aloud, yet none knew why;
    The neighbours stared and sighed, and blessed the lad;
    Some deemed him wondrous wise, and some believed him mad.'

He was, in fact, not fully aware of his own capabilities,
and, step by step, was he unconsciously led on to celebrity and usefulness.   Had there not been a deeper power
in him than was surmised, he might have remained in
charge of book-shelves in Plymouth or in Exeter—might,
perhaps, have written a few miscellanies, or done work
for some of the London publishers.   But he would have
come short of that high excellence to which he ultimately
attained—an excellence, based as much on the nature of
his studies as on the success with which they were pursued.   As he has said in one of his Journals, ' Talent is
common, but the art of unfolding talent is not so common.   Those whom we call men of talent had, perhaps,
ten thousand contemporaries of equal talent, but who had
not equal art and facility in unfolding the gifts they possessed.'

His romantic connection with Mr Groves was the turning point of his life.   It opened up a new path of labour
in connection with the Church of England Missionary
Society.   Manual toil it was, but it awoke novel ideas and
prospects.   At length his journey to Bagdad fulfilled one
of his first dreams, and revealed to his quick eye the very
dress and manners of early times.   He saw the East, and
soon learned to perceive what biblical illustrations might
be gleaned from it.   The seeds of piety had been sown in
his heart by his kind and loving grandmother, but they
were quickened by the conversation and example of Mr

Groves; so that, when the time came, he took to biblical work as a congenial task, and therefore he rose in it to signal eminence. Again, his deafness aided him. It threw him ever on his own mental resources; led him to retire into his own heart, and commune with his Maker; and gave his mind that special liking for Scripture, and all about it, which fitted him so well to illustrate it. The mere love of fame, so natural to youth, gradually subsided, though the natural desire of appreciation still remained. 'I did,' he avows, 'earnestly desire to leave to the age beyond some record of my past existence, and thereby establish a point of communication between my own mind and the unborn generations.'[1] He has recorded his obligation to a member of the Society of Friends, who showed him great kindness when few thought of him, and especially impressed upon him this idea, 'that it was the duty of every rational creature to devote whatever talents God had given him to useful purposes.'[2] The counsel took effect, and, as 'a word spoken in season,' aided in producing large results.

Had Dr Kitto been born in such affluence as to receive a good education, and to have been enabled to live among books, and occasionally to compose a biblical paper for amusement, he would have been regarded as a literary phenomenon. Had he done even a tithe of what he has done, without any such disadvantages as he had to contend with, he would still have been entitled to no little thanks. But he had to fight for life as well as for learning, had to work sore and hard for food and raiment, while slowly acquiring the elements of knowledge. His question was not what shall I eat, but how shall I get it—not what shall I put on, but how shall I contrive to provide it. Such a conflict might have absorbed all his energies, but the battle for

---

[1] Lost Senses—Deafness, p. 89.   [2] Ibid., p. 91.

bread only hardened him for the struggle after knowledge.
The late Duke of Sussex possessed a magnificent biblical
library, comprising many thousand volumes, and he could
occasionally talk of better versions and happier renderings.
Many gentlemen who have similar tastes, and are not without extensive information in the literature of Scripture,
can propose various readings, and defend ingenious translations. But study is to these dilettanti a matter of luxury
and pastime, and rarely do they produce much of permanent merit or utility. Kitto, on the other hand, had to
educate himself while wearied out with manual toil. He
had to gather his library with the fragments of his scanty
earnings, the crumbs that fell from his frugal table—had,
in fact, both to create his instruments, and teach himself
how to use them. He had to collect the clay and glean
the straw ; and not only has he made the bricks, but he
has built them into structures, stored with richer treasures
than were Pithom and Raamses.

There can be little doubt that Dr Kitto's infirmity increased his natural love of books. His own account is,
‘ Whatever acquirements I have been able to make, have
been built up in solitude upon the foundation of the taste
for and habit of reading, which I had acquired at an early
age, *before* I had lost my hearing. How it would have
fared with me had not this taste been previously formed, I
am afraid to conjecture.’[1] Books became his companions.
He did not simply handle them, he fondled them. A book
was a thing of life and fellowship to him. It spoke to his
heart in frank companionship. What a wistful eye he cast
on some favourite lying on a bookstall, when he painfully
knew the purchase to be beyond his means ! He seemed
to feel that the book instinctively understood his yearning
towards it, and sympathised with him. Day by day, as

[1] Letter to Mr Oliphant, March 30, 1850

he passed the spot, the book and he exchanged lovers' glances; and this coquetry would last for months. When speaking of Kirjath-Sepher, as meaning 'Book-city,' and therefore probably having some library within it, he says, with true zest, 'By the dear love we bear to books, which place within our grasp the thought and knowledge of all ages and of all climes, we exult in this inevitable conclusion.' Referring to the Pictorial Bible, he tells Mr Knight, 'Never was there any commentary that required more help from books, and yet perhaps no work of the kind was ever undertaken by a person with a more scanty library. It was my peculiar disadvantage, to have no books at all when I came to England. I had a very decent collection for a person in my circumstances; but I have never heard of it since I left it at Bagdad, to be sent home by way of India.'[1] Books, however, were gradually accumulated by him at no small expense, till he could boast of a library 'three thousand five hundred strong.'

The books common in his younger days were of a far inferior class to those in circulation in his riper years, and were also considerably dearer in price. 'To bring this home,' he calculates, 'let us see how I might now employ a weekly sixpence, which in those times would only have furnished me with about thirty-two loosely printed octavo pages, sixteen of quarto, or eight of folio, being a portion of a work to be completed in from thirty to a hundred numbers, and perhaps containing a cut in every fourth number. The same sum would now enable me to obtain regularly the Penny Magazine, one number; the Penny Cyclopædia, two numbers; the Saturday Magazine, one number; and Chambers' Edinburgh Journal, one number; leaving me, besides, an overplus of a weekly halfpenny, which, at the end of the month, would more than enable

[1] Letter to Mr Knight, Feb. 22, 1837.

me to obtain Chambers' Information for the People. Thus, for my weekly sixpence, I should have five distinct publications, containing a large body of interesting information, and comprehending about eight times the quantity of printed matter which my sixpence would formerly have purchased. Besides this, instead of one engraving for every third or fourth sixpence which I expended, I should now have from eight to twelve neat and instructive cuts included with my printed matter; and, at the end of the year, I should be the possessor of six large volumes, containing altogether upwards of 2000 closely printed pages, and comprehending from 400 to 500 engravings.'[1]

Few men have made better use of books than Dr Kitto. All his productions teem with the results of his multifarious reading. Not that he multiplies extracts unnecessarily, either with slovenly profusion or with the parade of learning; for his selections tell at once upon the case in hand, and in their aptness lies their force. So appropriate are many of them, so exactly do they hit the precise point, that one is apt to compare him to the left-handed warriors of Benjamin, who could ' sling at an hairbreadth and not miss.' The awful stillness in which he lived, gave him special facility in consulting books, and his undisturbed attention enabled him to turn all that he read to the best advantage.

His deafness gave also peculiar power to his eye,—

> 'For oft when one sense is suppressed,
> It but retires into the rest.'

This ocular discipline was, indeed, a natural necessity. But it imparts a vividness to his descriptions. He excels in word-painting. He tells you what he has seen so distinctly, that you see it too. Every scene that he beheld seemed to be photographed on his memory. Even when,

[1] Penny Magazine, voL iv., p. 228.

as he quaintly describes it, he *saw* without *looking*, he could trust implicitly to his impressions. He adduces in proof, that his wife and he went to Woking to look out for a house, and that, when they began to talk about it afterwards—the day, indeed, before taking possession of it—she, who had been on a second visit to it, affirmed that the front was of plaster, while he maintained that it was 'good red brick.' He had merely seen, and not looked; but he was correct. 'I confess,' he adds, 'that I allowed myself to exult at this, as it was a very strong proof of the *distinctness* of the faculty of minute observation.' He had been in the habit of noting whatever he observed. At Bagdad, objects of natural history interested him; and his accounts, in his Journal, of the form, habits, and doings of certain species of wasps and spiders, have not a little of the quaint and amusing minuteness of Gilbert White of Selborne. In consequence of this faculty, one of his paragraphs is often equal to an engraving or a panoramic picture. The effect is the same, whether he describe a tree or a mob, a landscape or a portion of dress. His style is eminently pictorial, and, by a few masterly strokes, he paints what he has set before you. In this power he resembles another, who has raised himself to imperishable renown in physical science. When the late Hugh Miller figures in words a fossil fish, its jaw, or fin, or general shape; or describes the attitude in which it was found, the species of rock in which it is imbedded, or the scene in which the discovery took place, his reader comprehends the object or place as clearly as if he beheld it, and the pencil is felt to be almost a superfluous aid.

Dr Kitto's eye was one peculiar source of enjoyment to him. It drank in a rich and unfailing pleasure from the landscape. He loved, therefore, to traverse the Hoe at Plymouth, to saunter on the baraccas or high terraces at

Malta, and to gaze around him as he lounged on the housetop at Bagdad. A flower or tree was a special delight; nature, in all her visible forms, enchanted him. He liked to see the old trees swinging their great boughs in the storm, and 'to *fancy the sound.*' He could well comprehend the seductions of grove worship, from the sensation which he experienced among 'the endless fir woods of northern Europe, the magnificent plane trees of Media, and the splendid palm groves of the Tigris.' His study was usually selected, not so much for his convenience, as that it might enable 'his view to rest upon trees, whenever his eyes were raised from the book he read or the paper on which he wrote.'[1] He could describe, with astonishing vividness, not only what he looked on, but also any imaginary scene which appealed to the vision. What he saw in his mind's eye, he could tell as clearly, and with the same effect, as what he saw with those large and lustrous orbs. ·I can live again,' he assures us, 'at will, in the midst of any scenes or circumstances by which I have been once surrounded. By a voluntary act of mind, I can in a moment conjure up the whole of any one out of the innumerable scenes, in which the slightest interest has been at any time felt by me. If I wish to realise a scene, or to conjure up the view of a place, it comes before me, peopled with the very persons I saw in it.'[2] Paintings delighted him; but he could not endure such glaring improprieties as painters of Scripture scenes too often commit—'the Prodigal Son in trunk breeches, and king Joash as a half-naked mulatto;' or, we might add, the Jewish high-priest, in full pontifical costume, immolating Jephthah's daughter; blind Bartimeus with a violin on his arm; or the angelic choir over the common of Bethlehem, chanting with a music-book spread out on the clouds

---

[1] Lost Senses—Deafness, pp. 56, 57.　　　　[2] Ibid., p. 68.

before them. His eye had also a special quickness, and its informing glance told him what question you were about to propose. The writer was struck with this peculiarity when he met with Dr Kitto. The moment he saw you looking at anything, he divined at once what you meant to ask, or what had attracted your attention. He read the thought as unerringly as if he had heard the question. Long practice had produced a facility, which had all the promptness and sureness of an instinct. The vigour, in short, of many of his descriptive passages, is owing to the use which he was forced to make of his vision, to supply, as far as possible, the service of the organ which had been so utterly destroyed.

Yet there is no question that this defect told upon his composition in another form. His sentences sometimes want rhythm, the clauses are occasionally rugged, and his manuscripts exhibit a word or an epithet recurring in contiguous members of the same sentence. He had lost so far the feeling of sound, and his eyesight could not guide him. His poetry exhibits this aural defect of 'halting, hopping feet;' and he admits that he could not recognise or rectify it, and that he had always a misgiving on the subject. The effect of such verbal repetition could be learned only from reading, for though he might read aloud himself, he heard no syllable. A strange mystery—to use what were sounds to others, but none to himself; to speak, with what tones he could not tell; and to articulate, with what results he could only faintly remember or dimly imagine. He was sensible of this defect, and sought sometimes to prove his MSS. by fancying the effect of reading them. Still he had sensations which appeared like those of sound. Perceiving, on one occasion, that I did not fully comprehend his deep guttural speech, he said at once, 'I feel that I am not in good voice to-day.' 'I have often,' he assures us, 'calculated that above two-thirds of my vocabulary consist of words which I never heard pronounced.' The words of his first vocabulary he continued to pronounce as he had done in boyhood, and he could not get over the provincial pronunciation of *tay* for *tea*, though he was perfectly aware of the error. Uneducated people are apt to write words according to their sounds; but he was liable to pronounce words as they are written, and as he generally brought out all the syllables, German strangers, having some acquaintance with English, usually understood him better than his own countrymen.[1]

But while we ascribe so much to the disaster which befel him, we must not forget his extraordinary diligence and perseverance. What he did, he did with his might. It was not a feat, and done with it, but patient and protracted industry. He did not spring to his prey like the lion, but he performed his daily task like the ox. He did his work with considerable ease, but he was always at his work. He was either fishing or mending his nets, either composing or preparing for composition. From his earliest days he could not be idle; his repose was in activity—not unlike the swallow, which feeds and rests on the wing. He wrote to Mr Woollcombe, in 1827:—' I have no peculiar talent; I do not want it; it would do me more harm than good. I only think that I have a certain degree of industry, which, *applied to its proper object*, may make me an instrument of usefulness—of greater usefulness, perhaps, than *mere talent* can enable any man to effect.' He declares also to the same friend from Bagdad:—' All the fine stories we hear about *natural ability* are mere *rigmarole;* every man may, according to his opportunities and industry, render himself almost anything he wishes to become.' At a later period, in 1841, he asserts to Mr Knight, ' I am quite

---

[1] Lost Senses—Deafness, pp. 23, 24.

sensible that I am in a condition to undertake what others would shrink from. I am fitted, by a variety of circumstances, for hard work. From my predilection for study and composition, it is not easy for work to become labour to me.'

Though under the pressure of a calamity which would have broken the fortitude of many, he resolved, not so much to be famous as to be useful; and, though numerous providences seemed conspiring to thwart him, he boldly acted out his resolution. He often felt exhausted, and sometimes dispirited, on the rugged and up-hill path. But though 'faint,' he was still 'pursuing.' Every time he fell, he rose with renewed vigour. His stout heart and indomitable perseverance carried him through. 'Perhaps,' said he toward the end of his career, 'few men are more contented than I am. I have attained the object of youthful aspiration—I am satisfied with the position I have gained, and which I feel to be *mine*—I have to work, but, unlike very many men, my work is what I would do for pleasure, though I were not obliged to do it.'[1] Will any one blame him for feeling that he had achieved something, and done good service to his age? After the traveller has climbed the hill, may he not, as he gazes on the scenery beneath him, contrast his present elevation with the humbler position which he occupied at starting? We remember how amused and gratified he was, when we took a venerable friend, the Rev. Dr Beattie of Glasgow, with us to see him, and who paid him, through Mrs Kitto, such a compliment as this:—'Madam, I am disappointed in your husband's appearance exceedingly. I had thought, from the amount of information he possesses, that he must be double the age he is, and, from the quantity of labour he

---

[1] From a journal of some of his more remarkable sayings, kept by his eldest daughter.

has gone through, that he must possess twice the physical vigour.' Yet, in spite of many temptations which naturally sprang out of his singular career, he maintained his humility as deeply as when he said, in 1832, to Mr Woollcombe, 'I know perfectly well that many thought you and my earliest friends not justified in their original kindness toward me. What is more, I soon began to think so too myself.' But he had won his position by toil, in season and out of season, toil such as no constitution could long sustain. 'The working day of the Museum,' he wrote to Mr Knight, 'is six hours—mine is sixteen hours.' What physical frame could long bear up under such continuous strain and pressure? 'A merciful man regardeth the life of his beast;' and Dr Kitto's soul should have had compassion on its 'earthen vessel,' and not worn it to death.

It is true that, in his latter years, there were great demands upon him. The cares of a numerous family summoned his pen into perpetual motion. He told me, when I saw him during the period of the Great Exhibition, that he had not been across his threshold for about six weeks. It was a manful struggle which he maintained in order to support a wife and ten children, by his literary labours. Such toils are not the most remunerating—very unlike the lighter works of fiction, which often draw a princely revenue. 'They are of the world, therefore the world heareth them;' but treatises like those of Dr Kitto, though they bear upon the highest interests of mankind, neither awaken the curiosity, nor gratify the relish, of the common circle of readers. They are set aside as serious productions, to be read perhaps by and by, but when or where the unwelcome study may be forced upon him, their rejecter does not know. There seems every reason to believe that Kitto's head had sustained some serious internal injury, and there was, therefore, all the more need that every precaution should be taken that labour should not deepen into drudgery, and that, along with intervals of entire relaxation, the amount of study should be meted out with rigid regard to constitutional capability of endurance. The bow should have often been unbended, that the cord might not be speedily snapped, or become so flaccid as to be useless. Less work—longer work, should have been the motto of his life. His memory began to fail under those attacks which so prostrated him—first the memory of names, and then the scraps of poetry which had been so abundantly stored up, 'leaked out.' He was to some extent aware of this danger. 'It may not,' he is obliged to confess, 'be always prudent or safe for a man to be constantly on the stretch, doing all he can.' Yet with this conviction, we find him, during his residence at Woking, saying to Mr Tracy, 'I fancy that I must soon trundle into town, notwithstanding the disinclination to motion which results from the corpulency engendered by my sedentary habits, which are so rooted that I can seldom bring myself to move beyond my garden once in three or four weeks.' This reluctance to physical exercise had always made travelling a species of self-denial, even though he had enjoyed such benefit from it. 'I would not,' he says to Mr Burnard from Bagdad, 'give five *para* to see the finest city in the universe, unless I could see *without going to see.*'

It is somewhat remarkable that one is able to trace in Kitto's early boyhood the visible germs of those tastes and habits by which he was afterwards distinguished. Few lives are moulded by merely accidental circumstances. Childhood often supplies the key to the interpretation of ripened character. The soul has its 'seed in itself,' and its growth is the result of a thousand invisible influences. Kitto's mind contained within it a strong formative principle, which was fostered and strengthened by causes apparently the most unpromising and disastrous that can well be imagined. His love of books was almost an infant passion. A cordwainer's recitation of juvenile stories set him to buy them. He tasted, and his thirst was never quenched. Mrs Barnicle's shop-window became the scene of daily and intense gaze and wonderment, finding, however, a more formidable rival in a book-stall in the market. The boy begged or borrowed volumes wherever he could find them. The money that other youths threw away on sweetmeats, he cheerfully spent on books. This book-love resisted every temptation—even that most tempting of luxuries to older palates, the clotted cream of Devonshire. And the passion was a lasting one. In his Workhouse Journal, he stated his highest ambition to be, to gain a livelihood by means of a circulating library. A very short period before his death, he said to a friend, who declared his relish for the country, because it afforded hunting, fishing, and shooting—'I like hunting too, but in London; I hunt books—*they* are my game.'

Not only so, but one who reads the story of his boyhood, may discover in it the foreshadow of his authorship; nay, the special form of literature which he should prefer was thus early indicated. Copies of the Pilgrim and Gulliver's Travels with illustrations, had been very attractive to him, and he daubed all the engravings with his mother's washing indigo. The story book he wrote on one occasion for his cousin, was decorated by a *pictorial* embellishment. Boys usually like pictures, and often amuse themselves with drawing. Kitto, however, not only painted, but he did it with energy, and to good practical purpose. Pictorial works were his subsequent masterpiece. His early shifts were also, as it were, typical of his later forms of industrious ingenuity. He wanted a penny, and he bargained to write a book to his cousin for it. Really, what else did he do during his life?—he still wanted a penny, and he still bargained to write a book for it. If he wished anything, he was seldom baffled in obtaining it. The deaf boy, unfit to work, and abandoned to himself, used to wade at low-water in Sutton-pool, to fish out pieces of rope or scraps of iron. Treading on a broken bottle, he was laid up; and then he resorted to painting, having expended twopence on paper to set himself up in business. When the first method of exposing his wares had lost its novelty, he next erected a stall at Plymouth Fair, and threw open to public gaze his Art exhibition. Then he fell upon the device of printing labels, and was so engaged, when, to keep him from utter misery, he was lodged in the 'Hospital of the Poor's Portion.' It was much the same with him afterwards. If one thing failed, he tried another: the conclusion of one labour was the beginning of another—either shoeing people's feet in Plymouth or repairing their mouths in Exeter; setting types in Malta or nursing and tutoring little children in Bagdad; writing for the Penny Magazine at Islington, editing the Cyclopædia at Woking, or completing the cycle with the Daily Bible Illustrations at Camden Town. His letters to myself teemed with projects to occupy him when this last work should be concluded; and they were all more or less connected with Eastern life or biblical illustration. His industry was unceasing—from the period when his thrifty grandame taught her quiet and delicate charge to sew patchwork and kettle-holders, to the period when he felt the week by far too short to turn out in it the expected and necessary amount of copy. He liked to have his hands full, and they were sometimes too full; it puzzled him what to do first, though the indispensable 'penny' had often summarily to settle the question.

> ' Thus from its nature will the tannen grow,
> Loftiest on loftiest and least sheltered rocks,
> Rooted in barrenness, where naught below
> Of soil supports it 'gainst the Alpine shocks
> Of eddying streams; yet springs the trunk, and mocks
> The howling tempest, till its giant frame
> Is worthy of the mountains from whose blocks
> Of rude bleak granite into life it came
> And grew a giant tree : this life has proved the same.'

His literary projects were truly multifarious. In prospect of finishing one work, he generally sketched a
score of successors.   Before the Daily Bible Illustrations
were concluded, he had in view a Bible for the young,
with three volumes on Joseph, Ruth, and Esther, for the
purpose of expounding at length the customs and institutions of the patriarchal age, the daily rural life of the
Hebrew nation, and the connection of the exiled people
with the court and kingdom of Persia.   He proposed also
a series of great dictionaries.—I. One of Ecclesiastical
History, including not only sects, dogmas, ceremonies and
usages, but ecclesiastical geography and chronology, antiquities and liturgies ; II. Dictionary of Christian Biography,
containing fathers, martyrs, heretics, missionaries, popes,
and divines ; III. British History and Biography of the
Nineteenth Century.   The two first works, had they been
combined with the materials of the Cyclopædia of Biblical
Literature, would have formed a work not unlike the
great German work in course of publication—the Real-
Encyclopædie, edited by Professor Herzog, with the assistance of a numerous circle of famous scholars and critics.
Kitto's gigantic plans of literary labours seem to be
equalled only by those of Antoine Court de Gebelin, one
of the illustrious French Protestants who lived and suffered under Louis xiv.—one who not only read with astonishing voracity on all subjects, and who might be seen

with the Complutensian Polyglott on one side of him, and
a Treatise on Mathematical Infinitudes on the other, but
who sketched a prodigious repository, in twenty or thirty
volumes, to be called the ' Primitive World Analysed and
Compared with the Modern.' The first volume was to
deal in Eastern allegories, the generating principle of the
ancient religions ; the second in universal grammar ; the
third in the natural history of speech ; the fourth in the
history of the Calendar, etc. etc. ; the three next being
etymological dictionaries of the French, Latin, and Greek
languages. ' Why, it would take twenty men to do all
that,' interrupted an astonished auditor, as he listened to
a partial detail of the plan up to the tenth volume.
' Twenty men, you say ?' replied the smiling projector, ' I
begin to be reassured ; Mons. d'Alembert asserted that it
would require forty.'[1] Dr Kitto equalled De Gebelin in
laying out plans, and, like him, thought of executing them
too by unaided effort.

Though Kitto, in his youth, had seasons of melancholy,
yet he was buoyed up by sanguine anticipations. ' The
question was,' he says to Mr Knight (1837), ' whether I
should hang a dead weight on society, or take a place
among its active men. I have struggled for the latter
alternative.' Even when he was seated on Mr Burnard's
tripod, he displayed an innate vitality, and lived in the
ideal regions of his own creation. Occasionally he pictured
to himself what he might, by God's grace, become ; and he
laboured hard to realise his picture. He looked to the
future, and lived in it.

> ' I slept and dreamed that life was beauty ;
> I woke and found that life was duty:
> Was then thy dream an idle lie ?
> Toil on, sad soul, courageously !

[1] See The Priest and the Huguenot, by Bungener, p. 215. Edinburgh: Nelson
and Sons, 1854.

> And thou shalt find thy dream to be
> A noon-day light and strength to thee.'

Indeed, he revealed his own secret, when he said to a friend, in 1853—' If you dreamed, you should not have awoke ; you should have striven to make your dreams realities. The very act of dreaming these aspirations and desires, shows that we possess the power to make them so.' He never wholly renounced faith in dreams, though his own recorded ones may be traced to an active imagination giving sphere and form to its waking thoughts and fancies. He dreamed, and then he dared. Nothing was too arduous for him. ' I am,' says he in his Eastern Journal, ' not myself a believer in impossibilities.' When he lived at Woking, and wished to have some means of livelihood of a more permanent and regular kind than literary labour could secure, he had serious thoughts of applying for the wardenship or secretaryship of a new cemetery to be established in his vicinity. ' The writer remembers how he wished him to make interest with one of the directors, and especially what plans and contrivances he proposed to ward off the objection about his deafness, and to meet the auricular demands which such an office would necessarily bring upon him.

The reader is not to suppose from these statements that Kitto was a mere bookworm—a dry creature speckled with dust, and living in the congenial brotherhood of moths. He was a recluse from necessity, not from choice. He valued society, and keenly felt the loss of being, as he has phrased it, ' shut out from good men's feasts.' He did not condemn festivities, though he could not join in them ; nay, he expressly vindicates them, as ' one whose infirmity frees him from all misconception' on the subject. In his Workhouse Journal, the boy records that, on a visit to his aunt, she regaled him with ' a baked pig's ear,' and the man was never an ascetic skeleton. Many who deem themselves the victims of circumstances, too often think that they owe society nothing but a grudge, and they make war on the world. But Kitto yearned for brotherhood, ay, and sisterhood too. He loved 'children, especially girls.' When in Exeter, he encouraged the girls to whom he gave tracts, and whom he otherwise laboured to instruct, to indite short essays and letters to him ; and, as his Journal shows, he wrote them earnest, faithful, and beautiful replies. His heart was in no risk of ossification. Benevolence was a distinguishing feature in his nature. One of his last acts, before leaving London for Germany, was to take some wine and a few confections to a poor invalid incarcerated for debt, whom he had often before relieved, even when in pressing straits himself. This prisoner was the son of Mrs Barnicle, whose little books had enraptured him, and who had been kind to him in his boyhood. Out of tenpence which he gained when toiling as a shoemaker's serf in 1821, he records that he gave 'a halfpenny each to five little children' —a large proportion, for he expended only double the sum for paper and books, the idols of his soul. He was fond of his native country, and what he had seen abroad but endeared it to him the more. The account of what he suffered from the savage to whom he was given out as an apprentice, reveals also the depth of his emotion. There was no stoicism, real or affected, with him. He did not morosely retire into himself, though he was forced to spend so much time by himself. When she whom he had wooed and won broke her plighted troth, his letters referring to this sad disappointment reveal a crushed spirit overflowing with tenderness, moaning under an agony which refused to be comforted, and so smitten, as to be anxious to travel out of view into a dark and solitary future.[1] He felt that this condition of mind was morbid and 'unhealthy,' and he

[1] See page 147.

2 D

prayed God to revive him. And when the wound was healed, and time had brought him one who has proved a help-meet in so many respects, no one more enjoyed his home. His trials had taught him that 'if we are wise, the fruit comes after the blossom has departed, and that, although less pleasant to the eye than the blossom, is much more useful.'[1]

So far, then, from being, as some might imagine from his history and labours, an inkstained recluse or a living mummy, Kitto was a man both of heart and humour. He enjoyed a good story, and could also tell one. So unexpectedly did his wit break out, that it lost nothing by his apparent gravity. When a friend quoted the lines of Pope as the motto of his desires—

> 'Give me, again, a hollow tree,
> A crust of bread, and liberty,'

he archly replied—'I would rather have a good dinner and a comfortable library.' After he had felt what it was to be tried and crossed, he composed a specimen of a new Lexicon, to be called Love's Dictionary, with illustrations in prose and verse. Three examples may suffice :—ADHERENCE—a word well-known to the ancients, practical meaning now forgotten ; ADVICE—that which those who are in love never take ; ACHE—indispensable in the idiosyncrasy of a lover's heart, etc.

The eloquence of the following paragraph is equalled only by its pleasantry :—'I have had but an indifferent taste for anything which travel offered (mountains and trees excepted), save man, and the circumstances by which he is surrounded ; and even ruins have been interesting to me, chiefly as circumstances belonging to men of a past age, and I have cared for them only as I could read man in them. Oh, how it has delighted me to take a man, dis-

---

[1] Letter to Rev. F. F. Tracy, June 1847.

tinguished from his brother man by a thousand outward circumstances, which make him appear, at the first view, almost as another creature—and after knocking off his strange hat, his kullah, or his turban—after helping him off with his broadcloths, his furs, or his muslins—after clipping his beard, his pigtail, or his long hair—after stripping away his white, black, brown, red, or yellow skin —to come at last to the very man, the very son of Adam, and to recognise, by one " touch of nature," one tear, one laugh, one sigh, one upward or downward look—the same old, universal heart—the same emotions, feelings, passions, which have animated every human bosom, from the equator to the poles, ever since that day in which the first of men was sent forth from Paradise.'[1]

He was fond of poetry, and occasionally wrote it himself. A fine conception or a glowing image afforded him intense pleasure. He had met with the following verse from Longfellow, as a motto, in some book he had been reading—

> ' Art is long, and life is fleeting,
>   And our hearts, though strong and brave,
> Still, like muffled drums, are beating
>   Funeral marches to the grave.'

He committed the lines at once to memory, and advised his eldest daughter to do the same. ' I would,' added he, ' give £50 to be the author of that verse. He has done something for the world ; he has given it a fine and beautiful idea.' A quaint humour, as we have already said, peeps out occasionally in his writings, and often in the Daily Bible Illustrations. ' Lamech had his troubles, as a man with two wives was likely to have, and always has had.' ' When Jacob kissed his fair cousin, he lifted up his voice and wept. . . . Had the faults of Jacob been

[1] Lost Senses—Deafness, pp. 150, 151.

greater than they were, we could forgive them for these tears.' 'Laban's daughter was a match for her father, even in his own line.' 'In dreams, we not only see, but *hear*.' 'A razor is itself a good thing, especially if it be a good one'—a reminiscence of the earliest craft which he was sent to learn. Describing the frontal ornament of the women of Lebanon, he affirms, that the horn from its height and weight, 'needs as many forestays and back-stays to keep it in position as the mainmast of a seventy-four!'[1] In reference to Solomon's prayer for wisdom, he avers, that 'if twelve men were taken, whether from our colleges, or our streets, or our church-doors, not more than one would say, as the Hebrew king said, "Give me wisdom," most of them would think themselves as wise as Solomon. It has not occurred to us in all our life, not now scant of days, though, alas! scant in accomplished purposes, to have met with one man who avowed any lack of wisdom, or who therefore would have made the choice of Solomon, had that choice been offered to him.'[2]

He went once up to the gallery at the top of the dome of St Paul's, and was exceedingly nervous in ascending, and especially in descending ; but he accounts for his fears by saying, 'My old experience in falling may have had some effect in producing this trepidation.'[3] The attempt to explain away the miracle of the manna, by referring it to the gum of the Tamarisk falling round the camp six days, and intermitting the seventh day, is, says he, 'much harder of belief than the simple and naked miracle—much harder than it would be to believe that hot rolls fell every morning from the skies upon the camp of Israel.' Refer-ring to a kind of rough and ready water-cure, applied to persons under fever in the East, he writes, with consider-

[1] Daily Bible Illustrations, vol. v., p. 165.   [2] Ibid. vol. iv., p. 47.
[3] Lost Senses—Deafness, p. 66.

able naiveté—' We have ourselves received exactly this treatment, under the orders of a native physician, in a fever that seemed likely to be fatal, and we certainly recovered—though, whether by reason of this treatment, or in spite of it, we know not.' In the sublime contest between Elijah on the one hand, and the hundreds of Baal's priests on the other, the conclusion agreed to was, ' the god that answereth by fire, let him be God.' The commentator argues that the Baalite priests could not, with a good grace, refuse to abide by such an ordeal, seeing that ' Baal was none other than the sun, whence it should have been very much *in his line* thus to supply them with the fire which they wanted for his service.' According to his own account, he was four feet eight in stature when a lad of sixteen—and certainly he never attained a much greater altitude. He is hard upon Samuel for admiring Saul on account of his being a head taller than any of the people, and he is rather satirical in the sentence which follows :—' Even we want not experience of this in the involuntary respect with which tallness of stature and powerful physical endowments are regarded among ourselves by the uncultivated—and, indeed, by persons not wholly uncultivated, if we may judge from the not unfrequent sarcasms which we may meet with in the most " respectable" monthly, weekly, and daily publications, upon the shortness, by yard measure, of some of the most eminent and highly gifted public men of this and a neighbouring country.' He is witty on the ponderous folios of Caryl upon Job—a book so awfully large, that a clergyman's son, on going to India, left his father reading it, and found him by no means near the end of it when he returned. ' Life in sheep,' said he on one occasion, ' is merely salt to keep them fresh, till they are wanted for eating.' Describing the unearthly sort of noise he made when speaking in the open air, he represents people as starting and staring in astonishment; and adds, that, in the Burlington Arcade, 'the preternatural rumble of the voice is heard afar, and the wonder really is, that all the busy inmates of that industrious hive flock not forth from their cells to learn what calamity threatens their flimsy habitations.'

Allusions to himself are sometimes found in the Daily Bible Illustrations, and his loss is incidentally mentioned. Still he felt it, even in his resignation:—'Very cheerless was the lot that seemed to be before him.' Describing the peacocks imported by Solomon's fleet, he says of the original name, that it is probably imitated from the cry; and, as if he had ventured too far, he adds, 'but we do not know, for *we* never *heard* it.' Illustrating the phrase, 'the wheel broken at the cistern,' he introduces a machine which might be referred to by the royal sage—one which was at work every morning in front of a house he had dwelt in on the banks of the Tigris; and he adds, as if painfully reminded of his 'slain sense,' 'it is *said* to produce a creaking disagreeable noise.' In alluding to Zacharias as struck dumb, he at once puts in, as if it were an extraordinary alleviation of the judgment, but 'he was not deaf.' As if the sentiment did deeply gratify him, he announces:—'Some of the most eminent men of ancient times were subject to infirmities—Moses had a stammering tongue, Jacob was lame, Isaac was blind—yet they were not the less chiefs of the chosen race, and accepted of God.' And we might venture to say, that the terseness of the following sentence has its edge from the pangs of boyish experience:—'The sight of the pottage was pleasant, and the odour overpoweringly tempting to a man ravenously hungry.' Esau knew that, if he did not get it, he must wait some time—'an age to a famishing man.' Such remarks might be indefinitely extended. The samples which we have given tend at least to show, that Dr Kitto was of no peevish or misanthropic nature, but was kind, social, frank, and generous—attached to domestic comfort, and well fitted to enjoy it. His hours in his parlour were as pleasant as those in his study; and when you saw him of an afternoon, with the festive cup in his hand, so happy and so much at ease, you could not have thought that that hand had held a pen for eight or ten hours previous to your pleasant interview.

It would be excess of eulogy to say, that Dr Kitto was a paragon of scholarship, though certainly his attainments were extraordinary in proportion to his opportunities. He had as much knowledge of Hebrew, Greek, Latin, and the modern tongues, as sufficed for his purpose. His English style is pleasant, and, on the whole, correct. Occasionally, it has a tendency to diffuseness, and it has many sudden changes, as if the writer were holding a conversation with himself. He thought, however, that his style was 'rather sententious than conversationally fluent,' a style for which, in reading, he avows a decided preference. As his mind was somewhat poetical, many pathetic and beautiful fancies adorn his compositions. The reader is never at a loss for his meaning; whether you agree with him or not, you always understand him. He wrote with great ease—an ease not always consistent with vigour. Sheridan's remark, that 'easy writing makes hard reading,' does not, however, apply to him. His references to books and authorities are unusually accurate, and quite trust-worthy.[1]

---

[1] But even 'good Homer' occasionally nodded. An amusing instance of oversight occurred in the paper on 'God's Retributions,' in the first edition of the Bible Illustrations. Wishing to show that the Romish Church still maintains its ancient persecuting principles, he inserted a quotation, very pat to his purpose, from a recent pamphlet, purporting to be written 'by the Bishop of Bantry,' and having much the appearance of a genuine Roman Catholic document. On his attention being called to it, and the pamphlet placed in his hands, with the intima-

His mind was sagacious and well balanced, and he had one faculty in a very high degree—that of constant appropriation. Naturalists tell us, that though the zoophytes are fixed to one spot, yet they are for ever tossing their arms about them, and drawing in to themselves whatever minute nutriment floats within their reach. It was so with Dr Kitto. He was well aware that there wrought within him ' a strong faculty of mental association, which enabled him to discover illustrative analogies where few would perceive them, and thus gain constant accession of materials not commonly thought of or usually available.' ' Recognition, recollection, and research,' were his ' threefold cord.' In his Daily Bible Illustrations, there are many facts taken, not only from the class of works usually referred to, but also from current literature—from books he happened to read in the course of his labours. Not only have we Benjamin of Tudela, but we have also Beldam and Bartlett ; verification is brought from Hollinshed, and likewise from Lord Claud Hamilton ; contribution is levied from Sir Charles Napier, the Indian commander, and from Emerson Tennent, the governor of Ceylon ; Napoleon III. and Abd-el-Kader, the prince and the exile, are both pressed into his service ; Marco Polo and Mayhew are alike at his command ; the ' Fair Maid of Perth ' and the Arabian romance of ' Antar ' do him equal service ; the ' school at the end of the street ' gives one example, and the temple-palace of Karnak affords another ; ' our own house ' is put in contrast with ' the old lady in Threadneedle Street ' and her nightly ' guard of bearskin-capped grenadiers ;' sculptured slabs from Koyunjik at Nineveh figure by the side

tion, 'not by the Bishop of Bantry, but of *Banter*—the thing is a *jeu d'esprit*'—leaning his cheek on his hand, as was his wont, he looked amazed for a moment or two, and then, as he turned over a few pages, its true nature flashed upon his mind, and he burst into a hearty laugh, exclaiming, 'Well, this is the first time I ever fell into such an absurd mistake.'

of sepulchral tablets from the catacombs at Rome ; extracts are given from such passing publications as Notes and Queries, and the Missionary Record of the United Presbyterian Church ; Sanchoniatho stands at the one extreme of reference, and the Times newspaper at the other.   The same faculty was in active exercise, even to his latest days. When he was at Cannstatt, and smitten by bereavements, he loved to study the processes of the vintage going on around him, which, he says, ' have made clearer to me many of the allusions of Scripture on the subject—all being here conducted in a primitive style.'   But he concludes, in mournful tone—' I find myself unable to enter into these matters with the eager zest of former days.'   Yes, his work was over.   He needed not to be detained by the cutting of the clusters, and the treading of them in the press, for he was so soon to drink of the fruit of the vine new in his Father's kingdom.

Sentiments both beautiful and striking sparkle in his pages.   Had space permitted, we might have quoted the long eulogy which he has pronounced on Moses—' the greatest of woman born, with the exception of One only, and that One more than man.'   Or we might have referred to the admirable summing up of the character of Joshua —' an Asiatic conqueror, without personal ambition, without any desire of aggrandisement.'   Or we might have selected, for illustration, the concluding paper on the book of Esther, in which he refutes and tosses away the frivolous objection against this old historical fragment—that the name of God does not occur in it.

In fine, what point and truth are there not in the following paragraph ?—

' There are many who pride themselves on their deep " knowledge of human nature,"—that is, being interpreted, on their keen appreciation of the dark things and the foul things of the human heart. The Lord preserve us from too much of this knowledge ! He who has none of it is little better than a fool, and he who has most of it is much worse than a man. For we usually find among men the highest degree of this knowledge united to the lowest degree of appreciation of—a moral incapacity of apprehending—a total inability of feeling, that which, through the grace of God, is divine and spiritual, and therefore good and holy, in the soul of man. . . The most perfect master of this learning is Satan, and he is at once the most consummate example, and the most egregious dupe of that ignorance. It were difficult to find the man in whose soul some faint glimmering of faith in God or man does not linger. But Satan has none. He is the most finished pattern of knowledge without faith. This is his character: HE HAS NO FAITH. This is his weakness and his shame. In this possession and in this want, he has reached heights and depths impossible to man.'[1]

The power of religious principle was the mainstay of Dr Kitto's life. The reader will not have forgotten the sublime prayer which he wrote after his introduction to the workhouse, nor his great desire to be confirmed at the bishop's visitation. Early impressions were deepened by the Divine Spirit ; and the Bible, which had been a sealed book, was then read by the guidance of a new sense, and welcomed with the aspirations of a new heart. The ardour of Mr Groves communicated fresh impulse, and the terrible visitations which crowded upon him at Bagdad— plague, famine, inundation, and blockade—threw him, unreservedly, into the arms of his heavenly Father. From Exeter he wrote, in 1824, to Mr Harvey:—' I did think of religion *now* and *then*, but I did not make it the constant subject of my thoughts.' In 1834, he said to the

[1] Daily Bible Illustrations, vol. v., pp. 63, 64.

Rev. Mr Lampen :—' I never talked about religion less than I do now, but there is much about religion which I never felt so decidedly and deeply.'   His faith in God ever helped him on.   Rescued from any crisis, he 'thanked God, and took courage.'   Assured that God had work for him, he never wholly lost the assurance that He would bring him to that work in the right place, and at the right time.   He had long studied the Bible, for itself and its spiritual benefits, and not with any view to its public illustration.   It had been to him the Book of Life before it became a text for pictorial comment.   He had searched the Scriptures, and discovered the Christ which they reveal, ere he invited others to ascend the hills or traverse the valleys, mark the manners or investigate the antiquities, of the Lands of the Morning.   ' On coming home,' he humbly and thankfully states to Mr Tracy, in 1847, ' I was enabled to lay all that I had during long years of silent study acquired, and all that I had gathered together in foreign parts, upon God's altar ; and I sometimes venture to think, that He has been pleased to accept and honour even that humble offering.'   He had a firm faith in the plenary inspiration of the Bible, and he knew full well that mere truthfulness in those Oriental allusions, which he was so happy in illustrating, is not, of itself, as many have erro‧neously supposed, any proof of a Divine origin.   Agreement with the ' form and pressure of the age' around it is demanded of any production, and the want of it in Scripture would certainly be fatal to any higher claim.   But historical veracity is not identical with canonical authority, though essential to its evidence.

His trust in God was unwavering :—' There is One,' he solemnly writes, ' higher than the highest, whose honour is not to be the second or the third, but the FIRST matter for consideration.'   It was very natural in him, who referred all things to God, to ask, on a review of the 'sad passages' of David's life, ' How is it that we hear no more of David's asking counsel of the Lord?' And he nobly records :—' Thirty years ago, before "the Lord caused me to wander from my father's house," and from my native place, I put my mark upon this passage in Isaiah, "I am the Lord : they shall not be ashamed that wait on Me." Of the many books I now possess, the Bible that bears this mark is the only one that belonged to me at that time. It now lies before me ; and I find that, although the hair which was then dark as night, has meanwhile become " a sable silvered," the ink which marked this text has grown into intensity of blackness as the time advanced, corresponding with, and, in fact, recording the growing intensity of the conviction, that "they shall not be ashamed that wait for Thee." I believed it then, but I know it now ; and I can write *Probatum est*, with my whole heart, over against the symbol, which that mark is to me, of my ancient faith. " They shall not be ashamed that wait for Me." Looking back through the long period which has passed since I set my mark to these words—a portion of human life, which forms the best and brightest, as well as the most trying and conflicting in all men's experience — it is a joy to be able to say, " I have waited for Thee, and have not been ashamed. Under many perilous circumstances, in many most trying scenes, amidst faintings within and fears without, and under sorrows that rend the heart, and troubles that crush it down, I have waited for Thee ; and, lo ! I stand this day as one not ashamed." '[1]

During a period of great straits, in 1848, he penned these words to a friend :[2]—' My sensations have become less acute, not because my burden is less heavy, but be-

---

[1] Daily Bible Illustrations, vol. v., p. 203.   [2] Rev. Mr Lewis.

cause I have become more accustomed to its weight. . . . .
It has not yet pleased God to relieve me from the great
present distress, in which I have been so long plunged;
yet I still wait day by day for this help, believing that He
will not suffer one who has been enabled to trust so much
in Him to be ultimately confounded. I shall learn one
day the lesson He designs to teach me ; and I know that,
when the lesson I am to learn has reached my heart, He
will stay His hand. My heart had fainted long since
unless I had believed in that fatherly care, which has never
yet failed me, and never will. None but those who have
been tried in the furnace of affliction can tell or conceive
the bitterness—greater than the bitterness of death—of
the trials which one day after another brings to me, and
under which I sit still in a depressed and sorrowful, but
not in a despairing spirit. I have hope, but it is " hope
deferred." '

We present only another illustration, the sentiment of
which has its source in his own domestic experience, and
the number of his ' olive plants :'—' There are tens of thousands among us, who would by no means be thankful for
such an intimation as that which the angel of God brought
to Manoah and his wife. How is this ? Alas, for our
faith ! which will not trust God to pay for the board and
lodging of all the little ones He has committed to our
charge to bring up for Him. Good old Quarles, who was
himself the father of eighteen children, enters feelingly into
this matter :—

> " Shall we repine,
> Great God, to foster any babe of Thine !
> But 'tis the charge we fear ; our stock's but small :
> If heaven, with children, send us wherewithal
> To stop their craving stomachs, *then* we care not.
> Great God !
> How hast Thou crackt Thy credit, that we dare not

Trust Thee for bread ?   How is't we dare not venture
To keep Thy babes, unless Thou please to enter
In bond for payment ?   Art Thou grown so poor,
To leave Thy famished infants at our door,
And not allow them food?   Canst Thou supply
Thy empty ravens, and let Thy children die ?" "[1]

The last days of his life were clouded, as we have narrated, by successive family bereavements.   In that land of
strangers whither he had gone to die, his youngest child,
and then his eldest one, the lovely and bright-eyed Shireen,
preceded him to the tomb.   The trial shook him with
intense agony.   But though he mourned, he did not murmur—looking to Him who ' healeth the broken in heart,'
and wipes away the tears of the bereaved.   There pressed
upon him, too, the consciousness of physical disability ;
and the sad thought, that, at the end as at the beginning
of his life, he was dependent on the bounty of others.
He cannot, indeed, be classed among the *infanti perduti*—
authors noted for misfortune and sorrow.   His works, as
he says, had a steady, though not always an immediate
sale ; but his calamity lay in failing health and occasional
want of employment.   He was, however, no exception to
Sir Edward Bulwer Lytton's statement—' For the author
there is nothing but his pen, till that and life are worn to
the stump.'

Dr Kitto was in connection with the Church of England,
but he was a man of catholic spirit.   He was wont to say
that he belonged to the Church Universal, meaning that
he had no sectarian leanings, and that he was not, and
could not be, a constant and visible worshipper in any
sanctuary.   But he punctually attended the Episcopal
Church on communion Sabbaths, for this reason among
others of higher moment, that with his prayer-book ' he

[1] Daily Bible Illustrations, vol. ii., pp. 425, 426.

could follow the service.' He thought, too, that this absence of ecclesiastical bias tended to recommend his writings to all classes of the community. The example of Mr Groves was not in this respect lost upon him. 'Talk,' said this worthy man, 'of loving me, while I agree with them. Give me men that will love me, when I differ from them and contradict them.'[1] Every Christian was a brother to Dr Kitto, and he loved the image of the Master wherever he saw it. On parting with Mr Pfander at Bagdad, he sets down this meditation in his Journal :—
' The personal separation of Christians, even in this life, is less complete than that of other people. There is a spiritual intercourse which still subsists when their bodies are widely separated. There is also the feeling of being children of one common Father, who Himself sees and loves all *His*, whilst they are unseen to one another ; and who thus, so to speak, becomes a medium of intercourse with their spirits, which all centre in Him. *Him* whom I love, they love also ; *Him* to whom they look every day, I also look to daily, and I see them in Him ; and He who talks to my heart, talks with theirs also. No! thus members of one body, we cannot be completely separated.' Nay, he had a strong desire to serve the Lord in what he justly reckoned the highest form of earthly service, that of an Evangelist to a heathen country. His want of hearing, indeed, disqualified him ; but, even with this drawback, he felt the handling of types to be a sacred duty, from its connection with Bible circulation, and he looked on his journey to the East in the light of a missionary tour.

Dr Kitto's life was marked by gratitude to all his friends and patrons, and he rejoiced to make prompt and cordial declaration. His early epistles are full of his thanks ; and, in his last letter, referring to the public subscription in

[1] Newman's Phases of Faith, p. 37. Fourth Edition.

process of being raised for him, he writes :—'I am deeply
thankful for what has been already done, and for the most
kind attentions of which, under these circumstances, I have
become the object.'[1]   This dying testimony at Cannstatt is
only the echo of his first acknowledgments in the Plymouth
Workhouse.   Mr Tracy, at the time one of the surgeons
of the Public Dispensary, visited the boy who had fallen,
and ' his sympathetic and good-natured face' being the
first that met the poor patient's gaze on a momentary return to consciousness, was never effaced from his recollection.   ' Are you Mr Tracy?' scribbled the little cobbler
on a slate, as that gentleman was afterwards passing
through the wards of the Almshouse, for the questioner
was anxious to recognise and honour him.   In 1847 he
wrote to him :—' Thirty years ago—is it possible that it is
thirty years ago?—I lay before you as one dead.'   ' Ten
years after, I saw you in London.   I went and returned,
and now we meet again.'

The only objection which can be brought against our
statement is, that Dr Kitto does not, in any of his works,
make allusion to Mr Groves: not only in places where he
refers to his journey to the East, but even in the Lost
Senses, where many of the changing pursuits of his life are
described.   We believe that Mr Groves himself, on visiting
Kitto in London, asked why his name had never been mentioned by him in any of his writings, and that Kitto replied,
that the silence was in accordance with his own peremp-
tory request before the separation at Bagdad.   Mr Groves
then made some explanation as to the meaning and purpose of his injunction, to the effect that it was not intended to forbid all mention of him, but only the mention
of him in connection with his religious history and mission.
This awkward misconception, if it were one on the part of

the deaf author, is but another example of the loss sustained through his infirmity—which prevented, as we have said more than once, all supplemental talk with him ; and, in deed, he confesses, in a note to Mr Blackader, that he 'had always an unfortunate turn for taking people at their word.' This same tendency led him to express his own opinions in a bold and unmodified style. We have referred to the foregone conclusion which he ascribed to Professor Robinson ;[1] and he asserts with equal bluntness of Sir Gardner Wilkinson, in reference to the question of human sacrifice in Egypt, that, throughout his work, ' he keeps the subject as much as possible out of view, for a very pardonable unwillingness to bring forward into broad light a matter so disparaging to the civilization of a people whom he has made it the business of his life to comprehend, and, from the influence of that devotedness to a single object, to extol and magnify.[2]

Dr Kitto was, at the same time, of an honest and independent nature. Though he had been so much patronised, he had never learned to cringe. In July 1823, he began thus to Mr Woollcombe :—' I commence my letter with telling you, that I have ever been accustomed to write my opinions with freedom, and that I should deem myself unworthy of your patronage if I could be so base as to sacrifice my intellectual and moral independence at the shrine of interest. Much of my future welfare depends, I believe, on you ; yet, were I certain that you were my only friend, and that on you rested my every hope of earthly comfort, I would not seek the way to your continued favour by endeavouring to accommodate my opinions to yours.' What the lad, who had just thrown off the poorhouse livery, said so firmly, the man continued to assert and exemplify. He was too self-reliant to be servile. All he sought was

[1] Page 322.   [2] Pictorial History of Palestine, vol. i., p. 584.

opportunity to put forth his energies. He was noted for his uniform candour and truthfulness, and for his kindness to all his correspondents and coadjutors. He had no jealousies of others, and he loved to encourage promising talent. Perhaps, from his peculiar situation, he might imagine slights where none were intended; and that persistency which made him what he was, must have sometimes assumed, in the view of others, the character of obstinacy.

In whatever aspect we view him, he is a wonder. It is a wonder that he rose in life at all; a wonder that he acquired so much, and that he wrote so much is yet a higher wonder. Many have excelled him in the amount of acquisition, but few in the patience and bravery which he displayed in laying up his stock of knowledge, in the perfect mastery he had over it, and in the freedom and facility with which he dispensed it in Magazine, Review, or Treatise. Most certainly he hit upon the moral of his life when he couched it in these vigorous terms :[1]—' I perhaps have as much right as any man that lives, to bear witness, that there is no one so low but that he may rise; no condition so cast down as to be really hopeless; and no privation which need, of itself, shut out any man from the paths of honourable exertion, or from the hope of usefulness in life. I have sometimes thought that it was possibly my mission to affirm and establish these great truths.' We do not mean to place him among those men, of whom the Italian poet sings—

' Natura il fece, e poi ruppe la stampa ;'

' Nature made him, and then broke the die ;' but, take him all in all, he was a rare phenomenon—an honour also to his age and country. He struggled manfully, and gained

---

[1] Lost Senses—Deafness, p. 73.

the victory; nay, out of his misfortune he constructed the steps of his advancement. Neither poverty, nor deafness, nor hard usage, nor ominous warnings, nor sudden checks, nor unpropitious commencements, nor abandoned schemes, chilled the ardour of his sacred ambition. He lived not to a long age, but he had not lived in vain; and when death at length came, it was but the Master saying, as of old, to the deaf one, ' Ephphatha—be opened!' and his spirit, which had so long dwelt in distressing silence, burst away to join the hymning myriads whose song is—

> ' Louder than the thunder's roar,
> Or the fulness of the sea
> When it breaks upon the shore.'

THE END.

MURRAY AND GIBB, PRINTERS, EDINBURGH.

www.ingramcontent.com/pod-product-compliance
Lightning Source LLC
Chambersburg PA
CBHW030952110726
47900CB00004B/1240